Sorcerous Moons

Books 4–6

by

Jeffe Kennedy

"It's going to be an epically magical ride!!"
~Happy Tails and Tales

Table of Contents

The Forests of Dru   1

Oria's Enchantment   187

Lonen's Reign   371

The Forests of Dru

Sorcerous Moons – Book 4

BY

Jeffe Kennedy

An Enemy Land

Once Princess Oria spun wicked daydreams from the legends of sorceresses kidnapped by the barbarian Destrye. Now, though she's come willingly, she finds herself in a mirror of the old tales: the king's foreign trophy of war, starved of magic, surrounded by snowy forest and hostile strangers. But this place has secrets, too—and Oria must learn them quickly if she is to survive.

A Treacherous Court

Instead of the refuge he sought, King Lonen finds his homeland desperate and angry, simmering with distrust of his wife. With open challenge to his rule, he knows he and Oria—the warrior wounded and weak, the sorceress wrung dry of power—must somehow make a display of might. And despite the desire that threatens to undo them both, he still cannot so much as brush her skin.

A Fight for the Future

With war looming and nowhere left to run, Lonen and Oria must use every intrigue and instinct they can devise: to plumb Dru's mysteries, to protect their people—and to hold fast to each other. Because they know better than any what terrifying trial awaits...

Acknowledgements

Thanks to Susan Conley, longtime family friend and knower of All Things Art, for coming out of Facebook lurkage to suggest that "retablo" was the word I was looking for. Yes, exactly – and it added so much to the story.

Copyright © 2017 by Jennifer M. Kennedy

This is a work of fiction. Names, characters, places, and incidents are either the products of the author's imagination or used fictitiously, and any resemblance to actual persons, living or dead, or business establishments, organizations or locales is completely coincidental.

Thank you for reading!

<u>Credits</u>
Content Editor: Deborah Nemeth
Line and Copy Editor: Rebecca Cremonese
Back Cover Copy: Erin Nelson Parekh
Cover Design: Steam Power Studios, www.steampowerstudios.com.au

~ 1 ~

"WE WON THE war and this is still the best the king's table can command?"

Nolan poked at the meat with a sour scowl, and Arnon clapped him on the shoulder. "Not much of a homecoming, huh? You could have brought us game from the far forests and done better."

"I brought the King of the Destrye instead." Nolan shrugged him off. "That seemed more useful at the time."

Lonen, that selfsame King of the Destrye, didn't adjust his position to ease his aching side, lest his brother misinterpret that as a sign of discomfort with the topic of conversation. Nor did he miss the sidelong glance from Nolan that suggested he might be reconsidering Lonen's inherent usefulness. Not that Lonen could argue much otherwise. Being laid up in bed recuperating for more than a week didn't lend itself to high-profile—or even marginally effective—rule. Nevertheless, some remnant of his youthful self cringed, wishing he could do something to earn his older brother's approval rather than his scorn.

Mostly, though, he longed to be back in that bed, under the furs with Oria, sharing her warmth, basking in the surety that she slept beside him. To be there when the strange dreams woke her.

Oria hadn't wanted him to be up and about yet, but Nolan—believed lost in battle, now miraculously returned and restless with unsatisfied expectations—had decided he'd waited long enough for explanations. Rather than risk having Nolan barge into his bedchamber and interrogate Oria, Lonen had conceded to the lesser of

7

the evils and gotten himself to this private dinner with his two remaining brothers. The last three of Archimago's line, sadly diminished in robustness of every kind.

But three was one more than they'd thought they had.

That had to be a good thing. A blessing from Arill herself. Somehow, though, under the sharp scrutiny of Nolan's piercing blue stare, Lonen nursed a few doubts.

He gave in and shifted, easing the pinch in his gut. The infection no longer poisoned him, but the massive tissue damage had yet to replace itself—however much it ever would—despite Oria's foolhardy attempt to give her life to heal him. That side of his body sagged inward, as if part of him had been carved out.

Which, come to think of it, it pretty much had.

With a grimace for that, he forced himself to finish the slice of stringy roast on his plate, then picked up his warmed wine and drank, hoping to mute some of the ache.

"It's not good for you to be upright in a chair like this," Arnon said, frowning at him. "I can see it pains you."

"Father would say a warrior can suffer far more than a bit of pain, especially in the service of Dru," Nolan replied, gaze never wavering from Lonen. "He would have expected his successor to be sitting the throne and handling the pressing issues of the Destrye, not lying abed with a foreign mistress."

"You mean Her Highness, Oria, Queen of the Destrye?" Lonen didn't raise his voice, but his tone carried all the iron resolve of his battle-axe. Enough that Nolan sat back slightly, a hint of surprise flickering through his eyes before they sharpened again. *That's right. I am not the same little brother you knew before the war.* He might not be ruling impressively, but neither was he a pushover. Not anymore.

"She is Báran," Nolan said flatly, tempting Lonen to remark on his brother's powers of observation. But this was no time for levity. This conversation had been a long time coming and Nolan clearly intended to have it out now. So be it—and Arill hold him in her hand for this battle.

"I'm fully aware of that, Nolan, as I met her in Bára, where she is in fact, a princess and should be queen of her people by her own right."

"What exactly happened there?" Arnon put in, full of curiosity. "What?" He gave Nolan's frown a scowl of his own. "You're not the only one who's been sitting on questions while Lonen concentrated on *not dying*," he added pointedly. "You've dragged him out of bed for this, so we might as well get the whole story."

"I'm not interested in this Báran princess's *story*," Nolan snapped. "What I want is to break this foul spell she's employed to ensorcell our brother and king. We needed to get him away from her devious influence if we're to have a hope of that. *Stories* can wait."

"I am not ensorcelled."

"She's a witch, Lonen—you know this."

"A sorceress, actually." Surreptitiously, Lonen scanned the shadows near the ceiling. Sure enough, the emerald gleam of Chuffta's eyes shone back from a high perch, his iridescent white body stretched into a low profile along the upper curve of a ceiling beam. Oria had sent her Familiar to spy on the conversation, even though Lonen had asked her to keep her friend and guardian close. He didn't like her to be alone. Not after what had happened to her without his protection when they'd arrived in Dru.

"You call it a pine, I call it an evergreen," Nolan replied. "It's the same Arill-cursed tree."

Lonen regarded his brother calmly. One benefit of battling hordes of golems, running out of water in the desert, and countless other ways he'd nearly died horrifically—it had become abundantly clear to him that arguments over minor details like semantics paled significantly as anything to get excited about. He'd have thought Nolan would have learned that lesson, too, during his trials and journeys.

"Trees are sacred to Arill," Arnon put in, ever the pedant, "so it's not technically correct to call it an 'Arill-cursed' tree."

Nolan turned on Arnon with a snarl, proving that temperance had not been one of the lessons he'd learned. Ironic, as Nolan had been the dreamer and thinker before the Golem Wars. Whereas Lonen, solidly third in line for a throne he'd thought he'd never have to sit, had been the irresponsible, playful one their father had despaired of teaching discipline to. Perhaps tragedy and the horrors of war worked to change people. Fire tempered some weapons to greater strength and destroyed others.

"Queen Oria is a sorceress, yes," Lonen said before his brothers could come to blows. "She wields powerful magic, but she does so with heart and conscience." He eyed Chuffta in the shadows, certain her spy would be faithfully relaying the conversation, and chose his words carefully for both audiences. "Instead of staying in Bára as their queen, Her Highness married me and journeyed here at great risk to herself, sacrificing her own throne out of a sense of responsibility to the Destrye, in order to help us." And to keep a personal vow to him, but that should remain exactly that—personal. He held her promises to him close to his heart, treasuring them alongside her confession that she loved him. Precious gifts from a prickly and dangerous woman. They did not need to be scrutinized by others.

Particularly those who couldn't—or wouldn't—understand what lay between him and the foreign bride who'd brought a bright face to the terrible magics wreaked in the wars, and light into his own darkened heart. She might have made the difference in him becoming the tempered weapon, rather than the warped one.

Nolan sighed heavily. Pushing his plate aside and leaning elbows on the table, he laced his fingers together except for the index fingers, which he pointed at Lonen. "Your obvious sentiment aside, let's discuss the legality of this marriage."

"It's a legal marriage, Nolan."

He waved that off. "Only according to Báran law, which is not ours. We do not recognize it."

"I recognize it, and I was there." The onerous ritual had nearly knocked him unconscious and had left Oria in a dead faint. The magic connection hummed between them, Oria a warm flame inside him. The only time since their marriage that he hadn't felt it was when they'd been separated, both near death. Something he never intended to endure again—and something else he wouldn't attempt to explain. Before he'd experienced it for himself, he wouldn't have understood it either. Nolan opened his mouth and Lonen held up a hand. "A moot point anyway, as I intend to rectify any lingering legal qualms by marrying Oria in Arill's Temple, just as soon as we can both stand upright for the entire ceremony." *And dance afterwards*, he promised himself. Oria would see how a wedding—and wedding night—should be properly celebrated.

He flicked a glance at Chuffta, hoping Oria had gotten that particular message. She could be stubborn, but he'd have his way in this.

"Well, let's discuss that," Nolan said.

"No."

Nolan made an impatient sound. "I want you to hear me out on this."

"No."

"There is no need for you to marry her, Lonen! Keep her as a trophy of war, if you must. Our warriors have a history of that. It's somewhat outdated, but the tradition is an old and stirring one that celebrates Destrye victory. We can play it to the people that way and they'll see you as all the stronger and more vital for it. Don't ask them to accept a foreigner—the enemy!—as their queen. There's no reason to do so and it makes you look weak. Your people deserve a Destrye woman as their queen."

Lonen shrugged. "They won't get one."

"Can she even quicken with your seed? We have no way of knowing if Destrye can breed with her kind. She could leave you without heirs."

"There are Ion's sons, if so."

"It's one thing for that to be a last resort, another for you to go in knowing she won't give you heirs."

"What man knows such things for certain when he marries?"

"What about Natly?"

Lonen tightened his jaw. "She's irrelevant to this conversation."

"Hardly. She waited for you to return, believing the two of you to be engaged. She could still be your queen."

At Nolan's suggestion, Arnon dropped his face into his hands. He and Lonen had spoken about Natly before, with Arnon arguing strongly against Natly as an appropriate queen.

"It seems to me," Lonen said slowly, measuring Nolan, "that you, yourself, rejected Natly as a suitable queen."

His elder brother had the grace to wince. "Yes, well. It need not be Natly, but—"

"It's a moot point. I've made vows and I intend to keep them. Would our people want a king who breaks his vows?"

"You mean like your betrothal to Natly?" Nolan shot back.

Lonen clenched his teeth against returning the bite. "I never promised. She assumed."

"Perhaps you are becoming the politician, parsing terms and dividing rope fibers."

"Perhaps so," Lonen returned, ignoring the sneer in Nolan's voice. The accusation was a fair one. "But I *am* king. I realize I shouldn't be. Arill knows our father died too young and this crown should be his." Lonen waved a hand at the wreath of hammered metal leaves he'd worn to the dinner. He didn't much care for it, and he'd worn it mainly as a reminder of his authority to his elder brother. At least it was light, even if he felt vaguely like an imposter wearing the thing. "Ion should have lived to succeed him, as we all believed he would. And yes, Nolan—you should have been king in his stead. Would have been, had we but known you lived."

Nolan's jaw flexed and he sat back, crossing his arms. "It wasn't as if I had a way to send a message. It took us weeks to find our way out of those caverns. If not for the underground lake that cushioned our fall, we would have died of thirst." He shook his head, a ghost of his old smile crossing his mouth behind the neat beard. "I tell you, it pissed me off mightily that I might die of *drowning* of all things."

"What did you do for food?" Lonen asked.

"You haven't gotten to hear this tale." Arnon poured them all more wine, clearly cheered by the turn in conversation. "It deserves to be set down as an epic ballad of its own."

"You tell it." Nolan took his cup, staring into it. "I'm weary of it, myself."

Arnon, who never met a topic that wearied him, grinned with enthusiasm. "So, there they were, Nolan and his regiment, on the north flank of the city. Fireballs hurtling through the air, golems everywhere, whirlwinds whipping through the center of the battlefield, while lightning forked overhead."

Lonen adjusted his position, sitting back to enjoy his brother's tale—and not bothering to point out that he'd been there, too. No sense interrupting the story's rhythm. He kept an eye on Nolan, however, darkly brooding over his wine.

"Then *crack!*" Arnon slapped his hands together, making both of his brothers jump and grinning at it, Arill take him. "The ground shook and opened up. Nolan and his men raced away from the edges, but no man can outrun the earth itself. The ground disappeared beneath their feet, and they fell, plummeting to certain death."

Nolan wiped a hand over his forehead and Lonen nearly called a halt to the story, but Nolan caught him looking and pierced him with a stare so challenging he knew it would only give insult. Instead he silently toasted his brother's bravery. After a slight hesitation, Nolan dipped his chin.

Oblivious to the exchange, Arnon continued. "Our hero, Prince Nolan, managed to grab a handhold and cling to it, as did a few other men. But the ground continued to shake, crumbling beneath their hands, while horses, supplies, even golems rained around them. They fell, too, sending a prayer to Arill to guide their steps to the Hall of Warriors."

"My prayer was nothing so coherent," Nolan interrupted.

"Shut up, this is my tale now," Arnon replied easily. He was doing this on purpose then. Telling the elaborate story to defuse tensions. Good on him. "But instead of waking in the Hall of Warriors, our hero plunged into icy water, cold and black as the sea. He drove for the surface, hampered by the rocks, men, horses, and supplies also teeming in the water."

"Grim," Lonen said, and Nolan raised his brows in acknowledgment of the observation. There. A bit of connection. Lonen would have to tell his brother the story of swimming through the bore tides of the Bay of Bára, carrying an unconscious Oria, nearly drowning all of them.

Or perhaps better not to.

"No light penetrated so deep in the earth," Arnon described with ghoulish glee, "but Arill held our hero in her hand, guiding him to swim to an unseeable shore."

"I mainly tried to swim *away* from flailing hooves and falling rocks," Nolan pointed out acerbically.

"Do *you* want to tell the story after all?" Arnon rounded on him.

"No, no—you go ahead. Never mind the fact checking."

"Thank you. Prince Nolan, chilled to the bone, exhausted and aching from the fall, at last dragged himself onto a dry shelf of stone. A few other men made it also, along with several horses—still with their packs, thank Arill."

"How many men?" Lonen asked out of habit before he caught himself. "Never mind, it—"

"About three dozen survived the fall," Nolan answered, gaze glittering. Out of a regiment of more than a thousand warriors. Horrifying indeed. Of course, they'd thought none had survived the chasm at all, so there was that. "Ten of those didn't survive the first few hours, and we lost three more on the journey to Dru. I brought fewer than two dozen home."

Lonen closed his eyes and sent a prayer to Arill to fete the lost soldiers well in the Hall of Warriors—and to forgive him that he felt some relief at the smaller number of bodies to feed and keep warm through the winter.

"You're jumping the story," Arnon accused.

"Apologies, brother." Nolan at least sounded less dour.

Arnon grunted, but continued. "Only three dozen men survived the fall," he intoned, "and ten of those didn't survive the first few hours."

Lonen passed a hand over his mouth to hide his smile.

"In the blackness of the caves, they might have been lost had Prince Nolan not been an educated man, as well as an experienced woodsman and hunter. Discovering that a phosphorescent fungus grew on the rocks, he reasoned that, like the moss on trees in the forests of Dru, it might grow more densely on the north face, and he navigated accordingly."

Lonen whistled, impressed, and Nolan refilled his goblet, shaking his head slightly, but not interrupting.

"As they continued, they discovered a well-worn passage. One that led more or less directly to Dru, and in fact emerged into a dry lake bed somewhat north of us." Arnon waited, expression expectant.

The wine evaporated on his tongue and Lonen found himself sitting upright, the pain in his side a minor consideration. "Wait—an underground passage from Bára to Dru?"

Nolan gave him a long look. "At least to the region north of Dru, but it appears so."

"That's how their golems traveled here. And how they drained the lakes so quickly before we became aware, sending the water back to Bára."

"The passage might have acted like an aqueduct, an underground river carrying water from our lakes to theirs until it had drained completely. They might have made others over however many years, with many routes to the surface, which would explain how the golems managed to pop up so unexpectedly and disappear again," Arnon agreed.

"Why didn't you tell me about this before?" Lonen demanded.

So many possibilities. How could they use this to their advantage? Of course, they'd thought the golems had been eliminated following the fall of Bára and that their major problem now lay in incursions by the even more deadly Trom, who needed no underground passages, instead flying in on their enormous dragons that scorched crops and Destrye alike. But he had nearly died under the fangs and claws of a band of golems he and Oria had encountered on their journey. "If we could—"

"*Why didn't we tell you?*" Nolan interrupted in a tone as scathing as dragon fire. "There was the small problem of an enemy princess in your bed. She of the people who sent the cursed goblins. We could hardly discuss such sensitive matters in her hearing. Arill only knows what her plans are or what information she'd send back to—"

"Oria is a not a spy." Lonen set his teeth against saying more. Steeled himself not to look up at her actual spy, concealed in the beams above.

"How do you know that?" Nolan demanded, angry and bewildered. "*Think,* man! You acknowledge she's a powerful sorceress. She could easily work magics to cloud your mind. She could be here to finally and completely undermine Dru. What better way than to capture the attention—and, incredibly enough, the hand in marriage—of our king? How is it possible this has *not* occurred to you?"

"Because I know her," he snapped. And he knew the many reasons she'd fought against him bringing her to Dru. Ones not at all politic to divulge. "I know what goes on in her heart and mind."

Nolan threw up his hands. "No man knows what goes on in the heart and mind of a woman, and that's if she's Destrye and not a foul Báran sorceress."

"Be mindful how you speak of your queen."

"I have pledged that woman no fealty."

"You will," Lonen replied evenly, putting the weight of command behind it. "Or do you mean to challenge me as king?"

"And bring civil war to Dru, on top of everything else? Oh, that's a grand idea."

"Are you asking me to abdicate in your favor?"

Nolan's face was perfectly neutral, an impenetrable mask. "Are you offering?"

"It's been suggested that I should abdicate in favor of Ion's son, Mago. His claim takes precedence, even over yours."

"That was before the Trom attacked," Arnon cautioned. "We discussed it as a peacetime proposition because we believed the war had ended—and because Salaya campaigned for it. I never thought it was a good idea, even if it might ease her widow's grief, and would not support that measure now. We are as much at war as ever and Mago is too young to bear such a heavy responsibility. In times of war, a warrior must lead."

"I am a warrior, and not too young." Nolan gave them both long and pointed stares. If all had gone as it should, he would have been crowned king. It never should have been Lonen and they all knew it.

"By Destrye law, I became king the moment my father and older brothers died," Lonen spoke slowly, feeling the weight of it himself. "I believed you dead and grieved your loss, brother, with never a thought that you might have survived." Not exactly true, but the haunting terror that his brother might be trapped beneath the earth, broken, bleeding, and slowly dying without succor wasn't worth plaguing them with. "I took the sword of the Destrye from my father's dead hand. A hand that had been turned to jellied flesh by a monster so heinous it dropped my father and his heir with a touch, reducing every bone in their bodies to pulp. I had to wipe the hilt clean of unnameable substances just to keep my grip."

He paused to gather himself, his brothers watching with ill-disguised horror.

"I didn't want it, never sought to be king, but I took that responsibility," Lonen told Nolan. "I assumed the weight of it over their dead bodies, as my heritage demanded I do, and I negotiated our truce with the Bárans." He put down the wine goblet with a thump when Nolan opened his mouth. "It doesn't matter that the truce was violated by *some* of their people. I did my best by the Destrye, as our father would have wanted. We came home to a decimated people, but I kept going. It was on me to find a way to save us and by Arill, I have tried."

"You've done more than most men could have," Arnon said. "The aqueducts. Planting the late crops. Rationing food and water. Planning for winter. Nolan, he nearly killed himself, and this after a long and exhausting campaign."

"I don't question any of that," Nolan replied.

"But you question my competency now."

"I think you should consider that you might be compromised."

Silence fell among them, sharp-spined and treacherous to navigate.

"And you, Arnon—what do you think?" Lonen asked his younger brother.

"We don't know her," Arnon said quietly. "You ran off to Bára to demand answers, to hold this princess to her vow that they would observe the peace and no longer attack us, steal our water, burn our crops. I looked at that sword every cursed day and made myself consider that you would likely never return for it. Every time I made a decision in your name, I dreaded the day we'd reconcile ourselves to your death, and I'd have to hold the throne for Mago. If the Destrye survived long enough to for him to grow up.

"And then you returned—more than half-dead and apparently married to this Báran sorceress—who for all we know sent those attacks, who has swayed your heart and mind to the point that you snarl at us for asking the simplest of questions. We try to give you space to recover without her influence, and you barge into the ward for Arill's Blessings—the women's ward, even, where men are expressly forbidden to enter—you terrify our head healer, roar orders in all directions, install the sorceress in your bed, and refuse to admit anyone but a few servants. If not for them we'd wonder if the sorceress yet lived. You won't even admit our healers to tend you, though you need it badly."

"That was you who ordered Oria sent to that charity ward, who kept her from me?" Lonen gripped the arms of his chair, rather than strangle Arnon.

"We decided together," Nolan said, jaw tight.

"You had no right to—"

"This is the first time since you've returned that we've been able to talk to you." Arnon thumped a fist on the table in a rare show of frustrated temper. "What in Arill do you expect of us, Lonen?"

"I expect you to believe in and support me. If not because I'm your brother, then because I am your rightful king, whether any of us are happy about that situation or not."

"It's not that, Lonen, dammit." Arnon raked his hands through his already messy brown curls. "If it were one of us, you would do the same. If you believed we'd been captured and controlled by a sorcerer—and up until recently, you agreed their magic was an abomination against Arill, too—then you would fight to help us also."

"And I'm telling you that I am not controlled and I don't need your help. Oria is here to help *us*, to protect us from the Trom. You'll see."

"See what?" Nolan spread his hands wide. "They're gone and the damage has been done. You lost most of the unharvested crops. We have no nearby fresh water supplies for all these people hunkered down for the winter under the wings of Arill's Temple. You've made little progress in shoring up what was supposed to be emergency construction and not long-term housing. And there's no indication these 'Trom' and their 'dragons' will return. We have nothing left worth taking."

"Any number of people can bear witness to what the Trom and their dragons did," Lonen said. "Don't try to make it sound like a child's tale."

"My point is that we have bigger problems than you dreaming up some implausible cause for your sorceress wife. If I were king, I—"

"But you're not." Lonen cut him off and Nolan's piercing gaze flashed with anger before he directed it ferociously at his wine. Lonen choked back the temper and sighed. "We're all stuck with me being king, like it or not."

"There is legal precedent," Nolan said, not looking up, but staring into his cup, "for a king to be deposed by another with an equivalent or more potent claim to the throne."

"That civil war you mentioned?" Lonen tried to keep it light, but the implicit betrayal stung.

Nolan flicked a sharp glance at him. "Nothing so large scale or destructive. A duel would allow Arill to select her champion, according to the old ways."

Arnon drew a sharp breath. "Lonen is barely out of his sickbed. He cannot duel with you, even if Arill's priestesses agree to such an archaic ritual."

"If you wanted me murdered, brother," Lonen replied, holding Nolan's gaze, "you would have done better to leave me at the spring. I could have died in peace and you would not have had to sully your hands with my blood."

"I've thought back to that day." Nolan's eyes were dark. "And sometimes regretted my part in it. Particularly that I brought that viper of a sorceress here instead of leaving her there to fertilize the forest as I should have."

"I would have killed you for abandoning her."

"A dying man held no threat to me."

"I'm not dying now."

"And you may yet get the opportunity to try to kill me," Nolan replied, with no apparent emotion.

"Brothers—" Arnon began.

"I've had enough." Lonen cut him off. He drained his mug and eased to his feet, no longer bothering to hide the wince of pain. "Such a heartening interlude this has been. So worth leaving my sickbed for."

"Go back to her then," Nolan called after him. "She is pretty enough to distract you for a while. But you have to get out of bed sometime."

"Lonen." Arnon caught up to him, expression earnest, eyes grave. "Let the healers tend you. Give us that much."

"Not Talya," he growled. If he saw the woman, he might strangle her.

Arnon held up his hands. "Fine. Not Talya. Who?"

A fine question. "Baeltya."

"Isn't she a junior healer?"

"Yes. And she tended me when I was but a junior prince. She has a good manner." A quiet one that might not disturb Oria too greatly. "Send her."

"I will." Arnon gripped his shoulder. "We're on your side, brother."

"Then show it." He shrugged out of Arnon's grasp and strode away.

Alby, Lonen's lieutenant, met him outside the doors. He made no comment, but stayed closer than usual. Perhaps he thought he needed to be ready to catch Lonen if he fell, which meant he must look nearly as bad as he felt. Lonen would not let himself fall, however. They walked slowly down the long hall, as Chuffta slipped in through a crack in the ceiling and winged his silent way ahead of them.

~ 2 ~

"H*E'S LEFT THE dining hall and is coming your way,*" Chuffta spoke into her mind. "*He's not happy.*"

Oria restrained a sarcastic reply. As wise and clever as her derkesthai Familiar could be, the intricacies of human interactions sometimes escaped him. He'd faithfully relayed Lonen's conversation—if you could call it that—with his brothers, but that didn't mean he'd understood the nuances of all that had been said. So, instead of snapping at him, she vented her righteous anger by pacing in front of the stone fireplace. The room wasn't as big as her old rooftop terrace, but it gave her a decent amount of space to work out her annoyance. Especially since she had only her own emotional energy to wrestle.

One upside of having figured out how to shut out the chaotically overwhelming input of the wild magic: she didn't run the risk of overload of that variety. Small compensation as that also meant she had no way to replenish her magic, either. Nothing to be done about that.

She didn't blame Lonen's brothers for being suspicious of her—in fact, she'd warned Lonen countless times that his people wouldn't welcome her with open arms. She loved the Destrye warrior immensely, probably unwisely, definitely without meaning to—and that included his propensity for irrepressible optimism—but for once he should have been able to predict this inevitable outcome.

Things didn't turn out rosily just because he was so sure they would.

No, of course his brothers had questions—but the way they'd sneak-attacked Lonen had her burning with fury. She'd met them both only glancingly. *We don't know her.* Arnon's words echoed with quiet menace in her head. Along with the others they'd used. *Sorceress. Foul. Viper.* They didn't know her, but they distrusted, even hated her. Fine. That was to be expected as their people had been enemies for so long.

How could they show so little faith in Lonen, though? The Destrye warrior was everything that was noble, honest, and stalwart.

The doors to the outer chamber opened and after a moment, Alby stuck his head in to check the bedchamber, gave her a nod, and then stepped back for his king to enter. The lieutenant at least always treated her with neutral deference. He closed the door, leaving them alone. Lonen moved stiffly, with more than physical pain. Composing herself—restraining the impulse to go help, which would only get her snarled at—she arranged the supporting pillows in his favorite armchair near the fire and picked up a wine carafe.

"No more wine, love," he said, dragging the wreath of hammered metal leaves from his hair and tossing it on a chest, then unclasping his indoor furred cloak and throwing it on top. He made his way to the chair and eased himself into it. "My mind is foggy enough. I've apparently lost my head for drink these last weeks."

"Not surprising, as you've fallen out of training for it."

He snorted, the fresh scar over his right eye creasing as he stared into the fire where it leapt behind the intricately designed metal screen. Chuffta arrived from somewhere and settled himself into his favored nest on the hearth. The servants had quickly gotten over their fear of the winged lizard and had taken to spoiling him outrageously, with Alby setting the lead, bringing him all sorts of meaty nibbles and soft furs sized just for him. They assumed he was a pet, more like a favored hunting hound, and Lonen and Oria had decided it was best to let them continue to think so.

"Are you comfortable? There are more pillows."

"Don't fuss."

Aha. Those barbs aimed at his warrior toughness had lodged under his skin. Fine then. "How was the meeting with your brothers?" She tried to sound idly inquiring, fiddling with her own goblet of well-watered wine. She greatly missed her favorite fruit juice, but it was never among the food and drink served them and she wouldn't ask, lest Lonen feel guilt over something else he couldn't provide her. They might not have any fruit at all in this frozen realm.

No guilt in him now, he eyed her with some acerbity. "You're going to pretend Chuffta didn't relay every word?"

Ah, the guilt was hers, staining her cheeks with warmth. *"You were supposed to stay hidden."*

"I tried. There are not many places to hide in these enclosed rooms of theirs—and Lonen deliberately looked for me. No one else knew I was there."

Lonen was watching her still, knowing in his uncanny way that she conversed mentally with her Familiar. "I asked you to keep him with you."

"Clearly you suspected I'd disobey, as Chuffta says you searched him out," she replied stiffly.

Lonen massaged the scar. It had healed cleanly, but the way it crossed the path of that other, older scar made the skin around his eye pull. He'd developed a habit of rubbing at it when distracted or in thought. "I *requested* it of you because I don't want you unguard-ed."

She shrugged that off, tucking her hands in her sleeves. They were always cold in this wintery place. It might also be a sign of her slow failing without a source of purified sgath. Something else she couldn't change. "You know perfectly well he doesn't always listen—and he's found all sorts of ways in and out of your wooden rooms and passageways."

"Oria," Lonen said in that patient tone that mean he didn't buy her explanation. "Can we dispense with this? I've had enough verbal fencing for the time being."

"Yes," she replied, chagrined. Thoughtless of her. "I'm sorry."

He slanted her a crooked smile. "There's your one apology for the day. Will you sit or are you determined to pace about like Buttercup stuck in a short stall?"

She huffed a breath at being compared to the massive black warhorse. "I'll sit, if we can discuss what your brothers said to you."

"Deal. Bring your brush and pull the stool over."

"My hair doesn't need brushing." What it needed—quite desperately—was washing.

"It soothes us both."

Which was true, so she fetched the odd brush he'd arranged for her to have. With a handle and back made of wood, carved into delicate, intricate vines, it fit nicely in the hand. The business end, however, was made from some kind of animal bristles. It seemed fur shouldn't be so stiff, but these forest pigs Lonen described apparently sported such stuff. Strange as it was, her hair liked it well, and it pulled at the tangles far less than the one she'd left in Bára when they fled. Along with everything but the clothes she'd worn, all now consigned to the rag pile.

She tried to think of herself as unencumbered, gifted with a clean slate, rather than dependent on Lonen for every little thing.

Handing him the brush, she sat on the low cushioned stool between his knees, staring into the fire. He undid the knot she'd put it in, then the tie that held her braid and unraveled that. "I think you should leave your hair down," he commented, not for the first time.

"It gets in my way," she replied. Maybe he didn't notice that it needed washing. Hoping so, she refrained from saying anything about it, lest she lessen his pleasure or dull the moment.

Gathering the long fall of her hair, he ran the brush through, making a wordless hum of pleasure. Because of her particular limitations, they couldn't touch physically—not skin to skin—so his solution of indulging himself in touching her hair served as a substitute, however poor. It did relax her, however, and seemed to make him happy. As much as a sexless marriage could. His brothers just had to bring up Natly, Lonen's former lover. Oria had yet to see the Destrye woman in the flesh, though she'd glimpsed her in Lonen's mind.

A bitter irony, though, that Nolan had asssumed Lonen couldn't pry himself out of bed for luxuriating in sex with her, when they'd never had actual intercourse at all. One of a number of things about her Lonen had not divulged.

"I notice you let them believe I have my full powers," she finally said, since he didn't seem to be planning to speak first.

He remained silent a bit more. "It's better if they fear reprisals from you. And I'm confident you will yet regain your magic."

"Does nothing dim your optimism?"

"It's not optimism," he replied with hushed ferocity. "It's necessity. You're too thin, too pale. We need to find magic for you, and soon."

His intensity took her aback. "Well, I don't know where I'd get it from. I can barely touch the wild magic before it knocks me unconscious." And left her burnt to the core. Like trying to light a candle and having a bonfire blow up in her face.

"I have some ideas. Now that we're better, we can explore them."

"I'm fine. You were winded simply walking down to the dining hall."

"You're not fine," he said quietly. "You grow more wan by the day. Do you think I can't see it?"

She had hoped.

"Finding you a sustaining source of sgath is critical," he continued.

"Preparing for the inevitable incursions of more golems and Trom is critical," she retorted. "You and I both know Nolan is wrong—they'll return, and soon. Now that he's King of Bàra, with almost unlimited power, Yar won't waste the opportunity."

"Do you think he knows about those tunnels?"

The brush whispered through her hair as she thought, grateful that he allowed the change in conversation topics. Such an extraordinary revelation, the tunnels. "I really don't know. I didn't know about them—or that lake—but my father, even my mother, kept their secrets well. There was a great deal I didn't know before the siege. It's difficult to say what they might have shared with my brothers. With Yar the youngest and always..." Not easy to pick a single word to encompass Yar's character flaws. Understanding her pause, having helped her battle her younger brother for the crown, Lonen patted her hip, giving her tacit permission to move past it, too. "Anyway," she sighed, "I can't see that they would have shared information that sensitive with him. And if they knew we had a lake beneath Bára, why steal water from Dru?"

"That occurred to me, too."

"Perhaps it was a secret among few that was lost," Chuffta put in.

"True. Chuffta points out, rightly so, that the tunnels might have been built long ago to carry the water from your lakes to Bára, and even her sister-cities. The lake might not even have been for storing the water itself, originally."

"What do you mean?"

There had been a time she would have hesitated—no, absolutely refused—to share temple secrets with the Destrye. Moot now, along with so much else of her previous life. "You know how I explained that the coherent source of sgath lies below Bára, and that all her sister-cities have something equivalent?"

"Though each city is slightly different, which was why Gallia couldn't access Báran sgath as well as you could."

"Not right away, anyway." Hopefully Yar's beleaguered new bride had found a way to do so. She had enough trials stacked against her as it was. "But yes, each city is different—so I was taught, and Gallia's experience bears that out—though I don't know why that would be. It never occurred to me to wonder how the sgath got there. It always just *was*." So much she'd never examined closely enough, determined as she'd been to gain *hwil* and receive her mask as a priestess. Those goals seemed superficial and … juvenile now. "The priestesses replenished it, but that was a slow trickle compared to the enormity of the sgath stored."

"You think it has something to do with the lake?" Lonen broke into her thoughts.

"Maybe? Sgath is often correlated with water—it accumulates like a pool filling, it's dark, ever yielding, passive."

"Female."

"Yes." She laughed a little at that. They'd both learned that wasn't necessarily true.

"And grien, the male magic, is more like fire—active, forceful, bright."

"So the metaphor goes, yes."

"Then there's you, who somehow ended up with the ability to wield both."

"Against all reason and precedent."

"*As far as we know and you were told,*" Chuffta said. He appeared to be asleep, rounded white belly up before the fire, wings half splayed and rear talons curled in contentment, but his mind-voice remained animated and alert. "*I still think there wouldn't be such a strong prohibition against a woman wielding grien if it weren't possible. Has it occurred to you that there's no law against a man using sgath?*"

"*Because they can't—*" she began, then stopped herself. Or could they?

"*Exactly.*"

"Of course," she said aloud, to return to the point, "neither sgath nor grien are actual physical forces, so all of these descriptions are only analogies."

"But they exist in the world and affect physical things, so they must be physical."

She contemplated that. "I didn't realize you were such a philosopher."

"I'm not. Really we should put this to Arnon. He's the one who understands physics and such. He's the one who got us across the

Bay of Bára by charting the bore tides and the influence of the moons' phases on them. Since you associate sgath with Sgatha and grien with Grienon, maybe he'll have ideas on how the moons affect the magic flows, too."

"You've been thinking about this."

"Long hours abed lend themselves to contemplation, even for those of us not much inclined to philosophy." He sounded drily humorous. A welcome sound. He'd once had an irrepressible sense of humor, even at the worst of moments. His extended convalescence had managed to drain him of that as nothing else had. Convalescence and worry for her.

"I'm thinking Arnon will not be inclined to discuss how to replenish the magic that frightens the Destrye so badly."

Lonen's turn to be quiet, sifting her hair through his fingers. "He'll come around," he said finally. "Nolan's been at him, that's all."

She bit her lip on asking, then gave voice to her most salient fear. "Will Nolan truly challenge you to a duel for the throne?"

Lonen grunted noncommittally.

"A real answer, please."

"Only Arill knows. It would be extraordinary, but we live in extraordinary times."

"Is it a duel to the death?" she asked quietly, as if saying it softly would give the words less power to evoke the reality.

"One can't have defeated kings hanging about to rally the disaffected."

"So that's a yes."

"The whole duel is theoretical."

"But possible—even likely," she insisted.

"A fine turnabout that would be for us, yes? First your duel for the throne of Bára, then mine for Dru."

"Hopefully yours would turn out better than mine," she muttered.

"Hey." He set the brush aside and coaxed her to turn to face him, touching her only over the thick fur robe she wore. It both kept her warm and cushioned her from casual contact. Lonen settled his hands on her hips. "You won your duel in spectacular fashion. You defeated Yar handily—it's not your fault the temple intervened and called your use of grien anathema. You're a sorceress of rare and amazing ability. I haven't forgotten it and neither should you."

"*Was* a sorceress, of unreliable, untrained, and unpredictable ability," she corrected. "I appreciate the support, Lonen, and I won't pretend that when you say such things, it doesn't turn my head, but you can't—"

"Oh yes? Tell me how I turn your head," he murmured, his mood shifting into languid desire, as he tangled his fingers in the hair falling over her shoulder, and leaned in to breathe against her cheek. "If it's anything like how you affect me, it must be dizzying indeed."

"It is." Well and truly dizzying, exacerbated by being so close to him. With her portals so tightly closed, she didn't feel his thoughts and emotions nearly as easily, not unless he projected strongly or they were very close. Skin to skin opened up all the channels from another person into her—to an unbearable degree that strained her to the point of collapse and coma if sustained too long, almost like contact with wild magic—but skin a whisper apart from hers sent the feel of him into her on a manageable level, much as his warm and spicy scent filled her head.

The anger his brothers had stirred up brooded dark in the background, but above that swirled a potent mix of affection, admiration, and pure lust. His masculine exuberance had drawn her to him from the beginning, even back then, when it overwhelmed her ability to vent the energy again. With his slow return to health, each day immersed her in more of the vital wash of his presence. Though she welcomed that as a sign of his recovery, it also made it more and more difficult for her to contain her own longing for him.

"Lonen..."

"Yes, love?"

"Stop." She tried to pull back but his hand wrapped in her hair anchored her there. "We can't do this."

He lifted his head, studying her face. "Because you don't feel up to it?"

"No, that's not it." That was the thing. She really did feel more or less fine. Kind of out-of-body sometimes, but not terrible. *Wan.* That described it well. "We just can't—"

"We're doing it," he murmured. "So it must be that we can. You're so lovely in the firelight, Oria. The flames make your hair shine like a copper drum hit by the golden light of sunset. You look good in my furs, too. Perhaps you have ensorcelled me, as the least glimpse of you makes me want to chuck all of this nonsense and run back to the oasis. Maybe I should never have made us leave."

The memory of that peaceful place—and the magical buffer that had allowed them to touch—made her ache with nostalgia, and more. If only she hadn't been too ill from the wild magic for them to truly be together. "Don't joke about that—it's not at all funny."

"That's the thing. I don't think I'm joking. The need for you burns in me stronger than anything else. Make love with me, sorceress."

She laughed breathlessly. "You're impossible. We can't do any more than this."

"This much is good, but we can do more. Remember?" He lifted the hair he held and kissed it stroking the locks along his cheek above his neat beard. "This is me, kissing you, caressing your skin, making you tremble."

She did tremble, going as hot and wet as when he'd said such words to her when they consummated their marriage. *I would be kissing you now. I'd start with light ones, like butterfly wings on your lips, lulling you in until you felt safe enough to open your mouth ... Your lips wet and plump and pink from meeting mine ... By now you'd have opened your mouth to me. My tongue would be inside you, tangling with yours.* The memory he deliberately evoked shredded her recalcitrance. "Lonen..."

"Ah, I love it when you say my name that way," he murmured, sliding the other hand that had lingered on her hip up to cup her breast through the fur robe, pinching her hardening nipple. The fur lining that had been so plush a moment ago became torturously stimulating. "This is my mouth on you, warm and soft, then my teeth, nipping so you squirm."

She did squirm. "Stop this. We can't."

"We can. We are." He projected an image of it, parting her robe to bare her breasts, his dark head bending over her, mouth teasing her nipples. She pressed her thighs tight together against the ache, putting her hands in his hair just as he envisioned, careful not to touch his scalp, but tugging away the leather tie he favored—the one he'd once left behind in Bára and she'd kept for him—so his curls flowed free in her grasp.

"You're avoiding the conversation about the duel," she managed as he used his grip on her hair to tug her head back, exposing her throat along with the breast he wasn't tormenting.

"Please, Arill, yes," he answered. "Spread your pretty thighs for me, love."

"We shouldn't."

"Why not?"

She couldn't remember.

Then the door opened in the outer chamber. "Your Highness?" A voice she didn't know called out.

~ 3 ~

WITH ANOTHER GASP—NOT of the lovely sensual variety, either—Oria jumped up and drew her robe back together, retying the heavy sash. "That's why," she hissed.

Lonen's gray eyes glittered, silvery with arousal and amusement. "I *am* the king. All we have to do is tell her to go away."

"You can tell me to go, Your Highness," a woman said from the bedchamber doorway, her expression neutral, but lively curiosity in her eyes as she surveyed Oria, "but if I don't report back that you let me treat you, Prince Nolan will have Head Healer Talya in here. I understand you don't want that. Otherwise I wouldn't have interrupted."

"You're not interrupting," Oria replied, hoping her face didn't look as hot as it felt. Imagine if she'd capitulated and let Lonen continue. Worse if he'd taken it in his head to tie her to prevent accidental skin-to-skin contact—and for their mutual pleasure, as he'd discovered how well that worked for her, with those long-held and ill-advised fantasies of capture by her barbarian warrior. Yes, her face was likely bright red. She turned her back on the healer to hold her hands out to the fire, discovering Chuffta had slipped out at some point.

"I'm nearby, but if you're not going to play with your mate, I'll come back. Your fire is the nicest."

Because Lonen had Alby bringing wood by the armful and the servants keeping it extra hot, for her and her Familiar both. Chuffta had wanted to mind the fire himself, but Lonen ruled that out as unwise—given the derkesthai's tendency to become obsessed with bigger and brighter—and also technically difficult, as the heavy metal screen that kept sparks from leaping out was beyond Chuffta's power to move. The possibility that the screen could be left ajar gave all the Destrye horrors. Indeed, the stone that lined the fireplaces was the only she'd seen in the otherwise wood-built palace. Lonen compensated by tasking the servants to keep the blaze burning hot at all times. A thoughtful and considerate man.

"I'm closeted with my wife," that considerate man was grumping at the healer. "There's no pressing reason to treat me right at this moment."

"On the contrary, there is concern that being upright and attending the dinner took a toll on you, Your Highness," the healer returned, calm and remorseless. "I'm tasked to give you a full examination or treatment, and that's going to happen now. Concern for the king's health trumps his commands. It's me or Talya—take your pick."

"Yes, come back," she told Chuffta, to help things along. Lonen would not stomach Talya being around either of them, not after the way the head healer had treated Oria. He might have many sterling qualities, but Lonen also held certain … 'grudges' wasn't exactly the right word. Convictions, perhaps. Okay, he was the most obstinate man she'd ever met.

"I'm upright now," Lonen pointed out, digging in, so Oria turned back. The healer met her gaze with some exasperation. She wore a lighter green veil than Talya had, and her dark hair spilled out in curls that tumbled down her back and escaped around her face in a way that reminded Oria poignantly of Juli, her waiting woman back in Bára. Though Juli's curls were red-gold, and the Destrye woman's strong frame and capable, square hands were nothing like the Báran priestess's. Her dark eyes held determination, and a clear call for action from Oria.

"Lonen," she said, moving to him and laying a hand on his shoulder so he'd look up at her. "Part of being king is making sure your people are confident and unworried. You know this. Let the healer do her job. She can only help you heal faster and grow stronger. And it will reassure your concerned brothers," she added, her tone more wry than she'd intended.

"I'm glad to hear of your confidence," he replied. "Then you'll be happy to have her do the same for the Destrye queen, too."

She opened her mouth to protest, but he'd neatly trapped her with that one.

"I keep warning you that he's a clever man," Chuffta said, dropping from some vent he'd discovered and landing on her shoulder. Lonen had had the robe reinforced with padding for just that purpose, so the derkesthai's formidable talons wouldn't pierce through to her skin. Chuffta wound his long tail around her arm in affection, the iridescent white scales gleaming against the mahogany and chestnut shades of the fur. *"Probably cleverer than you are, so keep that in mind."*

"I shall, along with your questionable loyalty to me."

"I love you best, of course," her Familiar replied with equanimity, *"but it's my job to avail you of my considerable wisdom."*

She snorted with laughter and had to cover it with a cough. Though it was unlikely that the Destrye healer could do anything for her peculiar condition, this young woman possessed a compassion that Talya lacked. Maybe she'd abide by the strictures not to touch Oria, anyway. At the moment, the healer studied Chuffta, rapt with fascination. "The healer might not agree," she cautioned, speaking to the woman. "She's here for you."

The healer's dark gaze shifted to hers. "I'm willing. Please call me Baeltya."

"Agreed then. You'll treat the king first, of course."

Lonen gave her a narrow look of disbelief and she smiled back in all innocence. She'd outmaneuvered him for once.

"If you'll undress, Your Highness?" Baeltya suggested, not delaying in seizing the opportunity. She reached to help him, acting like a humble servant to the king, then narrowing her eyes, sharply noting the pained look on Lonen's face as he shrugged out of the furred vest, then lifted his arms to pull the shirt over his head. Bracing himself on the arms of the chair, he levered up, strode to the bed with a vigor made almost entirely of bravado, shucked his boots and leather pants, and stretched out naked.

Baeltya covered Lonen's groin with a towel, probably more for Oria's sake than Lonen's. Bárans weren't exactly prudes—they used communal baths, after all—but neither were they as casual of nudity as the Destrye. Or, more precisely, as Lonen was. Like all Destrye, he lived in a natural harmony with his body, and his natural confidence, an outgrowth of his exuberant presence, made him completely unselfconscious.

Oria drew up behind Baeltya in order to see better, but keeping a careful distance back. The healer kept her thoughts and emotions quite self-contained. Her native calm and reticence made her unusually restful for Oria to be around. Still, long habit and prudence had her observing a more formal space than others might. Chuffta snaked his long neck to peer at Lonen, too.

At least he'd gained back some of the weight that he'd lost during their harrowing journey. Lonen had complained that he grew soft and fat, lolling about and not yet able to resume the strengthening exercises she'd spied upon in Bára, but there was nothing flabby about him. His chest, arm, and shoulder muscles shone with clear definition in the warm light, the sprinkling of dark hair that covered him not disguising the hardened ridges. He was every inch the massively muscled warrior she'd first encountered storming the gates of Bára.

Except for the one side of his abdomen, where the golem bite had festered. There the skin collapsed over the missing parts of him like wet silk, wrinkled and folded. If only she'd done a better job of cleaning the wound initially, when she'd had all of those fallen golems with their packets of sgath to draw from. Or if only she'd realized he hid the infection from her and acted before the corruption destroyed so much of his flesh.

She tore her eyes away from the evidence of her failure to protect the man she loved, to find his gaze waiting—granite gray and flinty with it. He watched her with steady attention and she very nearly opened her portals just a sliver to read the thoughts and feelings behind his opaque expression.

With her eyes closed, Baeltya ran her hands over Lonen's body, probing the bad side, but also pausing over his lungs and heart. Oria couldn't sense what magic—if it was magic—she used on him. Mostly it annoyed her to be both superfluous and unable to touch her husband as the healer did so casually.

As Baeltya worked, Lonen's gaze softened, going from granite to fog, the lush black lashes lowering until they draped over his broad cheekbones. His breathing deepened and mouth slackened into sleep. A soft snore dragged out of him and Baeltya stood, turning with a smile.

"There. That will help," she said.

"How is he?"

Baeltya stretched her back. "His Highness is healing, albeit slowly. Rebuilding the organs and muscle he lost to the infection simply takes time. I'll return in the morning to give him another treatment. But he needs to be resting, not meeting with his brothers, or he'll begin to backslide despite my best efforts. I'll tell Prince Nolan as much."

"No—don't," Oria said before she thought better. Nolan might push things that direction, to better his chances of winning this duel he considered.

"Or he might treat the news that Lonen is improving as a reason not to try to depose him."

"I think either way it's better for Nolan to hear Lonen is healthier than he thinks."

"And that he's not ensorcelled by you."

"Can anyone even do that?" she snapped back mentally. If so, it would be handy to ensorcell Lonen's brothers out of their doubts.

"Once you have your magic back, perhaps you can try." Chuffta's mind-voice was dry.

Baeltya had her brows raised, both for Oria's preemptory command and the silence after. Her canny dark eyes flicked to Oria's Familiar and back to her face. "I must report back my observations. That was one of my three directives."

Three? "What were the others?"

The healer gestured to Lonen. "To assess the king's health and give him a healing treatment."

"What exactly did you do?"

Baeltya spread her hands. "I am pledged to Arill, the goddess of the earth and all growing things, so I channel Her nurturing power into the patient so they can heal."

Hmm. It sounded like nonsense to Oria. If a goddess truly existed, why would such a being care to give her power away? But if that was the Destrye analogy for magic, why hadn't she felt it?

"I didn't feel anything, either, but Lonen looks better."

Indeed, his color had returned, a healthier glow replacing the pastiness of exhaustion. He slept deeply, his body relaxed, not twitching with pain or nightmares.

"And the third part of your instructions?" Oria asked, though she suspected she knew.

Baeltya's wide mouth twitched, not quite smiling. "To assess the Báran sorceress, look for signs of enchantment, and ascertain her hold on our king."

Oria sighed mentally. Being right should be more fun. "And?"

"I haven't decided." The healer studied her. "I'll know more after I examine and treat you."

"I'm fine."

"Don't stiffen up. Part of my vows are to do no harm. Besides, you promised His Highness."

She had. Lonen must trust this woman. He'd likely thought he'd be awake for this, however. She could lie to Lonen and claim she had accepted a treatment.

Baeltya watched her, amusement sharpening her gaze. "I'll tell," she warned.

"So will I."

"You can't talk mind-to-mind with Lonen outside of the oasis.

"I have my ways."

"Traitor."

"I love you, too."

"All right then." Oria moved to the bed and drew up the fur blankets, covering Lonen to the chest, but leaving his arms outside it, as he preferred. She smoothed them over him, touching him the only way she could. Well, not quite the only. She brushed back a few of the curls rioting around his face, since she'd freed them of his hair tie. He looked so much younger in sleep, with none of the anger or bitterness war had carved into his face.

"You love him," Baeltya said, some surprise in her voice, and Oria whirled, tucking her hands behind her back as if caught by a senior priestess while looking at some illicit illustrations in the temple archives at Bára. She wasn't sure what to say—or if the healer saw something more than her gestures. Did she have something like a goddess-given version of sgath sight?

"Let's go into the other room, so we won't disturb His Highness," Oria suggested. Baeltya studied her with that discerning gaze, then nodded.

"Will you stay here with Lonen?" she asked Chuffta. *"Let me know if he stirs or needs anything."*

"Of course. I'll be right here if you need me."

The derkesthai uncoiled his tail and half-flew, half-hopped to the bed, snuggling into the furs and curling carefully against Lonen's side. Baeltya watched that, too, with the same bright interest, then led the way into the outer chamber when Oria gestured for her to. Oria pulled the door tightly closed. If Baeltya planned to make things difficult, Oria didn't want Lonen to overhear and be concerned.

"The dragonlet," Baeltya said, "he's quite intelligent."

Mentally, Oria rolled her eyes. Not as intelligent as Chuffta liked to think himself, she wanted to say.

"I heard that."

"Mind your own thoughts. And Lonen."

"I can do both of those things and mind your thoughts, as I'm so intelligent."

She contained the laugh. "He's a good companion," she temporized.

"You communicate with him somehow, don't you?" Baeltya said. "Sit here, please."

Oria sat in a chair before the smaller fire in the sitting area, keeping her expression remote. She might never have achieved true *hwil*, the perfect state of emotionlessness the priests and priestesses of Bára claimed to attain, but she had faked it well enough to fool all of them. She could easily hide her surprise—and an uneasy sense of exposure—from the Destrye healer. "Naturally. It would hardly be appropriate to keep an animal indoors if it could not follow simple rules and instructions."

Baeltya smiled, closed mouthed. "I suspect he's more of a companion to you than that."

"Is this part of your interrogation?"

The healer put her hands on her hips and sighed. "That was curiosity, and an attempt at friendly bedside manner so you'll relax. I've never met a Báran sorceress before, nor have I seen a winged lizard that seems as intelligent as our hunting hounds. Or more so. Believe it or not, my purpose—and calling—is to help."

"And to ascertain the magical hold I may or may not have on your king."

"I thought it would be better to be honest about that. Frankly I don't know how to assess such a thing if you have an agenda beyond your obvious love for him, and that he's never behaved with any woman that I know of as he does with you."

"Have you known Lon—His Highness for a long time?" She'd seen so little of this place and its people. Difficult to imagine what it had been like for Lonen, growing up here.

Baeltya smiled with some nostalgia. "We're of an age, so I first met him when I was a young apprentice and he had to be treated for a broken arm because he fell out of a tree. His sword arm, too, so his father, King Archimago, stood over him, berating him throughout the healing treatment."

"And you mended the bone?" How extraordinary.

"Not me and not entirely, but the head healer then was able to knit the bone within a week, with repeated treatments." She gave Oria an expectant look.

Fine then. "All right. Point made. What is your plan?"

"What I promised His Highness I'd do—evaluate and treat whatever problems I find as I did him." She moved toward Oria, who held up her hands to fend off the healer.

"You have to do it without touching me."

Baeltya stopped, studying her. "My art works through physical contact. I can't help you without touching you, and now the king has given me the go ahead. You don't command me. He does."

"He's asleep," Oria returned. "Or he'd back me on this. He understands."

"Understands what?"

"That you can't touch me," she said, with what she hoped sounded like patience.

"Is this some kind of Báran custom? I understand your nobility keeps far more formal practices and manners than we do." Though her voice remained neutral, Baeltya clearly found the idea off-putting. She wasn't incorrect, though those manners were driven by practical reality, not snobbery.

"It is customary—and absolute. You can't touch me."

Baeltya frowned. "I can promise that I'm objective. I don't derive sexual pleasure from it or anything like that."

The throbbing spot between her eyebrows begged to be rubbed, but Oria sat straighter to resist showing any weakness. "It's not that. There are real impacts."

"Explain this to me." The healer was as relentless as Lonen with her questions. Perhaps it was a Destrye trait.

"You wouldn't be able to understand." Oria sounded stiff and imperious to herself. Better than desperately cornered however.

"Do you need me?"

"No, I just need to find a way to make this healer go away."

"I can burn her. That always scares them."

She suppressed the smile. *"Not this time, but thank you."*

"I'm a smart woman," Baeltya was saying, her eyes snapping with offense. "I assure you I can understand a great many things, if you'll deign to explain them to this uneducated Destrye healer."

Giving in, Oria pressed her middle finger between her brows, discovering she'd broken into a fine sweat. So much for faking *hwil*. Any priestess of Bára would have spotted the cracks already. "I apologize if I gave offense." Apologizing to someone else shouldn't break Lonen's rule of one per day for each of them. And he wasn't awake to hear anyway.

Baeltya knelt beside Oria's chair, her dark eyes softer, full of sympathy. "Look. Oria. Am I saying it correctly?"

"Because you won't call me 'Your Highness'?"

The healer closed her mouth on something. "I can't. Not yet. Not without an oath of fealty. Work with me here."

"With a long 'i,'" Oria said, relenting. Talya had been vicious, but Baeltya seemed reasonably sincere. She couldn't treat them all like her enemies, not and live among them, be their queen, even, as Lonen so optimistically believed would happen. "Ohrr-eye-ahh."

"Oria," Baeltya repeated, mimicking the non-Destrye vowel twist perfectly. "I want to help you."

"You can't help me," Oria said as gently as she could. "I simply need to eat more and regain my strength from the journey, and from being unconscious for so long."

"You've been eating, so the servants report, since you awoke and His Highness brought you from the ward for Arill's Blessings. I don't know the norm for your people, but your weight appears to be quite low, you seem to be chilled, and your skin and eyes lack luster."

"Gee, thanks," Oria bit out. "This is a cold place. And I'm sweating now."

Baeltya surveyed her. "Nerves. And something more. That's a greasy sweat from imbalance. Your system is off; I can see that much without knowing you. Why not explain to me about Bárans and touch, and see if I can do something to put you on a path toward healing?"

Her perception surprised Oria. Perhaps there was something more to her goddess-given practice than superstition.

"If I explain, will you promise not to reveal my secrets to anyone?" Oria asked.

Baeltya nodded somberly. "You didn't need to ask. My vows to Arill and my calling prevent me from revealing anyone's medical condition."

Oria raised dubious brows. "Other than your report to Prince Nolan."

"I know how to give superficial information while redacting the personal," the healer replied easily. "Now, have I passed *your* test?"

It had been one, Oria realized, and she smiled ruefully. "I apologize again. I feel...somewhat embattled here."

Baeltya smiled, full of charm. "I can only imagine. It can't be easy to have come among us under any circumstances, let alone as one of the hated enemy, near death and suspected of seducing and ensorcelling our king. Some say that you're a shapeshifter who can become one of the Trom and your pet can grow to a full-sized dragon."

Oria blinked, assimilating that. "That's quite the story."

"Oh, there's lots more rumors than that," Baeltya replied cheerfully. "How about you let me in on some of the truth?"

How to begin on such an enormous topic? "Being a sorceress means I absorb magic from the world."

Baeltya nodded encouragingly, so she continued.

"If someone touches me, it creates a kind of conduit, their skin conducts to mine and all sorts of stuff comes in. Thoughts, emotions, without filter. Depending on the sort of person they are, it can overwhelm me."

"Hmm." Baeltya looked thoughtful. "Are all Bárans like you?"

"Only the magically inclined. And I'm unusually sensitive."

"So the magically inclined don't have children—because you can't touch anyone," she reasoned.

The healer did possess a quick mind. "Your logic is sound, but there are exceptions. Some people are … better suited. Our mothers and fathers don't impact us. They're more in harmony, in a way."

"I see. So, despite the differences between our peoples, you found this harmony with His Highness and so are able to be his lover."

Oria didn't bother to correct the healer on that. If Lonen's brothers suspected the truth, that she could never fully be Lonen's lover and bear him heirs, they'd take it as one more reason to depose him. If she'd found an ideal match among her own people, she might have borne children. "There are other possibilities, too," she continued. "Some people have developed control of themselves so they don't leak nearly so much."

"Aha. Control. I'd wondered about that. Can you sense my thoughts and emotions from there?"

"You just believe me on all of this?"

"Why would you lie?" Baeltya shrugged. "We're working on the assumption of trust here. You trust that I want to help, that I'll keep your secrets and I'll trust you in turn not to harm me and to tell me the truth."

"Harm you?"

"You're a powerful sorceress. I've heard the stories of what magics your people can wreak. I've treated many warriors returned from your walled city, wounded by forces difficult to comprehend."

It's better if they fear reprisals from you. Oria understood Lonen's reasoning there—he wanted to protect her—but she'd never wanted to be feared. "All right. At this moment, I'm not reading your thoughts and emotions. The closer you are to touching me, the more I can sense, particularly if I try."

"You can control how much you receive then?"

"Yes, to some extent." She found herself smiling. "Lonen doesn't much care for me prowling around in his head."

Baeltya grinned back. "I can just imagine. Let's try this. Over your sleeve is okay, yes?" When Oria nodded, the healer put her hand on the longer fur of the cuff of her robe, very close to the skin of her wrist. "What can you sense?"

Oria drew in a breath and allowed her senses to open ever so slightly. She wasn't as attuned to Baeltya as she was to Lonen, but the woman's presence resolved crisply and suddenly in her mind's eye. Resonant with bright green energy, her emotions shimmered like leaves in a spring storm. Sincerity, curiosity, a desire to help, a sense of urgency. Images followed: Baeltya as a girl, making her vows to the goddess, the sense of Other filling her, making her whole again. Not so alone. There she was even younger, an orphan, weeping over her parents on a farm, their bodies sliced to ribbons, livestock similarly dead and bleeding everywhere. Old, deep grief.

Oria yanked herself back, meeting the healer's calm gaze. "You were so young," she said. "The golems. Our golems—they did that, killed your family, destroyed your farm?"

Baeltya yanked her hand back as if burned. "You saw all of that?"

"I'm sorry. When I said I can control it, that's an exaggeration. Sometimes I see more than I mean to. I didn't intend to invade your privacy."

"No, it's all right." Baeltya rubbed her fingertips together. "I wanted to show you what the goddess-sent healing feels like. The rest must be attached to that."

"Strong emotions can be that way," Oria agreed. "Tied to old memories. We can stop there."

"No, no—that was a first step. To find the baseline, if you will. Now I want to try something else." Baeltya closed her eyes as she had with Lonen, stilling herself. Her presence drew back palpably. Much like a Báran meditating to nourish a state of *hwil*, Oria realized with a sense of dislocation. The Destrye knew of such practices? But how, and why did the temple—"All right," Baeltya broke into her whirling thoughts, her voice even, slightly remote, "I'll touch your sleeve again."

She did. Oria waited for the return of the Destrye woman's presence and memories.

"Anything?"

"No." How curious. Not even a breath of that green vibrant energy.

"I'm going to touch your skin. Tell me if it pains you."

"Believe me," Oria replied, bracing herself for the agonizing onslaught, "you'll know."

Baeltya smiled slightly, then slowly moved her hand onto Oria's. Anticipating the jolt of searing invasion she'd experienced before, Oria jumped a little at the shock of contact. The healer opened her eyes in concern, but didn't move. "Yes? No?"

To her astonishment, Oria felt nothing from the woman. Just a warm hand on her skin and a hint of something, like the faint scent of the inside of a leaf. "That's amazing. I'm fine. How did you do that?"

"I kind of reversed what I normally do, so I wouldn't flow into you. Now I'm going to see if I can do an assessment without changing that flow. Is that all right?"

Oria relaxed back, stunned to feel so reassured by the soothing contact. "Yes. Go ahead."

The healer's energy flowed through her, but without invasion. Like a soft evening breeze that sifted over her skin, but never stirred her hair. In its wake, warmth lingered behind, a hint of the desert sun Oria missed in her very bones, along with a kind of well-being she hadn't felt since her father died and her mother collapsed. She nearly melted into the chair with the sweet surcease of it.

"You're starving."

At Baeltya's words, Oria forced open her heavy eyelids to find the Destrye healer standing before her, rubbing her hands together in a way Oria recognized—a method for shedding accumulated magic.

"Why are you starving?" the healer mused, almost to herself. "I've done what I can for you, and you napped for a bit which did you good, but you're going to have to help me here. We don't have much food, what with the rationing, but you clearly need more than you're getting. Or do you need a different kind of food?"

"I don't think any kind of food will help," Oria told her. At least whatever the healer had done for her helped fend off the specter of despair.

"Oria—I'm not sure you understand. I've seen people who've starved to death who weren't as far gone as you are. We need to take action or you won't last much longer."

"How much longer?" Lonen asked from the doorway, startling Oria. She hadn't heard him open the door. Nor had Chuffta warned her.

"You were sleeping. It was good for you."

Lonen strode in, barefooted, wearing only his leather pants, his hair hanging down his back, and took Baeltya by the shoulders. "Tell me straight. How much longer?"

~ 4 ~

HE MISSED ORIA immediately when he awoke, knowing with some deep sense he'd acquired that she wasn't in the room. The warm weight nestled against his side stirred, and Chuffta lifted his head, emerald green eyes shining like jewels in his narrow, triangular face. He'd liked being able to hear the derkesthai's thoughts—snotty as they'd been at the time—because reading the expression in that reptilian gaze wasn't easy. As if understanding, which he might, Chuffta cocked his head and lifted his wings in a very human-seeming shrug.

Lonen chuckled and lifted a tentative hand to scratch the spot between the golden horns that curved out of Chuffta's head and rub the surprisingly soft white ears that flanked them. The derkesthai leaned into his hand, making a rumbling sound of pleasure that sounded much like a cat's purr. Not an easy spot for Chuffta to reach, that little valley, Oria had explained, and Lonen could see why. After a moment, though, Chuffta pulled away and looked at the door. A murmur of feminine voices where there had been silence.

"Best see what's up, eh, Chuffta buddy?" He levered himself up, feeling considerably less winded, his side moving more easily as he pulled on his pants. He could be the better man and admit they'd been right about treating him. That would be the answer to ending this enforced inaction. He needed to get into top form—okay, at least working condition—to find Oria a sustaining source of magic.

The rest could wait, Arill take them.

Opening the door, he heard the tail end of the conversation, words that chilled his blood. *...or you won't last much longer.*

"How much longer?" he demanded. Oria whirled in the big chair that dwarfed her slight frame, her mass of hair crackling, strands rising with static like the flames leaping behind her, copper eyes enormous in her white face. So much thinner. He'd noticed it before, but her unusual appearance always struck him as exotically beautiful. Now he could see how her high cheekbones stood out like knife blades, her skin seeming nearly transparent enough for them to cut through. Seeing her clearly, without the fog of love and relief at having her alive and with him, filled him with rage that he'd been allowing himself to live in a fantasy the last few days.

Does nothing dim your optimism?

Apparently, a dose of reality from a healer did. Baeltya's eyes widened, though not in alarm—concern?—as he took hold of her and asked how much longer.

"I can't answer that," she said.

He resisted the urge to shake the truth out of the woman. Baeltya had the sheen of Arill about her, as all the best healers did. She knew more than she let on.

"Can't or won't?" he snarled.

"Lonen." Oria was beside him, hand hovering next to his arm, where normally she'd touch him if he'd remembered to put on a shirt. "Baeltya helped me. She can touch me without harm. Don't break her." A smile ghosted around her lips.

He let go of the healer. "I didn't hurt her," he grumbled. "Wait—she could touch you?"

"Yes." Oria nodded with a broad smile. "Something to do with her healer's control, like our *hwil.*"

"Is this something I can learn?" he demanded of Baeltya. The possibilities whirled in his mind, while the healer gaped, clearly thrashing for an answer to the odd question from her king.

"It would involve meditating, no doubt," Oria teased him. At least some of her mischievous spirit had returned.

"To lie with you, I'd learn even that," he told her with fervor, and she shifted, flicking a cautious glance at Baeltya. "Fine. We'll pursue that later. I want my straight answer."

Baeltya held up her palms, unruffled. "I can't answer, not won't. Oria isn't just foreign, she's different from the Destrye in many ways. Her physiology and energy feel unlike anything I've encountered before. I'd hesitate to predict anything with her."

"But you said you could compare her to other patients, who you knew to be starving."

Baeltya frowned in thought. "Yes, I can discern that much, though even that is odd. She 'feels' malnourished to me on both those physiological and energetic levels. I don't understand it."

"Then you should have a sense of how long she has."

"I don't. I have some ideas that might—"

"Stop hedging, healer. How long?"

"She should be dead already!" Baeltya snapped. "If she were Destrye, she would be."

It took a moment for his stricken heart, to catch up to a regular beat. "You have to help her."

"I am working on it, Your Highness."

"Enough of this," Oria put in with some asperity, her voice cutting. "I do happen to be standing right here. I'm not one of your horses that you can be debating whether it's too ill to be put down."

"Of course not, love," he said, with some chagrin. Baeltya noticed the endearment, drawing in a breath, and looking between them. Better to make that clear, too. He'd kept them closeted too long. His people—and his family—would soon learn that he would not budge on his feelings, or on Oria's place in his life. He'd abdicate first, if they forced him into it. "I apologize."

Oria smiled at him, copper eyes soft with an affectionate glow she reserved only for him and Chuffta. "There's *your* one for the day. Baeltya, you said you have ideas? I feel much better for your treatment, so I'd like to hear them."

"Well, let's start with the prosaic. Do you normally eat anything that you're not eating now?"

Oria's smile quirked a bit to the side. "That's an easy yes. Almost nothing here is what I ate before."

"Like what?"

"I never ate meat before this. Bárans eat lots of fruits, leafy greens, vegetables, grains. We do eat bread, like you do."

Baeltya cast him a look, making him feel abruptly like a careless boy again rather than King of the Destrye. "Why haven't you ordered these foods brought to her?"

"Meat is good for her," he grumbled. Arill knew he'd gone to enough trouble to force it down her stubborn throat. Now that he had her compliant on the matter, he'd kept up with it. Meat built muscle and bone, didn't it?

Baeltya sighed heavily for his idiocy, putting her hands on hips and shaking her head. "Your Highness," she began, as if using his title again would mitigate the scolding to come, "a person who's spent her entire life, whose physiology for generations—" she cast a glance at Oria for confirmation.

"At least," Oria replied.

"Whose physiology for many generations is acclimatized or even adapted to extracting nourishment from non-meat sources, cannot simply go to an all-meat diet and thrive on it. Her body isn't set up to process it effectively."

"It hasn't been all meat," he said in his defense, though really there wasn't any. "There's been bread, too."

Oria laced her fingers together. "I mainly eat the bread," she confided, and Baeltya threw up her hands.

"What?" Lonen stared at her. "What about all the meat I give you?"

She lifted her chin in defiance. "I can't eat all that. It makes my stomach hurt, so I slip it onto your plate when you're not looking. You need it, too."

He processed that, stunned. "Oria, if you think—"

"Arill save us," Baeltya interrupted. "All right, at least this I can do. It's the wrong season for leafy greens, but we do have stores of various grains, root vegetables, and dried fruits. What about fruit juices?"

"I would kill for some fruit juice," Oria replied with fervor.

Lonen absorbed her bright-eyed enthusiasm with a growing sense of betrayed injury. "Why didn't you tell me? You know I'd give you anything you asked for."

Baeltya cleared her throat. "I'm going to step out for a moment and get a nourishing meal on its way while you two sort this out."

Oria thanked her and waited for the outer door to close, returning her somber gaze to his. "Let's sit." She went back into the bedchamber and took her accustomed place by the bigger fire, curling her bare feet up under her, tucking them beneath the hem of the furry robe. Chuffta had also returned to his nest before the fire, the fine tip of his tail tapping in welcome, though he otherwise didn't move. The both of them, still adjusting to the cold. And it wasn't even deep winter yet. For himself, he left his shirt off as he sat, the fire almost too hot for him. A small sacrifice to make.

"Lonen," she began, twisting her fingers together, "this is a strange place for me to be."

"I know Dru is different, but you'll get used to it. You've barely seen this land. Wait until I show it to you."

"It's not that." She shook her head slightly, then tucked a heavy lock of her shining copper hair behind one ear. "I mean, I look forward to seeing Dru. From the few leaves I've seen, the trees must be enormous. And lakes! I want to see those, too. No, I mean, it's strange for me to be in this position where absolutely everything I need comes through you. Food, clothing, this fire, healing. My very life depends on you and I don't … like asking for more."

"You don't like it," he echoed, feeling a dangerous edge, though he tried to contain it.

She eyed him warily, far too sensitive to his moods. "Don't get angry."

"I'm not." Though he was and they both knew it. "Let me ask

you this—how can I know what you need if you don't *like* asking for it?"

Her eyes flashed hot copper. "Don't pull attitude with me, Lonen. I'm trying to be honest here."

He flung himself out of the chair, pacing off the surge of … okay, anger. First his cursed brothers, now this. "Since you're being so honest, how about telling me why in Arill you still don't trust me? I thought we were past this. You're my *wife*, Arill take you. You know I love you; you say you love me. We're in this together. You're not dependent on me. Everything I have is already yours. Why can't you understand that?"

She had her face averted, and Chuffta raised his head, looking to her. She gazed back at her Familiar as they clearly exchanged some confidences, ones that left him out. "What does Chuffta say?" he demanded.

Oria transferred her gaze to him, her eyes pooled with unshed tears. "That you're a boor and a brute of a barbarian Destyre warrior and I'm better off without you!"

Lonen clenched his fists and growled. "He said no such thing."

"Then why did you bother to ask?" she snapped at him, tucking herself deeper into the chair and hugging herself.

"Oria." The anger drained out of him, like water lost from a broken vessel. He dropped to the rug at her feet and laid his head on her fur-covered knees, wrapping his arms behind her slim hips. "I am a boor and a brute. I'm sorry."

Her fingers drifted through his hair, soothing with the relief the caress brought him. "You're not. I shouldn't have said so. I'm sorry, too. There—we're even with each of us over by one for the day."

"Then we'll have to be sure to do nothing to apologize for to-morrow."

"That would be good," she said softly.

"I thought everything would be okay," he said, rubbing his cheek against the fur, "if we could just get to Dru. Back in the desert, even the oasis, I just felt so certain that, once here, we'd be all right, that everything would fall into place."

"There's your rosy optimism coming into play," she replied, though she didn't sound scornful with it. "I love that about you, Lonen, I really do. But things don't end as in the tales. There's no happy ever after in real life. There's just the ending of that time of trial, and then the people go on to face new trials. We maybe don't usually hear that part of the story, so we forget it."

He lifted his head, resting his chin on her knees, looking up at her. "We can go back to the oasis. You at least weren't starving for magic there."

"You said it wasn't sustainable—no game coming in, no fruits on the trees, or other food to gather."

"We'll take food with us. Chuffta and I can go hunt in the desert."

"And we'll do what? Just hang out and do nothing all day?"

"And have sex. Lots and lots of sex," he reminded her, massaging her back through the robes. "We can touch there."

A light, pretty flush graced her cheekbones. "Besides that. We married for duty, to serve our peoples, not to run off and indulge ourselves in sex."

"The latter is sounding better to me all the time."

"Be serious, Lonen—we have responsibilities. You said it yourself."

He regretted that, too. It had seemed so urgent to get them back to Dru, to save the Destrye. "That was before I knew Nolan had survived. He can be king instead. I never wanted it. He does."

"Nolan can't fight Yar or the Trom," Oria said gently, her expression oddly compassionate as she brushed a curl back from his forehead. His hair tie was around there somewhere. "You know that as well as I do. No matter what your brothers think, we both know this war isn't over."

"I can't fight them without you." The ache grabbed his throat. "Without you I won't even want to."

"Don't say that," she whispered. "You're not a man who stops fighting, not for any reason. Look how far we've made it. That's all because of you and your determination to get us here to Dru."

True. And part of that had determination had also been to save Oria. Maybe that had been rosy optimism, but he'd believed Arill's healers could help her, that she could find magic here. That they'd triumph. Somewhere, deep in his heart, he still believed that.

"You're going to get better," he told her.

She looked amused. "Is that an order, Your Highness?"

"It is, Your Highness."

"I take it you two have made up?" Baeltya said from the doorway. She had the grace to look slightly abashed at Lonen's glare. Healers claimed a certain autonomy that let them skirt even the more relaxed protocols of the Destrye nobility, but cheekiness went a bit far. "That is, the food is on its way, Your Highness, Oria."

"Your Highnesses," Lonen corrected.

Baeltya edged into the room. "Not under Destrye law, King Lonen."

"A formality only."

"A critical one," Baeltya pointed out. "And not my purview. Oria's health is, so let's discuss the energetic aspect of her condition."

He deferred to Oria on that one, who was naturally discussing it with her Familiar. She got a certain look in her eye when she did, an unfocused distraction that gave her away. Not that he'd reveal how he could tell, as it gave him a rare window into the thoughts of his sorceress wife.

Her focus returned to him. "Baeltya says I can trust her with my secrets."

It was a question for him. He stood, pulling on his shirt while he thought. Arill's healers did take a vow of confidentiality, but there were also plenty of stories throughout history of healers helping various political factions with the potent information they extracted. Without studying Baeltya outright, he considered her and checked his gut feeling about the junior healer. He'd picked her to attend him because she wasn't Talya—not necessarily a strong recommen-dation—and because her calm and steady reserve reminded him of Juli, who'd been good for Oria—which might be as good a recom-mendation as any.

"Oria has explained her skin sensitivity to me, and that it's part of her absorbing magic from the world," Baeltya said evenly, catching his eye. "I can guess that if she is starving energetically, that's because she's not able to absorb what she needs here in Dru, because we have no magic here."

"That's true," Oria said, not flinching when he narrowed his eyes at her in warning. "If it's a choice between trusting her and maybe living or not trusting anyone and dying, I'm going to take the risk." Her eyes held the knowledge of the same feelings he'd confessed to her. She wouldn't necessarily act to save herself, but she'd gallop headlong into every battle in order to save him.

He folded his arms and leaned against the mantel. "Go on, then. It's up to you to decide what to tell."

She nodded at him, her expression soft as a kiss, then spoke to Baeltya. "You do have magic here. It's everywhere, arising from all living things, pushed and pulled by the moons as they wax and wane. But here it's what we call wild magic. It's... chaotic. Very strong but also in a form I can't digest, to compare it to food."

"Like deer can eat bark but we can't, because our guts aren't set up for it," Baeltya supplied, thoroughly intrigued, judging by the light in her dark eyes.

"That makes sense. Only imagine the tree falling on you because you can't eat it. In Bára, we had a source of purified magic, called sgath, that we could all draw on."

"How did it get purified?"

Oria glanced at Chuffta, silent a moment. Then shook her head slightly "We don't know."

"We?" Baeltya pounced on that. "You *can* communicate with it."

"You Destrye and your 'its,'" Oria laughed, holding out an arm to her Familiar. He hopped up, craning his neck with interest at the healer. "His name is Chuffta. He's a derkesthai and, yes, I can talk to him mind-to-mind. He's slightly smarter than your hunting hounds. Ow!" She pulled her hair from Chuffta's mouth where he yanked on it. "Okay, much smarter. You can touch him, if you like."

Baeltya's face went reverent as she ran a finger down Chuffa's arched neck, and Lonen remembered that feeling well. He'd expected the scales to be hard and slick, not soft as talc. "As smart as we are?" she asked.

"Different," Oria hedged. "Don't you bite me. You know it's true. He is similarly intelligent, though he sees the world differently. His kind tell stories to transmit history, rather than recording them in books."

"Oral histories." Baeltya's shrewd gaze flicked to Lonen. "Once the Destrye were the same. Barbarians telling tales around the campfires."

"We've progressed in any number of ways since then," Lonen pointed out.

"And not in others," Baeltya retorted.

"A work in progress," he agreed without rancor. Oria looked back and forth between them, filing the information away in her own keen memory.

"So," Baeltya returned to business, still stroking Chuffta, who tipped back his chin for a scratching there from the healer's adept fingers. "You said, 'we don't know,' meaning you and Chuffta. He advises you?"

"Yes, he's my Familiar. He helps me manage chaotic magical input, gives me advice, and is my oldest friend. Neither of us knows how the sgath came to be below Bára, except that the part of the duties of any priestess is to take sgath she absorbs and feed it into the common pool."

Baeltya frowned. "That's circular. You pull it from this source and also put it back?"

Oria looked thoughtful. "I never thought of it in those terms. Some things you just grow up thinking you know, and then when you step back and evaluate them through other eyes, they don't make sense."

"I think that's part of becoming an adult," Baeltya replied, glancing at Lonen again with wry amusement, then away, as if remembering herself.

"Maybe one day I'll find out," he commented and Oria rolled her eyes.

"So, maybe you can purify the wild magic, create your own reservoir here," Baeltya prompted. "If you knew how to input to the one in Bára, you should have the instinct and ability."

Oria blanched at the mention of accessing the wild magic, a glimmer of fear she so rarely evinced. "I think… that is not an option," she said softly.

"Maybe you can find a way to both cushion the effect on yourself and then purify and store it. It seems someone in your ancestry must have done that in the first place."

"Oh yes? You sound very confident of that. Is that how your Arill-delivered healing happened? A priestess woke up one day and said, 'hey, I think I'll meditate a whole bunch and see if Arill will give me some of her divine power!'" Oria's eyes flashed with emotion as she said it, so Lonen didn't laugh, knowing that her fear spoke.

Baeltya regarded her steadily. "Actually the legend is pretty close to that. I'll tell it to you some day."

If he'd expected her to apologize to the healer again, she didn't. Instead she firmed her chin. "I'd be interested to hear that. It would be helpful if I had a similar legend to work off of. Everything I've been told is that wild magic means death—fast or slow—but death."

"Overload on one hand, or starvation because you shut it out?"

Oria inclined her head in acknowledgment, a rueful twist to her mouth—that became a smile for her Familiar. "Chuffta says the problem with humans is that we're too black and white, that it's not always one thing or another."

"So, is there another option?"

"There's one." Oria's coppery eyes, dark now with consideration, looked to his. "Though that solution has a number of moving parts also."

"We'll discuss that," he told her, certain she contemplated some plan of enticing golems through the recently discovered tunnels so she could steal the packets of sgath they carried. Perhaps the danger of that truly would be less than her wrestling the wild magic, but he knew fighting golems from personal experience. His side throbbed with the memory and the scar over his eye twitched. He wanted Oria far from the lethal creatures. "A possible back up plan, but even you have to admit it's far from a long-term solution."

"Then it's back to you purifying wild magic into a sgath source like you had in Bára," Baeltya pointed out in all practicality.

"It is some sort of cycle," Oria mused. "We've been wondering if the source in Bára has something to do with that underground lake."

"That Prince Nolan nearly drowned in?" Baeltya raised her brows. "That would be interesting. Though we have no underground lake here that I know of."

"We have other lakes." And he would take Oria to one. He should have thought of it sooner.

"Lake Scandamalion is a day's journey from here," Baeltya pointed out. "It's the closest with any water left in it."

"And that's not the one I have in mind." No, he'd take her to Lake Chenault, his favorite. If they only had a little time left—*don't think of it*—well, he wanted her to at least see it.

"Surely you're not thinking of going to—"

"Where I go is my business, healer. I'll remind you of your vows."

"Your Highness," Baeltya gave Chuffta one last caress and held up her palms in surrender. "Is that wise?" Her question held a volume of unspoken information.

"It's not," Oria put in crisply. "You cannot leave the palace now. Not with all that's going on."

"I am king," he told his wife, ignoring the healer. "I decide what

I can and cannot do."

"Don't pull out your 'hear my manly roar' bluster with me." Oria glared at him. "You might be a barbarian, but you don't frighten me."

"Maybe I haven't tried hard enough," he replied in a tone as silken as the robes she once wore.

Baeltya looked between them and, apparently deciding they were done, scrubbed her palms together. "I'm going to check on that meal. I think I heard the servants."

"Besides," Oria continued, "you have no idea if *your* plan would work either. Neither you nor I know where to begin."

"I actually do have an idea on that." One he'd been nursing for some time. If his memory served him correctly, he might have something of a place to start. "For tonight, though, you eat the food Baeltya has arranged. We'll sleep. Tomorrow, after another round of treatments, I will introduce you to my brothers, show you to the people, and settle matters there. The day after, if the healer approves, and if we've thought of nothing else, we'll set out on our journey."

"I agree that we'll talk about possibilities more then."

"There's but one viable possibility, if you're not too stubborn to see it."

"I don't know about this, Lonen."

"Trust me." He'd meant it to be firm, but an edge of a plea filtered in.

"I do." She trailed long fingers down Chuffta's back. "I promise that I do."

As much as she trusted in anything anymore.

~ 5 ~

THE FOOD DID help. The fruit juice, in particular, sank like a balm to some dried-out core of her, saturating her desiccated soul. Though the root vegetables were somewhat wizened, they still tasted nourishing, particularly with the salted cream that Lonen dolloped on the starchier ones for her. She hesitated to eat too much, thinking of how lean the Destrye stores must be, but Lonen gave her such a threatening scowl that she didn't voice it. With her belly finally full in a satisfying way instead of a gut-cramping one, she grew sleepy.

Lonen was groggy, too, from the healing nap, so they crawled under the furs together, the room lit only by the fire, and fell asleep. With Lonen's arm draped over her hips over the thick, quilted nightgown she wore, she slept deeply.

For a while.

Until the wild magic invaded her dreams, that was.

At first she thought she lived her life as she always had—which should have clued her in, because her life had become anything but normal. All of that was shattered and gone.

But the dream worked on her so she forgot all that, walking among the flowers and hanging vines of her rooftop terrace, atop her tower in Bára. The blue desert sky arced above, cloudless and hot. All around, the towers of Bára rose in fanciful spires, capped and scrolled in the colors of the sun.

Chuffta preened on the carved balustrade, a shimmering white so bright she squinted against his brilliance. He looked at her, the green of his eyes almost painful.

"Don't forget what I am, Oria. Or what you are."

She paused, trying to remember how to reply mentally, but her brain felt mute, stuffed with silk.

As she struggled to move, to think, trapped and mesmerized, the reptilian black slits of the small dragon's pupils widened, expanding so his eyes became matte pits that consumed his narrow head. His skull and body swiftly caught up. Then his eyes grew. Then the body and wings again, leapfrogging each other. He swelled until he filled the terrace, and beyond, overlapping the balustrade, squeezing her out, until she hung perilously over the precipice, pinned between the abyss of the city and his black eyes, now larger than herself.

"Don't forget," his mind-voice grated over her brain, burning into it, setting her on fire with its leaf-dry, knife-edged hiss. *"You've taken not one, but several steps farther down your path."*

"No." Her mouth muffled it, refusing to work, just like her mind. "No!" she tried again, pushing out the shout that was only a mutter.

"We come when summoned. Don't forget."

"Never!" She arched away, the dizzying drop threatening to devour her. "I won't."

"You will. Queen Ponen. Don't forget."

"Let me go!" She screamed it, wrenching away, and fell. She plummeted from the tower, stretching her arms to become wings, wild magic swirling in, exploding her body, transforming her into a dragon so black she became a hole in the sky.

She burned with the power. Arching her neck, she trumpeted it to the sky. Fire, thick and turbulent, welled up like vomit, billowing from her lips. She screamed her triumph after it, the coal of terror sending agony through her heart.

Burn!

"Oria!" A stinging slap to her cheek brought with it a searing impression of Lonen—and a font of his emotions slamming through her. Anger. Despair. Terror. Love. Desperation. The tumult shook her, but also made sense, human sense, in a way the wild magic didn't. "Arill, take you, Oria, wake up!"

"I'm awake!" she gasped. Then gasped again, dragging at the air. She couldn't breathe.

"Lonen is sitting on you." Chuffta's mind-voice—his real mind-voice—fluted through her head, real and reassuring, too.

Lonen leaned close to her face, looming over her, a shaggy, wild silhouette against the dimming fire. He had her pinned by the wrists, thighs clamped on either side of her hips, his weight crushing. "Breathe!" he demanded.

"Get. Off. Me." She managed while struggling to draw breath.

In a flash, he was off her. Off the bed. Now a standing, naked silhouette between her and the blazing torches of the Destrye guards who'd pounded down the door and poured into the bedchamber, Alby in the lead.

"Your Highness!" Alby skidded to a halt. "What—"

"Stand down," Lonen said, voice gravelly, but firm. "There is no danger. Go."

"But Your Highness—"

"Go!" he thundered. The boom of his rage echoed through his voice, making her flinch. She sat up and Alby's eyes fell on her, wide and startled. Then he and the men saluted and fled, Lonen following after, practically chasing them out.

"I would never push you off a tower." Chuffta sat on the carved wooden footboard, gripping with his talons, head cocked in question. His mind-voice had a hesitant sound. *"Or say those things."*

"I know," she replied aloud, too frenetic and drained to try for the concentration of replying mentally. She held out a hand to him and he hopped onto the blankets, hop-flying onto her lap, coiling his tail around her wrist and helping to relieve the pressure of the magic and the aftertaste of the nightmare. "It was only a dream."

"Not only."

"Only?" Lonen echoed Chuffta unintentionally, striding back

into the room, carrying a hammered metal cup that glinted in the low light. "That was the goddess of all nightmares."

"You're one to talk," she muttered.

Lonen crawled up onto the bed, steadying the cup as he did, then handed it to her, concern creasing his shadowed face. "Yes—thus I know what I'm talking about. Drink this."

The liquor, sweet and bright, burned in her throat as the fire had in her dream.

"It doesn't really burn like that, breathing fire," Chuffta noted. *"Your throat hurts because you were screaming."*

"I was screaming?"

Lonen raked a hand through his hair. "Froze the blood in my veins so the lumps nearly stopped my heart. You took years off my life, love. What in Arill brought that on?"

The wild magic. Perhaps the conversation had suggested it, or opening her portals to Baeltya had made her more vulnerable. The narrowing of her senses that had allowed her to shut out the wild magic instead of absorbing it was far from a practiced skill or a precise art. She opened her mouth to apologize for waking him, for bringing the guards running, then remembered that, even if it was after midnight, she'd already used up her apology for that day, too. Not sure what else to say, she closed her mouth again.

"Talk to me, Oria," Lonen growled. "Let's not rehash this."

"I don't always know the answers to your questions." She'd wanted to snap out that reply, but it dribbled wearily.

"But you know this one. Even I can guess. It's the wild magic, isn't it? You're vulnerable to it no matter what. It invades your sleep, when your guard is down. Just as happened on the journey here."

Oria took a long swallow of the liquor. It burned less this time. "I didn't realize you knew about that."

"I knew. I just didn't say anything." He slid his fingers through the hair that spilled over her shoulder, tugging a little when he met a tangle. She must have been thrashing in her sleep, too, as well as screaming.

"I don't know *how* you knew." She met his steady gray gaze.

"The pair of us, both restless in our dreams—one recognizes the other. I only guessed." He said so, but her jangling sensitivity to him showed it to be a lie. Not maliciously told, but the visceral truth nevertheless pulsed along the marital bond between them. He *knew.* Lonen somehow accessed some deeper knowledge about her, something she hadn't expected from their alliance. Were all temple-joined marriages like this? She didn't think so. She'd never heard any of the priests and priestesses even in ideal marriages speak of this kind of subconscious *knowing.* Of course, given how Yar had treated Gallia, who was supposed to be his ideal bride, like a trophy, it would be difficult to imagine him being sensitive to much about her at all. Also, the priests and priestesses weren't given to spilling any intimate secrets.

With a nearly physical pang, she abruptly missed her mother with a deep and desperate longing. Rhianna would have answered her questions.

"Maybe. She didn't always. And the influence of the Trom is unprece-dented, at least in recent memory. Odd how their words invaded your dream."

She really hoped Lonen hadn't witnessed any details of the dream as Chuffta had. Though normally Chuffta didn't comment on her dreaming thoughts.

"Because I don't usually hear them. When you sleep, I hear you in my mind, but without focus. As if you're very far away. This was different."

As if it hadn't really been a dream at all. Lonen still gazed at her, as if reading her thoughts in her eyes, his fingers wound in her hair, stroking one lock caught between his thumb and forefinger. "Yes, I think the wild magic gave me that … nightmare." She offered that like a confession.

He tugged her hair with affection and shrugged as if none of it mattered a great deal. "I think you have no choice," he put to her, rising and fetching another goblet.

"No choice?" About him seeing the inside of her head?

"About confronting the wild magic," he said. "Even if you went ahead with this unlikely plan to lure golems through the tunnels so you could steal their sgath, the wild magic will continue to work on you any time your defenses are down. You have no choice but to learn to manage it somehow."

"Or learn to improve my subconscious controls so they stay in place when I sleep." That seemed far more feasible.

"You have a plan for that?" He drank deeply, head thrown back to drain the liquor, the column of his throat strong beneath his neat beard.

"You know I don't."

He smiled slightly, a quirk of shadow in the flickering firelight. "We proceed with the plan then. We cannot ignore the wild magic, so we'll have to face it."

She didn't at all like the sound of that. "You mean I will."

"No, *we* will. We're in this together."

She had no immediate argument. Not a coherent one. "We already agreed that we'd talk about it more tomorrow."

Tossing aside the empty goblet and taking hers, Lonen slid under the furs again, snugging her against him. "We can talk all you like, love—within the deadline we already agreed to—but it seems there will be no escaping this truth." Despite his uncompromising words and tone, his touch soothed, his empathy for her fears shimmered in her heart, a shining and solid comfort.

"You're always so sure things will turn out well," she accused, but drowsiness—and the warmth of his nearness—softened her words.

"One day you'll accept that I'm always right." He kissed her hair.

Rather than arguing, or giving him the satisfaction of agreeing, she focused on shutting her portals tight, before let herself fall back to sleep. The morning would be soon enough to examine the walls of the trap she found herself in.

AS IF THEY'D broken a seal on the oasis of Lonen's chambers with a three-part ritual—Lonen going out to dine with his brothers, admitting Baeltya, and the inrush of guards brought by her night terrors—with the advent of daylight, the outside world began pouring in. And much like the cracks in her mental and emotional portals let in the wild magic, the Destrye brought chaos of all levels with them.

The morning began serenely enough. Lonen was already up when she awoke, doing some stretching and strengthening exercises before the fire, which she took as a good sign. Baeltya soon arrived, along with a hearty breakfast of stewed fruit and grains. More healing treatments and a nap in the chair by the fire fast gave way to a thorough invasion of her sanctuary. Women of all stations, it seemed, arrived with various supplies and implements—dresses, clothes, grooming aids, advice—all of which seemed to be more excuses to look her over with their critical dark eyes.

Lonen, the traitor, abandoned her with a kiss to the top of her head and a whisper to have courage. The way he kept his expression deliberately neutral, though his mouth crooked at the corners suspiciously, told her all she needed to know about how seriously he took the female attack. Since he went to be briefed on the situation facing Dru, she supposed her own troubles paled in comparison.

Still, it was her first real encounter with the women of the Destrye court, and she knew full well these situations were quicksand of their own variety.

Even Chuffta fled the center of the scene, taking a perch on a high beam and watching with a keen-eyed gaze, making laconic comments in her mind, which she studiously ignored. Lonen might insist that the Destrye conducted themselves far less formally than Bárans, and he'd be largely correct, but the female politics seemed uncannily akin to the undercurrents of temple jockeying for power and position, all under the serene guise of *hwil*.

These women, however, made no pretense of any sort of emotional control. At first they whispered and murmured to each other, but once they determined that Oria couldn't follow the twisty Destrye dialect, they spoke more boldly, chattering amongst themselves and occasionally erupting into passionate arguments— once over the difference between two spools of thread, to all appearances. For her part, Oria took the opportunity to observe their ways, while concentrating on sustaining her own *hwil* that also served to keep her portals tightly closed.

They were careful, at least, in not touching her. The seamstresses laid their measuring tapes over her light bed gown. Lonen, or Baeltya, had passed the word and they observed the protocol scrupulously, whatever they might believe to be the reason for it. Several maids staggered in heaped with furs, leathers, and some heavier materials that gleamed with deep color, and the seamstresses fell into animated discussion that seemed to involve how best to use the fur as lining.

Apparently Lonen intended to see her warmly clothed, a tremendous relief. The ladies had returned her fur robe to her and one indicated a metal pot of something hot warmed over a candle flame encased in a metal-screened box. Oria nodded and the girl, younger than the others, with eyes of a blue that reminded Oria of the flowers that bloomed only in the first cool of morning, poured her a mug. Oria sat by the fire, cupping it in her hands to warm them. The pot was of a hammered coppery metal that caught the light, making her blush to recall the times Lonen had brushed her hair, praising the sheen and color. The liquid seemed to be a brew of fragrant flowers and perhaps a spicy bark. It warmed her from the inside out, leaving behind a sense of bright well-being, which made her wonder if it came from Baeltya.

Like jewelbirds when a raptor flies over, the chattering women fell suddenly silent, bowing their heads as a tall woman entered the room. She wasn't particularly richly dressed, but she carried herself like a high priestess or queen. Unlike the other women, she wore her hair short against her scalp, the curls in black whorls against her lighter skin. Without the elaborate fall of coiled hair like the others, her deep blue eyes stood out large under arched dark brows. They held a solemnity echoed by her full lips, both bracketed by etched lines of grief.

She studied Oria with bold appraisal, not acknowledging the silent women around her. Oria fought the urge to rise to her feet, or even make obeisance. Lonen had been quite clear that he expected her to conduct herself as the Queen of the Destrye. The battle would not be that easy, of course, but if Oria had learned little else, she knew that faking the appearance of station took one a great deal of the way to actually having it. So she stared back at the woman, her own face a mask of perfect *hwil*, raising her brows ever so slightly in inquiry, as her mother would do. The woman seemed to wait for something more and Oria mentally cursed Lonen for insisting there were no particular protocols to learn.

Men could be so obtuse.

"Human males," Chuffta corrected with a hint of a sniff. *"I am most perceptive."*

"Can you read anything from her?"

"She is very sad. And angry. Also, surprised by you."

Oria had no opportunity to follow that up, because the woman spoke, her voice surprisingly deep. "I am Salaya," she said, in Common Tongue.

"I am Oria," she replied, using the same phrasing and intonation. Lonen likely would have wanted her to add "Queen of the Destrye," but that felt like too much of a declaration of war with this hard-eyed woman. Who was she? Salaya. She didn't recall hearing the name spoken. At least she wasn't Natly, but Salaya's unfriendly demeanor didn't bode much better.

Salaya said nothing more, but neither did Oria offer anything further. Something else she knew—how to wait out a high priestess who hoped for the least lapse in *hwil* to pounce upon as further proof of Oria's deep unsuitability. If Salaya thought to intimidate with brooding silence then she'd be in for further surprises. Oria had withstood worse.

"You're a bit of a thing," Salaya finally said. "I imagine I could break you in two with my bare hands."

Oria smiled thinly. "If you managed to lay hands on me."

"Ah, yes. You're a sorceress, they say. And, I imagine, like all your people, willing to deal death with a crook of your little finger, and no thought to the consequences."

"Have I done so?" Oria asked in her mildest tone. Honey to trap the stinging insect. "It seems to me that I, personally, have done nothing to be treated as the enemy."

"We don't know, do we? Such things are done from behind golden masks and high walls. Perhaps you *were* the one to strike down my husband." Salaya's voice vibrated with rage and her hands shook until she clenched them into fists at her sides. The other women looked askance, pretending not to hear, to be busying themselves with their tasks. But every ear was riveted to the exchange—and if the Destrye were remotely like Bárans, everyone ready to spread the gossip as soon as they left the room. If Oria wanted to establish a fearsome reputation among these people, this would be the time. And yet, something in Salaya's mien spoke profoundly of abject grief. They'd all lost so much.

"I've never struck down any man," she said, willing the Destrye woman to hear the honesty of her words. After all, Oria had only ever killed a woman. "Who was your husband?"

"As if you don't know," Salaya spat.

Oria held up her open palms. "I honestly don't. I am new to your realm and have been ill."

Salaya's mouth turned in disgust. "Yes. Ill and weak. A sad and sorry excuse for a queen. Had Ion lived, he would have succeeded his father and *my* sons would inherit the throne. Strong boys from a real Destrye woman. Now we are to accept you instead." She popped open her fists in a spray of fingers that dismissed the likelihood of such a scenario, adding a word in Destrye that communicated her derision.

This was Prince Ion's widow then. The moment came back to Oria, in horrific detail as if she'd witnessed it from much closer than from atop her high tower. The dragon landing at the edge of Ing's Chasm, snaking its sinuous neck just as Chuffta would, creating a living bridge across. The Trom rider stirring at the wing joints, then walking along its steed's neck over the chasm to the palace side. The Destrye king—Lonen's father—confronting it, then falling to its lethal touch. Ion had been the other man, leaping to defend the king and crumpling also, his sword and strength useless against the Trom's ancient magic.

"I am very sorry," she told Salaya, in all sincerity. "I saw Prince Ion fall. He died bravely, defending King Archimago. But it was not a Báran who killed him; it was one of the Trom. I can only say that it happened very fast. He would not have felt pain."

"Ion would have relished pain!" Salaya hissed, but she'd lost some of her fire. "These Trom, the same who flew on dragons to burn our crops—you also claim they kill with only a touch?"

"Did not your own warriors bring back the tales?"

Two of the women murmured in a far corner and Salaya threw them a glare. Absurdly it pleased Oria to share some of the widow's ire with others. "Warriors," Salaya scoffed. "They tell us what they think we wish to hear. They send us off on a fool's journey to find a new home and then spin stories of fantastic magics, hollow victories, and painless death."

"The Trom are real." Oria took up her mug of tea, now cooled. "And their touch *is* death. Fast, painless, and unstoppable. I'm very sorry for the deaths they dealt your people."

"They kill with a simple touch, you confirm it." Salaya's gaze held a speculative gleam. "And His Highness has declared that none may touch you. Perhaps you are one of these monsters."

Interesting, if convoluted, logic. And yet some truth in it unsettled Oria. No one seemed to be sure where the Trom came from—or the answer lay in the temple texts she'd barely missed being able to access—but they were human-like, if not actually human. Their magic, too, bore some resemblance to what the Báran priests and priestesses used. Her sgath vision had shown their magical presence as a densely powerful black sun, both familiar and not. Some visceral part of her had recognized it. Just as they'd recognized her. The Trom had touched her and it had done nothing beyond making her skin crawl in revulsion. Those matte black eyes, as in the nightmare, had stared into her heart and found a mirroring darkness. *Queen Ponen*, it had called her. *Someday you will call to us and your understanding will deepen.*

Much as she craved answers to the questions that burned at her, she dreaded that such a day might come.

"His Highness makes commands for his own reasons," Oria replied. "I did not kill Prince Ion, nor am I one of the Trom."

Salaya's fingers twitched and she took a half-step forward. "Prove yourself then. I'll touch your skin and find out for myself what sort of poison you ooze."

"You have sons, Salaya," Oria cut into the woman's fugue with words sharp as any blade. "Would you leave them motherless, also?"

Salaya paused, lips trembling then firming, and she swallowed something down. "I… My boys are so young."

It seemed like a non-sequitur, but Oria somehow followed. She nodded. "The children are innocent of all crimes. We owe it to them to bring them up as best we know how. Your sons need you."

"They should have been princes." Salaya sounded almost pleading. She reminded Oria forcefully of her own mother, the labyrinthine drag of grief and helpless anger at events beyond anyone's control.

"They are still princes," Oria said firmly, belatedly realizing this might not be true according to Destrye law—or Lonen's current policy. Though if Lonen wanted her on board with his rule, then he'd have to let her in on discussions and information. She supposed getting actual clothes so she could leave his bedchamber would be the first step. What had Lonen said to her though, back on her rooftop terrace when she first proposed this crazy plan for a marriage of alliance between them? *My older brother left two sons behind when he ascended to the Hall of Warriors. By Destrye law, the crown passes to my father's children first, before going to the next generation. But if I have no sons and Arnon persists in his refusal to be my heir, then Ion's sons would be next in line.* All right then. "They are still princes," she repeated, "and Dru needs all its heroes. Look how much has already turned upside down. Who knows what the future may bring?"

"It's true," Salaya breathed. "You are not yet queen. And not yet with child, I think." Her gaze fell to Oria's midsection, and she made herself stay upright and unflinching, resisting the urge to wrap an arm protectively around her empty womb. She also declined to confirm or deny Salaya's supposition. Soon enough they'd have to confront that she could not bear Lonen any heirs. But that fell beyond much larger and more daunting obstacles. "Then you—" Salaya broke off at someone's approach.

Baeltya entered the room, bearing a basket of supplies, and she paused, raising her brows at Salaya. "Lady Salaya. How encouraging to see you out and about. Young Mago and Kavon will be delighted to see their mother."

If Oria had not been long practiced at keeping an impassive expression, she would have winced at the sweetly couched accusation. As it was, Salaya flushed and ran a trembling hand over her hair. "Have they… my sons have asked for me?"

Baeltya softened. "Yes. Go to them, Salaya. There's no need for you to be here."

Salaya cast Oria a speaking glance. "I am not the worst of your problems. Look to your husband, Báran sorceress. There are others who weave their spells today." Seeming pleased to have scored a point, Salaya stalked out of the room.

~ 6 ~

"**N**OLAN IS NOT joining us, I take it?"

Arnon shook his head, shrugging cheerfully. "He said he had a stop to make and would meet us at the storage silos. He's happy, though, that you're taking stock of the situation here in Arill City. We're both glad to see you out and about."

Lonen had to admit, getting outside and into the bracing air of the forest was doing him good. Buttercup, too, pranced with high spirits, the great warhorse also pleased to be released from the confines of the stable. Even Alby, riding behind, ever loyal and attentive, seemed more relaxed. Much as he didn't care to leave Oria alone, Lonen had yielded to Baeltya's well-couched arguments that his hovering made Oria seem weak and in need of protection. If he wanted her to be accepted as Queen of the Destrye, then he'd have to treat her as he would any Destrye woman. Which had always meant leaving them to their own devices and Arill only knew how women spent their time. He'd certainly paid little attention to what Natly was up to when they were not together.

Mostly he'd been happy enough at her absences, as her presence had been distracting at best and infuriating at worst. He'd never missed her as he'd begun to miss Oria the moment he left his chambers. As if he'd forgotten something critically important, like his iron battle-axe, some part of him kept triggering a minor alarm. Enough so that he kept setting a hand to the worn wooden handle before he remembered that, yes, he did have his favored weapon and that, against all reason, he'd deliberately left his heart behind.

You have to get out of bed sometime. Nolan's voice snickered in his head, echoed by Ion's long-ago taunt, *Don't let a bit of foreign pussy make you think with the little head instead of the big one.*

Oria had been an addicting fantasy from the moment he first saw her, and his obsession with her had only increased over time. He'd even entertained for a while the idea that she had cast a spell on him, to occupy his thoughts so, waking and dreaming. But his connection to her had only deepened since she'd depleted herself of magic. For whatever reason, he loved her with everything in him. More than he loved his own people. A truth he'd never speak aloud, though Arill undoubtedly knew his heart.

Arnon glanced over with an assessing expression. "You look better. Baeltya says that, with continued treatments, you should be back to your robust self soon."

Lonen grunted at that. He did feel better. It had been foolish, in retrospect, not to have called in a junior healer to tend him and Oria sooner. But then, he hadn't been quite right in the head. More like a frenzied wolf, pacing the den to protect its mate and allowing none close enough to aid either of them. Some of it he could put down to fever. The rest...

Back to Oria and his crazed feelings for her. At some point he'd stop questioning them and simply accept that he wasn't at all rational where she was concerned. He'd have to factor that in, like a warrior subject to the red rage might. Every man had his weakness and—no, not that. Oria was not his weakness. His unreasoning passion. Before her, his life had become a bleak landscape of death, grief, destruction, and toil. Oria brought magic with her.

That could only be good. For him and the Destrye.

"Baeltya says the sorceress is also stronger," Arnon continued in a such a bland tone that Lonen bristled internally.

"Her Highness, Queen Oria?" he asked. "Your sister by marriage, you mean? You could inquire after her health. That would be the civil approach."

"Don't pick a fight with me," Arnon replied mildly. "It's not me who has an issue with your marriage to the Báran princess."

"Then you've decided I'm under no spell?" A flock of ravens took off from the bare branches above, croaking out their scolds and warnings, sifting ice crystals down upon them. Oria would like seeing them, perhaps enjoy the taste of melting snow. He could envision her, pale skin pink with the chill, her copper eyes bright with delight as she tipped her fine-boned face to the sky to catch snowflakes on her tongue.

"Oh, you're under a spell all right, just not one born of Báran magic, I'm thinking." Arnon gave him a rueful smile. "Nolan doesn't recognize a man in love when he sees him."

"And you do?" Lonen retorted, a bit stung and exposed by that.

"I do now," Arnon agreed with good cheer, not at all daunted. "Remember, I watched you with Natly, and there's no comparison. For whatever reasons you've given yourself that you married the— that you married Oria, the primary one is clearly how you feel. For good or ill, it seems we must accept that reality."

"And you think it bodes ill."

"Not for you, no—though Nolan does." Arnon closed one eye, peering at the dark lace of branches above. "But you and I both know it could mean trouble for Dru. If you're blind to that, then I might have to change to Nolan's view."

"I thought you were the one who warned me against making Natly queen. Would any woman please you, or are you so jealous?" The wounded wolf in him leapt, quick to anger. And the reproving look Arnon shot his way made Lonen immediately sorry for it.

"Natly *would* make a terrible queen," Arnon agreed without rancor. "I stand by that opinion. But this foreign sorceress? She's turned your head in a way Natly never did, no matter the wiles she worked." He held up a hand to forestall his brother's reply. "I'm not saying it's magic. I'm only asking you to listen to yourself. To *think*. Setting all else aside, answer this: will Oria make a good queen for the Destrye?"

"She is a sorceress of great power. We need her to protect us from the Trom. They will return. Surely you do not doubt that. Her brother Yar is king of Bára, worse than his forebears. Oria knows him, knows how to fight him. He wants Dru's resources and won't hesitate to strip us of them—and to strip us to the bone in the process."

Arnon nodded, looking thoughtful. "I don't disagree. In fact, I'm sure you're correct on that. Today will show you where we stand on making it through the rest of winter as long as there are no further incursions. But, Lonen—I say this as your brother and your friend— the sorceress need not be queen to accomplish any of this."

Lonen clamped down on his immediate jerk of protest. Arnon was right. And Oria herself had made the same argument, that she didn't need to be queen in Dru. But she did need to be Queen of the Destrye to shelter the people within her magic—yet another thing that would be difficult to explain. Still, she didn't have to be his only wife to accomplish that. Being brutally honest with himself, Lonen could see how part of his desire to make Oria queen lay in his boyish wish to give her the best, to prove to her that he could. He might not be able to return her to the elegant life she'd lived before, but he could build her towers to live in, make her a garden that would at least thrive in summer. He might be nothing more than a mind-dead barbarian, the furthest thing from the ideal sorcerer-mate who would have lifted her to magical heights, the husband she'd dreamed of, but he could dress her in the finest furs and give into her hands the might and power of ruling the Destrye.

Not honorable thoughts, none of them to his credit. All born of pride and vanity.

But there were honorable reasons, too, not the least of which that Arill Herself had guided his footsteps in this. The goddess had bound him to Oria both in blessing and as retribution for the terrible acts he'd committed in war. Arill meant for Oria to be Queen of the Destrye. He'd vowed as much in the goddess's name and he would not be forsworn.

"As long as I am king," he said, letting his trust in Arill suffuse the renewed vow, "then Oria is my wife and queen. I will not set her aside for any reason."

Arnon sighed. "You always were the stubborn one among us. I told Nolan as much."

"He put you up to this?"

"He wanted me to suggest setting the sorceress aside as queen, yes."

Lonen swore at that, but Arnon reined up and put a steadying hand on Lonen's forearm. "I want you to think about this, and this is only me talking. Forego making Oria queen. Marry Natly instead if you must. Or marry Salaya and make Ion's sons your heirs as would please the people and perhaps Arill Herself. Keep the sorceress as a mistress. None would question that she is your trophy, least of all Salaya, who would likely not want to share your bed regardless."

Lonen gripped his brother's shoulder, looking hard into the younger man's intelligent brown eyes. "Is this what the Destrye have come to? For decades we've worked to shed our past. We are no longer barbarians to abduct women and keep them as trophies. I vowed to Oria to be her husband. Would you have me go back on that, dishonor all we've done to become better men?"

Arnon returned his gaze. "Would you embrace that honor and be dead? Because that's what it will come to. If you do not set aside the sorceress, Nolan will challenge you and you know he is the superior fighter. He'll kill you. Not because he wants to, but because he believes it's best for Dru. Isn't that also honorable?"

When Lonen dropped his hand, shaking his head, Arnon persisted. "He's not wrong and you know it, Lonen. You say this is about honor, but isn't it more about your affection for this woman?"

"It can be both."

"And you can be both right and on the side of honor—and it might still come down to one more of my brothers dead. Dru needs us all. We can't afford to be killing each other. Think about that when you weigh your decision."

"I've already made up my mind."

"Of course you have." Unexpectedly, Arnon grinned, though weariness mixed with the affection in it. "When have you ever *not* been set on your path? I'm asking you to think long and hard about whether this is the right time to be stubborn, the right thing to be stubborn about. Your certainty is a strength. Don't let it be your curse."

"I'll think on it," Lonen conceded, mostly to end the conversation.

"Thank you." They rode on for a bit, the dense trees giving way to brighter light that signaled a clearing ahead. "One more thing for you to weigh," Arnon lowered his voice, glancing at him, back at Alby and his squire, and away again. Lonen braced himself, for the set of his brother's jaw signaled his unhappiness. "Perhaps it hasn't occurred to you, but I am the one who should serve as my brother's second in any duel. And I can't be second to both of you at once."

"Are you saying that you'd choose Nolan's side?" Lonen asked the question evenly and without emotion. Oria would be proud.

"I'm asking you not to make me choose." The weariness crowded out all affection in his voice, and Arnon didn't look at him as he said it.

BY THE TIME Lonen returned to the palace, he too was weary in mind and heart, as well as body. Although he felt better than he had the day before, and it seemed possible that soon a short outing wouldn't exhaust him.

Holding on to hope that everything else would improve proved more daunting.

Despite the depredations of war on the numbers of warriors and the trials of the Trail of New Hope on the rest of the Destrye population, he still had far more mouths to feed than food to put in them. The decimation of the crops in late fall by the Trom and their dragons had done them in. At the current rate of consumption—already strictly rationed—they'd run out of food easily two months before the earliest crops could yield fruit, and that was hoping for a gentle spring. Even if they sent hunting parties further afield, to forests where they hadn't thinned the game beyond the herds' abilities to recover, and grimmer math predicting losses to hunger, disease, and cold, that only bought them maybe another month.

Ironically enough, the reservoirs Arnon and his engineers had constructed held plenty of water to see them through, even keeping in reserve several to irrigate crops through the summer. Heavy snows had fallen early and Arnon had wisely tasked teams of otherwise idle warriors to gather the snow from the fragile rooftops of the hastily built wooden city sprawling around the temple and palace—both relieving the structures of strain and supplementing the water reserves.

But if they were to make it through the winter, they'd have to slaughter the egg-laying poultry and brood livestock. The short-term solution would only leave them worse off the next winter.

Die now or die later, Nolan had commented with a malicious smile. *We'd have done better to perish on the battlefield and have at least taken those cursed Bárans with us.*

Lonen had left his brothers bickering over the math, citing very real fatigue. He hated how Nolan's inquiry after his health sounded like another calculation, this one counting down the days until the duel. The lightweight wreath of hammered golden leaves weighed heavily, and he nearly handed it to Alby along with his outdoor fur cloak on entering the heated palace, remembering even as he lifted his hand to it that his responsibilities could not be shed so easily.

Or perhaps they could. He could abdicate—in Nolan's favor or in Mago's. Surely kings had done so before him. It might not necessarily be a failure. Wasn't there wisdom in knowing when to retreat? If he dueled with Nolan, he'd almost certainly be defeated, which meant death. Either way he'd lose. And so would Oria and the Destrye.

The only path he could see through the dense forest of decisions was to take advantage of his powerful sorceress wife. They needed her back at full health and magical strength.

Dismissing Alby, he turned his steps, taking the branching passage to the bridge to Arill's Temple rather than hastening back to Oria. There was some kingly discipline. It could be enough to know she would be there, waiting for him when he returned. He'd make it be enough.

And it was time to take his questions to the goddess.

He made his way to the royal family's chapel, the sacred chamber where all their private prayers and rituals were conducted. He'd walked it so many times, his feet knew the way of their own accord—though they'd often dragged when he'd been a boy, his small and sullen rebellion against the boredom of the enforced visits. Back then the corridor had seemed excruciatingly long, the chapel dark and even somewhat scary. The carving of Arill over the altar had always reminded him of his mother, who had wielded her disappointment and disdain with devastating accuracy.

By the time he reached the age of five, he'd far preferred facing his father's anger or even his brother Ion—older by seven years— gleefully dealing bruises with the flat of his sword than one of his mother's heart-to-heart discussions. She'd had a knack for laying open his failings, gently but ruthlessly exploring his character and suggesting improvements. How a reckless boy might think ahead to the consequences of his actions. How a careless boy might slow down and pay attention to his lessons. That, while the illustrated tales of past deeds might be exciting, the son of a king had better ways to spend his time.

In the quiet of the chapel, Arill's painted visage stared down at him with gray eyes exactly like Queen Vycayla's. Her slight smile seemed both knowing and—while forgiving—also pained that he'd needed forgiveness in the first place.

Arill knew his blackest heart, had borne witness to all the dark deeds he'd done in the name of war and in the name of lust. After the siege at Bára, when he'd returned home an unwilling king and starving victor, he'd repented to Arill, purging himself in Her harshest ceremonies. Something in Her smile, however, always left him feeling some taint remained, the certainty that not only had he never measured up, he likely never would.

Her eyes forever mirrored his mother's disappointed love. Perhaps that was the answer he sought—that he should abdicate in favor of Nolan or Mago. No one had meant for Archimago and Vycayla's carefree third child to govern the Destrye.

Is that Your message, Arill? Should I step down and let my betters rule?

Arill's sad smile spoke of Her grudging approval. Her open palm offering a heavy-headed stalk of grain gave him surcease. And yet… Her other hand held the scythe. The goddess both grew the crops and harvested them. The gleam of the fine-edged blade drew him, always had. He was a warrior, not a farmer.

His had been a battlefield promotion and, now that the battle had ended, he could demote himself again. But the hair prickling on the back of his neck told him the war was not yet over.

Something about Her hands though… There was another image of Arill, one he'd always loved, and She hadn't held the grain and scythe, had She? In that one She'd looked not disappointed, but benevolent. And Her eyes were tawny gold, Her hair fair and fiery.

A scuffling sound startled him enough that he'd half-drawn the battle-axe out of reflex before he caught himself, resheathed it, and turned. *No golems here,* he reminded himself. *Not yet,* the hairs on his neck whispered.

Priest Robson eyed him with disapproval from under silver-white brows, spider-leg long with age. "I took you to be praying, Your Highness. Have Arill's children fallen so far back into the old ways that you come before Her armed as if for battle?"

With some chagrin, he shrugged, the weight of the axe heavy now between his shoulder blades, but the priest's question resonated oddly with his own forebodings. "I've carried it so long, my axe has become another limb. I forget it's there until I reach for it. So perhaps so, Rhiten. Perhaps I am regressed to our barbaric past." *A careless boy. A reckless boy.*

"Is that why you've come here today?" Priest Robson asked, more gently. "It's no feast day, nor a day for regular observance, but neither have you been to pray to Arill since your return to Dru."

"I've been ill," he replied, feeling more than a little defensive. Did everyone want something from him? Of course, he knew the answer to that.

"And so you have. But the spirit requires healing from despair as much as the body does from injury. You've sent for a healer. Why not your spiritual guide, your rhiten?"

He couldn't very well say that it hadn't occurred to him. Or that when it had, it had felt like the lowest of priorities. Instead he met the priest's keen gaze. "I'm here now."

"Then let us pray."

"Rhiten, I don't really have time to—"

The old man pushed past him and, leaning heavily on his staff, knelt before the altar. He looked over his shoulder with some impatience. "Do you tell Healer Baeltya you have no time for her treatments, to drink her teas? I thought not. Kneel down and clear your mind, boy."

Setting aside the pull of restlessness, the urge to get back to Oria, he obeyed old rules and knelt beside the priest, attempting to clear his mind. The memory came back, vividly bright and clear, of kneeling like this in the temple at Bára, preparing to wed Oria. She'd teased him, copper eyes shining with magic and laughter, telling him he was supposed to be meditating.

"What in Arill does that mean?"

"Like... praying to your goddess. Silently."

"Now what?"

"Keep doing it. And be quiet."

"Why would I keep doing something I already did?"

"You're supposed to be contemplating!"

"Contemplate what? I already made the decision about the step I'm about to take. There's no sense revisiting it."

Like praying to his goddess. Only he'd never much seen the point of that either. The purging rituals, the sacrifices—those made sense and consumed all of his attention with their grueling demands. Strange to look back on that moment, to taste again in his memory that certainty. He had made the decision to wed Oria despite the wide array of reasons not to, and he hadn't needed to revisit it.

Yes, her arguments had made logical sense, once he got past the shock at the audacity of her idea, but that hadn't been why he'd ultimately gone along. Even when he'd questioned his own sanity, even wondered—like his brothers did, he had to admit—what sort of magic she might have used on him, he'd never lost the bone-deep certainty that she was meant to be his wife.

A gift from Arill.

Or a punishment from the goddess.

His, either way. No matter what.

Casting his eyes up at Arill's image, it seemed Her smile held only approval, Her gray eyes alight with challenge.

~ 7 ~

"THIS IS A bath?" Oria gazed at the steaming basin of water—no deeper than the first knuckle of her forefinger and the size of her hand—with some dismay. The pot Baeltya used for tea held more fluid.

The young serving girl with the morning-flower blue eyes twisted her fingers together. "I beg your pardon, my lady, but… yes. The water restrictions—"

"Surely don't apply here," another serving woman interrupted. "Let us bring out one of the queen mother's tubs and fill it. That's what Lady Natly—"

"No." Oria held up a hand, and not only because she didn't want to hear what Natly did or didn't do. That was all she needed to improve her reputation among the Destrye, to prove herself a wastrel as well as the enemy who'd deprived them of their water reserves in the first place. She needed to stop being so thoughtless.

"You're not thoughtless. This is all new to you."

"And you are too generous with me."

"Because I love you. I suggest rolling in hot sand—that cleans my hide nicely."

"Leaving your scales dry and peeling. You'll be in need of oil."

"I am itchy," her Familiar admitted, and she felt another pang for having neglected him.

Time to take more control of her situation. Her hand still in the air, the serving women eyeing her with breath held and faces anxious, she studied their glossy curls, shining with volume and vitality. Surely the palace ladies had ways of washing their hair, if only to keep the vermin out. The very thought of insects breeding in her hair made her skin crawl as if a Trom had touched her.

"I would pick them out for you."

"Ah...Thanks. How about we save that for a last resort?" Out loud, she asked, "How do you all cleanse your hair?"

The ladies exchanged nervous glances. "Us? Or the noble women?" the blue-eyed girl ventured.

"Both. Either, since it seems there's a difference."

The girl gestured to the bowl. "The noble ladies use a cloth and bowl, as such."

"Even to wash their hair?"

She giggled, more nervous than anything. "We do that in spring, traveling to the lakes when they've thawed. Or some women of the outer buildings have been gathering snow and melting it."

"In winter we use powders to soak up the excess oils," another put in, eyeing Oria's hair with some doubt. Even with it knotted up again, she could feel it heavy with the sweats of sleep and sickness. The wiry and curly hair of the Destrye women clearly withstood far more oils than her mass of fine, straight strands. They had no mirrors, it seemed—she recalled Lonen's fascination with hers back in Bára—so she could only imagine how awful she must look. It made no sense to dress her up to dine in the fine clothes and furs being industriously sewn for her, when the person inside the pretty garments stank with filth. How she longed for the steaming baths of Bára.

"Perhaps I should cut my hair short, like Salaya," she suggested, nearly taking a step back when they exclaimed in horror.

"Begging your pardon, my lady," the blue-eyed girl said. "Lady Salaya's hair is shorn out of mourning for her husband's death. If you were to do such a thing..."

Ah. It would appear that she considered Lonen dead. Even though the popular opinion seemed to be that they weren't truly husband and wife. It would be nice if the Destrye would make up their minds about that.

"If you don't do the bowl and cloth method, what *do* you do?"

"The aswae in Arill's Temple," blue eyes replied, ignoring the others, including the senior servant who tried to shush her. "But it's public and all the common women go there. The more refined ladies bathe in private."

"How does it work—what is an aswae?"

"It's a wooden room with benches. And they build up the fire very hot. We rub oil on our hair and skin, then scrape it off again. The sweat from our bodies makes it quite cleansing."

"Sounds delightful."

"You would like that." But she agreed that the prospect of being warm enough to sweat was enticing indeed. "All right. Will you take me there?"

The other serving women looked aghast and fell to muttering among themselves, but blue-eyes nodded, her chin firm. "I will. And I'll tend you myself. Let me find you something to wear."

While Oria waited, she wandered about the chambers, sipping her tea and eavesdropping on the Destrye women as they conversed. From what she could pick out, several seemed to find Oria's proposed visit to the aswae quite scandalous while others shrugged it off.

The helpful serving girl returned with a plain gown of thick material. "It's not a lady's dress," she explained, "but decent for a trip to the aswae, if you don't mind." Oria did not mind a bit. The outing had begun to feel like an adventure—and a welcome respite from the crowding of her sanctuary. Wearing the gown, an additional cloak and her fur slippers, she held up a hand to Chuffta, who glided down from his perch on the ceiling beam, to land on her shoulder. He looped his tail around her throat, more out of affection than anything else, as the thick cloak gave him excellent purchase, and delicately poked his nose at her hair.

"I don't see any vermin," he commented.

Before she could frame a tart reply, the serving girl, eyes wide and shocked, blurted out, "You don't mean to bring your pet!"

Several women fell silent, some shooting glares at the girl, as if to admonish her for impertinence, the others avidly interested. "Yes," Oria replied, finding it easy to remain serene on this one. "Chuffta needs cleansing and oiling, too. And he loves the heat."

"All right," the girl replied, shrugging for the vagaries of crazy noble ladies. "It's not like they'd dare criticize you, anyway."

Not to her face, that was.

The girl led the way out the door and into a corridor. Like all the rooms Oria had seen thus far, the hall was built entirely of wood, long strips of it fitted together along the long sides, arching up from a flat floor, then bending overhead to form a point. The colors shifted in a subtle spectrum from dark to light and back again, like a rainbow of brown. Oria trailed her fingers along it, the texture not like wood or bark at all, but smooth as sueded silk. They must do something to it, to make it feel so fine. Smaller pieces in various shapes and colors made up the flooring, the swirling pattern giving her a curious sense of swaying branches.

Destrye guards that had been outside the doors now followed after, not speaking to her but also not commenting to each other as the serving women might have. Alby had no doubt gone with Lonen, as he always did.

"What is your name?" she asked the girl. None of the serving women had offered their names, although she wasn't sure if they observed some sort of protocol, believed she wouldn't be interested, or had some other reason.

"Pilaryh," she replied without hesitation.

"Why didn't you offer your name earlier?"

"We weren't sure of your customs. Báran ways are strange." She cast a glance at Oria, the blue of her thickly lashed eyes a vivid contrast with her golden skin and burnished dark curls. They were very nearly the same height, which made Pilaryh short for a Destrye.

"Báran custom is that you should call me Oria," she said. No matter that wasn't strictly true. She tired of hearing the deliberate omission of honorifics. Not that she blamed the serving women. They all found themselves in a snarl.

Pilaryh led them over a sort of bridge that Oria vaguely recalled from Lonen's rescue of her from the healing ward at the temple. Tacked-down hides covered large holes cut at regular intervals in the walls. One had come loose, flapping in a chill breeze, so Oria paused, lifting the corner.

"That should be fixed," Pilaryh noted. "In the summer the Bridge of Seofe is open to the warm breezes and the view is quite nice. But this time of year it's too cold."

"May I look anyway?"

Pilaryh cocked her head, giving her a funny look. "I'm pretty sure you get to do whatever you want, my... Oria." She gestured to the guards. "Remove this hide so the sorceress may look out."

One man stepped up and made short work of it, standing back and holding the hide while Oria stood in the open frame, the chill pouring in. On her shoulder, Chuffta lifted his nose, scenting the breeze. He'd been in and out, taking in the sights, telling her some of what he'd seen, but he had a peculiar perspective at times. And though she loved the cloistered warmth of Lonen's chambers, she'd greatly missed the vistas she'd lived with all her life.

Now it seemed she stood high among branches. Naked of leaves, they twined like black snakes against a gray sky, rattling against each other with thin-boned murmurs. On one side of the bridge, a graceful construction of wood surrounded the largest tree she'd ever seen. It wove in and out, echoing the lines of the branches and limbs. Arill's Temple. At the other end, where they'd come from, an uglier structure squatted. Made of heavy wood, it looked like the fortress the palace was. The warrior counterpart to the elegant, airy goddess.

All along its walls, below the bridge, at the base of the temple and radiating out in every direction, more wooden buildings sprawled. These were not made with any design or the most basic nod to decoration. None seemed to be square. Even the simpler cubes weren't perfectly aligned, and they often branched into triangular wings or sprouted narrow passages. They piled on top of each other, the ceiling of one the apparent floor of another.

A haphazard series of catwalks and ladders allowed people to move among them, which they did. Children with dark curling hair ran shrieking up and down the passages, sometimes leaping from one level to the next, making Oria catch her breath in dismay. They seemed to be partly helping, partly getting into trouble among the adults who worked on the topmost roofs, which sported slanting boards that shunted snow into troughs. The people looked to be gathering it up and giving to others to carry away. To be melted, no doubt, as Pilaryh had mentioned.

Snow and ice. She'd imagined it more beautiful than this. Not grimy and packed down. It didn't look like anything one would want to drink.

"It's prettier when it's fresh. It snowed several days ago and not since. When it's fresh, it looks like sand, drifting and smooth." Chuffta showed her an image of it.

The conglomeration of the Destrye city rose and fell in waves. She could see it as not unlike sand dunes, with a ridge at the distant edge, the buildings there high enough she couldn't see past them, though here and there, breaks between revealed some sort of a deep pit beyond.

"What is that?" She pointed, edging aside for Pilaryh to see.

"The moat." Pilaryh darted her a glance. "You know—full of sharp spikes, to stop the golems."

Ah. Oria stepped back, allowing the guard to reattach the hide, almost sorry that she'd looked. She had not imagined the exuberant, free-ranging Destrye living so crowded together, in such unlovely conditions. What had she expected, though?

"I think they did not always live this way, that may be why you expected otherwise."

That could be, though she hesitated to ask Pilaryh about it. That was how the city looked—like the place a hunted and terrified people might hunker down in to fend off an implacable enemy. Not planned.

The temple itself further confirmed that supposition, with its lovely, arching halls and attention to beauty. Everywhere she looked, some detail adorned the least nook. Leaf and branch designs trailed along lintels. Fruits and sheaves of grain decorated wall panels. Tapestries in vivid colors showed vast meadows and forests of with animals of all types. Branches and twigs from the tree that formed the core of the temple poked through seamlessly, a few still sporting fiery leaves. Here and there, dried leaves scuttled across the wooden floors in the wind of their passage, and Oria recalled how one had fallen onto her in a lazy spiral when she'd first awakened. How the head healer, Talya, had taken it up and set it in a bin.

Picking up one of the dry leaves, she examined it. Larger than her head, it looked unlike the smaller leaves of the trees in her rooftop garden. Rather than a central spine, this one had veins that rayed out like the fingers of a hand to pointed edges. It contained no color—not living green nor the dying oranges. Instead it had gone beige, nearly the color of the dirty snow outside, thinner than the most delicate glass vessel the master forgers of Bára could produce, and it gave off a scent like Baeltya's tea. She brushed her fingers over the sandy surface, producing a sound like she'd touched the finest of scrolls.

"My lady?" Pilaryh asked, a puzzled line between her thick brows.

"It's beautiful," Oria said, a kind of an explanation.

"It's a leaf."

And thus ordinary to a woman who grew up surrounded by these massive trees. They were the counterpoint to that squalid jumble of huts. Holding the leaf, closing her eyes, it seemed Oria could almost sense it out there—a sort of holy silence where the forest breathed softer than sand whisking against glass. A verdant, ancient magic, the quiet unheard heartbeat behind the yammering tangle of wild magic.

She inhaled, taking it in, savoring. It didn't flood her, not like the chaos of the wild magic, nor did it surge in great waves like the sgath below Bára. It infiltrated, another kind of satiation, quenching a deep thirst. Swallowing the unexpected gift, she held it in her heart and belly, keeping it safe.

"Oria?"

Oria opened her eyes to find Pilaryh and the two guardsmen all watching her with suspicion and concern. One guard fingered the hilt of his sword.

"You were standing there meditating for a while. I think you confused them."

"Did you feel it—the forest song?" Abruptly she recalled that delirious moment in the water at the oasis when she'd listened to the enchanting sound of the stars brushing against each other as they danced across the sky. She'd forgotten it mostly, as one did with dreams, checking them off mentally as not real and therefore not worth remembering. But now…

"Would you… like to keep the leaf?" Pilaryh asked gently, the way one would mollify a temperamental child. Or a crazy sorceress.

"Can I?" She did want to keep it. Perhaps work with it to reach for that holy sensation again.

"Well, sure." Pilaryh held out a hand for it. "We normally throw them away." She gestured to a bin in the corner, brimming with leaves that had been crushed as someone tamped them down to make more room. "You can have as many as you like. Or do you want to keep *this* leaf, in particular?"

Oh well, they already thought she was crazy.

"I know I do."

"Which makes you so very clever." She added aloud, "I'd like to keep this one."

Pilaryh stepped to the wall and rang a little brass bell. It made a sound, too, like the stars. Why was everything suddenly reminding her of strange things?

"You're waking up. Now that your body and mind are healing, your natural abilities are resurrecting, searching out the magic to sustain them."

"How could you possibly know that?" She mentally rolled her eyes at Chuffta.

"I am wise in many things," he replied in a smug tone. *"Heed my words and you shall go far, sorceress."*

"I think maybe your mind needs healing." The laughter bubbling up inside felt good. Light, fizzy, and cleansing. Soon she'd be clean all over. Maybe there was hope, as Lonen in his infernally stubborn way always insisted.

A young girl, not old enough to have had her first visit from Sgatha, ran up to Pilaryh, nodded at the instructions and held up her palms reverently for the leaf. Black curls in ringlets spiraled down her back, thickly fringed lashes surrounded crystal clear gray eyes that were enormous with wonder as she stared at Chuffta on Oria's shoulder. Without a word—and without taking her gaze off the derkesthai—she accepted the leaf, bowed and walked back toward the bridge to the palace, moving as carefully as if she carried a precious vessel.

"I would have introduced her to Chuffta," Oria said as they resumed walking.

Pilaryh cast an oblique glance at the Familiar, who snaked his head around the knot of Oria's hair to study her. Probably with a mock fierce glare, knowing him. "It wouldn't ... hurt the child?"

"No." Oria nearly laughed, then thought better of it. And of Lonen's warnings. "Not if I command him not to."

"I hear and obey, worthy mistress." Chuffta managed a dead-on imitation of one of the more obsequious Báran council members.

"Ooh, I like that. Grovel more and maybe you'll earn your dinner."

Chuffta tightened his tail around her throat, only for a moment, but a more subtle move than his usual trick of pulling her hair.

They'd descended far enough that she supposed they must be underground. The light had dimmed and the air smelled moister, earthier. The branches that occasionally surfaced in the corridor ceiling and walls could actually be roots. If roots grew as big around as a Destrye warrior's body. Which, she supposed, they'd have to do, to support those enormous trees.

At a set of wooden doors, banded with gleaming metal, the guards paused and took up stations. Pilaryh knocked on one, and it opened, just enough for Oria to slip through. Pilaryh gestured her in. The heat hit her immediately and she blinked at the relative brightness of the room after the dim corridor. They seemed to be in a sort of antechamber. Shelves lined the walls, divided into cubbies, some with shoes and bundles of clothes. A metal brazier in the middle of the room glowed with hot coals, smelling of herbs that cleared her nose and soothed her mind.

"I like it here!"

Oria put a restraining hand on Chuffta's taloned foot. *"Not yet. Stay with me and let's learn the rules."*

"I was just going to look," he muttered, but he stayed put as Pilaryh barred the door behind them. A stooped older woman craned her neck to peer at Oria, then back at Pilaryh, asking something quietly. Pilaryh replied at some length and the keeper shrugged and nodded. How had that explanation gone? *Here's the king's foreign mistress claiming to be queen. She's probably insane, but she's also a sorceress, has a dangerous pet and doesn't know any better. So just play along.*

In any case, play along the woman did. She waved Oria to a corner, pointing a crooked finger at Chuffta, then to a bench there, and he obligingly half-glided to the perch. The woman undid Oria's cloak, shaking her head when Oria tried to help, fixing her with a menacing glare from one tawny eye, an unusual shade among Destrye. The other eye appeared to be injured—or missing—the white lines of old scars making a starburst around it. She undressed Oria, deftly folding her clothes and setting them in a cubby, along with her furry slippers. Pilaryh had disappeared into some other corner.

The crone demonstrated that Oria should hold her arms out

from her sides, so she did, a little self-conscious at being naked in front of the strange woman. But when the attendant brought over a bowl of golden fluid that had been warming on a shelf under the brazier, dipped her hands in it, Oria stopped her. "Please, don't touch me."

The woman frowned at her and said something. "No," Oria replied. "I'll do it." She reached for it, but the attendant held the bowl away, studying her with that one startling black eye. She nodded to herself, set the bowl back to warm and shuffled off. Returning, she held up her hands, showing Oria she wore hand covers made of leather. She dipped her leather-covered hand in the oil, and stretched it toward Oria. A test then. Holding her breath, Oria held out an arm, bracing for the impact, but the oil smoothed on thick and warm—with no intrusion from the old woman's thoughts or emotions.

She released the breath in relief, then nodded and shared a smile with the woman. Then she lost all caring except for how wonderful it felt.

If the fruit juice had felt like it quenched a core-deep thirst, the oil sated an encompassing one. At first it seemed odd to smear oil over skin that already felt unforgivably filthy, but it sank into her pores with a delightful simmer. With hands surprisingly gentle and deft despite her knotted fingers, the old woman massaged the oil into every inch of Oria's skin, even over her face and between her legs. Instead of feeling intrusive, however, the massage made her feel cared for, loved even.

"*Me too?*" Chuffta asked, and for a moment she thought he meant being loved, but he held out his wings hopefully. Oria pointed at the bowl, then to her Familiar, making as if to dip her fingers into the oil. The woman snatched it away, however. Before Oria could apologize to Chuffta, the attendant tottered over to him, filled her hands with the oil and began smearing it over his scaly white hide, as if she did it all the time. The woman noted Oria's surprise, winked at her with the good eye, then pointed her chin at a metal teapot simmering on a low flame inside a screened box.

Oria almost demurred, feeling quite full of healing teas, but the crone called out something in Destrye. A naked Pilaryh appeared, her hair now knotted up too, her robust body gleaming with oil. She hastened to pour a cup for Oria, then herself. "It helps bring up the sweat." She smiled over the rim, as natural as if they weren't drinking tea in the nude.

The old woman was working oil into Chuffta's wing membranes with deft grace, and the derkesthai had his eyes half closed in utter pleasure, his thoughts a murmur of delighted commentary. "Will your pet want some tea, too?" Pilaryh asked, all politeness.

"I don't think he sweats," Oria replied gravely.

"Derkesthai glow," Chuffta noted in such a prim tone that she nearly snorted tea. *"But tell Pilaryh thank you for the consideration. And Rachyl that she has a wonderful touch."*

"You caught her name?"

"Mmm."

"Would you thank the attendant for us?" Oria asked Pilaryh, deciding discretion might be better.

"Rachyl will continue to serve you both. At the end, you can gift her to show your appreciation."

Oh wonderful. Oria had nothing to give. Perhaps she could have Lonen send something. Finished with Chuffta, Rachyl took Oria's hand again and held out the other for Chuffta. He didn't usually go to strangers, but he hopped up onto her wrist, carefully wrapping his talons around the old bones so as not to pierce her skin, raising his tail for balance. She grinned at him, then at Oria, a smile missing several teeth, and said something.

"What did she say?"

Pilaryh shook her head. "Something in her tongue. Arill only knows."

"She's not Destrye?"

"Not even a bit, but she's been here forever. This way for the aswae."

Pilaryh opened another door and Oria, Rachyl leading her by the hand still, entered yet another room. Both hotter and dimmer, this one seemed to be lit only by bloodred coals gleaming in metal grates positioned around the room. About a dozen women, all naked, lounged around on benches.

All of them stared at Oria.

Pilaryh seemed not to notice, finding an empty tier of three benches attached to the wall. "Start at the top. If you feel too hot, move down to a lower one. But try to resist. Just keep sweating."

At least lying down, Oria felt less conspicuous. Chuffta arranged himself perilously close to a brazier of coals, belly up and wings spread to their fullest extent, sighing happily. Oria tried to emulate his ease, stretching herself on the topmost bench. She was already sweating profusely, her perspiration mixing with the oil and sliding across her skin. It felt like the hottest afternoon in Bára, without the sun. There, however, they'd never deliberately tried to be hot. Everything had been about cooling—the ices, juices, fruits, shades, and fans.

In this, too, then, the Destrye were opposite. But as the heat penetrated her bones, she felt warm for the first time in what seemed like ages. Rachyl had been tending other women, moving about in the shadows. Oria hadn't really been watching. She returned to Oria, gesturing her to stand again. Working swiftly, she took what looked like a wooden knife, scraping it over Oria's skin, then wiping the dull blade and tossing the refuse onto the coals where it hissed, sending up a smoke that smelled of dark spices and a roasted scent she only then identified. Human skin. Oh joy.

"Humans don't smell so bad once you get used to them," Chuffta's snotty comment lost something in the blur of contentment.

Other attendants worked, too, or some women tended each other, some scraping as Rachyl did for her; others rubbing on oil and massaging. Sure enough, once Rachyl finished scraping every crevice on Oria's body, including behind her ears and the bottoms of her feet, she slathered on more oil and waved for her to lie down again. Rachyl set to work performing the same service for Chuffta, who predictably loved every moment. Oria had long oiled his hide to keep it supple in the desert heat, but it had never occurred to her to scrape it this way. Maybe she could get one of those wooden knives and learn to do that for him.

"Or we could just come here. Every. Day."

She chuckled at that, but tended to agree. The aswae felt wonderful. After a while, Rachyl returned, this time with a cup of fresh water. Oria sipped it as Rachyl scraped her, no longer minding the smell of old skin burning on the coals. She imagined it as all the filth she'd accumulated and it seemed fitting to burn it. Old pains and sorrows, burnt and turned to smoke.

This time, Rachyl took her empty cup and had Oria sit on a lower bench. She took Oria's long hair down and, tugging Oria's head back, poured hot oil through it. The sensation melted through her, leaving utter lassitude behind. This time, when she lay down, her hair once again reknotted, she fell into a deep sleep, free of dreams.

When Rachyl woke her, fewer women occupied the chamber. During the time they'd been in there, women had occasionally left through a second door, and Rachyl, after a final scraping, took her and Chuffta out that door. This room was brighter and almost startlingly cool. Women chatted in louder tones, sliding her glances and conferring as they rubbed themselves and each other down with rough-looking cloths. Rachyl took up a metal flask with a curious attachment and sprayed Oria with a liquid so cool and stinging that her nipples instantly hardened and she squealed—making several of the women laugh.

"It's always startling the first time," Pilaryh said, appearing at her elbow, dark nipples tight with a similar response. "It's like... I don't know the Common Tongue word, like wine, only different. It closes up the pores again."

Rachyl cackled, said something in her tongue which, now that Oria paid more attention, was clearly not Destyre, and sprayed her back, following with the cloth that was rough indeed. Then she applied a lighter oil that smelled of the same spices but absorbed into the skin. Oria herself rubbed down Chuffta, skipping the alcohol spray as it probably wasn't good for him, but using some of the same finishing oil.

Finally, Rachyl sat Oria on a bench with a high back that had divots to rest her neck in. Rachyl unknotted Oria's hair and combed it out, the wooden teeth gliding easily through the thick oil. Oria cracked open her lids at the murmurs, to discover a ring of Destrye women watching. They spoke amongst each other, Pilaryh with them.

She caught Oria watching. "No one has seen hair like yours, like fire," she explained. "They want me to ask, if it won't cause offense. Are all Báran women colored so—or only the sorceresses?"

As her hair had to be nearly black with dirt and oil, she couldn't imagine how they could even tell. "Our hair tends to be much lighter than yours, but not always my color," she replied, closing her eyes and resigning herself to the interrogation. "Ask whatever you like. If I don't want to answer, I won't."

"Your skin, is everyone so fair?"

"Pretty much, yes." Rachyl poured some kind of grit into her hair, massaging it into her scalp. It actually felt good, in an odd way. Stimulating and refreshing after the lulling oils.

"Your nipples are pink," Pilaryh pointed out, and Oria cracked an eye open again.

"Yours are brown," she replied, resisting the urge to cover her breasts. Pilaryh translated for the ladies, who started giggling, cupping their breasts and showing each other. All of them were more endowed than Oria, much in keeping with their larger frames and robust musculature. They had wider hips and voluptuous thighs. One was heavily pregnant, her breasts large and belly swollen. Oria felt like a wraith compared to them. *Wan.*

"It's easy for us to understand now," Pilaryh said, a wistful sound in her voice, "why King Lonen is so obsessed with you. You are the most beautiful woman any of us have ever seen. Perhaps you are the most beautiful woman in the entire world."

Oria nearly choked on that, though maybe that was the powder Rachyl seemed to be dusting through her hair, then brushing out into clouds. "Surely not," she replied. "I'm nothing special. I'm just exotic to you. I would love to have hips and breasts like all of you do." These women looked built to bear children easily and often. Even if Oria could find a way to get with Lonen's child, it seemed impossible that her body could swell to carry such a burden.

Rachyl misted some of the spray onto her hair, then gestured for her to sit up again, draping Oria's hair over her shoulder in a long fall. Impossibly it gleamed brighter than ever, nearly glowing with a healthy sheen. Oria smoothed it, giving Pilaryh a grateful smile. "It worked!"

Pilaryh nodded knowingly. "King Lonen will be most pleased." She patted her own flat belly. "And soon you will swell with his heirs, perhaps even starting one tonight, lovely as you look."

If only it were so simple.

~ 8 ~

LONEN COULDN'T VOUCH that spiritual healing did anything real. Nothing like what Baeltya did, removing pain and reenergizing his body. But he did feel as if he'd shed his despair. He still wasn't certain of the best decision as far as remaining King of the Destrye. But he also didn't feel that bone-deep weariness just contemplating the choices.

And returning to his rooms, seeing Oria, felt more like a delight to anticipate, rather than fleeing to the comfort of her company to hide himself away.

The guards outside his chamber doors bowed to him. As he strode into the outer chamber, however, he would have doubted that Oria was within if they hadn't said so. The teeming hordes of ladies, maids, and seamstresses who'd driven him out to begin with had all apparently fled. The rooms had been neatened, too, with ashes carried away from the fireplaces, and fresh fires burning, the wood furniture gleaming and furs fluffed.

He supposed they had let it get a bit stale.

"Oria?" he called out, doffing his indoor cloak, tossing aside his wreath of office, and unsheathing his axe to set by the bedroom door. As he entered the room, she rose from her accustomed place by the fire, a lovely flush on her high cheekbones.

"Sorry—I must have dozed off. One day I won't fall asleep at the least opportunity. I went to the aswae and talk about relaxing. It was so warm and they put oil on you—have you done it?—it's so purging and—what? What's wrong?"

He'd been staring. At least he hadn't let his mouth actually fall open, though his tongue felt unaccountably dry. "Oria," he breathed. "You look gorgeous. I mean, you're always beautiful, but—"

She laughed, interrupting the tumble of incoherent praise. Then she stepped out from behind the pair of chairs, held out the skirt of her crimson velvet gown, and twirled. "Isn't it wonderful? I don't know how they knew to make it red—maybe from the rags of my robes—but it's perfect, and I feel almost like myself again."

She spun again, the full skirts belling out, emphasizing her narrow waist and the elegant fullness of her breasts. The high neckline was trimmed with white fur, framing her delicate jaw, and the long, tight sleeves ended in similar cuffs, with long fringes of fur that trailed over her slim fingers. Her hair hung loose and perfectly straight down her back, nearly to her bottom, not billowing in a cloud as it sometimes had in the dryness of Bára, but in a liquid fall as perfectly shining as a newly forged sword.

"And look!" she was saying. With a bright and saucy smile, she picked up a pair of matching velvet gloves from the table between the chairs, which also held a carafe of wine and two mugs. She drew on the gloves and held them up. "I can touch people without worrying about it."

She moved to him with something of her old restless energy, that impetuous grace she'd lavished on every movement back in Bára, and framed his face in her hands, brushing her thumbs over his cheeks, smoothing his beard. Her copper eyes, wide and gleaming, full of light, seemed to glow with her pleasure. "I can't feel, but at least I can touch," she added, her voice throaty.

He encircled her waist with his hands, brutally aware of the swell of her hips below his fingers, the narrow path of her ribcage that begged him to slide his hands up and cup her lovely breasts, tease her nipples until that teasing pretty mouth begged him both to stop and for more. His cock hardened with almost painful ferocity, his darker nature seething to toss her on the bed and throw up her skirts, plundering her until they both wept with exhaustion.

Oria narrowed her eyes slightly. "What are you thinking? You haven't said a word since your astonished observation that I look good."

"Gorgeous," he reminded her quietly. "I said you're gorgeous. And you smell of qinn."

"They put all sorts of stuff on me. I'm not sure which that was."

He knew. Natly—well, all of the Destrye women—used the spice in their soap and oils. It smelled to him of home and comfort. And it did crazy things to his brain to scent it on Oria.

Clearing his throat, he added, "They made the gown red because I told them to. All of your state garments will be red, unless you request otherwise."

She blinked long and slow, a considering closing of her eyes. Her lashes were copper, too, and long, but rarely showed until she lowered her lids like that, and then they stood out against the faint scatter of freckles on her cheeks, an almost invisible constellation of fawn stars. Then the full sun of her eyes bored into his again. "Why?"

"A sorceress should have her robes, no matter the material. I have no silk to give you, but you wouldn't be warm enough anyway."

"True," she murmured. "Thank you, Lonen." Her gaze dropped to his mouth. "I wish I could kiss you."

He nearly groaned at that. 'Wishing' didn't come close to how he felt about it. "We'll find a way."

She didn't smile, exactly, but her eyes danced with amusement. "You always do, my Destrye warrior."

Which only reminded him. He let her go and stepped back with a massive effort of will. "Shall we have a glass of wine? There's time before we eat."

"Yes. And you can tell me what's preying on your mind. How was the excursion with your brothers?" She poured him a mug of warmed wine and handed it to him, cupping her own in her gloved hands. "Also, you might change clothes."

He took a swig of wine and set the mug aside. "I no doubt smell of Buttercup, who says hello, by the way." He'd meant to tease her about her attachment to the warhorse, but she looked pleased, as if the steed really had sent a message. "Where is Chuffta, by the way?"

"Stretching his wings. The aswae made him feel frisky, so he's exploring. He'll be back to accompany me to dinner. Enough stalling—what has you worried?"

"What doesn't have me worried?" he shot back. But he told her about the state of Dru as he shucked the day's clothes, found the washing bowl and sponged himself clean of the worst of the day's sweat, then pulled on the clean clothes Alby had left out for him.

Oria listened gravely, asking questions here and there. Finally, she gave him a considering look. "All of this is serious news, but none of it is new. You knew all of this when you left this morning. Before you left to confront me in Bára, in truth."

"I didn't know the exact extent of it," he argued, knowing as he said it that it wasn't the full truth. He *had* known. Somehow hearing the dire facts recited by his older brother, all of them laid squarely at his feet as if he'd created the situation from his utter carelessness as king, made it all that much more painful. He reached for the wreath of metal leaves, realizing he'd left it in the other room. Some king, forgetting his crown.

Then Oria was in front of him, a staying hand on his arm. "Talk to me, Lonen." Her lush mouth curved in a sly smile. "We're in this together."

He shook his head, laughing under his breath at her ways, then indulged himself by sliding a hand through the sheet of her hair. The ladies had oiled it—probably the source of the qinn, then—which gave it that heavy, silky feel. She gazed up at him, her face so magically lovely that he hesitated to say anything that might dim her regard for him.

"You can't say anything that will make me think less of you," she said softly.

"Reading my thoughts, sorceress?" The prospect, which had once made him uneasy at best, strangely heartened him.

She looked thoughtful. "Not the way I used to, but… some? Maybe. I felt something today, something in the trees…" She shook it off, her hair sliding thick through his fingers. "Never mind that. Tell me what has you so churned up."

"I think," he said slowly, searching for a way to articulate his turbulent thoughts. "Maybe I should abdicate to Nolan. Or to Mago, with Nolan as regent."

"Because of me?" She asked it evenly enough, but he scowled at her.

"No. Because of me. Because I'm … I'm not a good king, Oria. I was never meant to be one. The Destrye deserve a good king. Not me. I'm careless, undisciplined, reckless, my head always in the canopy."

She tilted her head, considering. Then shrugged. "I don't know this man you're speaking of."

"I'm trying to explain that this is who I am. You haven't known me long, but I—"

"Oh nonsense!" She broke in and broke away, once again that imperious princess who'd laid out his options with ruthless clarity while the quiet towers of Bára stood sentry around them. "I'd venture that I know you better than anyone else, just as you know me. We've crossed the desert together, nearly drowned in the bore tides together, fought back to back, saved each other's lives and listened to each other's deepest fears when things seemed bleakest. You have flaws, Lonen—I won't deny that. You're ridiculously stubborn, won't leave well enough alone. That you remain so optimistic in the face of impossible odds never ceases to amaze me."

"So you've mentioned," he said drily. "And the point is that I'm not feeling that now. I'm not sure… Oria, I might not be up to the task."

"All right then," she said, pouring them both more wine, then clinking her mug against his with a sunny smile he could see right through. "Back to the oasis then? Or to one of Bára's sister-cities? It might not be so bad crossing the desert this time, if we actually take some water and food along."

"That's not what I—"

She set down her mug, threw up her hands, and began pacing. "Oh, you mean stay here? What a great idea. You can let Nolan lord it over you for the rest of your days that he got you to knuckle under and admit he's the better ruler. That will be fun."

The image made him want to growl. "I never said he's the better ruler."

"That's *exactly* what you're saying," she snapped back, skirts whirling out as she reached the wall and spun to pace in the other direction. "Whether you step down for him to be king or regent, it would be an admission that you think he's the better man."

"Maybe he is the better ruler!"

"Fine." She shrugged elaborately, like it didn't matter a whit to her. It rankled a surprising amount.

"That's it? No sage and wifely advice to offer?"

She paused, giving him a long look. "My advice? I think, Destrye, that it was easier for me. I had no doubt that Yar would be a terrible king. My potential inadequacies as queen blew away like so much sand in the face of what his rule would mean, for both Bára and Dru. I don't know Nolan. I barely recall him from when he rescued us. Certainly I owe him my life, but other than that, he's a cipher to me. I'm very interested to take his measure tonight. I *do* know you—and you're none of those things you cited. You are canny, wise, deliberate, noble. Even from the beginning you've never been anything but careful with me. You act decisively, yes, but never recklessly, with the possible exception of when you decided to sacrifice yourself fighting an army of golems to save my life."

"I visited Arill's Temple just now, and wondered once again if She sent you to me as a blessing or a punishment," he said in a wry tone.

She beamed with impish glee. "Can't I be both?"

He strode to her, catching her by the hips. "You are both."

She sobered, her gaze intent on his. "And you are King of the Destrye. Accident or challenge from your goddess, it doesn't matter. You don't need to think about if you're good enough to be king, because you *are* king. More—you're the best warrior I've ever seen and your people need a warrior to lead them. You and I both know the war is far from over."

"Yes," he agreed with regret. "Which Nolan doesn't see."

"Maybe he can't. He missed so much. But you see and you know. If you need to worry about something, worry about being the best king you can be. The best man you can be. Though you're already the best there is, to my mind."

"In all the world?" he teased, to cover how much that touched him.

"Well, I don't know. I haven't seen all the world. Once the war is finally over, maybe you can show me."

When the war is finally over. "Do you think we can truly end this conflict and find peace for our people?"

Her smile dimmed and she regarded him seriously. "I think we have to. Or die trying."

Her words riffed over him with premonition. "It could come to that. If Nolan challenges me, I could lose. It would mean my death."

"Then if it comes to that, we'll have to make sure you win."

~ **9** ~

THEY'RE ONLY PEOPLE, Oria chanted to herself as they progressed down to the formal dining hall. *Only people.* But she clung gratefully to Lonen's muscled forearm beneath her gloved hand. Chuffta's tail spiraled down her arm over the crimson velvet, a perfect match to the white fur trim. His iridescent scales often reminded her of a series of bracelets, but against the Destrye gown, his coiled tail looked more like jewelry than ever.

They'd make an exotic sight for the Destrye court. Talking with the women in the aswae had bolstered her confidence considerably. A good thing, as she'd been in a stronger place to give Lonen the pep talk. He moved with more of his usual swagger, his bold masculine exuberance wafting around her.

Now if she could hold up her end of things.

"You will. These Destrye barbarians will be dazzled by their Báran sorceress queen."

"Now you sound like Lonen."

Chuffta mentally preened. *"I have plenty of fire, too, if we need it."*

She stifled a giggle. *"Let's try not to burn anyone."*

"I said if," he replied in wounded tone.

The conversation had distracted her long enough to get them down a flight of stairs. She hadn't been this way before—at least, not while conscious. The lower parts of the palace had no windows, not even the hide-covered ones of the upper levels. And the walls seemed to be built entirely of enormous logs. Not the occasionally surfacing living branches of Arill's Temple, but cut trunks of whole trees—three or four of the massive things forming one wall to the ceiling. But surely, they weren't—

"Originally, the palace was a fortification," Lonen murmured to her, following her gaze. "Before the Destrye learned to take only dying trees and deadfall, we cleared parts of the forest for farming. We used the felled trees to build several forts, in various quadrants of Dru."

"Then the walls are...?" she asked faintly, unwilling to sound silly by suggesting the ridiculous.

"Are as thick as each log is tall, yes. No windows. Only a series of doors and portals. This part of the palace, at least, is virtually impregnable."

"I'm amazed the golems could get to you at all."

He looked thoughtful, gaze roaming the walls up to the ceiling beams—made of trees a quarter of the size, but still enormous. "Holing up in here is pretty much the only thing that saved us," he agreed. "But we can't fit all of Dru into the forts. Plus, it did us little good to save ourselves while your—while the golems stole all of our water and slaughtered our livestock. The Destrye used to be much more scattered throughout Dru—lots of small communities and farms. As they were overrun, people came here, or to the other forts. When you see it... Well, the city around the palace and temple are nothing so beautiful as the towers of Bára."

I think they did not always live this way, Chuffta had observed and she winced for both the truth of that and the apology in Lonen's voice. *"You were right,"* she told her Familiar.

"Yes," he replied, but for once did not sound pleased about it.

They didn't enter the grand hall so much as make their way to that end of the enormous fort. It differed from the part they'd passed through in that it had fewer subdivisions. Otherwise, the massive tree trunks dominated the room, dwarfing even the high table built onto a raised platform at one end.

The roomful of people—along with those at the high table— rose to their feet as they entered. Arnon she recognized from the council chambers at Bára, when their respective peoples had negotiated their all-too-temporary truce. She might have recognized him anyway, as he looked like a younger, leaner, and more relaxed Lonen. To his right stood Salaya, her fine-featured face set off by her short hair, her expression clear and remote. She stared off into the distance, perhaps thinking of days when her husband might have sat beside her.

For all that Salaya had been unpleasant, Oria felt for her. She couldn't imagine facing a formal dinner like this with her late husband's family. Too much to endure on top of the grief. Oria would have sent her a commiserating smile, but Salaya never looked her way.

The man to Arnon's left, on the other side of the empty chair between them, she would have guessed to be a relation, but not Lonen's elder brother. He had to be Nolan, though—cleaned up—as he looked nothing like what she recalled from her brief glimpse of the grizzled, travel-worn man in the forest before she'd passed out.

He had a hard face, his dark beard trimmed ruthlessly short, and his eyes such a sharp blue that the color showed clear across the room like the noonday sun through stained glass. A beautiful Destrye woman stood to his left, her black hair in elaborately piled swirls, studded with metallic bands and glittering jewels. She stared at Oria, lustrous dark eyes full of hatred, until she wrenched her gaze away to smile at Lonen, her full mouth pouting seductively. Her clinging gown revealed her voluptuous curves as she seemed to pose with both studied indolence and sensual grace.

Natly. Lonen's former betrothed. Oria knew her face well, from glimpses into his mind when her abilities worked with such keen activity that she picked these things up without meaning to. Which meant that, even worse, she had images in her head of Natly naked, writhing with sexual abandon in the very bed Oria now slept in, those luscious lips closing around—

Oria shook her head abruptly to clear her mind of the image, suddenly aware she dug her gloved fingers into Lonen's arm. And that he'd covered her hand with his, enfolding it tightly in reassurance.

"Brothers," he said, not pausing in the acknowledgment. "I see you've miscounted—there's one chair where there should be two."

"Your Highness." Nolan stared at her as he spoke. "Surely you don't mean to seat your—"

Lonen went deathly still, the rest of room as uncannily silent. She almost imagined ears growing longer to better hear. "This dinner was your idea, Nolan," he said, as quiet as a snake's hiss. "Consider carefully the steps and words you choose."

"Or what?" Nolan's blue eyes glittered. "Will you call insult?"

"If necessary," Lonen replied easily.

Arnon looked as alarmed as Oria felt. He pointed to the people to his right, making them shift down, an annoyed warrior at the end leaving to find another seat. "Your Highness, you've yet to properly introduce me to your wife," he said, adding a smile that looked a bit too much like a grimace, but still there. He gestured to the now-empty chair he'd been occupying. "Would you care to sit, sorceress, and dine with us?"

Lonen still vibrated with tension, so Oria took the situation in hand. "Thank you. I'd be most pleased. Lonen, would you perform the introductions?"

Some of that got through to him, because he glanced down at her, gray gaze wary, but not flinty. "Oria, love, meet my younger brother, Prince Arnon."

She ignored the reactions of the others to his endearment—one she'd passed off as meaningless initially, but it appeared to carry even more impact than she'd come to believe—and inclined her head. "A pleasure to meet you, Prince Arnon."

Arnon's smile warmed. "We encountered each other glancingly ... in the past, sorceress, but it is truly enchanting to get a chance to know you better. Welcome to Dru. We know you traveled great distances and suffered harrowing trials to help the Destrye in our hour of need."

Lonen's bemusement wafted over her, but she focused on No-lan, whose expression had decidedly soured at Arnon's speech.

"And Prince Nolan," she said, taking the initiative and emphasiz-ing his title ever so slightly, "I have not had the opportunity to thank you for saving my lord husband's life. Please accept my gratitude for your timely intervention."

Nolan's mouth thinned. "You thank me for his life and not yours, sorceress?" What had sounded like an honorific from Arnon's mouth became an epithet on his brother's tongue, but Oria smiled with all the calm tranquility she'd learned to muster in the face of priestesses far more toxic than this Destrye.

"My life is my own," she answered, pleasantly enough but let-ting him hear the steel beneath. "It was never yours to give or withhold."

He gazed back at her, not frowning, but sorting through her words. "And your loyalty, sorceress—who owns that?"

Lonen stirred. "Is this a dinner or an inquisition?"

"The question is easy enough for me to answer, love, even if we haven't even been served wine yet." She smiled up at her husband, at his surprise that she returned the endearment and how much that obviously pleased him, then allowed her smile to sharpen as she returned her focus to Nolan. *It's better if they fear reprisals from you.* "I am pledged by binding vows to my husband, Lonen, King of the Destrye—where his loyalty goes, mine follows. His friends are mine. His enemies? Also mine."

"Is that a threat, sorceress?" Nolan asked on a queer intake of breath, a waft of old fear in the air. He'd been on the battlefield at Bára and thus witnessed the mighty—and showy—battle magics of the priests. And he'd nearly died there. No doubt he suffered night terrors, too, as Lonen still did, from the things they'd witnessed. She misliked playing on those wounds, but she'd spoken true: her loyalty lay with Lonen. Or rather, with what was right and true, though she hadn't been able to think of a way to say that without sounding naïve. Fortunately, she and Lonen agreed on what those things were.

She hoped. It didn't bear thinking what she might do if they diverged on that.

"A threat?" she echoed with a bemused smile. "How could that be, if we are among friends?"

Lonen didn't stir, but his amusement—and a hint of annoyance—filtered from him. "Let us sit," he declared, holding the chair Arnon had vacated for Oria, giving her an opaque look from eyes gone to granite.

"I thought it was funny."

"Thank you."

"But my people have a saying: if you singe the wolf's tail, be ready for his teeth to follow."

"Derkesthai like to battle wolves? Seems… unnatural."

He sniffed mentally. *"It's true that it's unfair. They stand no chance against us. But it can be a fun game. For younglings."*

She folded in the smile at that and stroked his tail, beyond glad to have him with her in this.

"Really, should there be animals at the table?" Natly's question pierced the general shuffling of everyone reseating themselves. She possessed a voice as lush and sultry as her figure, but the querulous undertone made Oria want to wince. "After all," Natly continued, "the Destrye no longer allow hounds and fowl to pick at our table leavings. We don't behave like *barbarians*."

"At least, not in the last week," Arnon quipped. "The journey from brute to civilized man seems fraught with pitfalls and backsliding. Back in the day, allowing women at the table was considered the height of weakness."

Oria, at last gratefully sipping the wine a servant poured, nearly choked on it. Her gaze flew to Arnon who leaned around her to send his verbal sally to Natly. He gave her a twitch of a smile, which broadened when Natly made a noise between a shriek and a growl.

"She is a woman, too!" Natly stabbed a finger at Oria that flashed with a long, pointed, and painted bejeweled nail.

"This 'she' you refer to is my wife and queen." Lonen's voice, on the other hand, was pure growl. "You will show—"

"That is a matter of debate and—" Nolan spoke over him, then broke off when Lonen spun on him, nearly nose to nose.

"Respect. You will all show respect and behave like adults, not children, before *our people*, for at least the span of time it takes to eat a meal. Our father would expect that much of us." He leaned around his brother. "That includes you, Natly, though you are not, I might point out, a member of this family."

"I wondered when you'd acknowledge me," she pouted.

"I don't even know why you're here."

"How can you say that, after what we've been together?"

"I spoke to you about this, Natly, at length. That was meant to be the end of things."

He had? When had that happened? Lonen had mentioned nothing about it to Oria. Though she supposed that wasn't an easy tidbit to drop into conversation. And his personal business. She didn't envy him that confrontation.

"You don't get to just tell me things are done," Natly gritted out.

"I'm king," Lonen said simply and turned back to Oria, dismissing his former betrothed with studied disinterest. Waving away a servant who sought to serve Oria from a platter of meat, he signaled to another who brought a special plate just for her. A large bowl of grains in a simmering broth, loaded with vegetables and graced by a puff pastry made golden with the Destrye butterfat, it made her mouth water and her stomach leap with interest.

"Thank you," she whispered to Lonen, enjoying the way his silvery eyes lingered on her lips. He smiled at her.

"Scary sorceress," he murmured, gaze glinting with pure humor.

"Lady Natly is here as my guest," Nolan cut into the moment.

"How nice for you." Lonen's eyes went flat again, his voice all polite boredom.

"It seemed insulting not to include her," Nolan continued. "To simply let her languish. She might not be actual family, but she's as near to it as any might be. Some might say more so than others at this table."

Beside her, Arnon made a quiet choking noise, but Lonen methodically cut his steak, forking up neat bites. "I seem to recall you firmly rebuffing Natly's attempts at becoming 'part of the family,' brother. Let's see—that was after Ion declined her offer in favor of Salaya's fair hand—" he nodded to Salaya, who still stared into the middle distance, not eating "—but before she moved on to me."

"You seemed happy enough to savor the rewards settling on you," Nolan retorted. "I recall you extensively savoring Natly's many charms before we left to destroy the Báran predators, and I understand you continued to lead Natly on after you returned, promising her that you and she would marry. You must address the question of the honor you owe her. Our father would expect that much of us." He bit out that last, looking tremendously pleased with himself.

Lonen heaved a sigh, then looked at Natly, who continued to sulk, though it seemed her eyes glittered with a kind of excitement at the attention as she looked past him at Oria. It made Oria feel oddly old and weary—especially odd given that Natly was likely older than she. But the Destrye woman did have a legitimate grievance, as she would have married Lonen had Oria not maneuvered him into a marriage of state with her. She couldn't blame Natly for being hurt and angry, particularly at losing a man like Lonen. Oria needed to keep that in mind—that she had what Natly had wanted, had been promised, and lost through unfair means—and keep in her heart compassion for his jilted fiancée. In Natly's place, she would likely not behave well.

Never mind that the bickering felt juvenile at this point. Being honest with herself, she completely reneged on her initial offer for Lonen to keep his former fiancée as a lover, or even install her as Queen of the Destrye while Oria remained in Bára. No one need know about that ill-advised idea. It took her aback at the ferocity of her own emotions on imagining such a situation—to the point that she'd fight tooth and nail to keep Natly's jeweled nails off Lonen.

"Or with fire," Chuffta suggested. *"Burn all her hair off."*

Oria stifled a snort of laughter. *"Don't like her, do you?"*

"'Animals at the table.' I'll show her what real *claws can do."*

She concentrated on eating the truly excellent meal, the grains having soaked up the rich broth so they almost melted in her mouth. Baeltya had outdone herself in instructions, if not actual cooking. Lonen, Nolan, and Natly were arguing in hushed voices, though the harsh cadences came through clearly enough. Destrye at the nearby tables, both men and women, ate in silence, doing their best to overhear the discussion, no doubt.

In Bára, the people would be equally eager for juicy tidbits to feed the gossip mill, but the royal family would never eat in public thus. Of course, for her family, eating had meant doffing the eyeless, mouthless golden masks of their office, something done only in privacy. With a pang of nostalgia, she missed those formal, elegant occasions. The ritual of removing their masks and setting them on the tiles beside their plates, made for that purpose. The relaxed intimacy of those meals.

"I miss Bára, too. Your rooftop terrace."

"The sunshine and the view."

The voices beside her grew in volume and intensity, and she felt Lonen growing commensurately angrier. A passionate, emotive people, the Destrye. Just as well she had her portals so locked down that she didn't get much of it. Mostly she experienced the edges of Lonen's dark and brooding anger, a familiar river that ran deep in him, only occasionally rising to the surface.

"They'll come to blows if we don't stop them," Arnon commented in her ear, strangely cheerful, considering the circumstances.

She'd kind of forgotten about him. "The duel?"

He gave her an odd look, pursing his lips. "Talked to you about that, did he? But that's an interesting point. Not the challenge. Not yet, anyway. I meant Lonen and Natly. Though perhaps we shouldn't try to stop them. A good knock-down, drag-out would serve as a fine pressure release and distraction from Nolan badgering you. Or making any hasty challenges."

She swallowed, glad that eating reminded her not to gape in surprise. "Lonen and Natly...might physically fight...at a formal dinner?"

Arnon grinned crookedly and curled his fingers, making a swiping motion. "Those nails aren't just for pretty. She's like a tree cat with them. Left her mark on more than one warrior hereabouts."

Oria and her brothers had squabbled plenty, but they'd never gotten physical. That would have been a grave lapse in *hwil*, even for a youngling, and if she could've borne even the slightest touch. Of course, her brothers had delighted in laying magical traps for each other. And she'd been too fragile for any such tussling, watching mostly from afar. Forever outside the inner circle.

"It hardly seems appropriate," she murmured to Arnon, "for my husband, the king, to publicly quarrel with his former fiancée." Not only because it put her on the outer edges, yet again.

Arnon stroked his beard thoughtfully. "You're not just for pretty, either, are you? I suspect this is exactly what Natly hopes for. What are you going to do about it?"

"Me?"

"No one else is going to." Arnon dug into his steak with relish, chewing ostentatiously.

"Meaning you won't."

"I'm not the one who's being tested tonight."

She sat back abruptly, Chuffta spreading his wings slightly to rebalance, grumbling at her. "This... scenario is for my sake."

"Lonen always did get easily sucked into Nolan's taunting. And yes, that's the question, isn't it? How much is our brother's mind clouded by love for you—or by your magic. What better way to push him than to dangle his former mistress in front of him? And you."

She forced herself to eat, though Natly's tone wavered between pleading and strident, growing loud enough for certain words to be audible. Love. Wedding. Arill. Loyalty.

"Why are you helping me?" She asked Arnon. "I thought you didn't approve of me either."

"Is that what I'm doing?" Arnon's happy-go-lucky smile dropped, showing the canny expression beneath. "I think I'm just interested in your true colors, as well."

"I don't know what to do." She really hoped Chuffta had wise advice for this.

"Hair-burning is still an option."

"You are supposed to advise me! Make yourself useful."

"I submit that hair-burning would put an end to this very quickly. But," her Familiar added hastily when she mentally growled at him, *"it seems to me this is all theater, right? That's what Arnon is telling you. Lonen's brothers are playing old games, pulling on his tail to make him lose control. He'll look weak, unable to decide between his females. Not something a king should do."*

She agreed with that. *"I still don't know how I play in."*

"If you were what they think you to be—a spy, controller of their king, pursuing your own agenda to expose the Destrye so the Bárans can triumph—what would you do?"

"I'd encourage the chaos. If a scenario weakened Lonen, I'd work to increase that pressure."

"So, do the opposite."

Gah. More easily thought than accomplished. She needed time to think, which she didn't have, as the argument continued to escalate. Natly stood now, nails flashing as she gesticulated. Nolan pounded his mug on the table, face screwed up as he scowled at Lonen, stabbing a finger at his chest. The people of the hall watched with avid delight, as if witnessing a mummer's play. Arnon sat back, sipping his wine, not watching the passionately involved trio, but observing her. Even Salaya seemed to have woken from her daze, her gaze alert and interested.

"They planned this—Arnon and Nolan."

"Oh yes, I think so."

Her temples throbbed, the relaxation of the aswae lost to the violent emotions churning around her with such potency they penetrated even her tightly closed shields, as if seeping into the pores of her skin like the warmed oils. She'd become permeable. Far from her home, far from the magic that had always sustained her. And for what?

These people respected nothing but strength. Much as the Bárans respected only power. They were the same thing, really—one physical, the other non-physical. Both with huge impacts.

She didn't have to pretend to be something she wasn't, to show herself to be truly on Lonen's side. She was as much the enemy of the King of Bára as any Destrye. Never mind that he was her brother.

That just made it more personal. The seething rage that burgeoned at the thought of Yar helped bolster her.

"Okay, fly about, breathe some flame—don't set anything on fire!—but make a spectacle. No hair-burning."

She caught barely the edge of Chuffta's glee as he surged off her shoulder with a clap of wings—and a keening howl unlike any other sound she'd ever heard him make. The cry morphed into a stream of fire that followed his path in a spiral, lingering in the air almost like smoke, to then sparkle gradually down on the ducking, and utterly shocked, Destrye.

Even Lonen fell silent, staring in astonishment.

Oria might have, too, had she not been concentrating on her own show. Keeping her focus on that sense of the silently breathing forest, she reached for the gift it had given her, and spun the living sgath—for sgath it was, just of another flavor, something to contemplate later—channeling it into active grien. Never having been trained in the supposedly exclusively male magic, she didn't have many prepared tricks up her sleeve, but she'd improvised before. Tossing her spoon into the air, she hit it midflight with a burst of grien, infusing the wood with growth energy long lost from its cells, but not forgotten. She stuck with the easiest path, letting it be what it had always been—so it sprouted tufts of new leaves, bright green with distant spring. Catching it neatly in her hand, she stepped past a wary Lonen and astounded Nolan, and offered the leafy twig to Natly, who gripped the arms of her chair, glossy red mouth in an O of horror or shock, or who knew.

"Natly," Oria said, "I owe you the gift of an apology. You've graciously given up the right to the promises King Lonen made you so that our people might be joined in peace. Please accept this token of my regard. It will remain ever green and bring you luck, prosperity, and fertility." She hoped so, anyway. If not, Oria would do her best to infuse the twig with new feedings of grien as often as possible.

Finally, tentatively, Natly lifted a hand and took it, at first touching it as she might a snake. Then a slow smile twitched at her mouth, spreading into something warm and genuine. "We grew these trees on my home farm."

Sheer luck there. Perhaps Lonen's goddess did smile on them. "Keep it in good health, for good memories."

The room remained hushed, so Oria picked up another wooden spoon, tossing it into the air and hitting it with another dollop of judicious grien. This one burst into blossom, small, pink and sweet, carrying the hint of crisp fruit to come. Oria took it to Salaya. "Princess Salaya. Nothing can replace the husband you lost, the father your sons will never know, but please accept this gift from me. May we come to know each other as sisters, and our joined families blossom as this does."

Salaya, dark eyes soft with welling tears, took the flowering twig, spinning it between her fingers. Oria left her with it.

And swiped Arnon's spoon on the way. She smiled at Lonen, who narrowed his eyes at her in some sort of warning, though admiration glinted in them, and tossed the spoon to the straw-covered floor behind the king's chair. Using the last of the magic she'd pulled in, she poured all of it into the dead wood, urging it to put down roots, to grow again.

At first nothing happened, except that the spoon seemed to worm its way through the straw, disappearing into the earth. Perhaps she'd miscalculated and the earth beneath the Destrye palace fortress remained too frozen for anything to grow.

But then, with a huge cracking sound, a sapling shot from the floor, fast as lighting and with the attendant rumbles. No, that was the awed murmuring of the gathering.

The sapling thickened, growing fatter, then taller, then fatter again by leaps, sprouting twigs like a fuzzy crown of baby's hair that rapidly became gracefully arching branches. The sound of the crowd grew, people leaping to their feet to point, and Lonen rose, taking her by the arm over her plush sleeve. The tightness of his grip communicated something, the excited leap of his emotions telling her more.

She would have slowed the astonishing growth, but couldn't. She'd given it everything she'd collected from that solemn chorus of breathing forest, and had nothing more to offer. Nor could she take it back. The limbs attenuated, draping from the central trunk nearly like vines.

Then, with a nearly audible chime, the umbrella of draping branches burst into a constellation of golden flowers, their sweet perfume bursting through the room.

The people gasped, then sent up a roar.

Lonen gripped her arm harder. "What have you done?"

~ 10 ~

A HALIGNE TREE. How had Oria known—or had she? She gazed up at him, copper eyes lustrous with the magic she'd wielded, though already the shadows deepened around them with its spending, face pale with trepidation at whatever she saw in his.

Up to him to explain this last gift then. She'd done it to stop the brewing fight—for which he was grateful, so far as observing protocols, even as he burned with frustrated ire to battle it out with them already. Nolan and Natly had baited him, yes, but he was Arill-cursed done with their poking him at every turn. *You don't need to think about if you're good enough to be king, because you* are *king.* Why couldn't Nolan just accept that reality?

And Natly. Of course she wouldn't give up without a struggle. The Destrye women might not be the sort of warriors who rode into battle, but they fought as fiercely as any man—and as tenacious-ly. He supposed he couldn't fault Natly for showing the same determination that won Bára for Dru, despite all odds.

But he'd see to it that she conceded defeat now. Oria had tem-porarily disarmed her. Salaya also, which made him wonder what encounter they'd had. Oria would be explaining a great deal. Once they extracted themselves from this fraught dinner. For all he knew, golems would spring from the earth next.

As soon as he thought it, he sent a swift prayer to Arill to guard against such an event. Knowing about the tunnels...if Oria could root a tree in the floor of the great hall, what would stop a burrow-ing golem from getting inside. They'd have no place of retreat then.

"And this tree, my queen?" he asked in a raised voice that commanded attention. "A gift to all the Destrye, Arill's own Haligne tree, carrying her sacred bloom. A promise of spring and bounty to come."

Her lashes lowered slightly in acknowledgement and perhaps relief. "Yes, Your Highness." She opened her mouth to say more, closing it again as Chuffta landed on her shoulder. Probably wise.

Nolan struggled to his feet, gripping the back of his chair and staring at the tree, looking both ill and awed. Arnon stroked his beard, arms otherwise folded, deep in thought.

"She can do this?" Nolan forced between his teeth, face darkening with anger. Here it came. "Your pet sorceress has the ability to grow fruit trees from nothing at all."

"Not nothing," Oria corrected, "I used—"

But Lonen, realizing he already held her arm in a fierce grip, released it and stopped her words by putting his arm around her shoulders. "One of Oria's magical gifts, yes, but—"

"All this time," Nolan grated out, his voice rising, "you've led us to believe that she'd wield battle magics to drive off mythical dragons, and you knew she could have been growing food right here in this very hall."

"Except for the minor issue of her being unconscious and weak from her journeys," Lonen shot back.

"She doesn't look weak now. And she's hardly been an unconscious prize in your bed, fucking your brains out while you let your people starve."

"That's not exactly how—"

"Then how *is* it, little brother? Explain this to me because as I see it, I'm looking at a selfish man fatally distracted by a bit of foreign pussy when he should be serving his Arill-cursed people!" Nolan thrust a clenched fist at the stunned silent room. Arnon started forward, stopped himself.

Lonen, also, fought himself, wanting nothing more than to strike a blow across his brother's mouth that spoke so foully of Oria.

Nolan and Ion, both, so certain that could be his only attraction to Oria. Unless his mind was controlled by her magic. Or whatever trumped-up reason they devised for what they simply didn't understand.

Couldn't understand because he still didn't dare expose Oria's weakness. How she'd summoned this much magic, he didn't know, but it had obviously tapped her out. Just in case, he asked, only for her ears, "Can you access more magic right now?"

She shook her head slightly, lips pressed together, tinged violet with fatigue.

"We're waiting for this answer, Lonen, and—"

"Your Highness," he corrected, overly loud but there it was. "I am your king, brother, whether you like it or not and you will address me and my wife with the appropriate respect."

"I do not like it!" Nolan roared. "This foul sorceress who toys with us and taunts us with Arill's sacred objects, profaning them with her Báran magic, she is no wife to you and you are no king of mine."

Silence, thick and jagged, fell hard across the room like a tree dropped by ice.

Very softly, Arnon groaned low in his throat. Oria held still as death against Lonen's side.

"Do you challenge me then, brother?" Lonen kept the words low enough to be between them, but the sound carried in the avidly listening hall.

"You have forced me to it," Nolan replied, stiff, head high, looking past Lonen to some vision only he could see. "I have no choice."

Now Arnon did move forward, taking Nolan by the arm. "You *do* have a choice," he hissed in his brother's ear. "Don't do this to us, to the Destrye, to Dru."

Nolan shook him off. "I'm doing this *for* the Destrye and Dru."

"The enemy is out there, man, not in here," Arnon urged in a harsh whisper.

"She is also here in this hall, along with any who aid her," Nolan replied, his gaze on Oria.

"The sorceress can help us; don't you see?"

"I see. Oh yes, I see all too clearly. And she *will* help us. Make no mistake of that. She will grow the crops we need to feed our people, but as penance for her people's crimes against us, not from the luxury of our king's bed. She clearly must be properly governed and controlled. Not coddled by a weak and besotted fool." He spat the last at Lonen.

"I would never be ruled by you," Oria hurled at him. "You make a grave mistake by thinking so." Lonen squeezed her, not to silence her this time, but in reassurance. He wouldn't let it happen, but her ferocity in the face of such a grim fate made him proud. His Báran sorceress was a warrior, too, in her own way.

"Do I, sorceress? We shall see. And the goddess will decide." Nolan's eyes glittered as he tightened his jaw. "I think you will do a great deal to protect your love from the death he's earned. It's clear from tonight's demonstration that you do care for him, regardless of your other plans. So, I challenge you, Lonen, son of Archimago and Vycayla according to the ancient laws. May Arill bestow her blessing on her chosen king."

"I accept your challenge, Nolan, son of Archimago and Vycayla according to the ancient laws," Lonen answered in tones loud enough to ring confidently through the hall, though the prospect made him ill inside. By the expression on Arnon's face, he felt the same.

Then Lonen's gut dropped, remembering his younger brother's warning, as Nolan clapped a hand over Arnon's where he gripped his arm. "Brother, will you stand second for me?"

Arnon looked away from Nolan, to Lonen, quiet anguish in his shadowed eyes. Of course his younger brother had no choice. He had to stand second for one or the other—and Lonen could forgive him the betrayal where Nolan never would. They both knew it.

"Yes," Arnon said quietly. "Yes, I will."

LONEN HUSTLED THEM down the hall, apparently back to their chambers, fast enough that Oria grew breathless keeping up, though she'd never complain. He gave orders as they went, summoning various people, by the names she caught. Uncharacteristically for him when she was present, he spoke in rapid-fire Destrye rather than in Common Tongue. Expediency or old habit, it didn't matter.

Events had turned as grim as they could be.

"Well, they could *be worse,"* Chuffta noted. *"The Trom could attack."*

"Shut up, Chuffta, really."

"It would be an excellent time, is all I'm saying. With the Destrye divided by internal strife, Yar would have the perfect opening. It's almost as if you did do *what they suspected."*

"Not. Helping."

He seemed to realize the depth of her displeasure belatedly. *"Of course we all know you didn't."*

Did they? By the grim set of Lonen's jaw, he might not see things that way. *"Just...don't talk to me right now."*

She'd messed it all up entirely. They entered his chambers and she turned to him, "Lonen, I—"

"Go sit by the fire," he interrupted. "Have some warmed wine or your cursed fruit juice. You're cold as ice and pale as death."

Okay, then. She did as he ordered, trying to be meek and unobtrusive—and also because sitting by the fire would feel good. The warm clothes had helped, but the great hall had been chilly, even before she unwisely spent the magic that left her empty. She sent Chuffta to his rug on the floor and tucked a fur blanket around herself. Some thoughtful soul had left spiced wine warming over a small candle, so she poured a mug and cupped the metal in her hands. It quickly became nearly hot enough to burn her palms, but she welcomed the sting. In the outer room, Lonen's voice rose and fell as he spoke with someone. Then the door closed and silence crept in from the corners.

Punishment for her crimes.

At last he came in, no longer wearing his formal clothes, nor the wreath that named him king. He always took it off as soon as he could, it seemed, complaining of its weight. She'd picked it up once, when he was otherwise occupied, and it had felt light as a jewelbird in her hands. There could be all kinds of heaviness, though, she supposed.

Lonen sat heavily, bracing his forearms on his knees and lacing his fingers together, staring into the fire. He'd stripped down to a sleeveless shirt and breeches, his muscled arms and shoulders bare, along with his lower legs and feet. Old scars showed white against his tanned skin, the newer, still healing ones shades of pink and red, a map of his brutal history.

And now he'd fight for his life again, because of her.

Chuffta, curled in his blanket nest, but head up and alert, cocked his head, green eyes glowing bright with some thought he didn't send.

"Where did you get the magic?" Lonen asked finally.

She swallowed hard against the surprise. Not what she'd expected him to ask. "I… absorbed it earlier today. On the way to the aswae, we crossed a bridge and then in Arill's Temple I held a leaf and… it's difficult to explain."

He tilted a sideways look at her, gray eyes calm, expression so opaque she nearly opened a portal to read his thoughts. "Try," he suggested drily.

Fine. "I held this beautiful leaf—"

"That beautiful leaf?" He pointed to where the leaf she'd picked up sat on a lovely golden metal stand on the fireplace mantel.

"Yes." In all the flurry of preparation for dinner, she'd forgotten to look for it.

"It's a dead leaf, Oria."

"Remember five seconds ago when I told you it was hard to explain?" she bristled.

He chuckled, surprising her yet again, shaking his head. "Oh, good, you're still you. I was concerned someone had replaced my fiery sorceress wife with a milkmaid."

"I imagine milkmaids have challenges, too, what with cranky bulls."

"Milk comes from cows, not bulls," he corrected.

What did she know about livestock? "Cranky cows then."

"I'll allow as there are cows easily as mean as bulls out there." Now his eyes sparked with humor and she huffed at him.

"I don't know how you can jest at a time like this!"

He shrugged his shoulders, a slight roll, muscles flexing. "My father always said if you couldn't afford to despair, then your other choice was to laugh."

"Aha. This is where you get the eternal optimism from."

Lonen frowned slightly. "You know, I'd never have said so, but you could be right. He was the one who risked everything to take every able warrior to Bára on the word of a few scouts and with no hope of victory. It's amazing, really, that he convinced us all to go."

"Was there arguing—like tonight?"

"No. No one dared argue with my father. No one would have dared challenge him. He was a great warrior and king."

Her heart ached for the bleakness in his tone. "I'm so very sorry about tonight."

He glanced at her, raising his brows in surprise. "Why? It wasn't your fault."

It wasn't? "Sure it was—if I hadn't worked that magic…"

"It *would* have been helpful if you'd warned me."

"I didn't know myself! I only wanted to stop the brawl and it felt like I had enough magic—which, yes, I somehow absorbed from communing with the leaf and feeling this sense of—don't laugh—the forest breathing sgath into me."

He didn't laugh—instead he grinned. "Aha! Just as I'd hoped."

"What? Hoped how?"

"I told you before I thought you could absorb sgath from the trees. They're very old and powerful. And I kind of know what you mean. I've had that feeling when I've been in the forest—the usual sounds fall away and there's this deep vibration, like an enormous heart beating at a pace so even and slow that we aren't really aware of it most of the time."

She regarded him thoughtfully, taking a long sip of the warmed wine. "You're an odd man, Destrye," she finally said, and he tipped his head in acknowledgment.

"You wouldn't be the first to think so."

"And I thought you wanted me to absorb sgath from the lakes."

"We'll try them, too."

"We—when? What are you talking about?"

He finally sat back, scrubbing his hands on his thighs. "We leave in the morning."

"We—I—you—" She was sputtering.

"Yes," he nodded helpfully. "You and me makes we, and Chuffta, too. And Buttercup. The old team together again." He sounded wry about that.

"But the challenge—are you forfeiting or… running away?"

His gaze went flinty. "Have you ever known me to run away from any challenge, Sorceress—including the formidable ones you set me?"

"No." Unaccountably a laugh welled up in her chest, but she held it down, savoring the bright sense of well-being it brought. It did her heart good to see him back to his arrogant self, though she couldn't account for the change in him. "Then what—"

"The sgath you got from that dead leaf, is it enough?"

"It wasn't just the leaf."

"Is it enough, Oria?"

"It depends. Enough for what?" But she knew.

"How about growing food in the hall—can you do that?"

"Well, not yet, but—"

"So we're going to find a better source."

"*But*, I was going to say, I'm working on it. I just need time to refine the technique, to meditate on it."

Lonen was shaking his head, his expression full of regret. "We're out of time, unfortunately. Not just for growing food. I need you to—"

"Your Highness?" An older man's voice called from the outer chamber and Lonen sprang to his feet.

"In here, Priest Robson," Lonen called out, waving to Oria to remain seated.

An older Destrye entered the room. Not a warrior, but tall as any of them, his wild mane of hair gone purest white with age. His brows, too, bristled with long white hairs that curled with untamed glee, as did his drooping beard and mustache. He wore deep green robes like Talya's and fixed interested pale blue eyes on her.

"Rhiten, may I present my wife, Oria, Sorceress of Bára," Lonen said in the most respectful tone she'd ever heard him use.

"Not your wife, boy. Not until Arill seals the union with her gentling hand." Despite his attenuated appearance, Priest Robson had a voice full of vigor. He never took his eyes off Oria.

"I made the vow," Lonen said, and the priest raised his brows, making the strands rearrange themselves into starbursts. "Arill's vow, warrior to wife."

"I know which vow you meant, boy," the priest replied irritably. "You had no business doing that without a priest or priestess there to witness."

"I didn't have one handy," Lonen replied in that dry tone of his. "And we'd already married under Báran law and magic, so it seemed … redundant."

Which vow was this? Oria cast back her mind. When she'd hesitated to confide the secrets that would get her killed, he'd knelt, kissed the hem of her robes and made a promise. *I swear by the magic that binds us, by the seed of me in you and the blossom of you in me, that I shall never betray you, my wife, whether by action or inaction.*

"'Redundant,' he says." The priest snorted and cast his eyes skyward. "Arill save us from impetuous boys who think they can decide which rituals to keep and which to discard. Báran, are you, girl?"

"Yes, Priest Robson," she ventured, though that answer seemed obvious enough. She felt wrong, sitting curled up under her blanket, but Lonen had told her to stay put, so she stayed.

"Hmm. Saw your display in the great hall. Quite the show."

She didn't know what to say to that, so she held her tongue and he transferred that pale gaze to Chuffta. "And this creature—it does your bidding? I've heard tell of witches who keep animal assistants to work magic for them, serve as repositories of power, that sort of thing."

A tingle ran down her spine. "I am no witch; I'm a sorceress."

He made a noise that might have been simply clearing a stopped nostril, though she doubted it. "What's the difference?"

"There's no such thing as witches," she replied evenly, "except perhaps in children's tales."

Priest Robson scowled and harrumphed, but let the topic drop there. He turned back to Lonen, opened a book he carried and began reading in the Destrye dialect.

Oria took advantage of the opportunity to confer with Chuffta. *"Have you heard of Familiars acting as repositories of magic before?"*

"Oh, am I allowed to speak to you again?" Chuffta's mind-voice reeked of disdain.

"Don't be a suck-sand. I needed a moment of peace is all."

"I'm sorry I said the wrong thing."

"Don't be. I was wrong to tell you to shut up."

"Then I have heard some derkesthai tales along those lines, but they always sounded like legends. Like the stories of derkesthai drinking from magic springs and growing to ten times their normal size."

Her skin went clammy. *"You mean… the size of Trom dragons?"*

Chuffta went very quiet. Finally, *"I never thought of it that way."*

"I thought you told me you're not related to those monsters."

"We're not!" He sounded fully insulted.

"You said it was like comparing a house cat to one of the golden desert jaguars."

"Exactly."

"But those are related creatures—just different in size and wildness."

"And intelligence. Don't forget that the Trom dragons are stupid beasts that lack derkesthai intelligence."

"How do you know?"

"Why else let the Trom ride them?"

"That's no answer."

He stayed silent a moment, then, sulkily, *"They* look *stupid."*

She was saved coming up with a reasonable reply to that by Lonen and Priest Robson turning to her.

"If you think she's up to it, boy, and you think you can get Her Eminence to assist, then I'll play my part."

"She's up to it," Lonen assured him.

Those spectacular brows drew together, sending them into an even more impressive pattern. "What say you, sorceress—you're willing?"

Oria looked past him to Lonen, who nodded encouragement. *Trust me.* Oh well, not like she had any other options at this point. "I'm willing."

"All right then. Travel safely under Arill's hand." The priest closed the text with a thump, nodded decisively, and left without another word.

Oria waited for the sound of the outer door closing. "What did I just agree to?"

Lonen came to her, standing behind her chair and filling his hands with her hair, sliding his fingers through it. She'd become so accustomed to this lulling ritual that her eyes half-closed, and she wanted to purr like one of Chuffta's house cats. "It means more than I can express," Lonen said, in soft, slightly rough voice, "that you agreed without knowing."

She shrugged a little, tipping her head back to look up at him through her lashes. Her fierce warrior. They were in it together, for better or worse. "You asked me to trust you."

"I appreciate the leap. I know that's not easy for you."

Perhaps not—but easier every moment she spent with him, it seemed. "So what did I agree to?"

"You're going to be my second in the duel."

Her eyes flew open wide. "I'm what? I can't do that!"

"There's no one else I'd rather have at my back. Priest Robson checked ancient law, and in the absence of other immediate family able and willing to serve as my second, my wife can fill the role."

"I'm no warrior—I can't fight your brothers."

"With magic you can."

"But…" She trailed off, realizing. *Travel safely under Arill's hand.* "That's why you asked if there was enough magic in the leaf. And why we're journeying to find a better source—or for me to confront the wild magic."

"Yes. Also, we need a sponsor for our wedding in Arill's Temple, since Nolan has lodged a protest to the marriage, along with tonight's challenge. We need someone with greater authority than he has."

"Don't you, as king?"

"I did, but no longer—not with the challenge live. Until we resolve it, we're equal in authority."

"That sounds like an unreasonable system."

"It's an old system," he admitted. "But typically a challenge would not be left unresolved for long. It would either be settled immediately or at first light the following day."

That's why he'd hustled them out of the great hall so fast. "So Nolan expects you to fight in the morning?"

"Yes, be we won't be here. Baeltya will be here soon to give us one more treatment that will last a while, then we'll sneak out before dawn."

"Won't that be you conceding the challenge?"

"No. Priest Robson confirmed that Nolan must wait seven days to declare me dead."

"He was thought dead longer than that," she pointed out.

Lonen rubbed the scar around his eye. "So many men lost in the war, we never got around to the formality of declaring all the missing as dead. It seemed unnecessary at the time."

"And now we have to sneak out of your own palace."

His eyes sparkled. "It'll be fun. Like escaping Bára again."

"That was *not* fun."

"You felt very nice bouncing on my shoulder, your breasts all soft on my back, your adorable bottom high in the air."

She closed her eyes and groaned. "Only you."

"You love me for it."

"Maybe," she conceded. "So who has this higher authority to sponsor a wedding in Arill's Temple?"

"Someone fortuitously living very near the lake I planned to take you to."

A note of hesitation in his voice alerted her and she squinted at him. "*Who*, Lonen?"

He gave her a lopsided smile. "My mother. Her Eminence, the former Queen of the Destrye."

All she needed. One more impossible Destrye woman to make her life miserable.

~ 11 ~

AS PROMISED, LONEN woke her in the early hours, when all was dark and still.

Though how *he* knew the time, she couldn't fathom. Even had the windows been uncovered, there wouldn't be any hint of sunrise yet. Pilaryh came to help her dress and pack her final things—something that surprised her, until Lonen curtly told her he wouldn't give anyone access to her who wasn't utterly loyal.

Apparently, although he'd told Oria numerous times not to be concerned about Nolan's challenge, Lonen had been expecting it. She'd been through the same with Yar. Hoping one's potentially traitorous sibling wouldn't do the worst was one thing. Being blind to the possibility was another.

Pilaryh dressed her warmly in layers, including wonderful wool stockings lined with fur that went all the way up to her crotch, held up by ribbons attached around her waist. Short bloomers would allow her to answer the call of nature without having to get chilled. Knee-high boots, also fur-lined, would keep her feet warm. Then layers of skirts and wool petticoats, the light indoor cloak she'd worn to dinner, and then another that Lonen produced, made entirely of incredibly soft white fur.

She stroked it, wondering at the texture. It wasn't alabaster white, but had a dappled pattern when she turned it just so in the light. A kind of faint striping of shorter beige and gray hairs mixed in with the longer ones.

"What kind of animal did this come from?" She wondered aloud.

"You're not telling me you're going to refuse to wear it," Lonen said.

"Did I ask after its name? I'm wearing half a dozen creatures' former skins already," she retorted. "I'm hardly going to draw the line now. I was simply curious."

He ran his hand down the fall of her hair. "I apologize, love—I'm on edge. It's a shadowcat. They live in forests farther north. The color and dappling makes it ideal for blending with the snow. There's a hood as well, to cover your hair."

"There's your one for the day." She smiled at him. "I'll hardly be invisible when I'm otherwise wearing scarlet clothing, riding a big black warhorse, and hanging out with a fearsome Destrye warrior."

Lonen grinned. "There are times to stay hidden and others to been seen in powerful ways. We'll be doing both."

THEY CREPT OUT of the palace, Chuffta scouting ahead of Alby—though the guards on duty who saw them looked steadily past. Lonen and his loyal attendants. How did he assess who would keep his secrets? She wouldn't have known in Bára. Well, at least she hadn't until the city fell to the Destrye and she found herself having to make decisions. At that point, most people had made clear where they stood. Some offered unequivocal loyalty, others—like her perfidious brother—made everything more difficult for her.

The tricky ones were those who seemed to change like a flower that follows the sun, forever adjusting to face whoever held the most power.

Banked fires lit a few rooms, but only enough to make the enormous log walls loom like sleeping giants. A few guards manned the great doors, opening them just enough when Alby spoke to them for their stealthy party to slip through, the snick of the locks behind them loud in her ears. She hadn't much liked being closed in, unable to look out of the windows, but by the time they exited the final door, Oria felt exposed, and not only because the chill settled against her skin.

Below, the shanty town gleamed here and there with lanterns. Mostly, though, the pre-dawn dark loomed with oppressive, cold quiet. To the side, Buttercup whuffed a greeting, steaming breath billowing out, and she skipped with glee to see him, cupping his big head in her gloved hands and blowing softly into his nostrils. The groom who'd brought him made a sound of distress, throwing out a hand to stop her, but Lonen told the boy not to be concerned.

Slipping off one glove to feel the warhorse's mind better, Oria leaned against him. Buttercup would never harm her. He smelled of sweet hay and heat, his mind fierce, eager—and excited for what the day might bring, much like Lonen's state of mind. Buttercup didn't think in focused words as Chuffta did, but he possessed a certain kind of sense. He seemed pleased to see the derkesthai, too, huffing and bobbing his head when Chuffta landed on the saddle and snaked his head around to peck at the horse's neck in affection.

"Up you go," Lonen whispered to her, grasping her by the waist and lifting her into the saddle, Chuffta winging up to clear the way. The groom held Buttercup still for them, so she didn't need to. Even with Lonen's height and strength, she had to grab hold of the saddle and haul herself onto the massive stallion. "Scoot forward," Lonen murmured, then was up behind her before she knew it.

"I'm riding in front?" she asked. "The saddle feels different."

"I had it redesigned." His breath caressed her ear as he leaned to speak into it, a warm shiver going through her. He rearranged her shadowcat cloak, more forward, snugging her up in the vee of his powerful thighs and adjusting his own cloak around them both. Wrapping an arm around her waist for good measure, he took the reins and nodded to Alby.

"If anyone asks," he said quietly, "you know only that your king requested his steed and left, nothing more."

"All know I do your bidding, Your Highness. There's no crime in that loyalty," Alby replied with hushed fervency. "May Arill hold you in her palm and grant your swift return to take and hold the throne, my king."

"Good man." Maybe Lonen's voice roughened a bit because of the need for quiet, but Oria suspected there was more to it.

They rode through the maze of buildings, hoods up, Buttercup stepping with that stealth so uncanny for his size and boisterous nature. They crossed a bridge over the moat. As Pilaryh had told her—it was filled not with water but with sharp spears all pointing toward the perimeter. The road crossed a short cleared area, then passed between two huge trees that stood as quiet and unmoving as the sentries back at the palace. As the lantern light disappeared behind them, the shadows of the deep, old forest settled around them, only the faint gleam of snow and Chuffta's ghostly form showing against all the shades of black.

Somewhere beyond that dense canopy of limbs, the moons would be in the sky. At least Grienon, in his swift passage. Sgatha might have lumbered already beyond the rim of the world, not to return for some time. Oria had lost track of the moon cycles, even time itself.

"More room," Lonen said, as if they'd only paused in the conversation, "to put the saddle bags and supplies behind me, and better for Buttercup to have the weight back over his haunches. Also," he squeezed her waist, "I feel better having you where I can hold on to you."

"I'm not going to fall off—my seat is much better than that by now. I could probably have ridden my own horse."

"This is faster and safer." He dropped a hand against her bottom and squeezed again, nuzzling against her hood. "And more fun. Though I'll agree your seat is excellent."

"Is sex all you think about?" she tried to sound tart, but his flirting warmed her. It was nice to be just them again, without all the people around.

"Not all," he sounded close. "When you're not anywhere I can see you or touch you or smell you, then I think about other things."

"Like redesigning saddles and which of your people are loyal enough to compile supplies and sneak us out of the palace."

"Those things, too," he agreed. "I also think up ways for us to pleasure each other, now that we're both healthier."

"Unfortunately, all your scheming has resulted in us no longer having a bed."

"I think something can be arranged."

"In the middle of a forest?"

"You'll see."

"Tell me." But he refused to say more about it.

She dozed a bit, then woke to growing light, perfectly warm between Lonen and Buttercup's combined body heat, along with the lusciously soft fur of her cloak. If only she could wear it all the time, she'd never get cold. Perhaps she could have more garments made of the shadowcat fur? She had to mentally shake her head at herself—what a long way she'd come from refusing to eat meat on principle to contemplating how to divest more shadowcats of their hides.

"We all live at the expense of something else," Chuffta pointed out from wherever he flew above or beyond them. *"It's neither good nor bad. It just is."*

"I just feel like I'm becoming more Destrye all the time—barbarian and predatory."

"Bára preyed on the Destrye, who definitely have names."

He had an excellent point. Perhaps she'd always been the worse predator, like the great cats, hunters so lethal they could afford to spend most of their time napping in the sun. An image uncomfortably close to how her life in Bára had been, lolling in the shade of silk screens during the heat of the afternoon, the lush luxury of her garden, the beauty of the city.

"You're forgetting all the time you spent studying, meditating, training to be a priestess and striving for hwil *in order to master your magic."*

She had sort of forgotten some of that, how intensely critical mastering her magic had seemed back then, how attaining her mask had seemed more important than anything in the world. As small as her world had been then, she supposed the mask had loomed that large. Since then she'd gained the mask and lost it just as quickly— and so many concerns loomed far larger.

Perhaps that's how life worked. She'd left the worries of her girlish self behind, maybe washed away by the bore tides of Bára, and she had the concerns of a woman now. One day she might have the thoughts of a queen, or a mother, or a crone. Strange to consider.

For now, it was good to be in the moment.

The light grew brighter, not just from the sun rising. The forest had thinned, with the trees slighter here, more spaced out. The road they followed approached a clearing. Though snow covered it all, the burnt remnants of what must have been a good-sized house tumbled black and collapsed. An extensive garden had been laid out, with barns beyond and still-standing fences that ringed empty paddocks containing only pristine snow. Nothing stirred.

It all reminded her forcibly of the images in Baeltya's mind, of the people and animals bleeding and crying all around the little farm. Not this one, but very like it.

"What happened here?" she asked, though she knew.

"Golems," Lonen confirmed. "Years ago, though. Before we set out to find Bára. And not necessarily an actual golem incursion. Most of these outlying farms were abandoned as water supplies dried up and because it was simply too risky to be so far away from help."

"Do you know that's what happened here for sure?"

"No, I don't know which family had this place. I never had much occasion to pay attention to such things." He had a frown in his voice for that.

"Then how are you so certain?" The road curved around the desolate farm, climbing a hill behind it.

"Mostly logic. We've been riding at a good pace for about three hours—and Buttercup's walk is faster than most horses. That means a rider going for help at a flat out run would take that amount of time to get to the palace and back, which is much too long. Also, the gates are closed on the paddocks, which means an orderly evacuation."

"But they burned the house?" She studied it again. Knowing how careful the Destrye were with flame, it seemed unlikely to be an accident.

"Ah." Lonen was silent a moment. This time when he snugged up against her, it felt more like him seeking comfort than flirtation. "That no doubt happened when the Trom attacked."

Oh. "They attacked here—this little farm?"

"Yes and no. Wait a moment, and you'll see."

They continued along the road, which ascended more steeply. The deep woods returned, the huge trunks full of their own quiet. But among them now were scattered boulders and the occasional jagged upthrust of rock. Granite, the color of Lonen's eyes. Buttercup's breath billowed in clouds by the time they reached the summit of the switchbacking trail, and the trees abruptly gave way to a startling vista.

The stood at the edge of a dramatic drop, the land below a flat stretch of snow-covered fields, patchworked by an array of wooden fences. Some sections of them had collapsed, others had burned and ended in nothing but snow. If she could reach out a hand to brush the snow away, there would be scars of burn and ash continuing in a line along the ground.

Lonen dismounted and held his arms up to lift her down, steadying her when her cramped legs protested, stiff after a few hours of riding. "I've already lost my riding endurance," she muttered.

"You'll get it back quick enough. The first day is always the hardest. And Buttercup might have a pansy name, but he's a big horse." Lonen slapped the warhorse on the shoulder with affection, sending him to lip at the snow in the pockets of grass along the otherwise windswept cliff's edge.

"It's not a pansy name—a buttercup is another flower entirely— and I don't see what his being a big horse has to do with it."

Lonen leered at her, patting her bottom. "Every woman walks funny after having a big stallion between her legs."

She swatted at him. "Get you out of the palace and you turn into a randy boy, all hands and dirty jokes."

He grimaced cheerfully at that. "You might have a point there, love. I feel like a new man, getting out of that place. The weight of all those decisions, everyone watching me all the time, wanting things from me, evaluating everything I say and do." He subsided, rubbing at the scar by his eye, then shrugged it off. "Anyway, come look."

"I can't help seeing," she said, but she walked to the edge with him and let him draw her against his side. Beyond the extensive meadows below, the forest resumed again, hills rolling in the distance, the trees blurring into a frost of brown merging with the gray sky. Chuffta glided on a thermal rising along the drop, humming his happiness at the lovely glide. "Is all of this Dru?"

"More or less as far as the eye can see," he agreed. "Though we don't draw boundaries as such. Once upon a time the Destrye had no settlements. Our ancestors traveled constantly, carrying their few possessions on their backs, following the game animals through the seasons."

"Raiding cities and carrying off foreign women," she inserted in a dry tone.

He hugged her and kissed the fur next to her temple. "If they got very, very lucky."

She had to laugh, but sobered. "So you traveled all this land, but eventually settled here."

"And near the other forts. These fields were Arill's first, cleared by the goddess's own hand to feed her children so that we might settle down and follow gentler ways."

She cocked her head up at him. He had his hood pushed back, so the frost accumulated on his dark curling hair, the haft of his battle-axe protruding over one shoulder, ever at hand. In this light, his face looked harsh, the scars standing stark in deep lines, as he gazed over the land as one of his fierce ancestors might have. "Enough with the nonsense, Destrye," she teased. "Surely you don't believe a goddess actually removed the trees so your ancestors could farm."

He glanced down, eyes soft gray with sober affection. "Why not? My powerful sorceress wife could do it."

That gave her pause. Lonen watched her with amusement while she struggled for a response. "There are differences between goddesses and sorceresses," she finally said.

"Such as?"

She punched his side, like hitting a wall with her gloved knuckles. "Divinity. Immortality. Unlimited power."

"There was a time we believed all of those things about the priests and priestesses of Bára."

And the Báran priests and priestesses liked to propagate that reputation, too.

"Think on this," he continued when she only hmm'd in thought. "Who's to say where the original concept of Arill came from? You ask me if I really believe that the goddess removed the trees with her own hands, and I don't know that I do. But I believe in Arill's teachings, that they mean something and come from somewhere. Or someone. Maybe some brute of a warrior Destrye carried off the wrong sorceress, fell in desperately in love with her—and who could blame him?—and she agreed to stay with him if he mended his more off-putting ways and didn't make her chase after deer all her life. Seems clearing a few trees would have been well worth the effort on her part."

"More than a few," Oria pointed out, but found herself measuring the distances, estimating what kind of magical resources it would take. Over time, it might be possible, even for one woman.

"They wouldn't have needed to do it all at once," Lonen said, echoing her thoughts. "They might have added a field at a time. By all accounts, the Destrye were not so many then."

Of course, they weren't so many now, but neither of them spoke those words aloud. "You've been thinking about this," she said instead. "This theory about Arill and sorceresses."

"Yes," he admitted. "I'm interested to find out if my memory is accurate—and to find out what you think when you see it."

"In the fields?"

"Oh no—we're not going that way. We could have reached the fields far more quickly by the low road. No, we're going that way." He turned her and pointed to where the hills rose higher and more jagged, ending in peaks, sharp against the sky. Fog swirled around them, then parted, a sun she couldn't see hitting the blinding white snow fields atop them.

She caught her breath, the bite cold in her lungs. "All the way up there?" she squeaked, making Lonen laugh.

"It's not so far as it appears."

"Is it as cold as it appears?"

"Yes, but not much colder than here. We'll stop for the night along the way and I'll keep you warm."

At least she wouldn't have to meet his mother on that very day. A small reprieve, but she'd take it. She returned her gaze to the fields. "Then down there is where the Trom attacked. That house burning was incidental. They did it on their way over the ridge— along with the crops and the aqueducts." Not fences then, but elevated wooden ditches to carry water to the fields. Refocusing her attention, she made out the paths of flame, where the edges of the forest had trees starkly black from fire, rather than winter. The pattern without the snow would be easier to see, but now that she aligned the view with what she'd glimpsed in Lonen's memories, the scene made more sense.

In her mind's eye, a stark black shape swooped over the fields, now golden with ripe grain. So easily fired, they leapt into gouts of flame, dark smoke billowing. The dragon sliced through it all, serene, graceful, and lethal. The figure on its back, a dark spider form, seemed to turn and look at her, matte eyes seeing deep into her mind.

We come when summoned. Don't forget.

She shook the vision away with an effort. They come when summoned. "What was their goal?"

"They burned our late harvest, and the aqueducts that brought water from the higher lakes." With his pointing finger, he traced for her where the aqueduct had ascended stepwise up a hill not far away. "The attack left us without that last crop and squelched any possibility of irrigating for a winter crop, even had the winter been not so cold. In the spring we'll have to do that much more work to rebuild the aqueducts. And that's if they don't come back to do it again. Which I think we both know they will."

She let him talk, though she knew all of that, had seen it. A memory drawn from what she'd glimpsed in Lonen's mind, one reconstructed from stories, or presentiment of the future? She didn't know. Some of all of that, perhaps. She let him lift her onto Buttercup's back. "But I still don't see what they hoped to achieve."

"Isn't that enough?" Lonen asked in that wry tone, vaulting up behind her. "Would you have had them burn the palace and Arill's Temple, too?"

"That would have made sense," she retorted. "If they wanted to destroy you utterly, that would have been a relatively simple step to doing so. Burn all the aqueducts—they made an easy visual line to follow. Instead, they did this patchwork attack—burn some aqueducts and not others. Burn that house but not the rest of the farm."

"What are you thinking their reasoning was?"

"I don't know. I don't understand the Trom, or the nature of the beasts they ride. They seem to do things for their own reasons."

"I thought they followed Yar's commands." Lonen urged Buttercup back up the road, and Chuffta shot overhead, an alabaster arrow. He said the flying kept him warmer than riding, but he'd be tiring soon enough and wanting to nap inside her furry cloak.

"Ostensibly they're supposed to," she mused, considering. "Though I don't know the mechanics of the summoning spell. The summoner—or summoners, as I think it takes both a male and female—command the loyalty of the Trom who respond, but I'm not sure how absolute that authority is. But even if we agree that Yar asked the Trom to come here to burn the fields and aqueducts, what purpose did that serve?"

"They did take water away."

"Which is a high priority for him. It means both life for Bára and power for him. But he could have had them collect the water without burning the crops. It would have been smarter not to burn the aqueducts and let you all do the work to make the water easily accessible."

"You're welcome." He sounded grim, so she patted his thigh pressed against hers, his muscle tightening in response.

"Not to be crass, but I'm trying to view it as he would."

"Understood. But it could be that the Trom simply like to burn things. When they arrived in Bára to save the city and drive us out, they killed Bárans and Destrye alike with their dragon fire."

"That's true." She shuddered at the horrible memory. "The Trom don't explain themselves. I was only told that they exact the price they wish to in exchange for their aid."

"So maybe they did it as a side bonus to grabbing some water for Yar. Burning us out here was fun for them." Lonen sounded neutral, but his old anger brooded dark beneath.

"Fire is fun," Chuffta commented. *"It's hot and bright."*

Oria didn't relay the troubling comment to Lonen, hiding even from her Familiar how much it unsettled her to contemplate his similarities to the giant and deadly Trom dragons.

~ 12 ~

THEY ARRIVED AT the chapel by midafternoon—sooner than his memories had predicted. It was only the pair of them, though, on a single horse. When he'd traveled this way in the past, it had always been with a mixed group, on steeds nowhere close to Buttercup's caliber. Their excursions back then had always been for pleasure, too, with much stopping along the way to picnic, climb trees, and take in the views.

Back before the golems came.

The chapel seemed smaller than in his memory, too, as if it had also shrunk along with the distance. Unlike most Destrye dwellings, this had been built of stone, the uneven rocks collected or hewn from the mountainside and painstakingly fitted together. Now that he saw it again, what he'd remembered as a fanciful design reminded him of Bára. Not in a way he could pin to specific details, but in the feel of it. As if it had been created to please someone with that aesthetic. Perhaps that boded well for the rest of what he thought he remembered about the place.

He dismounted, and Oria pushed back her hood, surveying the small chapel. The sun had finally broken through the overcast, and the rays hit her hair, radiating off the shining copper like a fire of the most benevolent kind. Her eyes, nearly as bright, held doubt, however, at the sight of the unprepossessing buildings. No indication she found it familiar. "We're stopping here?"

"For the night, yes."

Chuffta poked his narrow white head through the parting of her cloak, only the vivid green of his gaze a break in the alabaster on ivory shades. Oria smiled slightly, her expression changing as she conversed mentally with the dragonlet. Then she focused on Lonen again, the smile warming. "Chuffta says he sees a chimney in the cabin at the back and wonders if we'll need firewood." She arched her coppery brows in rueful amusement.

"There might be some stockpiled," he said to Chuffta. "But I'm guessing it's been a while since anyone has visited the place. We may need to chop more. How are you at chasing rodents, Chuffta man?"

Chuffta emerged fully, cocking his head with interest and shaking out his wings, nearly clipping Oria in the face with one. She was already choking on her reaction. "Rodents?" She squeaked out.

"They tend to nest in warm places like this," he told her in apology as he lifted her down.

"It doesn't look warm."

"Relatively speaking. We'll get a fire going and roust them out."

She nodded absently, face rapt as she turned in a slow circle. She felt it. He'd been certain she would. Okay, he hadn't been *certain*. Hopeful. "This is a good place," she murmured, almost to herself.

"Full of coherent sgath?"

Her face smoothed into that neutral mask. Her priestess face. Then her eyes fired again, full of keen intensity. "Not exactly. But something." She tipped her head back, following the spear of the straight, dark trunks to the blue sky, then closed her eyes, turning again and holding out her arms as she did. The parting of her white cloak over the scarlet gown beneath was like the sun breaking through the clouds all over again. She paused, facing away from the chapel to where the ground fell away to the gorge below, the peaks and lowering sun beyond.

Like Arill herself, some reverent part of him whispered.

Her eyes snapped open, startling him, they burned so incandescently in her winter-white face. "Is it safe here?" she asked.

"In what way?" he hedged, uncertain where she was going with this.

"I'd like to go deeper into the woods. By myself. To meditate." The smile she gave him at that was both self-conscious and teasing for his own dislike of the practice.

"I'll go with you."

But she shook her head. "I need to be alone. If that's okay with you," she added, with a touch of hesitation.

"Of course it's okay with me." He ran a hand over her shining hair, savoring the satin feel of it. It would give him time to set things up. "Take Chuffta with you."

"You need him for firewood. And rodent chasing," she added archly.

"I know how to chase out rodents."

"Yes, but you have him all interested now. I'll take him with me so he can see where I settle, then he can check back on me. I have a couple of hours of light left, yes?" She glanced uncertainly at the sun, which hovered over the far peaks.

He pointed for her. "It will set there, so yes, a couple of hours. Will it take that long?"

Her eyes sparkled and her face held a vivid anticipation he hadn't seen in her for quite some time. "It might." She nodded, as if confirming to herself. "Very likely. But Chuffta can rouse me if you need me."

"Sounds good." Wishing he could kiss her, he cupped her head and hugged her to him. "You won't get cold?"

She stepped back and pulled up her hood, tucking back the fire of her hair until none of it showed, tugging the alabaster fringes so they hung long around her face. "In my lovely cloak? Never."

Answering her soundless summons, Chuffta bolted from above, folding his wings to land neatly on her shoulder, talons digging into the pad he'd had them sew into it. She walked away, the dappled cloak dragging over the snow, blurring her footprints, the derkesthai a slightly more iridescent shape in the panorama of white, punctuated only by the sacred black sentinels of the trees.

The scene struck him as spooky and magical at once, sending that numinous shiver through him that he'd first felt upon spying her in a window in Bára.

"Oria?" he called after her, and she turned, adding fire to the frozen landscape again with her copper eyes. "I'll be here waiting."

Her lips curved in a gentle smile. "I love you, too, Destrye."

As he'd suspected, what little wood had been stockpiled had been scattered by wildlife during years of neglect. He found some dry pieces to start a fire with, however, buried under the snow in the lee of the cabin. Carrying it inside, he found the interior dusty, but thankfully unmolested.

Arill's followers built her waystations with care.

He laid fires in both the chapel and cabin, but waited on Chuffta to start them, as the little firebug enjoyed that so. Taking advantage in the interim, he opened all the doors to the cabin and attached chapel, removing the hides from the windows to shake them out, and allowing the cold mountain air to sweep through and clear out the stale.

He was tacking up the hides again—in spring, once the crops were planted, he'd have to send someone up here to replace them with newer, more supple ones, as these had grown brittle with cold and age—when Chuffta returned. Not for the first time, he wished he could talk to the derkesthai as Oria could, and ask after her. But what would he ask? Obviously she was fine, or her Familiar wouldn't be acting so relaxed. "She's a big girl," he muttered to himself. "And she survived just fine before you came along, buddy."

Chuffta flew up to him, hovering, and gave him a long look, then bobbed his head in that way that always made Lonen think he was winking at him. "Fires are laid, Chuffta man, if you'd like to do the honors."

With an enthusiastic spurt of green flame, the derkesthai shot over to the cabin fireplace, using quite a bit more than necessary to send the logs into an instant blaze. Lonen braced, half expecting the flames to escape the stones and attack the wood of the walls, but it settled back quick enough. Chuffta looked over his shoulder, as if to chide him for his lack of faith.

"In the chapel, too," he said, pointing through the doorway. At least that was all stone, so the fire-breathing dragonlet could go unsupervised. While Chuffta took care of that, Lonen found bedding in the chests made of insect-resistant wood, which had kept everything at least unchewed, and aired those out too.

Then he and Chuffta went to gather more wood. He'd brought a smaller axe, so he didn't have to shame his armsmaster's memory by using his weapon. He'd already rubbed down Buttercup and installed him in the attached stable, where the warhorse happily munched some oats he'd also brought along.

Journeying with supplies made everything worlds better.

He kept half an eye on the sun, feeling a bit like a fretful old nanny, but also cautious of becoming complacent. There was safe and there was *safe*. More predators than golems and Trom haunted these hills, especially in the crepuscular hours.

He made himself wait until the sun just touched the peak it would set behind, and was opening his mouth to ask Chuffta to check on Oria, when the purpling shadows between the trees shifted. Pale violet blurred into white—and she emerged.

She had her head bowed, in contemplation still or watching her footing, so he couldn't see her face past the furry fringe. Following impulse, he went to her and picked her up, holding her tight against him, his face pressed to her hood. She laughed, a bell-like melody he recalled from her garden in Bára, one he hadn't heard since. Magic ran through it, as if her happiness and pleasure grew out of her store of sgath, which perhaps it did.

Oria leaned back in his arms, arching to place her gloved hands on his cheeks, so she could search his face. "What's that for?"

"I missed you," he said simply, expecting a teasing reply, but she sobered, her laughing smile softening to a tender one.

"I missed you, too." The smile quirked to one side. "It occurs to me that we've not been much out of each other's company in the last days."

True. And the small separation had left him a little hollow. Not how he'd ever expected to feel about a woman. Well, about anyone. Needing to reconnect with her, he searched for what to say. What did one ask of a sorceress who went seeking meditation? It felt like she'd been hunting and he should inquire if she'd gotten the trophy bull she sought, though that metaphor was all wrong. Also, he didn't know much about magic, but it seemed like something that eluded her the more she forced it. The last thing she needed was more pressure.

"Did you find what you sought?" He finally asked.

She looked thoughtful, pushing at his shoulders, so he set her down. "Can we go inside? I *am* cold now."

"Of course." Surprising her, he picked her up again, but this time in the cradle of his arms, in the traditional style. Striding to the cabin, he kicked the door open, carried her over the threshold and set her on her feet inside.

"Now what was *that* for?" But she laughed as she said it, then he was saved answering as she took in the room with wide eyes. It had warmed up nicely, Chuffta vigilantly tending a fire that burned to the limit of the stone frame, thrilled to be given free rein. The freshened bed linens were turned back invitingly, furs piled at the end. The candles around the room in their shuttered lanterns scattered light with a warm glow and the table set for two boasted a small vase of bledsiae he'd found. She went to that, touching the hardy white blossoms. "Flowers?"

"They grow under the snow, at the base of the trees." He put his hands on her shoulders, looking at the flowers, too. "They reminded me of you."

She glanced up with narrowed eyes. "Small and frozen?"

"Hardy." He squeezed her shoulders, the bones light as a kitten's under the shadowcat fur, but with a similar tensile feline strength. "Able to survive and bloom in harsh conditions. Apparently fragile, fragrant, and lovely, but unstoppable."

"I feel like I've been stopped a few times."

"Not yet. You're still here, still going strong—and climbing higher."

"Why are you being so nice to me?"

"I'm always nice to you."

"No. Sometimes you're grumpy and taciturn." But she smiled as she said it, her tone teasing again. "Like in explaining to me why this place."

"Then I'll explain. There's something I want you to see." He took her gloved hand and tugged her toward the chapel. She dragged her feet, resisting.

"Am I going to hate this?"

"Why would you ask that?"

"Because this thing you want me to see is why you're being all sweet and seductive, I'm thinking."

Her instincts were good ones. Even without sensing his actual thoughts, she'd sussed him out pretty accurately. Or maybe there was more to it. "Are you able to read my mind again?"

"Some," she admitted. Then shrugged, an exasperated movement, pushing her hood back as she did. "To answer your question, I did get something from meditating in the woods. Nothing like what I did before in Bára. Back then I meditated to calm myself, to try to control what I now understand was a constant inpouring of sgath that I had no idea how to manage or channel. This… this is much quieter in a way, like breathing in mist rather than standing under a waterfall."

He ran a hand over her hair. "It sounds easier on you."

"But a much slower way to build power," she pointed out. "And it's power we need and fast, not as slow as this."

"I'm sorry for that. We could—"

She held up a hand to stop him. "Your one for the day—and don't be. We've agreed this is the right course of action. The same course we've been on since you accepted my proposal of marriage. I just need to hold up my end of the deal."

"Next time, I'll propose to you."

She smiled, then squared her shoulders. His tiny warrior. "Show me this thing already and then you can feed me."

"We can eat first," he offered.

She arched her brows. "And delay the fun? Never."

"It won't be *that* bad," he muttered, pulling her along while she was feeling amused at him still.

She balked again at the threshold, peering into the darker hallway. "Will I need Chuffta?"

"I don't think so, but we can leave the door open so you can call him if you do." The derkesthai perched on a log he'd dragged to just in front of and beside the fire, digging his talons into it, perched like a bird of prey. At the moment, he'd swiveled his head backwards on his neck to gaze at Oria while they silently communed.

"All right," she breathed, and gripped his hand more tightly, interlacing her gloved fingers with his. The sensation felt very like actually touching her, with the plush velvet against his skin whetting his anticipation for the rest of the evening.

But first this. *Please, Arill, let this help her.*

The corridor between the cabin and the chapel wasn't long—more a vestibule to allow one or the other to be closed off, depending on whether any guardians lived on site, or if visitors wished to use the chapel in private. The air drafted a bit chilly from the larger building. With its higher ceiling and echoing space, it took longer to heat up. For this reason, the builders had put small fireplaces at intervals along the walls. Lonen had set alight only the one next to the altar. They wouldn't be in here long—he hoped—so he hadn't built it up as much as in the cabin. When Oria shivered and drew the cloak tighter around herself with her free hand, he regretted that choice, then realized her reaction wasn't to the temperature.

Her gaze, the copper flat with shock, was fixed on the retablo over the altar. She saw it, too, what had prompted him to bring his own sorceress to this place.

His memory hadn't failed or misled him—as Oria's astonished reaction confirmed. The woman in the center panel of the retablo looked like her. Looked Báran, rather. And similar to Gallia, a woman from one of Bára's sister-cities, with the high cheekbones, slender build, and fair hair of Oria and Gallia's people. More, she possessed a certain look to her eyes, as if the artist had observed and attempted to capture that glimmer of enchantment he'd so often glimpsed in his own sorceress's gaze.

Oria pulled away, moving closer to the painted wooden panel, and trailed her fingers over the edges, careful not to touch the old gesso. The illustration showed a sorceress of Oria's people, almost certainly. Though the edges of the retablo had crumbled somewhat with age, the gessoed layers of paint flaking away, it seemed clear what she carried in her hand, half hidden in her skirts: the gold mask of her office as priestess, dangling by the ribbons.

"Her hair isn't copper, like yours." His voice came out as a reverent hush, whispering back from the silent stones. "But when I saw you in that window in Bara, you reminded me of her and this place, without my realizing it. I only connected it consciously in Arill's Temple, thinking how the image of the goddess in our family chapel reminded me of you—but this illustration even more so. At first I thought it was only because of the framing, the way the side panels echo the pillars flanking that window you stood in. But then I thought, no, it's more. Ever since that memory hit, I've been trying to reconstruct what she carried, wondering if it could be a mask. It seemed like maybe it could be, though guess I never paid it that much attention. Usually Arill carries a stalk of grain in one hand and a scythe in the other. But this looks like a mask, like yours, the one you had, so that's significant, yes?"

"Yes," she agreed quietly. "This is Arill?"

"Not really. This chapel is dedicated to Arill's worship, but this woman was considered to be one of Arill's priestesses elevated to semi-divine status. An avatar of the goddess." He pointed at the words scrolling in painted text on the side panels. "That's what this bit says."

"It tells her story?" Oria asked in a strangled tone. Maybe he should have waited. Enjoyed their evening together and then shown her in the morning. But that wouldn't have been fair, knowing this was here and keeping it from her.

"It's a short piece in a longer history. It's written in an antiquated script, mostly about the deeds she performed that pleased Arill, so that when she passed on she went to serve in the Hall of Warriors."

"Will you read it to me?"

He cleared his throat. "I am not skilled at reading aloud—"

"I'm looking for information, not entertainment. Just translate the essence of it." Her voice came out taut, her profile sharp with some humming tension.

He focused on the words, letting her interpret the meaning of them. "When Odymesen returned from the Seven-Year Wars, he and his warriors brought with them many prizes, including fair-haired slave women from desert cities built of gold. As ephemeral as they were beautiful, many of the foreigners did not live long, but languished and eventually perished. The strongest among them, however, Odymesen's favorite, survived many years, bearing him fair-haired sons and bringing him and the Destrye joy and riches beyond their imagining. Beloved of Arill, she loved this place best, so she was laid to rest here, with highest funeral honors."

Oria was silent, contemplating. Then, "What was her name?"

He shook his head slowly, stalling on the inevitable argument. They'd gone round on this subject with his warhorse, somehow ending up with the ignominious moniker of "Buttercup," which was entirely his fault. This would have to go much worse discussing a woman of Oria's people. "It doesn't say."

"Why not? Her name must be recorded somewhere if this whole story is."

"Not if she didn't exactly have one."

Oria slid him a look. "Of course she had a name. You mean that this doesn't say what it was."

"Back in those days, women didn't have names, as such," he hedged. "So there wouldn't have been one to record."

Her copper eyes sparked, reminding him of the glass forges of Bára. "Like animals."

He winced. "An unfortunately accurate parallel."

"Incredible. I can't believe you just admit to it."

"As opposed to what, Oria?" he threw up his hands in exasperation. Nothing like wading directly into an argument you'd hoped to avoid. "I'm not going to lie about it. That's our past. Yes, an abomination, but pretending things weren't that way won't magically make it so that it never happened. The Destrye have a saying that a man who flinches from the shames of the past will never recognize the dark paths that lead back to them."

She punched her fists to her hips. "Fine. But a Báran woman or one from our sister-cities would have had a name."

He shrugged his impotence away. "It wouldn't have occurred to the Destrye then to ask for it or to record it. She was Odymesen's."

Oria ground her teeth at that. "If this place is dedicated to her, what is *it* called?"

He held her gaze, not letting himself look away or step back. "Odymesen'y Chapel. Putting the 'y' at the end of his name denotes his woman. That's why most traditional Destrye female names end with a 'y' sound."

The look she gave him could have frozen fire. "Are they going to write me in the histories as Lonen'y?"

"If so, it would be as an honorific," he suggested, hoping she didn't read in him the primitive thrill of pleasure the sound of that gave him.

"Well it sounds stupid," she hissed. No surprise they wouldn't have like minds on that one. "Never mind all that. What does 'highest funeral honors' mean?"

"It means that she was buried as befits a warrior—and that we believe she entered the Hall of Warriors, where only those Destrye who die in battle are admitted."

Oria blinked, long and slow, that considering veiling of her eyes that never boded well, magical tension coiling palpably around him. His system sprang to alert and, though he'd never draw his battle-axe on her, he stretched his fingers to disperse the instinct to reach for it. "What happens to women otherwise, in this brilliant afterlife," she asked in a lethal tone, "or to children who take ill, or those men not *fortunate* enough to die battle-axe in hand?"

"I don't know why you're mad at me," he replied as calmly and evenly as he could. "I'm only telling you what I was taught. I'm not the enemy here."

That keen sense of attack receded. His response had been instinctive—from the memory of that shimmering sense of lethal danger swirling around her, one he'd learned well in Bára. She was gaining her magic back, slowly or not. An exultant surge of triumph filled him, replacing his previous wariness. Bringing Oria to the chapel had been the right thing to do.

She turned in a circle, reminding him of how she'd done that when they dismounted, eyes closed, her face that serene mask, as if she listened or scented for something. Or reached with some other sense. "Answer my question, please," she said in an absent tone.

He let out a breath of regret. "It depends. Some say they go to serve the warriors in the Hall. Others that they're reborn, in hopes of living a life where they can die a warrior's death. Most think that the souls of those not admitted to the Hall of Warriors go back to the roots of Arill's tree, to provide nutrients."

She cracked an eye open. "You Destrye have serious issues."

"Fine. What do Bárans believe? You have a temple, but I've only heard you reference the moons. I've never heard you swear by any god or goddess. Who do you pray to?"

"Haven't you been paying attention?" She broke into a beatific smile, one that covered sharp teeth. "You're the one who pointed it out. I *am* the goddess—or my ancestress was—so who do you think the gods pray to?"

He shook his head at her, trying to look stern, but failing in the face of her saucy arrogance. "Do me a favor and don't let my council hear you say that."

"I wouldn't." She closed her eyes again, turning slowly. "I don't really believe that, for the record. If Arill was a sorceress, I'm sure they called her a goddess long after her death. Or this one—I'm going to find out her name, or give her one, as a last resort—she likely only wanted to help. Her Destrye barbarian lover and all his people. We sorceresses are apparently easy prey for that sort of thing."

"Not so easy," he muttered. "Not easy at all."

"What's that?"

"Nothing, love."

Her close-lipped smile deepened, showing the deep dimples in her cheeks on either side. They gave her a girlish, even impish look completely at odds with the questing magic coursing around him. "We don't pray to anyone," she said. "We pay respect to the moons, yes. Sgatha and Grienon, sources of magic, the female and the male, the waxing and waning. Death is the ultimate waning. Like the new moon, a spirit emerges again, a slim crescent that..." her words had fallen into an almost singsong chant and she trailed off, facing a niche set into a wall on the far side of the altar. "Where is her body buried?"

"It would have been burned and the ashes sealed into a vessel. I have to warn you that I won't let you disturb her—"

"I'm not interested in her ashes," Oria cut him off, going to the niche, her eyes closed still.

"What are you doing then?"

"I'm seeing with sgath sight. Physical vision interferes, so it's easier with my eyes closed."

"You do have it back then."

"Some. As I said, it's slow, but getting stronger." She moved her face, reminding him of an animal testing the wind a distant scent. "You're right—it's better here. My ancestress liked it here for a good reason. I just need to find her place."

"Is that what you're looking for?"

"What? No. Her meditation place—where she gathered and hopefully pooled sgath—will be outside somewhere. At least, it's not here in these two buildings or I'd feel it. I'll seek it out in the morning. I knew something called to me, but I wasn't sure what. Right now I'm looking for her mask."

That cursed thing. He'd hated Oria's mask, the way it hid her face from him. More, which he'd admit only in the darkness of his heart, the thing gave him the creeps. "Why do you want it?" he asked, carefully neutral. "It might not even be here."

"If it isn't, what became of it? It's solid gold, so I'd think you'd know if someone had it as a part of their art collection. If they burned her with it—as she would have asked—then it wouldn't have melted, so they'd have had to put it with her ashes. If this Odymesen really loved her—"

"He did." Lonen said it with too much force, startling Oria into turning toward him, though she didn't open her eyes, making him wonder what she saw in him with her sgath sight. "He loved her. No man would go to such trouble if not."

Oria smiled, opening her eyes to shower him with the warmth of her gaze. "This is something I've come to understand."

He shifted his weight, wanting to do something with the powerful emotion she evoked in him—though the impulse at the forefront of his mind involved utterly distracting her from her current task, so he held back, letting her finish whatever she was doing. When he had her attention, he'd command it undivided.

"I'm going to ask you for more trouble, love," she said, gesturing at the stone beneath the niche. "I need you to break that open."

~ **13** ~

S HE HAD TO give him credit. Though her Destrye warrior clearly seethed with impatience, shock at her proposed sacrilege—and with the smoky sense of frustrated lust—he firmed his jaw against whatever argument he longed to throw at her and surveyed the problem.

"Arill forbids grave raiding," he finally ground out.

"Do you think she'll smite you?" Oria almost regretted baiting him when he rounded on her.

"Did I laugh at you when you explained that your dual magical nature was anathema to *your* people?" he demanded. "Even though it makes no Arill-cursed sense when you are clearly all the more powerful for it?"

"Maybe that's why it's anathema," she replied, softly and pointedly. "Maybe our cultures make rules to prevent our worst natures from taking control. You say Arill's taming hand stopped the Destrye wandering and raiding—maybe the injunction against grave-robbing was simply a rule to stop your greedier ancestors from causing more grief by unearthing bodies and ashes simply to get the good stuff they were buried with."

He shook his head at her irreverence, but put his hands on his hips and studied the stone beneath the niche that whispered of the mask behind. It called to her, this ancient object of power. The Báran priests and priestesses didn't talk much about infusing inanimate objects with sgath, but that could be because the cities themselves served that purpose. She'd felt bereft ever since losing hers.

"Why do you want it?" he asked again.

"I'm really not sure. I have a feeling."

"Are you sure this 'feeling' doesn't have something to do with pride, with getting back what they took from you, what you think of as your rightful rank as priestess?"

"It *is* my rightful rank!" she fired back. Lonen gave her a mild look, raising his brows at her vehemence.

"Because his words didn't strike a nerve at all," Chuffta commented from the other room.

"Did I call you?"

"No. That's the beauty of my superior abilities. I can be ready to offer advice and *tend the fire in the other room."*

"Just don't burn the place down because you're distracted by eaves-dropping on me," she grumbled at him, and he sent her an affectionate thought, despite her crankiness. The exchange made her take a steadying breath, which her Familiar had no doubt intended.

Lonen had gone back to studying the sepulcher, but with a sense of patient waiting emanating from him. It grounded her in an unexpected way to feel more of his emotional presence, to again catch the edge of a thought. It felt beyond good to have sgath flowing through her, however mildly, to see the world again in the resonances beyond physical sight. She liked the power of it, far better than the weakness of being without. If that made her as power-hungry as her brother, as the worst of the sorcerers and sorceresses of Bára, then so be it. She'd manage somehow.

This is how I'm meant to be. For better or worse, I am this as much as Buttercup is a warhorse and Lonen is a warrior.

"And I am a Bringer of Fire!" Chuffta added an evil cackle.

"I worry about you. I truly do."

"I love you, too," he replied, and she realized he'd fallen into their same habit of using the expression of love as a way of offering forgiveness or appreciation. Which she supposed it was. And if anything could save her from becoming like her aunt Tania—

whatever it was that she had done—then Lonen's love, even in the form of nagging reminders about her prideful ways, would be it.

"I understand your point," she said to Lonen, "and I agree it's valid for you to caution me." There. That sounded very adult and reasonable.

"Chuffta agreed with me, did he?" Lonen didn't look at her, instead squatting to examine the stonework more closely, running his fingertips along the mortar between, but his lips twitched suspiciously.

"Fine. Laugh. Yes, he did. But, Lonen—" She moved into the edge of his vision, which brought her closer to the niche. The mask was there. Oh yes. Calling to her. "You know that before I left Bára I was but a newly made priestess, so there's a great deal I never learned. Still, something in me is certain that the masks are more than a demonstration that we can see without physical eyes. The masks are too solidly a part of the practice of sorcery. Why would they have been so determined to take my mask away for my magical crimes, if not to hamper me in practicing it?"

Lonen glanced up at her, nodded crisply. "Makes sense. I think I can get it out of there." He stood, uncoiling in his smooth strength, and took her hand, turning her back toward the cabin.

"Do you need certain tools?" she asked, confused.

He let go her hand and snaked his arm around her waist under the cloak. "Tools will help, yes, but I'm also waiting until morning to attack this test my sorceress wife has set me."

"It's not a test," she retorted.

"In the stories, the witch always sets challenges for the hero to overcome before he can claim the beautiful princess. In my case, I happen to have both in one. And I intend to enjoy my wife this evening, while I have her all to myself."

"If we're going by the stories, then you shouldn't get to enjoy the reward before you successfully complete the test."

"Good thing this isn't a story then."

"Yes, because I'm not a witch."

He snugged her against him, shutting the door to the drafty chapel. "Neither are you a princess, my queen."

HE'D SET THE stage for romance, which made her feel unaccountably shy. They'd truly done so little together sexually, though the enforced intimacy of travel, injury, and illness had made them familiar with each other's bodies in a way she'd never expected before her wedding. She'd had a naïve young woman's ideas about marriage—mostly about high-minded ideals and a sort of silk-draped, candlelit cleanness to it all.

Though little of her marriage to Lonen had worked out that way, he seemed to have read *her* mind and created something of that romantic ideal in the little cabin. The inviting bed spoke volumes, along with the candles burning softly. The table for two, with wine waiting. The delicately scented blossoms.

Lonen turned her, smoothing his hands over the fur cloak. "Are you warm enough to take this off?"

She nodded, unable to speak around her suddenly thick tongue. One day she'd feel easy and natural with this man, but that day had not yet come. With his gray eyes intent on hers, he undid the fastening, taking the cloak away. Though she still wore her layers of skirts and fur-lined gown, she shivered a little, feeling naked.

"Would it be easier to eat without the gloves?" he asked.

It would be, so she stripped them off, too, putting them into his expectant hand. He took them over to the bed, setting them on a table next to it—and next to several other things she couldn't quite make out. He caught her curious look. "You'll need them later," he said, with that cheerfully lustful grin that warmed her as if he'd caressed her between her legs.

"I'm going to keep Buttercup company," Chuffta said. *"Don't let the*

fire burn down because you're all distracted frolicking with your mate."

"You don't have to go. It's cold out there."

"Buttercup lets me sleep on his back—he's very warm. And you need privacy." Chuffta flew up to Lonen and hovered expectantly.

"Thanks, man," Lonen said, not arguing in the least. "I'll let him into the stable. Go ahead and sit, pour us some wine."

His brief absence gave her a moment to gather herself. She trusted Lonen utterly. When he'd pleasured her to consummate their wedding, he'd been exceptionally careful not to touch her skin. In fact, the lengths he'd gone to—and the sexually scandalous game he'd constructed around it—made her face go hot at the memory. As did her behavior at the oasis when she'd tried to seduce him and he'd refused her, for her own good. He no doubt had something in mind for tonight to let them safely enjoy each other. She let herself relax. Enough with fretting.

Anticipation, however, only warmed her further.

The door opened and Lonen returned, bringing a cloud of icy fresh air with him that helped cool her cheeks. Still, she kept her face studiously averted, lest he glimpse too much of her salacious thoughts—she wasn't *that* relaxed—and belatedly poured the wine into the hammered metal cups. If she ever made it back to Bára or one of her sister-cities, she'd bring back a case of glasses. Wine didn't taste the same drunk from metal or wood.

Lonen sat, giving her an opaque look, then lifted his mug in a toast. "To my beautiful witch-queen—may I never fail in the challenges she sets me."

"I'm not drinking to that," she said on a laugh.

He made a mournful face. "You wish me to fail?"

"I'm not a witch and I'm not testing you."

"No? Let's see how I do anyway." He retrieved something from the fire, putting on a pair of leather gloves to carry it, then set it on the table, removing the metal lid to display the contents. The scent of rich broth, roasted vegetables and cream rose out of it, and she lifted her gaze to his expectant one in delight.

"How did you do this?"

"Baeltya had the cooks assemble several casseroles like this and set them outside to freeze. We need simply warm them in a fire. Can't let you backslide in regaining those gorgeous curves."

She wrinkled her nose at him, but accepted the generous helping and dug in. "What about you? Don't you need meat to rebuild those mighty thews?"

He grinned easily, ladled still more onto her plate, then fetched another metal container from the fire, opening it to release a meaty aroma. "Baeltya made her plans for me, too."

"We're well taken care of, then."

Comfortable silence settled between them as they dug into their respective meals, the delicious flavor and welcome nourishment of the hot meal hitting her stomach making her voraciously hungry. Snacking as they rode had felt satisfying enough, but nothing like this. Lonen kept dishing more onto her plate until she sat back, groaning as she realized she'd eaten the entire thing. She splayed her hands over her distended belly. "I can't believe I ate so much."

Lonen eyed her with amusement, using the last slice of the warmed bread they'd shared to soak up the last juices of his. "Don't pretend you have anything like a pot belly. I'll be happy if I can get you out of concave."

"You'll see plenty of belly on me if I get pregnant," she retorted.

He went still. Then set his utensils aside, laced his fingers together, and propped his chin on them, gray eyes both grave and cautiously alight. "Is that a possibility?" he asked in a careful tone.

She tried not to blush, she really did, but to no avail. Still, the excitement of her realization in the chapel made it relatively easy to overcome any shyness at such a frank conversation with him. "Maybe so."

"Because you warned me, when we agreed to this marriage, that you would never bear me heirs."

"That was when I thought we'd never be able to have sex of any kind, and you've found plenty of ways around that."

His grin went wolfish. "I did warn you," he pointed out.

"You did," she agreed, feeling somewhat wolfish in kind. Him, wending into her. Or perhaps all herself, and her desire for him. "And since you've ably demonstrated your inventiveness in that arena, then I feel compelled to point out that Odymesen and his sorceress managed the deed. 'Bore him many fair-haired sons.' I assume she provided the world with a few daughters as well, and they simply weren't worth mentioning."

Lonen was staring at her, thunderstruck.

"Didn't catch that, did you?" Being the one to tell him gave her a decided thrill. Happy news for a change. "That's the problem with you barbarians. You're always focusing on—" she broke off with a little shriek when he pounced on her, lifting her out of the chair and carrying her to the bed.

"You were saying?" he asked politely, rapidly undoing the fastenings of her gown.

"I—I've forgotten," she stammered, losing the thought entirely as the fur-lined velvet parted, exposing her breasts, the nipples hardening almost painfully at the sudden chill.

Lonen's eyes were hot, gone silver with lust when he lifted them to her face. "Cold?"

"Not enough to cover up." She wanted this. Wanted his gaze on her and more.

"Good. Take that off." He reached for her gloves on the table, watching her as she shrugged out of the upper part of the gown, pulling her arms out of the tight sleeves, then pushing the whole thing down to puddle at her feet. He raised a brow at the petticoat layers still belling around her. "How many of those do you have on?"

"A lot. I lost count," she admitted. "But I was warm."

"Put these on and turn around." He handed her the velvet gloves again, then began untying her underskirts one by one when she did as he bade.

"I love it when you get all bossy," she teased him but it came out breathless, especially as the last of her underthings came off to his yanking, leaving her naked but for the tall boots and the elbow-length scarlet gloves.

"I know you do," he answered, in all seriousness, his voice throaty. "Bend over and put your hands on the bed."

She did, then gasped as his hands—cool and a little rough—ran over her bottom and then up her waist and belly to grasp her breasts. Looking down, she saw he'd donned gloves similar to hers, but made of thin leather. He snugged his groin against her rear, his erection pressing neatly into the cleft of her buttocks, rocking there.

"Is this all right?" he asked in her ear. Still dressed, he pressed his body all along hers, one hand massaging her breast, the other sliding down her belly, pushing against her mons.

"Yes," she breathed. It was working. She received a lot of input from him this way, but not the overwhelming kind from skin-to-skin contact. His exuberance, that simmering male arousal and strength filled her empty spaces, dizzying her. "It's good," she murmured, indulging in shimmying against his grip. "Another test passed."

"I'm so glad to hear it, witch," he growled. "Now spread those pretty thighs for me."

"I'm not a—" She squealed when he slapped her bottom, hard enough to sting. Perversely it made her sex heat that much more and she spread her thighs on a moan—dropping her head when his gloved hand dove into the opening, dragging through her slick tissues with nerve-shattering results.

"That's a good girl," he crooned in her ear, grinding his hard cock through his leather pants against her cleft again. "You're just a tame witch, aren't you? My tame witch."

"I'm not a—" She cried out and shuddered when his gloved fingers pinched her nipple.

"Admit it," he demanded. "You're mine. My tame witch." His other hand stroked between her legs, making her frantic.

"Yes," she nearly sobbed. "I'm your tame witch."

"Because you need this from me," he gentled his touch, teasing her nipple now, pushing the tip of a gloved finger inside her. The fever pitch of her arousal only intensified.

"I do. Oh, Lonen, please."

"I like it when you beg." He sounded all satisfied male. "You'll be doing a lot of that. Lie back on the bed and spread your legs for me."

"My boots and…"

"I like them. Leave them on. In fact…" He walked away, then came back. "You can stand up and face me."

With some chagrin, she realized she'd remained where he'd last positioned her, and stood up, her face hot. With a quirk of a smile he draped the shadowcat cloak over her shoulders, fastening it again at her throat and bidding her to lift her hair out so it streamed down the back. The cloud of soft fur teased all along her skin, another stimulation. Lonen ran his gloved hands over her, stopping to tease her nipples, stroking the skin of her thighs above the furry stockings, dipping finger into her aching sex.

"Your skin is a white like this fur," he murmured. "Except for this pink." He tweaked a nipple so she squirmed. "And this copper." He cupped her mons with his hand, lifting her to her toes, so she grabbed ahold of his shoulders. It brought them nearly nose to nose, his breath mingling with hers, hot silver eyes boring into hers. "My prize. My tame, captive witch."

"I want to touch you, too," she got out rocking her hips against his hand. "My warrior king."

"Then do it. Touch me. Tend to me." He let her down, leaving her sex empty and wanting. So she hurried to undress him, dropping his clothes to the floor in her haste, but taking the time to run her hands over his shoulders and chest muscles, down the flat of his abdomen, the velvet of her gloves snagging the whorls of hair. Standing again on her tiptoes—Lonen's hands going to her waist to steady her—she reached behind his neck to pull the leather tie from his hair. When she went to toss it aside, he stopped her, taking it from her and setting it carefully on the bedside table.

"It's the one you saved for me, in Bára, after I left," he said, as if explaining.

"That didn't mean anything…" She trailed off at the look he gave her, possessive and pleased.

"It did. It meant you thought about me like I thought about you." He wound a hand in her hair, tugging her head back, gently and remorselessly, so she had to look into his face. He trailed a gloved finger over her lips, his eyes following the movement. She smelled her own musky arousal on it. "It meant you wanted me, and waited for me to return."

She nearly protested, but that was all true. Though it had seemed unlikely that she'd ever see him again, even impossible, she'd kept the tie, dreaming over how he'd felt in her mind, and maybe fantasizing a little about her Destrye warrior.

His face tightened, reading something of that in hers. "Finish undressing me, witch."

Desire coiling hard in her again, she knelt to pull off his boots, then unfastened and tugged down his leather pants, helping him step out of them. His cock, freed, stood out from its deeper nest of hair, and she took a moment to study that part of him. From this angle his man jewels were more visible, hanging full and turgid beneath. Hesitant, she glanced up, to find him watching her with heavy-lidded, slumberous silver eyes.

"Go ahead," he told her, not playing his games, stroking a hand over her hair. The leather made it crackle like fire. "Explore, if you like."

"Spread your legs," she told him, smiling to herself when he obliged. Cupping his balls, she weighed them, fascinated by the way the firm insides, like eggs, moved inside the looser outer skin. Lonen groaned, hand tightening in her hair. "Does that hurt?" she asked.

"No. It's good. So good. Touch me, love."

So, she kept one hand holding his jewels, cupping and massaging them, taking his cock in the other, stroking the velvet over his shaft so it went smooth in one direction, against the nap in the other.

Both made him groan and shudder in turn.

"Enough," he gasped, urging to her feet and pushing her back onto the bed. "Spread your legs for me, as I told you."

She did, with not even an inkling of refusing him. There was a power in this, too, lying back on her fur cloak and parting her thighs for his avid gaze. He grasped her knees, pushing them wider apart and back. "This is pink, too," he told her. "Blushing for me like you do when you think about having me."

Of course, she blushed at that, that he read her so easily. An irony that she could feel shyness over that when she was so totally physically exposed.

"Hold your knees apart for me like that, so I don't accidentally touch you," he instructed, putting one knee on the bed and stroking the now wet and rougher leather down the tender skin of the inside of her thighs. His cock bobbed over her, enticing, and she wished she could put her mouth on it, or put him inside her.

"Why do you get leather gloves and I get velvet?" Her breaths came in pants as he toyed with her, brushing his fingers along the outside of her burning core, not quite where she needed it most.

His fierce silvery gaze lifted to hers, his hair loose now, snaking in curls around his strong shoulders. "You can have leather. I'll wear velvet. I'll have gloves made for us both in every fabric imaginable, so we can torment each other with the textures." He pushed a finger, made thicker by the glove, inside her. "How's this one?"

She couldn't answer, her eyes rolling back in her head, her breath stolen away. The invasion penetrated deeper than the physical, all of him coming into her. Having his finger, even gloved, inside her body permeated her with his particular energy, that core vibrance that had drawn her from the first moment.

He slid the finger in and out of her, mimicking the intercourse they couldn't have, and she lifted her hips in answer thrusts. "Yes?" he asked, a purr in his voice saying he knew the answer.

"Yes," she panted. "More."

"More," he echoed, working a second finger inside her. It

stretched her, the pleasurable ache making her keen. "Look at me," Lonen commanded and she opened her eyes. He'd moved so he hovered over her, bracing himself on an elbow next to her head, a breath away from laying himself on her. Below, beyond the plank of his body, his fingers thrust in and out of her, diligently building the fire within. But all she could see was his face, so close to hers, his gaze mirroring the love and desire that radiated through her, from his touch inside her and wafting off his skin along with his intense body heat. Consciously or not, he undulated with her, moving as she did, and she could almost believe he made love to her in truth.

She reached down and took his cock in her velvet grasp. His mouth fell open slightly, his face taking on a strained mien. Fingers thrusting harder, the hilt of his hand slamming against her, knuckle rubbing her pearl of pleasure, pressure building. Building.

With a crash and a scream, she orgasmed, funneling her convulsion into her grip on his cock, angling it toward her entrance.

"Oria…" Lonen gasped, straining to pull his hips back. "Love—"

"Yes," she demanded, working him faster.

He went rigid, neck arching back and face suffusing with blood, a guttural roar erupting from his throat. Liquid splashed against her entrance—she hoped. Between his thrusting fingers and her own copious juices, she couldn't be sure, but he knew. Veins bulging in his temples beside bright sliver eyes, he worked himself in her hand, echoing the movement with his fingers.

"This is my cock," he whispered, as he had on their wedding night. "Planting my seed in your fertile soil. My wife. My lovely sorceress. My queen."

With a fervent wish, she took him in. All of him, savoring and tucking it away, as she had with the forest breath. Keeping it safe. With any luck they'd made a child.

Arill make it so.

~ 14 ~

H E MADE LOVE to his wife twice more, until she fell into a deep sleep after the third round. All of her moods enchanted him. Submissive, queenly, angry, sweet, passionate, powerful, gasping and begging, fiercely demanding—he loved it all. From sleekly gorgeous, her slim, pale nakedness framed by the fur cloak, ribboned socks, boots and those Arill-forsaken scarlet gloves, to sleepy-eyed and rumpled, hair tousled from sex and sleep, every face of his personal goddess ruled his heart.

Putting his seed inside her, even if only by close proxy, had given him such a powerful rush. Totally unexpected. Absolutely transporting. He couldn't get enough of her.

He had big plans for another session in the morning when she'd recovered—which quickly ground to a halt. Because of him, not her. Though his cock was ready enough, when Oria pulled on a glove to grasp it, he swore viciously, knocking her hand away.

She blinked at him, puzzled and a little hurt. "What's wrong?"

Sitting back on his heels, he examined himself. Erect, yes, but also nearly as crimson as Oria's gloves. His cock glowed with more than aroused color. The entire shaft looked rubbed raw, the head bloodred. Now that her velvet grasp had awakened the nerves, his entire cock throbbed with agony. Not at all a smart thing to do. Good thing his brothers would never know, or he'd hear about this until his deathbed.

Oria raised dubious eyes to his, giving him a weak smile that became a grimace. "Too much chafing?"

Gritting his teeth, he nodded. Really stupid. And inconsiderate. "How about you—are you sore?"

Experimentally she pressed her thighs together, then shrugged a little. "Slightly. In a lovely way. I'll probably walk funny." She blushed as she made the joke, as if she hadn't panted and begged and screamed her pleasure, encouraging him to penetrate every part of her. "I think I had more…lubrication."

Of course she had. Arill shouldn't let his seed take root. He didn't deserve to reproduce.

Oria bit her lip in sympathy. Then he realized it was to keep from laughing. He scowled at her. "Laugh even a little and I'm flipping you over and spanking your bottom until it's the same color as my cock."

With an amazing amount of control, she swallowed every hint of amusement, her face smoothing into a serene mask. Never forget her ability to assume an emotionless demeanor. She sat up, clutching the furs to her breast. "Perhaps some salve of some sort?" she suggested with polite reserve.

The thought of *that* potential burn made him choke. "I'll take care of it."

"I could—"

"It's my cock," he snapped. "I'll handle it."

"I'm sure you will," she murmured as he yanked his shirt over his head, and he thought he detected a ripple of laughter in her voice, but when he whirled on her, she looked as demure as ever. The leather pants scraped his still-engorged cock abominably and he was hard pressed to keep from cursing further, willing the thing to subside already.

"I'm going to check on Buttercup and rescue Chuffta," he said. After the door slammed shut, a peal of laughter rang out, silvery magic riding it like frost on a mountain breeze.

Nice to know he could make his sorceress break *hwil* and laugh—even at his expense.

He stopped to make water on the way back, which turned out to be its own special nightmare. Worth it though. He shook his head at himself. What a night. He'd figure out something for the next time. Smooth leather gloves for her hands, maybe. And oil.

Lots of oil.

Setting those thoughts firmly aside, as they did *not* help with easing his arousal, he went back in to find Oria had already sponge-bathed with water warmed by the fire, and she had nearly finished adding all forty-seven layers of clothing. Why she didn't melt inside all of that, he didn't know, but the flushed and happy expression on her face—along with the sated and sensual smile she greeted him with—spoke volumes.

He could live his whole life happily this way—warm, passionate nights, mornings with laughter. Get through all of this and they would. He would make it happen.

Holding up the tools he'd brought from the extra packs stowed with Buttercup, he pointed to the chapel. "I'm going to do your grave-robbing. If Arill smites me, you'll have to get off the mountain on your own."

She nodded, giving him a serious look, though her eyes sparkled. "I'll stand ready to bargain for your immortal soul." Exchanging a thought with Chuffta, who lolled belly-up in front of the blazing fire, she lost the smirk and added, "Try not to touch the mask though, if you can help it."

He turned back. "Why not? I touched your mask, back in Bára."

She picked up his hair tie and went to him, bidding him to turn around. Gathering his loose curls together—which in truth he'd forgotten about—she tied it back for him. "I don't know," she finally said, a remote sound to her voice. "A feeling I have. Chuffta thinks so, too."

"Someone would have had to touch it to inter it with her ashes," he pointed out.

"Still." She went to get her cloak. "Why take the chance?"

"You're the sorceress. I'm just the muscle." He opened the door and entered the dark and considerably chillier chapel. Oria followed behind, bringing a lantern from the cabin. "I'd light the fire, but this shouldn't take long."

She nodded, shivering and drawing the cloak tighter around her, casting a long and pensive look at the retablo of her ancestress. "I wonder what happened to her children," she said, as he began chipping at the loosest part of the mortar at the top.

With any luck the cover stones would come free and they could extract the mask without further disturbing the ashes. Oria might like to tease him and imply that he was superstitious, but why risk angering the goddess? *Why take the chance?* Oria had said. Each of them with their own talismans for dealing with unknown powers.

"I imagine they lived out their lives," he answered.

"But wouldn't they have had a sensitivity to magic, being her get?"

"No temple to train them, though." The mortar gave a little, but not as easily as he'd hoped.

"That would be even worse. The magic comes to you anyway— and makes you kind of crazy if you don't know how to deal with it."

"Well, then they probably didn't survive long among the Destrye. I can vouch that crazy people are barely tolerated now— back then would have been much worse. They'd have been exposed to the elements as babes or young children, or left behind if the tribe moved. If they made it to adulthood, the boys would have died in duels and the girls killed by angry husbands. And that's only if the families managed to marry them off." With a grunt, he applied more leverage, and the capstone grated free. "Got it!"

The thing was heavy so he skewed it to the side, hoping to avoid lifting it off entirely. "Bring the candle here and see if—" He broke off, seeing Oria's face streaming with tears. "What? What happened? Did…" Oh.

She wiped the tears away with an impatient hand, bringing the candle closer. "Don't mind me. I'm just emotional for some reason. Being here, in her tomb, where she was buried so far from home among a people who didn't even give her a name. And then thinking of her children, killed so ruthlessly, because of something they couldn't control…"

He took the candle and set it down. His idiocy record for the morning continued in full strength. Putting his hand over hers where it rested on her belly—had she been aware of the gesture?— he ran his other over her shining hair, once again brushed smooth. "Speculation only. And that won't happen to you or our children. You have a name and I'll make sure all of Dru—and Bára—knows forever of the mighty Sorceress Queen Oria of the Destrye. Our children will be protected and blessed by both Arill and the magic you'll bring them. They'll grow up to be kings and queens in their own right. Maybe one in charge of every one of your sister-cities."

She laughed, a little watery. "Ever the optimist."

"That's right." He cupped the back of her head and kissed her hair just over her forehead. As much as he regretted her unhappiness, it also moved him a great deal that she already felt so deeply for their future children. The way she held her hand so protectively over her belly… well, it seemed women sometimes knew these things instinctively. Perhaps they'd made a baby last night. A child conceived in this sacred place, where warrior and sorceress had joined before, would have to be specially blessed.

"I should have told you," he said, waiting for her to look up at him, copper eyes dark with tears. He pointed with his chin to the opposite wall. "Odymesen's ashes are interred here, too. This isn't just her place, but their place. I don't know if it helps to know it, but she was never alone."

A smile trembled into place on her lips. "It helps."

"Good. Now come fetch your treasure."

Her eyes widened. "It's in there?"

"Of course it is. You knew it all along." The gleam of gold hadn't surprised him in the least.

"I guessed."

"Uh huh."

She wrinkled her nose at him, which made him happy to see her saucy again. Taking the candle over to the sepulcher, she leaned over and peered in. A long breath sighed out of her. "It is in there."

"On a tile like you had in Bára for yours, I think." He looked over her shoulder, the mask now clearly illuminated in the niche built for it. "Her ashes are sealed beneath, I suspect, so you'll be relieved to know there should be no smiting imminent."

"I am beyond relieved," she said in a dry tone. "Will you hold this?"

SHE HANDED HIM the candle, noting the tightness around his eyes. For all his joking, Lonen harbored concerns about this project still. More than his dislike of her old mask. But he'd set aside his apprehensions and helped her do what she asked of him.

And there it was. Radiating old power, hot as the sun on her face. Lonen might not have doubted what they'd find, but she hadn't been certain of what she perceived. With sgath sight, the thing didn't look like a mask at all. It reminded her of how the Trom appeared on that other plain, like black suns radiating a kind of nonlight. Not moonlight, not sunlight, but something the reverse of both.

The dreams came back to her, Chuffta's eyes going matte black, as if they absorbed light instead of reflecting it. Yar's eyes, looking like that after he summoned the Trom. *You've taken not one, but several steps farther down your path*, the Trom had said to her. Was this another of those steps? She shuddered with more than cold.

But the course hadn't changed. Lonen and the Destrye needed her. The Bárans back home, laboring under Yar's deranged regime needed her. Food, water, safety—all of that called for magic, and a great deal of it. Did she dare attempt to wrestle these ancient magics?

"I need you," she called to Chuffta and he winged in, landing on her shoulder. *"What do you think of this?"*

He snaked his head around, angling it from side to side, peering at the artifact with brilliant green eyes. *"It looks like any Báran mask to me."*

"Do you think it's safe for me to take it?"

"I think you have to." His mind-voice sounded unusually somber.

"Why?"

"Because you feel it. There's a reason you wanted Lonen to dig it out. A reason it called to you."

"I don't know what the reason is though. And… it could be more than I can handle."

"We shall no doubt find out." Now he lifted his head, looking at her. His long tail slipped up her sleeve, finding a spot of skin above the glove, coiling around, infusing her with his cool, dry presence. *"Go on, take it. I'm ready."*

"Here we go," she said aloud. Lonen unstrapped his battle-axe, holding it at the ready.

He shrugged a little self-consciously when she raised her eyebrows at him. "Can't hurt, right?" he said.

Her barbarian, ever ready to protect her, even from the unseen. Reaching in with her gloved hands, she took up the mask. Heavier than hers had been, the thing sang of the weight of centuries. What must have been ribbons crumbled away into dust as she lifted it out of its niche. The candlelight caught the gold, the flicker of shadows on the subtle molding of the eyeless mask giving the illusion of a face.

For a startled moment, she thought it smiled at her. Then it subsided, losing the momentary illusion of animation and becoming simply a mask again. Very old, very heavy, but only that.

Mostly. In the back of her heart, a soundless tune hummed. A chime, like the breathing of the forest or the chime of the stars dancing together at the oasis. She strained to hear it better, but it retreated, like a memory from childhood she couldn't quite reconstruct.

Holding the mask in one hand, she nipped at her glove with her teeth, drawing it off and letting it fall to the floor where it lay on the chill gray stones like the discarded skin of a scarlet snake. Hovering her fingers over the metal, the sense of radiation from it sang louder. Dragons roaring far away. A distant silhouette of wings. A bloom of fire. More. But not enough. She drew in a deep breath, reaching for all her *hwil*, bracing for the impact.

"Oria, love." Lonen gripped her shoulder, tense concern flooding into her. "Don't rush things. There's time for you to study it."

She gazed up at him, that craggy, scarred face, hard and yet tender. So beloved in such a short time. Time and time and time. "There isn't."

And she laid her bare hand on the mask.

~ 15 ~

THE MAGIC GRABBED at her, hard. Rather than a geyser, it yanked her under, the waters of the oasis closing over her head, crushing the breath from her lungs.

No—filling her lungs with water. Which should have drowned her but... then she could breathe it. It swelled in and out of her, her chest like a larger heart, beating the fluid in and out. Sustaining. Nourishing.

Oddly it reminded her of that dream again, of the fire burning her throat, and Chuffta saying it didn't really do that.

"I'm here. And yes. Same, but different."

She tried to frame a reply, but couldn't. Her mind-voice didn't work underwater. Only it wasn't water, it was sgath. A more viscous sgath, purified, but intense. So much. She worked harder to breathe it out again. Couldn't.

"Oria?"

"Oria!"

She opened her eyes and gasped, air burning into her lungs. Lonen's face loomed above hers, echoing on several levels of physical and sgath sight. Waking her from another nightmare? No— the clatter of the gold mask against stone still rang in the air, a harsh bell of warning, a tantalizing chime of waltzing stars.

"I'm here." She drew in more air as slowly as she could, using the physical discipline to focus on pulling *hwil* into place, shutting down all but physical sight. That steadied the world. "I'm fine."

Lonen's mouth firmed into a harsh line. He gripped her, and she realized she lay on the floor, half in his embrace. "I would greatly prefer," he began in a ragged voice that was nearly a shout, then paused to calm himself. "If you could not do the stopping breathing thing anymore. That would be much better for my continued sanity."

She reached up to touch his face, diverting her fingers to stroke his silky beard when she realized that was the naked hand. "I'll see what I can do."

"Yes." He took a deep breath, let it out, then offered a crooked smile. "Well?"

"She pooled sgath, all right." She struggled to sit up and his arms tightened briefly before he let her go with a sharp shake of his head. Not for her, but for himself.

"Here?" he asked, giving the floor a suspicious look, his fingers twitching for the battle-axe lying next to them. Even discarding it in haste, he kept it near.

"Not exactly, but nearby. It's hard to tell because there's a lot of it and it's very old. Like it's sat and … grown solid over time. Does that make sense?"

Lonen gave her an incredulous look. "Seriously? No. None of this makes sense to me, but I'll take your word for it. The mask?"

"Connected me to it, yes. I'll have to think about how to work with it. Instead of being like drinking from the geyser below Bára, or breathing the mist of the forest, this felt like inhaling stone."

He frowned over her shoulder—in the direction of the mask he'd dashed out of her hands, she realized. "That can't be good for you. We'll put it back for now."

"No." She pushed to her feet, finding her legs weak. With a resigned sigh, Lonen stood, too, helping her up with a hand under her elbow. "Where's Chuffta?"

"Here." His mind-voice sounded strange, and she turned even as Lonen pointed.

Her Familiar perched next to the mask, one talon hooked in a hole where the ribbons would be tied. *"Are you all right?"* she asked him, wondering as she did if she'd ever asked him that before.

"Yes. No. I don't know. I feel strange."

"Strange how?"

"Like I want to be bigger. Much bigger."

ORIA EVENTUALLY AGREED to let Lonen be the custodian of the mask. The fact that she didn't want to give it to him—and that Chuffta showed a similar reluctance to part company with the Arill-cursed thing—finally convinced her of the wisdom of it.

Left to his own devices, he would have sealed it back in its crypt. But Oria refused to even consider it. Her fervor, and the fiery burn in Chuffta's gaze, made it clear he'd have a battle on his hands if he insisted.

And Oria shone with magic again, her hair lifting as she moved, swirling in the unseen currents, her skin as radiant and shimmering as when he first glimpsed her. When she paused to draw her glove back on, the saint in the retablo seemed to gaze over her shoulder, the resemblance so uncanny they could have been sisters.

He handled the mask himself only with gloved hands, wrapping it in layers of leather and tying knots in the ties that bound it. Under the close watch of Oria and Chuffta, he buried the thing at the bottom of the saddlebags. If Buttercup danced sideways when he added the packs to the warhorse's back, that surely had to be because the steed was restive from being cooped up.

Oria would know if there was any reason to fear. And she would tell him. He glanced at her, the remote cool of her face, her gaze drawn inward, contemplating.

"Oria."

Her bright copper eyes, molten with magic, lifted to his when he spoke her name.

"I want you to promise me you won't use the mask without me present."

A line drew in between her brows. "I might need solitude."

"Then we'll figure it out, but no going behind my back on this. You or Chuffta."

She cast her gaze down, her cheeks pinking, revealing that she'd considered it. "Lonen, I—"

He gripped her shoulders, forcing her to look at him, her expression no longer serene, but cagey and assessing. "I mean it. If I have to be a brute of a barbarian about this, I will. But I'll have your promise on this."

Copper fire snapped at him, his skin tingling with the seething static of magic building like a summer storm in a densely hot afternoon. The kind that produced lightning and no rain. And blazes that devoured forests. "Oria, love, listen to me. You know I'm right."

She firmed her lips in mutiny, then the fire fogged and she cast a glance at Chuffta, perched on Buttercup's saddle. Huffing out a breath between pursed lips, she closed her eyes briefly, a sweep of lashes and gone, then smiled at him, her gaze once again more herself. Abruptly he remembered that dream in her bed, that first night he slept with her, when her eyes had turned Trom black.

The hairs lifted on his neck.

"You're right," she was saying, and he shook off the memory. Or was it premonition? "You have my promise. Neither Chuffta nor I will touch the mask without you. You are its keeper and…." She moved into him, wrapping her arms around his waist, burrowing against his chest. "It frightens me, Lonen." Her voice came soft and muffled.

He cupped her head in his hand, using the other to pull his cloak around her, though she hardly needed more warmth. "It frightens me, too," he admitted. "Let's leave it here."

"No." She raised her face, leaning into his hand. "We need it."

"We can find another—"

"Not 'we' as in you and me. We as in Bára, and Dru. Something here started long ago and we're simply picking up the threads of it. Even if we leave the mask here, the course is set. Can't you feel it?"

He could. He didn't much like it, either.

Her gaze went up to the peaks over his shoulder. "So, we ride on and up. And I'll practice with Tania's sgath along the way."

"Tania?"

"My long-lost aunt. I've decided to give her name to my ancestress-of-the-chapel."

"Is that wise?" The feeling of premonition still sat heavy on him.

Oria gave him a look. "I am *not* calling her Odymesen'y."

"I understand, but perhaps a different name…"

"Why—what objection do you have?" She gave no hint of what, but something about her wide eyes made him think she kept them deliberately guileless.

"I think there's something you're not telling me."

She laughed, the magic glinting through it, seeming to manifest in the air like crystals to shower to the ground. No, it had begun to snow. That's all it was.

"Come on, Destrye." She tugged him toward the horse. "Let's go see this lake and talk your mother into sponsoring this wedding you want so badly. And I'll tell you the little I know about my aunt Tania."

Chuffta took off as he lifted her into the saddle, white wings etched against the wintery sky. Oria lifted a crimson-gloved hand to her Familiar and he nipped at her fingers as he flew past. When she transferred her gaze to Lonen, as he settled behind her, she smiled with affection, dropping the hand to caress his cheek.

"It will all be fine," she murmured. "Trust me."

He did. But he held her close, and sent a prayer to Arill to hold them in her hand.

ORIA'S ENCHANTMENT

SORCEROUS MOONS – BOOK 5

BY

JEFFE KENNEDY

THE TEMPTATION OF POWER

No longer a princess and not yet a queen, the sorceress Oria welcomes the rush of power the ancient mask brings her—though the obsessive connection to it frightens her and alarms her barbarian husband, Lonen. But retreat is not an option. She must wrestle the magic to prevent an annihilating war, even if she must make the ultimate sacrifice.

A WORLD IN FLAMES

If Lonen wants to reclaim his throne—and save his people from destruction—he must return by sunset on the seventh day. What he thought would be a short and simple journey, however, leads them deeper into the mountains—and Oria deeper into the thrall of foul magic. Until he must choose between two terrible paths.

A HEART-WRENCHING CHOICE

Struggling with conflicting loyalties, Oria and Lonen fight to find a way to be together… lest they be separated forever, and their realms go down in flames with them.

DEDICATION

For Terri Beth Chenault Verrette,
Who accused me of ending the last book "mid-paragraph,"
And who became an insistent voice among many that I finish this
series.

Acknowledgements

Many, many thanks to Nathan Lowell, who asked me every time we talked (and we're both on the SFWA Board of Directors, so it was often) when I was going to finish this series.

Huge thanks, too, to all of the readers who emailed, messaged, tweeted, and mentioned how much they wanted the next book. I'm truly chagrined I made you wait two years for this—and also grateful for your "pestering." Always feel free to do that! Without all of you asking, I might never have made it back around to this tale.

Merci to Melliane for her work behind the scenes—and for sticking with me.

A special thank you to Carien, for an early read and excellent feedback. And for everything else, as usual, *ad infinitum*.

Very special and heartfelt thanks to Kelly Robson, whose daily presence online carried me through some difficult drafting. You always know what book I'm working on—and you always ask how it's going. That means more than I can ever say.

Love—yesterday, today, and always—to David, who shares my days and nights. I wouldn't change a thing, my dear.

~ 1 ~

THE MASK HUNG in her awareness like a blinding sun, scorching bright and enticingly hot. Not that the wintry mountain air made her all that cold. Her husband, Lonen, had gone to great lengths to make sure she stayed warm. No, this was like a physical craving. Oria thirsted for more of the golden mask's rich magic, starving for another taste.

With every stride of Lonen's warhorse, Buttercup, with every minute since that morning when she'd held the artifact in her hands, swept under by its immense power, she missed it exponentially more.

Naturally, she wouldn't tell Lonen.

It wouldn't help anything for him to know how deeply the mask affected her. She'd admitted to being frightened by it and that unwise admission had been more than enough. Freshly shaken from the encounter, she'd promised Lonen she wouldn't use the mask by herself. "Fear," however, didn't accurately describe her emotions.

"Greed" would be a better word—and now she deeply regretted that hasty promise. She wanted the mask with a longing unlike anything she'd felt before, except for perhaps during sexplay with Lonen. He had a way of stoking overpowering need in her. Perhaps if they could have actual intercourse, with skin-to-skin contact, that driving desire might be slaked. As it was, despite his inventive alternatives—or, more likely, entirely as a result of those frustrating games of his—their sexual interludes drove all rational sense from her mind, until she could think of nothing but begging for more and more and more.

She wanted the mask like that—but no amount of begging Lonen would work in this case. She had to find another way.

Even now, riding in the cradle of Lonen's arm, cozy in the shadowcat fur cloak, with the startling peaks of the snow-capped mountains rising against the jewel-bright blue sky, she couldn't rest content. The mask mentally tugged at her. After the session with it in the chapel, Lonen had taken the mask from her, holding it suspiciously in gloved hands—and keeping it out of hers. All because she'd lost a bit of time while communing with it, and felt a little ill and disoriented afterward. He flatly refused to give it back, too, and she couldn't match Lonen's physical strength.

Fortunately, she'd managed to persuade him that they needed the magical artifact and he'd agreed to bring it with them. She'd know how to handle it better next time.

There had to be a next time.

She didn't know what extremes she might've gone to if he'd insisted on leaving it behind. Or worse, if he'd walled it up again in that tomb behind stones too heavy for her to budge. Though, if he had gone to such an extreme, she could perhaps have used magic to change the balance of power between them.

She'd barely begun to practice magic in active ways before they fled Bára. Leaving her home—and the deep, ancestral well of sgath magic beneath the walled city—had stripped her of her birthright of power along with her crown. Now the short and overwhelming session with the mask had filled her with such immense reservoirs of sgath magic that she bubbled over with it. She had little experience, and no doubt even less dexterity, at converting passive sgath to active grien to use it as a tool, but she possessed plenty of punch.

Enough to overcome Lonen. Just to take the mask. That's all.

The unfamiliar power tingled in her fingertips, begging to be released, to be exploited...

No. She wouldn't do that. She'd risk harming Lonen, perhaps permanently. She loved him and would never hurt him. And yet...

The mask belonged to *her*. Lonen knew that as well as anyone. He'd taken her to the chapel because he recognized Oria's resemblance to the ancient sorceress depicted in the retablo paintings. It belonged to Oria and her people, not to the barbarian Destrye who'd stolen her ancestress away. Anyone who came between Oria and that mask would suffer just consequences.

The mask whispered to her, full of sweet, heady power she could sense, but that only trickled weakly since she couldn't touch it. Lonen had wrapped the mask in layers of leather, knotted the ties that bound it, and then buried it at the bottom of the saddlebags, which he all but sat on.

When they stopped to eat, however, he might answer the call of nature. While he was off in the woods, she could extract the mask and drink in its magic. It wanted her to. That morning, Oria had only been able to take in a bit, the mask had sat stagnant so long and her sgath portals had been jammed shut with disuse. Recovering from physical starvation had worked that way, too. Her stomach had shrunk so that when she'd gotten the right food, she'd had to eat slowly, to give her system time to recover. But she'd also eaten frequently. Refilling her empty reserves with sgath again could follow the same pattern.

Lonen, however, distrusted the mask too much. To be fair, she had lost control during that first session, but she knew better now. If she could get to the mask, even only for a few minutes, she'd prove that to him.

"I'd help. I could get the mask out faster than you. I have sharp teeth and sharper claws," Chuffta bragged, not idly.

Oria glanced up to where her Familiar flew overhead, as dazzlingly white as the snow all around them, but with iridescent rainbow shimmers in his scales. The winged lizard looked surprisingly at home in the wintry landscape, so far from his desert habitat. He cocked his head at her, piercing green gaze meeting hers over the downbeat of his translucent leathery wings.

"I look like I belong because I match the snow is all. It's far too cold

here. What we need is fire! I could burn the saddlebag and free the mask—it won't melt." He breathed a puff of green fire in demonstration.

"*We promised Lonen that neither of us would touch it without him,*" she reminded Chuffta silently, aware that she'd been perfectly ready to break that promise only a moment ago.

"You *promised,*" he grumbled. "*I didn't promise Lonen anything.*"

"*Only because he can't hear you like I can. He trusts me to speak for you.*" And he trusted her to abide by her promise. Her thoughts had gone far down a dark and twisting path. How could she have been plotting to break her word, so soon after giving it?

"*Lonen doesn't understand how the mask feels,*" Chuffta commented, a wistful tone to his mental voice. "*He's only a mind-dead barbarian. He'll never be able to understand.*"

"*Chuffta!*" She stifled a physical gasp of reaction at her Familiar's thoughts, an unpleasant echo of Báran attitudes toward Lonen's people.

"*You thought the same thing before,*" Chuffta complained, but sounded chastened.

"*Before I knew better. Now we* both *know better.*" But Chuffta had a point—that Lonen didn't understand magic. He couldn't. It would be up to her to show him. Just a taste of the mask's power. "*All right, let's do it. I'll suggest that we stop. But no destroying the saddlebags. There's stuff in there that we need.*"

"*People stuff,*" he grumbled. "*Derkesthai don't need so much stuff.*"
"*Lucky you.*"

"What are you and Chuffta discussing?" Lonen asked, his deep voice a rumble against her back.

She jumped inside her skin, but managed to conceal it by turning her startled and guilty jerk into a wriggle. Leaning against him, reminding herself of the protection that his strong body offered—and the affection and trust that came with it—she tipped her head back to look at her husband. Apparently impervious to the cold, he'd thrown back the furry hood of his cloak, so the chill breeze off the mountain peaks tossed his unruly dark curls, the bright sunlight only emphasizing the glossy blue-black of his hair, the ruggedness of his features, and the granite of his gaze. "How do you always know?" she asked.

He plucked a strand of her long hair that had blown across her face, carefully not touching her skin, and wound it around his finger as he studied her expression. "I don't always know, do I? Only sometimes do I realize you must be, and mostly from the way he behaves." Lonen jerked his chin at Chuffta, who'd surged forward to soar along the edge of a precipice, taking advantage of the rising thermals stirred from the valleys by the intense sun. "He looks at you, flies closer, breathes flame sometimes." Lonen raised his brows in question.

"He likes to brag," Oria explained.

"But you, your expression and manner don't often reveal much." His voice lowered, a certain suspicion in it.

"That was part of my training, as a member of the royal family and the priestess they expected me to become. I worked very hard to learn to compose myself so as not to reveal emotion."

"You're very good at it. Which worries me. You're acting strangely now."

"Now?" She suspected where he was going with this and asked the question more as a delaying tactic. Lonen saw through her far better than he pretended.

"Since this morning and your encounter with that ... thing."

His scarred eye twitched, and she lifted a gloved hand to his face, the scarlet velvet a startling contrast to his brown skin, and smoothed the nap over that brow. The newer scar over the old one, both crossing his eye above and below, pulled pink and new, and he sometimes rubbed it as if it pained him, though her barbarian warrior wasn't one to complain. If only she could truly touch him.

"I'm still me," she said, giving him a reassuring smile. "And I'm feeling so much better now. Especially with the magic from Tania's mask." She'd decided to call her unnamed ancestress after a long-lost aunt. If only she could persuade him to let her keep the mask on her person… "I'm excited to try again since the mask will—"

"Will stay in the saddlebags for now," he cut her off, narrowing his gaze on her face.

Annoyed, she turned away so he wouldn't see it in her, how much she wanted—*needed*—just another small taste. "I have to learn to work with it if we're to have a hope of saving Dru from Yar and the Trom."

"Yes, well," he replied, sounding drily amused but also resolved, "winning that war shouldn't be an issue in the next few hours, and I want you to have some distance from that thing before you go near it again."

"It's mine, Lonen," she replied tightly, curling her velvet-clad fingers against the urge to claw him. "Your ancestor may have taken Tania captive and bred children on her, but she was of *my* people, not yours."

"Oh?" He replied with lethal softness. "And here I recall a vow when you married me that you'd be my wife and Queen of the Destrye, that you would take Dru as your responsibility and the people as your own."

Curse his clever tongue.

"He does have a point," Chuffta said, sounding as chastened as she felt.

"Only partially." Speaking aloud, she said, "As your brothers and numerous other Destrye, including your Priest of Arill, have noted, I am *not* Queen of Dru and won't be unless we're married according to *your* goddess."

"According to *your* temple, your ways, and the evidence of my own senses," he shot back immediately, "the bond between us was magically forged and cannot be broken."

She opened her mouth with a vague thought of arguing, but the tightening of his arms around her stopped her words in her throat.

"Don't try to deny that, sorceress," he murmured in her ear, "because even this mind-dead barbarian can sense magic at that level."

"I didn't know you could sense the magic of the marriage bond so strongly," she said aloud. Had he told her that? She didn't think so. How odd.

"You're like a burning sun inside me, Oria," he murmured in her ear, his lips so close only the veil of her hair prevented contact.

With him so near, his emotions flew into her like arrows, and she narrowed her magic portals to control the onslaught. Love, desire, fear, worry… and hope balancing the razor edge of despair. Lonen was a man of passionate feelings, which he projected with the same exuberant force as his personality, and it could be too much for her to bear, on so many levels.

"It doesn't matter what my brothers or the priests say," he continued with grim resolve, "you're wedded so tightly to my soul I imagine you'll be there after this body is gone and blown to ash in the wind."

She shivered at the images. Too many of them too similar to her own thoughts.

"But," he continued in a more cheerful tone, thankfully giving her a bit more room, "their objections won't matter much longer because when we return, we'll be wed under Arill's hand as well. Then there will be no doubts."

"Do you think your mother will be willing to journey back with us and sponsor the marriage?" Oria did have doubts. Many of them.

"Yes." He said it with finality, though she wondered how he planned to convince this former queen who lived in some sort of exile or hermitage, far from her family and the forests of Dru. It had never been clear to Oria why his mother lived so far from the center of Destrye government and Lonen had ducked answering her questions. "I wouldn't be dragging you on this journey otherwise," he added, after a moment.

"I thought you brought me along because you wanted to show me Odymesen's chapel, because you thought the magic there might help me, and it did." She didn't need to remind either of them that they'd both feared for her safety in the palace without him there to protect her.

"True. I hope I don't regret that."

"If you're that concerned," she replied, stung, "it seems unwise to marry me any more than you already have."

His strong arm slid around her waist, pulling her back against him, though she remained stiff. "I don't regret finding magic for you, beloved Oria," he said quietly. "Only that the nature of what we found might jeopardize your wellbeing."

"It won't," she answered. "You have to trust me there."

Making a noncommittal sound, he didn't offer any guarantee. Silence fell between them, fraught with the argument neither of them wanted to continue.

"How long to your mother's abode?" she finally asked.

"We'll be there tonight. A day to persuade her, two days' journey back, and we'll return to the temple and Arill City in plenty of time."

"Your brother can have you declared dead seven days from when he issued the challenge—that's only two days of leeway," she worried.

"Two days we won't need," Lonen replied, as carelessly and confidently optimistic as ever. "Once that's done, we can end this ridiculous infighting with my family and face our true enemy."

"Our wedding won't guarantee your victory in the duel against Nolan for the throne," she felt compelled to point out.

"With my powerful sorceress wife as my second?" He made a scoffing sound. "I cannot lose."

If she could wield her magic effectively. "All the more reason for me to practice with the mask."

"Later, Oria." He nearly growled her name, punctuating it with finality. "You'll mess with that thing in small doses or I'll melt it in the nearest campfire."

The threat sent a pang of panic through her. "Chuffta says it can't be melted."

"Does he now?" Lonen sounded so interested that she realized she'd revealed too much, that he now knew she and her Familiar had been discussing the magical artifact Lonen already mistrusted so greatly. "I wouldn't be so sure," he continued when she didn't reply. "The Destrye have long since mastered the art of metal work of all kinds. We no doubt have a kiln that will do the job."

"You wouldn't."

"I absolutely would. Make no mistake, Oria—I will destroy that thing rather than lose you to it."

She wanted to laugh—even tried to—but made a strained sound instead, so stricken was she by the panic that he'd carry out that threat and she'd lose the mask forever. "You won't lose me to it," she replied, loading her tone with scorn to cover the urge to beg him to give it to her. "It's a tool, nothing more."

"Good." He spoke the word shortly, nearly a grunt. "Then, as with all dangerous tools, you will learn to employ this one carefully and gradually—and under my supervision."

She set her teeth, well past annoyed with him, the fury in her heart burning as bright as any kiln. That did it. He didn't have authority over her. He could take his "supervision" and—

"Oria—do I have your agreement?"

"Fine, yes."

"Good. Thank you, love."

"Do we have time for a rest break?" she asked as smoothly as she could. "I need to visit the woods."

"Of course. You have only to say." Responding to subtle signals, Buttercup eased to a stop. Lonen swung down, offering his hands to help her down, smiling with affection. It might be enough to make her feel guilty for what she was about to do, but not quite. "Can you make it through the snow?" he asked.

"Yes." She gave him a dazzling smile, knowing how it affected him; the lazy curl of desire emanating from him warming her. Chuffta followed above as she tromped through the snow, then he perched on a branch to guard her while she did her business. *Is Lonen still with Buttercup?*" she asked him.

He swiveled his head on his long mobile neck, snaking it for the best angle between the interlacing bare branches. *"Yes. He's getting something out of the saddlebags."*

Couldn't be the mask. Unless he was making good on his threat to get rid of it. Hurrying, she clambered back through the deep snow. It had a crunchy layer on the top, but the snow was fluffy beneath, so she sank to her knees in places. Good thing she had the tall boots and fur-lined stockings.

"Hungry?" Lonen asked as she reached firmer ground of the trail. He held out a packet of seeds, dried fruit, and buttery grains—thoughtfully provided just for her. For his part, he chewed on some dried meat.

"Thank you." She took it, feeling chagrined at his thoughtfulness. But not enough to go back on her plan. He started to pack things away again. "I can do that," she offered. "If you need to visit the woods, too."

He grinned for her euphemism, and ran a hand down her arm over the cloak. "Do the woods need more visitors?" he teased.

"You know what I mean," she replied, more primly than she might have if she hadn't been mentally urging him to go, afraid that if he delayed he'd see through her subterfuge.

Hesitating, he frowned a little. "I guess I do feel the need after all. Will you be all right waiting for me?"

"Of course," she said brightly, though a sick feeling wormed in her gut. Had she somehow pushed his will? She'd never been able to do that before, but…

"I'll be right back, love," he promised, and cupped her head to kiss her through the furry cloak on the crown of her head.

Oria watched him go, tension mounting. Moving so Buttercup stood between her and where Lonen had gone, she scrabbled through the open pack, hoping fervently that Lonen had put the mask in that one. Chuffta landed on Buttercup's saddle, craning his sinuous neck to see. Remaining on alert as Lonen had signaled the warhorse to do, Buttercup ignored them and watched the surroundings.

"*Hurry!*"

"*Is Lonen already coming back?*"

"*No, but hurry anyway.*"

With a gusty breath of relief, she closed her fingers around the oddly shaped bundle that was Tania's mask, hard metal within layers of leather, the potent magic of the ancient sorceress singing its siren call of sweet, pure power.

"*Yesss,*" Chuffta hissed with metal glee. "*Hurryhurryhurry.*"

Her fingers shook, fumbling at the tight leather knots, and she impatiently yanked off her glove with her teeth. The cold air and frozen hard sinew cut into her skin, and she was just about to let Chuffta cut it apart when the knot gave. Tossing the sinews and wrapping to the snow, Oria grasped the smooth gold metal fashioned to look like a blank, eyeless face.

As it had before, the magic grabbed at her, but she wrangled it this time, not letting it pull her under. Instead she inhaled, absorbed, consumed, gorging on the feast of it.

So much gorgeous sgath. Sustaining. Nourishing.

Overwhelming.

She began to suffocate under the force of it, to choke on the sheer purity of it. It bloated her, stretching her skin to bursting, her magic portals springing leaks. Swirling, she drowned in the rush of it.

"Oria! Arill take you, come out of it!" Lonen roared in her face, his grip bruising her arms as he shook her.

The sun scorched her vision, the blue sky and white snow all too bright. She put a hand up to cover her eyes and her fingers skidded wet and sticky with blood, sharp pain spiking.

"I could throttle you for this," Lonen grated out.

"*What happened—where are you?*" she asked Chuffta.

"*I'm here.*" Her Familiar sounded uncharacteristically meek and chastened. "*Lonen told me to get lost. He's mad at me, too.*"

"Me, Oria," Lonen said with a snarl. "Talk to me, not him. What in Arill's name made you break your promise?"

"Extracted under duress!" she fired back. "You do not order me, Destrye."

"In this I do. That cursed thing nearly killed you this time."

"I almost had it. I just have to learn to handle the mask so that—"

"Look at your hands." He glared at her with fury—but also fear and worry, enough to give her pause.

She looked, shocked to find her hands covered in blood, fresh and wet over caked and brown. Now that she'd regained awareness, her body throbbed with pain, her neck stiff and hair sticky. She put a hand to her ear, fingers coming away with more blood.

"You were bleeding out of your ears, eyes, nose, and mouth," Lonen informed her. "Even after I got that thing out of your grip— which ripped the skin off your hands, by the way—you wouldn't come out of the trance. You weren't breathing, Oria. Explain to me how that is *learning to handle it!*" His voice climbed to a shout at the end, his face wild.

But it was the sheer panic flowing from him that penetrated her indignation. Lonen so rarely showed fear or worried about much at all. Even when any rational person would. She'd managed to terrify her perpetual optimist, a warrior so strong nothing frightened him.

"I'm sorry," she said, infusing the words with all the sincere regret she could muster. "I was foolish and I won't do it again."

He held her still, looking a bit crazed as he searched her face, then crushed her to him. "I can't lose you, Oria. It would break me as nothing else could."

"I promise I won't do it again," she said against him, meaning it with all her heart. Still, she mentally asked Chuffta the question, *"Did he try to destroy the mask?"*

"No. It's in the snow where he threw it."

Good. Now to make sure Lonen agreed to wrap it up again and bring it with them.

~ 2 ~

"ABSOLUTELY NOT." LONEN folded his arms, staring Oria down. She'd scrubbed all the blood off with snow, giving her face a pink-cheeked glow, her bright copper eyes snapping at him.

Her physical injuries had turned out to be minor, which would be a good thing except that she'd rebounded so quickly. And now she crackled with magic, her copper hair lifting in the unseen currents of it as she faced him, a stubborn look on her lovely face. She might be small and delicate in build, but the magic snarling around her made him cautious. He didn't think she'd use that magic to attack him. Then again, he hadn't thought she'd break her promise either.

"I'll keep the mask with me," she repeated.

"You're lucky I've agreed to wrap it up again and stow it in the bags." He finished that wrapping, hating the metallic glint of the thing with every fiber of his being.

Oria stepped close, as if to snatch it from him, and he held it out of her reach. She had too much pride to jump for it, but the air between them thickened, almost seeming to produce sparks from nothing.

"Don't do it, Oria," he said softly, though he didn't know how he'd stop her if she did.

"I'm not doing anything," she replied evenly.

Ha to that. "I can feel you inside me," he reminded her. "Your magic snarling, sizzling. Would you strike me down, love? Because of that mask?"

"Because you're not my lord and master, barbarian," she replied with heat. "I'm not a helpless, captive Báran bride and you'd do well to remember that."

As if he could ever forget. It made him want to laugh, so he let it out, a hearty release that had her blinking at him in shock. "Oh, my copper-haired beauty, I am more like to forget my own name than the power of the witch I brought home from war and installed in my bed." He deliberately dropped his voice as he said it, to remind her of what they shared together. It worked, too, her anger turning into another kind of heat. "Nor do I forget how to tame her," he added, not above goading her, especially if it distracted her.

"Not fair," she hissed at him, clenching her small fists by her sides. "Don't you dare bring sex into this."

"You're the one who brought it up," he replied with an easy smile, picturing her naked, tied up and tossed over his shoulder, hoping she'd pluck the image from his mind. She must have, because she made an incoherent sound of frustration, with a nicely sensual edge to it. Working quickly, he secured the last knot and stowed the mask deeply in the saddlebag, wedging in everything he could fit on top of it. Not that he'd leave her alone with it again. "Ready to go?" he asked, turning his back to her.

Without waiting for her response, he lifted her onto Buttercup's back, then swung up behind her. They practiced the maneuver so often that they immediately and smoothly nestled together. At least their bodies were in complete harmony. Even blisteringly angry with him, Oria leaned into him without hesitation.

"How are you feeling?" he asked.

"Perfectly fine," she retorted, so fast he'd know it for the lie that it was even if he couldn't see the shadows under her eyes, through her waxy, translucent skin, and the too-glassy look in her eyes. She still sparked with jittering energy, the way some warriors did when they fought too long on too little sleep: running on purely manic energy that eventually buried them.

Oria had told him early on that her peculiar nature made her oversensitive. Without a way to bleed off magical energy, it crackled and fried inside her, hollowing her out into exhaustion. Well, he might not know magic, but he knew how to help her relax. He slipped a hand inside her cloak, cupping the luscious globe of her breast—then pinched the nipple that eagerly rose to his touch.

"My tame witch," he murmured in her ear when she gasped. "You are more than fine."

"I'm not a witch," she replied tightly, but she also pressed her breast into his hand, though perhaps unaware of it—or of how she pushed her tight little bottom against his crotch.

"You admitted it last night. Remember?"

"Lonen…" She spoke his name on a helpless breath, her body growing hotter against him. Oh yes, she remembered, just as he did.

"You said you were my tame witch because you need this." She wore layers of skirts and petticoats, but he knew his way through them. Giving Buttercup the signal to continue on, Lonen secured the reins to drape loosely and slipped his other hand to the thin layer of fine cloth between her spread thighs. The fur-lined stockings tied high on her legs kept her plenty warm, as did all the heavy layers, but very little shielded her open sex. She burned hot and wet against his hand as he cupped her mound, her sweetly plump sex filling his palm.

She moaned and sagged against him. "Lonen… please," she said on a sighing mewl of pleasure. She put her gloved hand over his, but didn't pull his hand away from her intimate flesh, instead rocking her hips against the light pressure—and consequently against his trapped and turgid cock. "Anyone could see," Oria said, though she had her eyes closed, shivering with arousal.

He laughed, not heartily this time, hearing the huskiness of desire in it, and working his fingers against her, knowing exactly how she liked it. "There's leagues of empty landscape all around with no one to see or hear. You could scream your pleasure if you like," he suggested. He loved it when she forgot herself enough in desire to sob his name like a prayer.

"I won't." But the words came out uncertain as she panted, squirming against his pinning hand.

"You did last night," he crooned into her ear. "Over and over. You begged me."

She didn't reply. Even Oria couldn't argue with that truth. He'd driven her wild, driven them both into a frenzy. She'd worn the crimson velvet gloves and he used his leather ones to torment every part of her, determined not to leave even so much as a fingertip of skin that he hadn't thoroughly possessed. Those firelit memories swamped him, lurid and sensual, both of them naked but for the gloves they each wore, how he'd stared into her eyes as he used his leather-covered fingers to penetrate her. How she'd come apart, calling his name.

With a sharp cry she barely stifled, she came against his hand, a wrenching convulsion that had her arching, thighs tensing as she shuddered helplessly. He held her through it, pushing her harder and higher, murmuring wicked things in her ear, until she sagged against him, boneless and unresisting.

"That's better," he said softly, kissing her hair. Clean now, and hot from the sun, it tasted sweet.

"What is?" she asked, her voice vague.

"You needed to relax."

"You can't use sex to handle me, Lonen," she said, though she sounded more sleepy than anything, languid in his arms.

"You're welcome to use the same techniques on me. 'Tis a time-honored tradition between lovers." He shifted behind her, adjusting the hard thrust of his cock, quite painful now that he wasn't distracted. "Though perhaps not now."

"Still sore?" she asked, sounding entirely unsympathetic, even giggling softly.

"Yes, witch." It wasn't funny at all to the possessor of the cock rubbed raw by her gloves. "Lesson learned that though velvet gloves seem soft, the eventual chafing puts the lie to that."

Her giggles rang out in girlishly light, even giddy notes, doing a great deal to lighten his own heart. "There was a definite resemblance in color," she pointed out pertly.

"Sure, laugh," he grumbled. "It's already less painful. Tonight you'll be making it up to me."

"Not at your mother's house," she said without missing a beat.

"My mother did conceive and bear four children," he commented, teasing her. "I expect she knows what people get up to in bed."

"Yes, but she doesn't need us doing that sort of thing under her roof," she answered in a prim tone. "I'd like to make a good impression."

"Don't worry about that," he said. He must've sounded gruff because she leaned back to look at him in that assessing way that meant she read his thoughts. He offered her a smile, though it felt false even to himself. No need to get into ancient history. "To answer your earlier question, my mother *will* agree to sponsor our marriage to the temple, but she won't be doing it because of any impression you make. This has nothing to do with you and everything to do with me."

"I don't understand." Oria frowned, then yawned.

"No, I imagine not. But you'll see." He set his jaw and lifted his gaze to the peaks ahead. "She owes me."

Oria fell asleep soon after that. She would have done so long before, if that Arill-cursed mask hadn't had her so obsessed. The magic infusion had helped her immensely, but Oria had a long recovery ahead of her and she needed rest to heal her emaciated body as much as she needed the right food and nourishing magic.

He'd regret having kept her awake so much of the night with their lovemaking, if that too didn't have such a salutary effect on her. She might not even be aware of how much that affected her, both energizing and soothing her. Oria might make acerbic comments about him controlling her access to the mask and how she used her magic, but he'd begun to wonder if he didn't have a larger role to play in her sorcery than either of them had imagined.

She sighed in her sleep, snuggling against him with all the trust she'd withheld when awake and angry with him. Her lovely profile stood out in pale contrast to the shining copper of her hair, fiery in the sunlight and framed in the dappled shadowcat fur so perfect for showcasing her exotic beauty. In sleep she seemed all soft and fragile woman, with little evidence of the immensely powerful sorcery that burned within her. It consumed her, that magic, like a fever thinning her skin—and affecting her mind with delirium.

He fervently wished he hadn't given in to Oria's wheedling that led to unearthing the mask from the tomb. Perhaps she'd been right to chide him for being superstitious about the old prohibitions against violating tombs, but often those warnings that seemed baseless contained dire truths. If he hadn't been so afraid for Oria, so worried that she'd die without access to the magic of Odymesen's sorceress wife, he would've been able to resist what he *knew* was a bad idea. But he'd given in, and the mask did seem to at least provide Oria with the magic she needed to survive. He'd also studied the inscriptions on the tomb of that ancient pair.

And he hadn't told Oria all of it.

Odymesen had loved his sorceress wife, yes, a woman of Oria's people, captured in war and brought back to the forests of Dru. She'd lived a long life among them—unlike her sister sorceresses who'd languished and died, much as Oria had been on the way to doing—and she'd brought great gifts to the Destrye during that lifetime. But the inscriptions also warned that Odymesen had been pressed to serve as guardian to those gifts, that his sorceress's magic could turn dark and deadly.

In the end, he'd killed her with his own hands, to stop her from some terrible, unnamed destruction. Looking at his lovely Oria, sleeping so trustingly in his arms, Lonen couldn't imagine harming her. And yet...

And yet he'd felt the magic of that mask in her. It snarled in her voice, like another being entirely, and fueled a fury not native to her gentle nature. For a few moments, at the height of her rage, he'd been afraid of her. Her magic had been a palpable threat, like a coiled serpent poised to strike him down. The mask gave her the fuel for her sorcerous abilities, but it also somehow influenced how she used them. Perhaps even corrupting her will.

The way she'd looked, collapsed in the snow, clutching that mask even as her blood poured down her unconscious face... He'd remember that gut-watering sight until the day he died.

Chuffta returned from his forays, swooping and circling over-head. Oria's Familiar always showed discretion that way, giving them privacy for sexual intimacy—though not for much else. The derkesthai Familiar had helped Oria get the mask, encouraged her somehow, Lonen felt sure. Chuffta gave him a long, almost speculative look as he slowed his circling, his green eyes glittering bright. Not a reassuring expression at all.

While he and Chuffta had established a friendly relationship, Lonen harbored no illusions that the derkesthai's loyalty belonged to anyone but Oria. He acted in her best interests, but Chuffta was also young and easily swayed by shiny and interesting things, like fire. Or powerful magical artifacts. Chuffta had been as attracted to the mask as Oria was—which meant Lonen could find himself fighting the pair of them.

Wonderful. He possessed no magic, had no Familiar of his own, unless you counted Buttercup, which he didn't. The warhorse, while uncommonly intelligent and certainly powerful, wasn't a magical companion on par with the derkesthai. He and the horse had only brute strength, stamina, and fighting excellence on their side of the arsenal. Yes, Buttercup understood him with near perfect communi-cation, but not in the same way.

Not enough to counter sorcery like he'd seen the Báran war mages employ. Hopefully he worried unnecessarily about a battle that would never come to pass.

Still, no matter that Oria teased him about his sunny optimism, Lonen had a hard time seeing how this would turn out well. For the time being though, he'd do his best to savor the moment. His beautiful—and healing—bride asleep in his arms, the scent of pine forest and fresh snow, the hot glance of the sun on his face.

All of them safe and well, if only for the space of an afternoon.

~ 3 ~

"O^{RIA.}"

The sound of her name pulled her from deep sleep and strange dreams. Not nightmares for once, but still odd visions of people and lands she didn't recognize. She'd been dancing around a fire to the throbbing beat of huge copper-clad drums, the hammered metal glinting with rose-gold light. Scantily clad, she'd felt sleek and sinuous, moving her body to the powerful beat while her husband watched, desire and fear in his dark eyes. He'd gripped the arms of his throne with powerful hands as the magic rose in her, a fire in her blood that drowned out all else.

The crown of Dru rested on his head, the metal leaves of the wreath twined through his thick dark curls, threads of silver at his temples and in his long beard. Her husband. Her king.

With the wrong face. Not Lonen, but some other Destrye king.

She blinked at him in drowsy confusion, Lonen's face like and unlike the man in her dream. The same broad cheekbones, the dark hair and beard, the same powerful mien of the Destrye warriors that even the illustrations back in Bára had shown more or less accurately.

The eyes, though, they were different. Lonen's were a deep granite gray, with lush black lashes that would be feminine on a softer visage. They held love without fear—and a delighted sparkle. Above his beard, his mouth curved in a mischievous smile of anticipation.

She'd fallen in love with him because of his humor. Well, for many reasons, but first for that. Even when the Destrye suffered terrible defeat in Bára, when he'd faced horrors monstrous enough to leave his skin ashen and his eyes dark as pits, he'd been able to laugh—and make her laugh in turn. As always unable to resist that impish charm in him, she smiled back. "What has you looking like the derkesthai that devoured a nest of eggs?"

"I only did that once," Chuffta mentally sniffed in offense. *"And I was new to Bára."*

"You ate the high priestess's clutch of prized songbirds," she reminded Chuffta aloud, for Lonen's benefit, keeping the amusement out of her tone though she grinned at Lonen.

"He did?" Lonen grinned, too, and flicked a glance at the circling Familiar. "Chuffta, man—bad form."

"I didn't know!" he complained, then added, *"but they didn't taste like prized anything. More important, there's something very exciting just ahead."*

"Chuffta says there's something interesting ahead?"

Lonen scowled. "Did he spoil the surprise?"

"No. He wouldn't." Just to be sure, she mentally reminded Chuffta not to tell her. He sent her a scornful, wordless thought in reply. She levered herself up, her body protesting and unexpectedly stiff. "I must've slept a long time," she noted, realizing she'd slipped down all but horizontal in Lonen's firm hold.

"Half the day," Lonen agreed, nodding his chin at the sun, which now lowered in the sky ahead of them. Afternoon then, and not morning at all anymore. He raised a challenging brow at her exclamation of dismay. "You needed the rest."

Apparently, but how thoughtless of her. "But you must be starving, and you haven't had a break from riding all this time." Then she caught herself, remembering what happened the last time she encouraged him to take a break.

He lowered his brows, giving her a patient look. "Oria, my love, I've been glued to the saddle without food or rest for far longer than this on campaigns. I hardly noticed."

She rolled her eyes at him, relieved that he wasn't going to castigate her further for what she'd done. "So stalwart and tough, my Destrye warrior."

"I'm glad you finally recognize this truth," he replied solemnly, then grinned when she made a huff of exasperation. "Look." He pointed. "Watch through those trees there."

Peering along the line of his blunt finger, she scanned the forest lining the path. Now that she'd become accustomed to the extraordinary sight of so many trees, tall and dense, covering the landscape in numbers as great as the grains of sand at Bára, she found the forest somewhat frustrating and claustrophobic. You couldn't see anything *but* trees. Their ranks of thick trunks bordered the paths, soaring above on all sides and carving the sky into small pieces. Only when they came to one of the great precipices could she see any distance.

She'd opened her mouth to accuse him of making sport of her when she caught a glimpse of another color between the rows and columns of black trunks and snow-covered ground and branches. There.

Blue.

A blue so vast and bright it reflected like another sky full of sunlight. Like nothing she'd ever seen. Straining her eyes, she searched for another glimpse… Then caught her breath with a joyous wrench of utter shock.

Buttercup had rounded a bend and the vista opened up before them. The forest fell away to either side, the path they followed snaking down a steep hillside, the valley below filled entirely with water.

More water than she'd ever seen in her entire life. More than she'd been able to imagine existed.

"Is it the ocean?" she breathed in wonder.

Lonen laughed, then kissed her hair in apology. "No, my desert lady. It's but a lake. Lake Scandamalion. Not as large as the ones we once had, but the largest that's left—that we know of."

She set aside the wincing guilt that it had been her people who drained the lakes of Dru dry, sucking away the water through tunnels and over time. Hoarding and squandering it, killing the Destrye by slow degrees. "Can we swim in it?" she asked, remembering how Lonen had promised her that.

They'd swum in the water at the oasis—well, he'd swum and she'd waded and floated—but that was nothing compared to the vastness of this lake. A vibration of amusement rumbled in him, though Lonen managed not to laugh out loud this time. Wrapping an arm around her waist and snugging her against him, he pointed toward the hills sloping down toward the water, tracing the line for her while Buttercup stood obediently still.

"See how the snow goes all the way to the water? The lake isn't frozen, but it is snowmelt water—which means it's bitterly cold. You could swim in it—and some like to test themselves that way—but I don't think you would enjoy it."

"No," she agreed fervently, trying to imagine what that might feel like. Back in Bára they'd used ice in drinks, and to freeze fruit sherbets, but it had melted so quickly in the fierce heat that the experience of chill had been fleeting. To immerse in it…

As they watched, Chuffta's small white form soared over the brilliant blue of the lake. Then he folded his wings and dove, spearing into the water.

"Chuffta, no!" she cried.

"*Cold!*" he shouted in her mind, his tone exhilarated. *"There's huge fish in here, too."*

She groaned, shaking her head, and Lonen laughed, urging Buttercup down the switchback path and taking up the reins again. For the most part Buttercup's thoughts reflected the disciplined stoicism of an impeccably trained warhorse, but just then his mind jumped with excitement at the sight of the lake and the tricky, snow-covered path to it. The horse didn't articulate his thoughts with the clear intelligence that Chuffta did, but he was smarter than many other animals. It always interested her that Lonen seemed to know when

Buttercup needed a guiding hand on the reins and when he could be trusted to behave well.

Probably a reflection of Lonen's intuitive nature, which he also employed to gentle her and coax her into behaving well, her body leaping eagerly to his caresses, as well trained as his warhorse and hunting dogs. Thinking of which, she suddenly realized she hadn't thought about craving contact with the mask since she'd awakened. She couldn't decide how she felt about that.

It might be the cowardly choice, but at least for the moment, she decided not to think about it at all.

Lonen regaled her with tales of expeditions to the lake in his youth—a far more carefree era for Dru—and plans to repair and extend the aqueduct network in spring, to bring water to the fields lower down. Neither of them mentioned what had happened to the previous aqueduct the Destrye had labored so hard to build a few short months before. The burn scars along the lakeshore where the wooden structures had been were clearly visible a short distance away. The Trom had burnt them with vicious thoroughness, a maneuver intended only to harm Dru, as Oria's brother Yar, Bára, and Bára's sister cities gained nothing from the move. It wasn't as if the water the Destrye used came out of Báran mouths.

Or did it?

"The tunnels Nolan traveled in, from the lake beneath Bára back to Dru," she wondered, "could they extend to here?"

Lonen halted Buttercup at the water's edge and swung down, holding his arms up for her. "I've thought about that," he replied. Of course he had. Lonen seemed to think of everything far before she did. Bracing herself on his strong forearms, she swung her leg over and he lifted her down as if she weighed nothing. He set her on her feet, but held her there, hands on her waist, a thoughtful expression in his eyes. "I don't think so. Nolan said the tunnels ended north of Arill City, in a region that used to have numerous prairie lakes. For the tunnels to extend all this way, they'd have to travel beneath most of Dru—and go through the granite bedrock of these mountains. Could the Báran sorcerers accomplish such a great feat?"

"I don't know," she admitted. Her knowledge of what the Báran men, even her own father and brothers, could do with their powerful grien magic was woefully thin and riddled with gaping holes. "I didn't know about the tunnels to begin with, or the underground lake beneath the city, until Nolan told us. Before that I would've said no, it couldn't be done, but now I'm not so certain…"

"Could *you* do it, do you think?" He studied her, asking the question in an almost idle tone, but with a certain intensity beneath.

"As a woman, I'm not supposed to be able to wield grien magic at all," she pointed out.

"But we both know you can. Now that you have a store of sgath again, you can maybe channel it into grien, like you did before."

She began to follow his line of thinking. "You want me to bore tunnels through bedrock, to carry water down to the fields. Then the Trom dragons will have nothing to burn."

"It's an ideal solution." His gaze wandered over her face. "If the cost isn't too high."

"With access to the mask, and *practice*," she emphasized, "I should be able to filter the wild magic indefinitely, ordering it into sgath. After that, it would only take time to gradually wear away the rock, I'd think."

He nodded, more confirming something to himself. "Something to consider."

"No sense considering it if you won't let me have the mask." She raised her brows at him, giving him a cold look to make certain he knew she hadn't forgiven him taking control of that.

"I did say we'd have to factor the cost." His hands tightened on her waist, the scar over his eye twisting with a slight tic. "It's not worth your life. Or sanity."

Arrested, she stared at him a moment. "I doubt the stakes are so high. I feel fine."

"I don't know about that." He let her go and turned to survey the lake. "Next summer, when the weather warms, we can come back and you can swim to your heart's content."

"That won't happen if Nolan kills you in a duel for the throne."

"Then I'll have to win."

"And even then, it won't happen unless we can defeat Yar."

"Then we'll do that, too."

"You're so bloody optimistic," she grumbled.

"A good balance for my pretty pessimist." He grinned at her. "See what a great team we make?"

"I see that you deliberately changed the subject."

"Absolutely. Look—Chuffta caught a fish."

"Oh no—Chuffta, let the poor thing go!"

"A big fish! I caught it myself. It's very heavy though." Even his thoughts sounded labored as he flew low over the water toward them, the silvery fish twice the size of Chuffta's body dangling—and flapping, and writhing—in his talons. *"It wants to get away, but it won't. Mine."*

"Let it go. It'll die out of water," she called.

"Yes, it will," Lonen agreed, clapping his hands together. "And will make for fine eating. Good work, Chuffta man."

Chuffta made it to shore and landed heavily, pinning the fish with talons and spread wings, while Lonen grabbed a fist-sized rock and dispatched the fish. Gorge rising, Oria turned away, focusing on the deceptively peaceful and lovely scenery.

"We have food," she pointed out, not looking, though the predatory glee of Chuffta's thoughts and the pleased anticipation of Lonen's kept her apprised of their actions. Both meat-eaters, the pair of them at least shared that hunter's excitement in the catch. At least the fish didn't have emotions, not that she could sense. This was, no doubt, why the magic-users of Bára had been vegetarians for generations. Though her brother Yar had killed human beings without seeming at all affected by it.

"We have some food, yes, but we don't have a fresh stardew," Lonen replied. "Here Chuffta, keep your snout clear of my knife or I'll nick you. The entrails are all yours once I get them out. More important," he said to Oria, "this will make a fine gift for my mother, and should go a long way toward putting her in the right frame of mind."

"And what is the right frame of mind?" Oria muttered the question mostly to herself.

"Generous," Lonen answered, in the same tone.

She wandered along the lakeshore, moving away from the impromptu slaughter—and Chuffta's carnivorous satisfaction. Of course she'd always fed him meat of various kinds, as that was his nature, but in Bára his meals had been delivered in innocuous bites arranged on platters. He'd only started killing for food since they left Bára, with the exception of his occasional youthful lapse. It shouldn't bother her, as she'd been the one to put him in this position. But the predatory glee in him felt something like the vicious killing rages of the Trom dragons.

"The dragons don't eat their kill," Chuffta said with implacable logic. *"They only burn and destroy. Totally different."*

She sent him an affectionate thought, tucking her doubt where he couldn't sense it. Was this how Lonen felt about her—this wary uncertainty? She loved Chuffta without reservation, but the glimpses of the monstrous in him unsettled her. Squatting down, she pulled off her glove and dipped her fingers in the water, startling a little at the biting chill. No wonder Lonen had laughed at her for suggesting they swim. Determinedly she sunk her hand in the water to the wrist, holding it there. If the fire-loving Chuffta could stand to immerse in it, she could take that much discomfort.

She sensed his approach before she heard him. For a big man, he had a habitual warrior's stealth. Lonen crouched beside her, saying nothing for a moment. "Is this a sorceress thing?" he finally asked, quietly, as if taking care not to disturb her.

Glancing at him, she took him in, so robust and in his element here. Without the responsibilities of kingship, he'd relaxed. The chill breeze had his cheeks rosy over the dark beard, and his gray eyes sparkled with spirit. Her hand had gone numb—so interesting—so she lifted it out of the water and shook the droplets off. The cold had made her pale skin even whiter, and the veins stood out blue. "Just testing what I can withstand."

"I think you've passed plenty of tests of strength of will," he noted with a wry smile.

"Have I?" She wiggled her fingers, which felt stiff and not like her own. "This isn't that difficult, once you get over the initial shock—it just goes numb."

He considered her, gaze thoughtful. "It's the easiest death, the Destrye say, to freeze. Some commit suicide that way—going off into the winter. They say that once you get cold enough, you start to feel warm and sleepy. You fall asleep and..." He tipped his head, studying her. "Never wake up again."

A wordless silence fell between them and she wasn't quite sure what they were saying to each other in this odd conversation.

"I have the fish packed up in snow," he finally said, "but if we want it to be fresh, we should leave soon. Plus the sun is going down and it will be getting dark, which brings predators I'd rather not face without a bigger force than ours. If you're ready."

Standing and pulling on her glove again, she nodded.

~ 4 ~

ORIA WAS OMINOUSLY silent. Of course, she tended to be a quiet person, expressing her restless curiosity in movement rather than volubility. Though she'd told him stories about her difficulties in Bára, about not being able to meditate or exhibit the weird, expressionless state they called *hwil*, Oria had more evident calm and emotional reserve than she seemed to realize. Certainly far more than the most controlled Destrye woman exhibited.

Oria had developed that reserve and used it like a shield that she retreated behind when she was displeased with him. He didn't know much about marriage—or women, really, since his relationship with Natly had been of an entirely different flavor—but he and Oria seemed to be growing farther apart rather than coming to know each other better. He'd thought if he could find ways for them to have sex, that the emotional and physical intimacy would bring them closer together. Instead, he seemed to be losing connection to her. As if with each layer of reserve he peeled away, she compensated by withdrawing behind other walls.

Like now. No time or opportunity to really deal with it, much as he'd like to broach the topic, because he hadn't exaggerated the dangers the approach of nightfall brought. He hadn't wanted to frighten her, but packs of wolves did prowl the mountains and his mother's hermitage still lay a distance off. Quite a distance, judging by the landmarks. Farther than he'd recalled. It had been so long since he'd made this journey, with so much happening in the interim.

Hopefully he hadn't badly miscalculated and put them in danger.

As if evoked by his thoughts, a wolf's eerie, hair-raising howl echoed through the dimming twilight. Buttercup danced restively, too well-trained to spook, but not complacent either. The warhorse had been raised in this area and knew that sound. Keeping his seat solid, his hands soft on the reins, Lonen flexed his calves in a signal to Buttercup. Were it only the two of them, this could be handled. Not easily, but he and Buttercup knew this sort of fight. Having Oria there changed everything.

The howl rang out again, joined by several more. Drawing closer. Wonderful.

"The wolves are that dangerous?" Oria asked softly, as if the creatures could overhear.

"I've fought them before. Nothing I can't handle," he assured her.

"I can feel your tension and anxiety, Lonen. Don't lie to me." She said it in that quiet tone, but the accusation stung. Nothing like having a wife who could read your mind.

"I didn't mean to lie, only to reassure you." The howls came from the side and—Arill curse them—from ahead. The wily creatures were outflanking them.

"If we're going to be a team, as you're always poking at me about, then you have to trust me to handle the truth," she replied, still sounding distant.

She had a point there. Perhaps that lay at the root of the barrier between them. They'd been coming closer to mutual trust, but then they found the mask and… With a mental wince he accepted that he might be the one creating that distance. "I'm not as civilized as I'd like sometimes," he admitted, squeezing an arm around her waist before reaching for his battle-axe. "Part of me is still the barbarian who'd like to wrap you up and keep you safe."

She glanced over her shoulder, her expression taking life with a soft—even affectionate—smile. "Will you throw me over your shoulder and outrun the wolves?"

"Tempting." The howls drew nearer, ringing them. "Though Buttercup can run faster than I can, and the wolves have us surrounded."

"Then we fight," she replied, as if suggesting a cup of tea.

"Or you could stay on Buttercup and escape while I hold them off," he countered, though without much hope.

"Oh no you don't." She twisted more fully, eyes flashing in the low light. "The last time you pulled that you ended up gutted by golems. You have me and you have Chuffta. Consider this practice for the duel."

It would be nice to practice as a fighting team without having their lives on the line, he thought sourly to himself, but he only nodded. "What does Chuffta say?"

The white form of the flying lizard winged through the deeply shadowed forest off to their left. "He sees ten wolves—three ahead, two behind, three to the left, two to the right. Ah, another ahead, so eleven."

Handy, he had to admit. "Can you feel the wolves' minds?"

She paused, disconcerted. "I can try."

He smiled to himself, pleased to have pointed out something she hadn't thought of. After a moment, she shook her head. "I can sense them, but remotely. To get a feel for the mind inside, I think I'd have to touch them, at least the first time getting to know them."

"That won't happen." Not while he had breath in his body. With a flex of his thighs, he halted Buttercup at a decent clearing—just wide enough for the horse to be able to maneuver, but ringed with dense trees that should funnel the approach of the wolves into a few directions. "What about defensive magic?"

"I suppose this is a good time to try." She sounded not entirely certain.

"Sometimes pressure brings out the best in us."

"I don't know what I'm doing, Lonen. I have no skill with grien magic."

"Blunt weapons work, too. Do what you can. Otherwise, don't worry about it."

Surprisingly she laughed. "Chuffta is eager to assist with fire. He's all excited."

"Tell him to burn away. I'll fight them best from the saddle. I'm used to avoiding Buttercup's head and neck. Be a burr and lie low against his neck."

"I could dismount."

The image of her on the ground, savaged by wolves, nearly stopped his heart. "No. You stay on, no matter what happens. Last resort, we run for it."

A howl pierced the forest twilight gloom, sounding like it was at his elbow. "Down!" he ordered. Buttercup, in full battle mode, spun at the flex of his knee and he swung his axe in an arc aided by the stallion's momentum—rewarded by the bite of iron into flesh and the pained yip of the wolf.

It dashed back. Just the scout, testing if they'd be easy prey. Yellow eyeshine glowed from the shadows ringing them, and he sent mental thanks to Chuffta for the count—otherwise his fear and the tricks of light might've made him certain there were far more.

Buttercup turned a tight circle, guarding all flanks. Three wolves charged at once. The horse reared, striking with iron-shod hooves, catching one wolf on the jaw and sending it flying. The other two struck in a well-timed pincer. Lonen got one in a solid, killing blow, but the other managed to sink teeth into the stallion's hind leg, attempting to hamstring him. Buttercup whirled, shaking it, and Lonen swung, sadly missing.

Four more wolves darted in on the open side, one going for the other hamstring, while several circled out and around, preparing to pounce at best opportunity. Too clever by half, using their numbers to worry them to death.

Chuffta's flame split the darkness, the green fire blinding as he swooped over the wolves, setting them alight. The agonized shrieking of the wolves rose with the stench of burnt fur and flesh.

Oria, always so sensitive to the suffering of others, moaned. He made himself ignore her, unable to afford any distraction. Buttercup threw down his head, shoulders bunching, and punched out a double-mule kick, sending a snarling wolf into a tree.

Lonen barely registered that it fell limp, though one remote part of his mind ticked off the tally. One dead. Three down. Seven to go.

He blurred into battle mode, he and Buttercup working seamlessly to spin, hack, strike, slice, bite. And Chuffta became part of the deadly dance, swooping in before and behind the sharp edges of axe and hooves, blinding the wolves with fire, driving them back.

Two dead. Four down. Five to go. Slowly but surely.

When a wolf caught the edge of Chuffta's wing, he knew it by Oria's scream.

She'd been so good, clinging to the warhorse's neck through all the stallion's twists, bucks and rearing strikes, as if she'd been born to riding. But now she sat up, lunging for her Familiar, overbalancing them.

"No!" Lonen thundered, dropping the reins to hold her in place. She thrashed in his arms like a wild thing as Chuffta went down, yanked to the ground by the snapping wolves, another pouncing to join the fray.

Oria shrieked wordlessly, but he held her with ruthless determination, urging Buttercup to attack. The stallion seized one wolf with his blunt teeth, immediately sinking his weight back. What the warhorse lacked in a piercing bite, he more than made up in sheer leverage. The wolf gave an agonized yelp, flying past them, abruptly silenced as Lonen ended it with a sweep of his axe.

Three dead. Four down. Four to go.

A wolf fastened on Buttercup's hind leg and the horse lurched. The one wolf still stood on Chuffta, snapping its jaws down as it dodged flame. Two wolves circled them, prowling closer, and another got up to join them, not dead yet, curse it.

Two dead. Three down. Five to go.

Lonen swung the axe back, trying to dislodge the wolf from

Buttercup's leg. If it managed to hamstring the horse, they'd all go down with Chuffta. The stallion kicked, ineffectively. Oria still reached for Chuffta, screaming words in Báran now, such was her panic.

Too many targets. He couldn't fight every front. Chuffta might be lost, but he could still save at least Oria. Taking the risk, he wormed the hand holding her inside her clothes, the bare skin of her thigh above her stockings the most accessible. Steeling himself, he laid his bare hand on her skin and gripped hard.

Her scream froze his blood. Ruthlessly, he held on, resisting the reflex to let go. Until she sagged, weakened by the impact of his skin on hers. Thrusting the reins into her unresisting hands, he kicked an attacking wolf and swung down, killing it with a downward blow.

Four dead. Three down. Four to go.

Bashing it over the skull with the flat of the axe, he knocked the wolf off Buttercup's leg.

Four dead. Four down. Three to go.

"Go!" he shouted. Buttercup's haunches bunched as the horse leapt to obey. A wolf launched itself at Lonen's arm, fastening on with vising jaws. One on him, one on Chuffta. Where was the other?

Buttercup swung around. Oria's hood had fallen back, her hair sweeping in a banner of bright copper in the dying light.

"Run!" he howled.

"I. Will. Not."

And a strange hush ensued, as if time itself paused.

He could see it all. The wolf at his feet. Seven others on the ground. One on his arm. One on Chuffta.

One leaping for Oria.

Too far. Too late. Too slow.

Her magic filled the glen like a bore tide, crackling and crowding out the air. The trees seemed to bunch and shudder, drawing in as if inhaling. Then a storm blew out, a tornado of wind throwing him against a tree with stunning force. The wolf on him dislodged, taking a chunk of something with it. With a snarl, Lonen managed to bring his axe down, cutting its head off.

Five dead… He'd lost track of the rest.

Whirling, he lunged for Oria's last location—and found her crouched on the ground, Chuffta's limp form before her. Buttercup stood over her in guard position. Good steed. And the wolves… all limp carcasses. None moved.

Oria wept with heartbreaking sobs.

He forced himself to her side, his knees giving way, painfully smacking as they hit the hard-frozen ground. A distant part of him recognized with grim amusement that he could notice that minor pain when he felt nothing from his other, far more serious wounds.

"I can't hear him at all." Oria was sobbing so hard that he could barely make out the words. Her hands shook violently as they ran over Chuffta's limp and bloody form. "I've lost him. He's gone and I'm all alone."

It was the grief and fear talking, so he set aside the stab of injury at her careless words. "Oria, love." He rubbed a hand over her back, scanning the small clearing for movement, the black depths of the forest for eyeshine. "We have to move."

She turned on him, face contorted with tears. "Do you feel *nothing*?" she hissed, the words sharp as daggers.

"What I feel isn't relevant," he bit out, trying for calm. "We can't save Chuffta if we're all dead and if we stay here, we will be. Blood calls to predators and scavengers alike. We're hurt, weak, and vulnerable. Now gather up Chuffta and let's go."

"Why does it matter? He's dead."

He would've snapped back if she didn't sound so broken. For all Oria had been through, she'd still experienced so little of the hard blows the violent world dealt with abandon. It had been a long time since he wept over a fallen comrade. Later, he'd mourn Chuffta— but he'd learned to save the luxury of grief for safety. And not to declare death too hastily.

"Can you hear Chuffta when he's sleeping?" he asked, knowing the answer, but walking her through it with all the patience he could muster.

Oria blinked at him, eyes wide and owlish in her pale face, almost a hint of eyeshine in them, though human eyes didn't do that. His sorceress wasn't entirely human, however, so maybe…

"Well," she said slowly. "Usually there's *something*, but sometimes I don't."

"Gather him up, love," he urged gently. "Wrap him inside your cloak and keep him warm. He may yet survive."

She moved so hastily then that he might've laughed, had their circumstances been less dire. Climbing to his feet with a groan for how much he'd stiffened up even during the short stint on the cold ground, he hung his axe on the saddle and ran hands over Buttercup's haunch where the wolf had bitten. Blood—and the stallion stomped when he probed the tendon—but he seemed sound enough to ride. Good thing, as walking would see them finished off, no doubt.

Oria moved next to him, Chuffta in her arms under her shadow-cat fur cloak. "Ready?" he asked. When she nodded, he lifted her onto Buttercup's back, grunting as his left arm nearly gave.

Oria caught herself, settled, and looked at him, her face pinched with concern. "You're hurt. I forgot."

"Nothing mortal," he assured her, swinging up behind her and sending the stallion into a fast clip up the trail in the same movement. Not a gallop or canter as the warhorse couldn't sustain that for the remaining distance, but a fast trot. "I'm more concerned about Buttercup. Anything you can tell me about how he's doing?"

She was quiet a moment. "He's hurt, too," she replied, sounding chagrined. "His hind leg pains him, and he's very angry. He's mostly picturing stomping on wolves."

"Can he make it?"

"He says he'll never let you down." She had an odd sound to her voice, kind of choked.

"Chuffta will be all right," he promised recklessly.

"It's not that." She swiped at her face. "I mean, it *is* that. I've never been through that, him crying for help in my head, and I felt his pain…" She trailed off. Took a deep, ragged breath. "I'm so angry with myself for letting *you* down. I utterly failed back there."

His heart squeezed, and he wrapped his good arm around her. "No, love. You did well."

"I panicked. I lost objectivity and just… lost control."

"You've never been in a fight like that before."

"How can you always forgive me?" She sounded almost exasperated, making him laugh.

"First, there's nothing to forgive. Second, I love you."

She sighed. "I'm not at all sure I deserve it, Lonen."

"That's the miraculous thing about love," he replied easily, pressing his lips to her hair. "It's there whether we deserve it or not." It felt good to say that to her, to remind himself of that truth. They could build trust over time, as long as the love remained.

She didn't reply and they rode a while in silence. She was sinking into a fugue of worry over Chuffta. He knew how that went, how the grief and despair could suck you under.

"What did you do?" he asked her, mostly to keep her talking. She'd used her grien magic in a different way—though still related to trees. Every bit of her grien magic that he could recall related to trees or plants, come to think of it.

"Do?" she sounded vague again, startled out of deep thought.

"Your magic—you did something to knock all the wolves down." And himself, too, though he didn't add that, as she'd only feel bad about it. The echo of those bruises throbbed through his spine.

"Oh." She shivered a little. "I'd kind of… forgotten."

A chill crept over him, too. Her magic hadn't been like this before, with the forgetting and losing herself. That foul mask played a part in it, no doubt.

"I was so afraid," Oria continued. "Chuffta was shrieking in my mind, calling me to help him, and I felt so helpless. And the wolf had you. I wanted them all to go away, just go away and leave us."

She sounded so afraid and tenuous, almost childlike, that he laughed, hoping the sound would hearten her. Smoothing a hand over her shining hair, he kissed it again. "You certainly accomplished that."

"What was it like?" she asked, after a long hesitation.

Surprised she didn't know, he chose his words carefully. It was tempting to gloss it, but that wouldn't help her learn the truth of her abilities. "Like time paused and all the trees inhaled, then blew out their breath all at once, in a fury."

She didn't reply to that, seeming to shrink inside herself.

"Oria?"

"That sounds so… unnatural."

Maybe he'd erred in describing it to her. "I recall at the battle of Bára that one of the sorcerers made tornados. Maybe that's how they start."

"That's right. I wonder if that's how it feels from the inside."

"Perhaps so."

Buttercup had begun to limp. The great-hearted horse couldn't carry them much longer. Had Lonen been alone, he would've walked. As it was, he might have to jog alongside, to keep up the speed. He could force himself to keep going that long, surely.

Just as he'd determined he'd have to, he caught sight of lights up ahead. Never had he thought he'd greet the sight of his mother's house with such a rush of sheer happiness.

"We're almost there," he said, to Oria, and to Buttercup, patting the horse's flank. "Only a bit farther, buddy, and you'll be in a nice warm stall with a pretty girl to tend your wounds."

Buttercup had his ears perked forward, picking up his already punishing pace with all the spring of a horse scenting food and rest.

"Your mother has girls as grooms?" Oria asked.

"My mother lives entirely with other women. Can you feel anything from Chuffta?"

"No, but he's still warm and flexible, so maybe he lives. I wish I knew more of how to tell. Even if he's alive, I don't know how to heal him." Her voice went ragged at the end.

"No worries there," he cuddled her close. "My mother will."

"Just who *is* your mother?" Oria wanted to know, sounding bewildered. They came around the bend in the path, and the hermitage stood before them, a single white candle alight in every one of the many windows. The double front doors opened wide, and rows of young women and girls spilled out, each carrying a lit candle, robes white as the snow that lay smooth and pristine all around the manse. A tall figure walked between them, her dark hair trailing on the snow behind her like a train.

"The question is," she called out in stern tones, "who are you, foreign sorceress?"

"Mother," Lonen called, wishing heartily that they'd arrived in better condition for this. "I'd like you to meet Oria. My wife, and Queen of the Destrye."

~ 5 ~

Lonen's mother gave Oria a long, hard stare. "Odd," she commented with a blandness that didn't fool Oria for a moment, "I believed I retained the title of Queen of the Destrye."

Oria had never met Lonen's father, the late King Archimago—she'd only ever glimpsed him from the height of her tower—but the family resemblance to her son clearly shone in this woman's face. Tall, with broad cheekbones like Lonen, she possessed the same level gaze, granite in feel, though Oria couldn't make out the color from this distance. Her dark hair, like her son's, though glinting with silver threads, flowed thick and full down her back. If it hadn't been so long—and Oria hadn't imagined anyone could grow their hair to such an extreme—it would have rioted in curls as Lonen's did.

Lonen sighed. With him behind her, wrapped around her, she felt it, though he kept it inaudible.

"You were the first to teach me that people change and that crowns move from one person to the next," he called back, his words fraught with meaning beneath the surface. Buttercup had halted and they moved no closer, though she knew both man and horse trembled on the edge of fatigue.

There was some line in the snow-covered yard that Lonen observed—and waited for the invitation to cross. Chuffta lay limp as old lettuce in her arms. Not since she was a little girl had she not felt him in her mind at all. The loss left a hole in her, a shivering aloneness that ached with an almost physical pain. After her devastating loss of composure during the fight with the wolves, she hadn't wanted to belabor her grief aloud to Lonen, but her control frayed at the edges. She had no patience for pettiness at the moment.

"Is that why you've come at last, my prodigal son?" Lonen's mother asked, lightly mocking. "All this time you haven't bothered to visit. Now I perceive you're only here to inform me that I've been replaced."

"You accuse me of recklessness, still? I am a man grown, and king."

"How could I know?" she replied in that lofty voice. "You might as well be a stranger to me."

Oria felt Lonen set his teeth, the frustrated roil of his thoughts palpable. "Surely we could have this conversation in private, Mother," he answered. "In the warmth. I brought you a gift of a stardew. Or will you deny us your hospitality?"

She raised her brows, the dark wings of feigned astonishment clear in the candlelight. "You came equipped with a bribe? I can't decide if you've finally learned manners or if this is an example of improved political calculation."

Lonen growled deep in his chest, still unlikely to be audible to anyone but her. He also flinched emotionally, the barb hitting its target with the accuracy only close family could muster.

Oria had had enough.

"Your Highness," she called out. "I am indeed foreign and don't fully understand the ways of the Destrye, but where I come from, we don't leave anyone, let alone family, standing out in the cold, especially when they are exhausted, hungry, and injured. Snub me if you find it warranted, but your son comes to you with an open heart. You complain he hasn't visited. He's visiting now, and it seems you are intent on refusing the very thing you claim you've wanted."

The dowager queen's gaze landed on Oria again. The distance didn't allow for a good scan of the woman's emotions, but Oria might've detected a hint of surprise—and grudging respect?

"At least you didn't marry that ninny, Natly," she replied. "Come in then, and be welcome at my hearth."

Buttercup, as if understanding the words, immediately moved forward. "Nicely played," Lonen murmured in her ear.

"You could've warned me she'd be like this," she muttered back.

"I never know what she'll be like," he countered enigmatically, then halted Buttercup at the foot of the stairs leading up to the enormous house. Oria had never seen a structure so large made entirely of wood. Not even Arill's Temple. The manse seemed like it should fall over, but the edifice gave the impression of age and solidity.

One of the young women in the white robes handed her candle to her neighbor, curtseyed to Lonen, and held out a hand, keeping it a safe distance from Buttercup. "May I, Your Highness?"

"Please." Lonen swung down and handed her the reins, giving the subtle signal for Buttercup to regard her as a friend. Or so Oria assumed—mostly she heard Buttercup's suspicious alert relax, and the hurt and exhaustion creep over his mind. "He's injured," Lonen continued, taking a hold of Oria by the waist and lifting her down, then snagging his axe, "though not too badly, I think."

Another young woman stepped up, bringing her candle. "I'll assist, Your Highness, and will bring in the packs."

"What happened?" The queen mother asked, waving the women on.

"We were attacked by black wolves not far from here."

"How many?" Her face sharpened with concern. Not as indifferent as she'd hoped to appear then. She turned and gestured them to accompany her inside. "And where?"

"Eleven. About an hour's fast ride."

Had it only been an hour? It had felt like forever. The cloistered warmth of the manse wrapped around them like a cloak, a vast fireplace in a large room clearly meant for receiving visitors emitted a blast of welcome heat. With a pang that felt far too much like mourning, Oria imagined Chuffta delightedly winging toward it.

"You fought off eleven wolves by yourself?" His mother sounded astonished. "Tell me—"

"I'd like to, and I will"—Lonen cut her off—"but we have a pressing problem for you."

"For me?"

"Show her, Oria." When she hesitated, he smoothed a hand over her hair. "You can trust her."

Oria highly doubted that, but she pushed the cloak back over her shoulders and presented Chuffta to the imperious woman. Devoid of his liveliness, the white scales not shimmering but dulled and spattered with blood, her Familiar looked much smaller than usual, limp in the cradle of her arms. She'd managed to fold his wings in before she gathered him up as Lonen had bade her, making sure the slender bones wouldn't pierce the soft, leathery skin, though she thought at least two were broken.

"Is that… a derkesthai?" In her hushed question, in her softening expression, wonder bloomed—and along with it a hint of a genuine woman under the cool exterior.

"Yes," Oria replied, relief along with the surprise. "He's my Familiar and a valued companion. Can you help him?"

"I can try, though I haven't seen a derkesthai in ages."

"I'm surprised you've seen one at all," Lonen commented.

His mother shot him an unamused smile. "Which only proves how little you know about me. Bring your Familiar in here."

She led them through the reception hall and through a doorway into a much smaller room, also furnished as a sort of parlor. With chairs, shelves of books, and another fireplace—though unlit at the moment—it looked to be a place for people to sit quietly. They moved right through it and into yet another room through a door on the opposite wall.

"No weapons in here," she directed, and Lonen didn't protest, leaving his battle-axe outside the door, leaning it against the wall blade-end down.

This room looked like it could be used for cooking, or perhaps some other craft that required clean surfaces. A large table sat in the center of the space, with no chairs, and taller than one useful for sitting. Lonen's mother nodded her head at it and went to gather tools from a far counter. "Lay him on there. I apologize that it's cool in this room."

As if summoned, another of the white-robed young women entered quietly and lit the fire already set in the fireplace at one end of the room. Just as unobtrusively, she left again.

Oria laid Chuffta, so fragile and nearly boneless, on the glazed surface of the table. The green of his eyes showed dully through his thin lids, more the color of the unripe olives from home, rather than the bright shine of new apples. She caught the sob rising in her throat, and Lonen put his hands on her shoulders, drawing her back against his strong body.

"Easy, love," he murmured. "My mother is the best there is."

His mother returned to them just then, flicking him a wry glance from eyes that were indeed the same shade of gray, and just as lushly lashed in black. They shone with incisive intelligence from a face far too imposing to be called pretty. She coiled up her hair with deft and practiced hands, pinning it with several sharp picks. The healers at Arill's Temple had used some sort of intuitive magic to assess wounds, but Vycayla turned to a tray of strange-looking instruments. She inserted something into her ears with long tubes that extended to a disk that she placed on Chuffta's little chest. Moving it around several times, intently listening, she made a hmming noise.

"Is he… dead?" Oria asked, needing to know, even as she dreaded the words. "Your Highness," she added hastily, hoping she hadn't further offended the woman in her anxiety.

"Call me Vycayla. And no, he's not dead, …" She raised her brows at Lonen. "Did you bother to name this sorceress bride you captured?"

Oria didn't wait for Lonen to reply, riding on indignation and a rush of relief at the news. "My name is Oria, and I give you leave to address me by it. And I was not captured but married Lonen willingly, out of duty to my people and obligation to the Destrye. I don't believe I've given you cause to insult me by implying otherwise."

"Prickly. And arrogant. Perhaps unwise, as I'm treating your Familiar." Vycayla's gaze passed over her, reassessing, then flicked to Lonen. "I like her."

"I'm relieved," Lonen replied, even more drily. Oria began to understand his attitude about his mother.

"He seems to be in a deep sleep. Alive, but with a lowered heart rate and respiration. Possibly a healing mode." Vycayla spoke in a dispassionate tone, her hands moving with professional expertise over Chuffta's body. She lifted her gaze to Oria's. "Is this something characteristic of derkesthai?"

"I don't know. He's never been injured before," Oria replied, feeling stiff in her embarrassment and ignorance.

Vycayla made a noncommittal sound, exactly like Lonen's. "Some internal damage, though light. The worst is these broken wing bones. I can set them so they'll heal cleanly, then treat him to accelerate the overall convalescence. For now I'll give him a bit of strength and let him rest, so he'll be in a better state for me to work on him."

"Thank you," Oria said with quiet fervor. "What is your price?"

Vycayla raised an amused brow. "Are you truly a sorceress?"

Lonen squeezed Oria's shoulders in some kind of warning, but she didn't see any reason to prevaricate. "Yes." She also wouldn't qualify it. Whatever she'd done in the forest, she could do again. And she'd pay any price to save Chuffta. She'd give herself over to the mask—even if she had to fight Lonen.

"Then I'll think of something appropriate you can do for me." A misty gray light glowed around Vycayla's hands, and Chuffta seemed to absorb it, his color moving closer to his usual iridescence.

When Baeltya, the junior healer back at Arill City, had treated Lonen, Oria hadn't been able to detect the flow of magic. She still sensed nothing magical, but seeing that light was new. "Are you an acolyte of Arill?" she asked, beyond curious. Behind her, Lonen choked a little, swallowing it down and squeezing her shoulders again.

Vycayla, hands still on Chuffta, gave her an arch look without lifting her head, the flash of silvery gray through her lashes almost predatory. "The Queen of the Destrye is the head of Arill's Temple. You don't know much, do you?"

"About Dru and the Destrye, no," Oria replied evenly. "Though I dare say I know more about your people than you do about mine."

"You dare a great deal, indeed," Vycayla said, straightening and rubbing her hands together, her penetrating gaze studying Oria.

"Mother, the customs of Oria's people—" Lonen started to say, but Vycayla cut him off, sharp eyes never leaving Oria's face.

"Don't let your husband speak for you," she advised. "If you're to be Queen of the Destrye, you must speak for yourself. And stand on your own feet."

Oria shrugged off Lonen's restraining grip. Loath though she might be to do what his mother commanded, she also didn't need to be seen as weak. It was a valid point. "Surely there's a difference between enjoying the support of the man who loves me and leaning on him."

"Is there?" Vycayla shook her head slightly. "I don't agree." Despite her sharp tone, she picked up Chuffta with infinite gentleness and carried him to a basket before the fire. "There, sir. This will warm you. All right," she continued briskly as she returned, "strip off your shirt, son of mine, so I may see to your injuries."

"Yes, Mother," he answered, his voice as wry as the look he gave Oria. Another she couldn't quite interpret. He untied his cloak, fumbling a bit as his left arm hitched. Oria moved to help him, and he gave her a soft smile. She laid the cloak over a chair, then helped him pull the leather shirt over his head. Vycayla watched, not moving to assist, though Lonen had to bend over considerably for Oria to get the thing off. It was a frustrating exercise, but they managed. Oria smoothed her hair out of her face and took a look at Lonen, her mouth falling open at the sight of his ravaged arm.

"Lonen," she gasped in dismay.

"Better my arm than my throat—or yours, love." He gave her an affectionate smile and hitched himself onto the table, where his mother, apparently unmoved, brought a basin of warmed water and began washing the wound.

"Be still," she told him, though he hadn't so much as flinched, then patted him on the cheek, showing the first glimmer of maternal affection. "And be quiet. I have questions for your wife."

When she turned away briefly to rinse the bloody cloth in the basin, Lonen rolled his eyes at Oria and grinned in encouragement. He'd paled, however, the glassiness of pain and blood loss in his eyes. Oria still held his leather shirt and the softer one he'd worn beneath, heavy with the blood it had soaked up. She put them both aside, feeling a little woozy. Better sit before she fell over. Taking a chair by the fire, she sat where she could keep an eye on both her Familiar and her husband. "Questions?" she prompted.

"Who are your people, exactly?"

"I come from Bára. I'm the only daughter and third child of Queen Rhianna and the late King Tavlor."

"So you are the enemy," Vycayla noted, her attention on Lonen's wound.

"Bára and Dru have been enemies, yes," Oria replied evenly, though the subject wearied her. "I never fought, personally. When the Destrye armies attacked Bára, my father was killed, along with my two elder brothers. As the next in line for the throne, I negotiated a peace with Dru."

"Then why aren't you Queen of Bára?"

Oria bit back a sigh, watching Chuffta for any signs of waking. She dearly missed his sardonic commentary. "It's a long and complicated tale, but suffice to say my style of sorcery was not approved by our city elders and I was exiled. As I'd already married Lonen as part of our peace treaty, I traveled with him to Dru."

"Who's on the throne in Bára then?"

"My brother Yar."

"I gather from your tone that you don't approve."

Oria had thought she'd spoken quite neutrally, but no sense mincing words. "I don't. He's self-centered and emotionally unstable, especially since he contaminated his magic by summoning the Trom—the creatures riding the dragons that ravaged Dru last autumn. Even if he hadn't vowed to destroy Dru entirely, he wouldn't be a good king for Bára."

Vycayla threaded a needle and began stitching Lonen's wounds. He stared steadfastly at the wall before him, showing no reaction, though surely it hurt.

"You married Lonen before you came to Dru?"

"Yes, in the temple at Bára, according to the ways of my people." Oria waited for it.

Vycayla straightened, staring her son in the eye. "You haven't married this girl in Arill's Temple?"

Lonen gazed back. "Am I allowed to speak?"

His mother narrowed her eyes. "Don't be cheeky with me. You may be King of the Destrye, but I changed your diapers."

"Or handed me to a servant to do it," he replied gravely, then burst out laughing at the look on her face. "All right, all right. No, we haven't married under Arill's hand because we need a sponsor. Nolan has challenged me for the throne, and Arnon is his second. For Oria to serve as my second and then to be queen, we need to marry under Arill also."

"So *that* is why you've visited me at last."

"Yes."

"Self-serving to the end."

"I didn't think I'd be welcome without a compelling reason."

"You wouldn't have been," she snapped back.

Lonen only gazed back calmly. With the two of them nearly nose to nose, they were so obviously alike in almost every way.

Except that Vycayla seemed to entirely lack Lonen's sense of humor or sunny outlook.

"On what grounds does Nolan challenge you?" she asked, going back to work with her needle.

Lonen grimaced—though for the pain or the forthcoming duel, Oria wasn't sure. "He believes I'm an inadequate king, that I allowed the Destrye to starve, and that I've failed to defend Dru." He left out the accusations that Lonen had been enchanted by Oria and wasn't in his right mind. Probably wise.

Vycayla snorted, a most unladylike sound at odds with her severe appearance. Perhaps she did possess some of the same humor. "What would Nolan have had you do—throw yourself bodily over the crops and aqueducts so the Trom dragons couldn't burn them?"

For a hermit far removed from the politics of Dru, Vycayla seemed to know a great deal about them. "He also disapproves of Oria and opposes having her as queen," he added carefully.

Vycayla glanced at her, but returned her attention to Lonen. "He'd send Oria back to the people that exiled her?"

"He suggested that I keep Oria as a concubine, spoils of war as the old traditions dictate, and take Natly as wife instead." Lonen spoke easily enough, but watched his mother closely. None of this conversation had been accidental then. He'd been carefully managing how his mother heard the tale.

Vycayla paused as she processed that, then she glared at Lonen. "Your brother said this."

"In front of witnesses."

"And Arnon supports him."

"Arnon had little choice unless he wanted to openly defy his elder brother."

"Hmm." Vycayla continued stitching with meticulous patience, but her posture revealed her anger. "Would Nolan drag the Destrye back to being barbarians in every way?"

Lonen smiled, glancing at Oria, satisfaction in his gaze.

"What is Nolan's plan to fight the Trom and the dragons when they return, especially if our Báran sorceress is unhappily enslaved rather than being Queen of Dru as you promised her?"

"Nolan doesn't believe they will return."

Vycayla stopped, utterly astonished. "Did that fall rattle his brains? Perhaps I should be treating him."

Lonen laughed. "You know Nolan was ever one for seeing only what's in front of him. He can deal with trees well enough, but he will never believe there's a forest unless you can show him where it begins and ends."

"Hmm," Vycayla grunted noncommittally again, slathering some salve on the wound. "I thought he might gain wisdom over time, but apparently not. Whereas as *you*, my careless, feckless boy, have grown into quite a bit more of a measured man than I ever anticipated."

"Why, thank you, Mother. I love you, too."

She glared at him, but this time Oria saw the love in it. "So, that's your plan? Drag me back to Arill City—where you know I never intended to return—so you can marry Oria, win the duel, and secure the throne. Then what?"

"We haven't made exact plans," he temporized. "We've had many things to deal with," he added defensively when Vycayla raised one eyebrow at him.

"Left yourself open to Nolan there, my boy," she said. "Unwise."

"Lonen couldn't make a definite plan until we knew if I could wield magic outside of Bára," Oria inserted, pushing to her feet. "Now we know I can." She threw Lonen a defiant look when he scowled. She *would* use the mask, to save them all.

"You're quite the tiger," Vycayla commented, "defending this warrior brute of a son from his little old mother."

Oria gasped out an incredulous laugh before she could restrain herself.

Fortunately, Vycayla's eyes glittered with appreciation. "You need a plan," she said to them both.

Lonen opened his mouth, but Oria stepped forward. "Once Lonen is secure on the throne of Dru, we'll set the strategy to retake Bára in the spring."

~ 6 ~

Before that moment, Lonen would've sworn that his wife and his mother were nothing alike. Now he gaped at Oria, slim and pale, her hair shining in the firelight and spilling in rivers of molten copper over the shadowcat fur. Large in her exotically beautiful and piquant face, her eyes shone with determination as she voiced this plan they'd never discussed.

"Retake Bára," he echoed, striving not to make it sound like a question.

She returned his stare evenly, tension in the delicate line of her jaw. "It's the only solution that makes sense. We have to remove the threat at the source. Otherwise we'll be forever defending Dru from Bára—and the Destrye will be absorbing all of the losses. We have to take the battle back to them. Strike them before they attack us, as your father did before you."

His mother grimaced. "The old fool."

Oria looked shocked, but his mother didn't fool him. "He missed you every day, too."

"Yes, well, I never said he didn't have excellent taste." She blinked back moisture and looked him over. "Just the arm, or anything on your lower half?"

"Just the arm," he confirmed. "I was lucky."

"You always were the best of fighters."

He had only a moment to savor the rare praise before she thumped the tip of her index finger smartly on the still tender scar over his eye. "This is new."

"But healing," he countered.

"Hmm." She made that sound he remembered well, making it clear she disagreed but wouldn't bother to argue about it. "What about this?" She probed his side, painfully digging her fingers into the sensitive new tissues there. "Something took a bite out of you."

Manfully, he held back all but a grunt of pain. "Golems," he ground out. "It's better than it was."

"I'd hate to have seen you when it was worse then," his mother quipped shortly. "Infection. And someone botched the healing of it. What in Arill were you thinking?"

"He nearly died," Oria volunteered. "He hid the infection from me until we reached Dru."

"Idiotic oaf like your father. I can't imagine how you thought you could win a duel against Nolan in this state. You'll be easy pickings for your brother unless we fix you up. I assume you're counting on returning for the duel before he can have you declared dead—how many days of the seven do you have left?"

His mother had always seen the bones of a problem quickly and concisely. "Five. Plenty of time."

"Hmm. Lie down. I'm going to do something about this. How's the derkesthai?"

Oria knelt, stroking Chuffta, lines of worry bending her mouth down. "He seems to be sleeping, as you said. Not so... dead-seeming."

"Excellent. I'll set his bones after I'm done with my son. You can go. Get cleaned up and eat. Go to bed if you like. I'll take care of these two."

Oria hesitated, her eyes owlish as they went to him in uncertainty at the abrupt dismissal. One of his mother's women slipped into the room, having been listening in case she was needed. "Come with me, milady," the woman said, curtseying.

"Go on, love," he said. "I'll be up soon. She doesn't eat meat," he remembered to add. "She needs grains, any vegetables you might have. Butter and cheese."

"Yes, Your Highness." The woman urged Oria out, and she went, his sorceress looking more than a little forlorn.

He'd have gone with her, at least to see her safely situated, but his mother's healing magic had already sapped his will to move. She'd grown stronger in the last years, and her power suffused him with Arill's green bounty—and his mother's sharp edges. A particularly strong surge made his innards cramp and he gritted his teeth against the gasp of pain.

"Yes, I know it hurts," his mother said, without the least bit of sympathy. She'd ever been that way. Even when he was a boy and ran to her with his skinned knees and the other small wounds of childhood, she'd never been the sort of mother to offer kisses or cuddle him on her lap. After a brisk lecture, she'd treat him—or oversee one of the junior healers—and send him on his way with a lecture on carelessness and orders to do better. "I'm going faster than usual," she explained, "or you won't make the seven-day deadline."

"I appreciate your help," he wheezed.

"Hmm. So, tell me how you ended up marrying a princess from Bára, of all places. A difficult little thing, for all she's pretty, in that exotic way."

"You don't like her," he said, not a question so much as laying it out there so they could get it over with. None of his family seemed able to see in Oria what he did. He'd grown resigned to it, but it still wearied him to have the same conversation over and over.

"Actually I do," his mother replied. "I said so, didn't I? She reminds me of me, in my youth." She glanced up with a wicked grin. "I never expected that you'd choose a wife so like your beloved mother."

"Oria is nothing like you," he said between his teeth. "She wouldn't abandon her family to go live in a remote place."

"No? I must point out, my foolish son, that's exactly what she's done. She left her Báran family to live with you in Dru."

He lay there, gritting through the waves of pain, contemplating that startling perspective. "It's not the same," he said, unable to muster a better argument.

"Hmm. How did you overcome her sensitivity to touch?" his mother inquired. She must've seen the answer in his face, because she chuckled. "Too rich. My son not only chooses a foreign princess, a magic-worker, but she's also a woman he can't bed. I'd love to hear the logic behind this thinking, since clearly you weren't thinking with your cock."

"Mother!"

"Oh, don't sound so shocked. I bore four children—I know how it works. Tell me why you made this astonishing choice."

"It wasn't exactly a choice at first," he admitted. "Father and Ion were dead, Nolan among the missing. I'd taken up Father's sword and crown. We lost so much going after Bára and I knew we couldn't withstand more conflict. When Oria proposed a marriage of alliance, I took it as the best solution among a bad lot."

"So you nobly sacrificed your future happiness and heirs to marry a woman you didn't love and could never touch?" His mother mocked him, but lightly. Distracted, perhaps, by the healing. She caught his eye, her gaze sharp, belying that theory.

"I love her," he confirmed. "I think I loved her the moment I laid eyes on her."

"Foolishly romantic, for you," she noted. "I'd never have predicted it."

"I know." He stared at the ceiling, remembering that moment, how he'd glimpsed Oria in that window, the magical winged lizard on her shoulder. "The war had gone on so long. We'd lost so many, been baking in that desert with no word from home. It's hard to explain, but even with Father and my brothers there, I'd never felt so alone. Hadn't known I could feel so utterly empty. When I saw Oria—it was like she'd stepped out of the paintings, like the one at Odymesen's chapel."

"Oria could be the twin of Odymesen's wife."

"Yes. And she's as powerful as those stories, or more." The

sharper pains began to ease, the worst of the cramps backing off into dull aches. He struggled against the sweet exhaustion swamping him. "She can save us, Mother. If anyone can, it's Oria."

"Hmm. And after she's won the war for you? You can't live your entire life being faithful to a woman you can't bed or grow heirs on."

"We'll find a way. She's already overcome so many other problems. We'll find a way through that wall, too."

"Now there is the son I recall. Ever the optimist. I'm surprised the long campaign didn't kill that, too."

"I think it's all that allowed me to survive with heart and mind intact. Nolan—" He tried to think of the right words. "He's not the same."

"I'm sorry to hear that," she said quietly. "When he loses the duel, I'll persuade him to come back here with me. Perhaps I can help."

He laughed, which became a cough—and something inside him loosened. An exquisite relief. "You're so sure I'll win."

His mother lifted her hands, then laid them on his cheeks, kissing him on the forehead as she hadn't done since he was a little boy, then gave him a long look—all Queen Vycayla. "You've grown into a good man, Lonen. You'll be a good king. And Oria will make a good queen. You two will bring together what was sundered. You'll win because you must." She patted his cheek with a bit of sting. "But stop protecting her so much. She's no fragile thing, and she won't grow the way she needs to with you shielding her. Sit up now— how's that?"

He pushed up, his abdominal muscles responding easily for the first time in what felt like forever, a sheer blessed relief. "You are a miracle worker."

"I know," she replied in a dry tone. "It's good you came. You had a great deal of scar tissue in there. When we return to Arill City, I'm going to have a conversation with Head Healer Talya. I'm not pleased with her work."

Somewhat sheepishly, he admitted, "I wouldn't let her work on me."

"Oh?" His mother raised that eyebrow, a world of questions in the gesture.

"She was … unkind to Oria. I was unconscious and they put Oria in the charity ward, where she nearly starved and froze, though I'd told them she was my wife. Talya tried to keep her from me."

"Ah, politics. I don't miss that poisonous shit at all. Only for you—and Dru—would I return to that snake pit."

"I'm sorry to ask it of you."

"We all make sacrifices. This will give me an opportunity to clean house. Now, go to your wife, eat, sleep. I'll see you in the morning."

He went to put on his shirts again, but found them hopelessly bloodstained, wet and heavy with it. No wonder Oria had looked so dismayed.

"Leave them," his mother said. "I'll have something sent to your room." She went to the fireplace and gathered up Chuffta, blanket and all.

"How is Chuffta, really?" he asked. The derkesthai did look better, but remained limp and broken-looking. When his mother raised a questioning eyebrow, he added, "Is there anything you withheld in front of Oria?"

"I don't protect anyone's feelings," she replied firmly. "You should know that."

"True," he answered wryly.

"I'll take care of Oria's Familiar," his mother said with more gentleness. "Your sorceress will need him if you're to do what you hope."

"What do you—"

"Go away, boy. Do as your mother says."

He bent and kissed her cheek, the scent of her like home. "Yes, Mother."

She snorted. "Music to my ears."

THE SAME YOUNG woman who'd escorted Oria met him in the patient waiting salon, rising to her feet when he emerged, seeming not at all perturbed by his shirtless state. Probably she saw people in need of healing in all states of undress. He still had his cloak, so he slung that over his shoulders rather than carry it.

His mother preferred silence, and her ladies all observed that restful quiet, so he and his escort climbed the vast stairways and moved through the candlelit hallways without conversation. Nobody was about, most of the ladies no doubt taking to their beds early given the long, cold winter nights.

She paused outside a set of doors in the guest wing, curtseying and gesturing him to enter. "Your things have been brought in," she murmured in dulcet tones that wouldn't carry, "You'll find food, wine, hot water for a bath, but ring if you need anything else, Your Highness, no matter the hour. Someone will be listening for you."

Lonen thanked her and went in. He didn't think he'd been in this set of rooms before, though most of the guest wing suites were much the same. No sign of Oria. A fire blazed in a fireplace tiled with a mosaic of lapis blues. Woven carpets and fur rugs covered most of the floors of gleaming wood, and a grouping of plush chairs and sofas clustered around the fireplace. On the other side of the sitting area, a carved wooden table set with two places held platters of food and jugs of wine and water. All apparently untouched.

"Oria?" He called out, crossing to the next room, which was a bathing chamber, tiled in more glossy blues, a large tub waiting and buckets of water steaming over another fire. Empty. "Oria!"

The bedroom held a large bed, draped in blue velvet covers and more soft furs. Tapestries of Lake Scandamalion in summer, under scorching blue skies and mountain peaks devoid of snow, covered the windows, hiding the snowy landscape with memories of warm weather.

Oria, still in her shadowcat cloak, sat in the middle of the bed, a small, still figure. With her head bowed, her hair fell shimmering around her like a second cloak. She might've been another tapestried illustration for all the life she evinced.

"Oria?" He took another step into the room.

And saw the gold mask gleaming dully on the coverlet before her.

Terror stabbed at him. Was she dead? Before he knew he'd moved, he snatched the cursed thing away from her. He'd forgotten it would be sent up with the contents of their saddlebags—a stupid, foolish oversight, one he hoped he wouldn't pay for. Or that she would.

But the mask had no blood on it, so he hid it in a fold of his cloak. Uncertain how to reach her, he called her name again. "Oria."

With the object of her mesmerized attention gone, Oria slowly came back to herself, like a statue of a woman coming to life. Movement returned in small ways, a hint of color flushing her pale cheeks. She lifted her head and stared at him, at first unseeing, then awareness returning. Her eyes, which had been mostly black, showed copper again as her dilated pupils shrank back to normal.

"Lonen." She blinked, long and slow, her lashes like coppery lace on her white cheeks. Then she smiled. Her smiles always transformed her, taking her from that intimidating otherness to lovely woman. Worry returned with awareness, too, her smile fading again as her eyes filled with it. "How is Chuffta?"

He shouldn't mind, that she asked after her Familiar first, since he himself was obviously fine. Still it stung a bit. "Mother is setting the bones now, but she believes he'll be fine by morning." Stretching the truth some, but better for her not to worry.

"Truly?" She searched his face for the lie. "Don't protect my feelings."

Like his mother, indeed. "Time will tell, but I asked my mother again after she treated me and she says she's not painting a prettier picture than there is."

"You look so much better." She crawled across the bed, a bit stiffly, bearing witness to how long she'd sat without moving, and slid down from the raised height. Her feet made no sound on the thick rug as she came around the bed to him. She still wore her fur-lined stockings—she'd at least had the presence of mind to remove her boots—and still wore her gloves. At least she hadn't touched the mask with her bare hands. He'd like to think she'd made that choice out of caution, or being mindful of her promises to him, rather than absent-mindedness.

Running those gloved fingers over his bare abdomen, she marveled. "You've actually regained muscle. This is incredible."

"My mother has considerable skill."

"So I see. I have many questions for you." She followed the caresses of her hands with her gaze, then looked up at him through her lashes, coppery eyes lively with golden flecks, her smile a sensual smolder. "You look even more like a barbarian like this, wearing only your fur cloak."

Helpless to resist her allure, he fought the flood of heat, his cock engorging. She hummed a little, no doubt sensing it in him, and slid her hands over his flat belly to the ridge in his pants. Tossing the mask onto the bed, he caught her wrists barely in time before she seized him and made him forget everything.

She tracked the movement, gaze going to the mask, then to his face, her expression both chagrined and defiant. Had she forgotten it was there? Hoped he hadn't seen her with it somehow? Or, most likely, this sudden seductive move had been an attempt to divert his attention. "What happened to your promise not to touch the mask without me present?" he asked.

"I didn't touch it," she replied with heat. "I only studied it."

"You and I both know you can commune with it without actually touching it. You're splitting hairs to cover that you're in the wrong."

Her face flooded with angry color. "You can't keep it from me, Lonen."

"I can." He kept ahold of her wrists, even when she tugged at them. "Especially if you won't keep your word."

She shrugged in his grip, nonchalant, as if breaking her word didn't matter, as if his anger didn't bother her. "You have no right to decide—"

"I have every right," he snarled, beyond frustrated with her. "More, it's my duty. Even if I hadn't vowed as your husband to protect and nurture you, even if I weren't your king and charged to see to your well-being along with all of my realm, even then I'd keep it from you."

Ceasing her struggles, she gazed at him in consternation. "I'm going to need that mask, if you want me—"

"Don't you get it, Oria?" His rage fell apart, leaving ragged desperation behind. "I don't care about any of that as much as I love you. None of it is worth that price to me. Dru and the Destrye can go hang if it means sacrificing you. I can't bear to lose you."

"You'd sentence your land and people to destruction—and mine, too, most likely—for one person?" she demanded. "That makes no sense."

"I don't care." He dug in, aware he was being hopelessly stubborn, unwilling to change his position.

"Lonen..." She said his name in a broken whisper. "Don't *you* get it? That's exactly what Nolan accused you of. He thinks I enchanted you, enough that you'll abandon your duty to your people for me."

"Not because of magic," he countered. "Out of love."

"It's the same in the end."

"It's not. Love is something good and pure, not some perversion of magic. If you'd enchanted me, it would be a kind of control, and you don't do that."

"Arguably, if I had that kind of hold on you, you wouldn't know it," she countered, resuming her struggles. "Let go of me, you brute."

"No." He held her easily, that dark side of his nature relishing that he could. His sorceress. Powerful, lethal, magical—but his. He drew her closer against him so that the silk of her hair and the shadowcat fur slid along his skin, the fullness of her breasts and litheness of her body an enticement that scrambled his brain. She glared at him, fury unabated, mouth pursed in rebellion. "If I could kiss you, I would," he told her, his voice coming out rough. "I'd kiss you until you forgot everything but me."

Stilling, she leaned into him, her face reflecting the same hunger that plagued him. "Then do it. Kiss me and make me forget."

With a groan he leaned in, beyond tempted. Only the memory of the way she'd screamed when he touched her thigh restraining him from the reckless need to try. How much worse would it be on her tender mouth? Instead he brushed his lips over her hair, at last letting go of her wrists to enfold her in a desperate embrace, crushing her against him. The need to touch her, to be inside her, ground at him with a deep-seated craving.

"I wish I could," he said. "You have no idea how much."

"I have some idea. And I love you, too, more than I can find words to say." Her voice was muffled where her cheek lay against the fur of his cloak. "But I think even with kissing and touching we'd still fight."

He laughed, kissing her hair again. "Yes, but the making up would be sweeter."

She shifted, and her gloved hand glided between them, gripping his shaft as tightly as he'd held her wrists, eyes sparking with delight at her revenge. "This is sweet as it is," she noted. "Unless you're still sore?"

Surprised to note he felt no pain, he shook his head. His mother must've healed that too. He only hoped that came as a residual effect of the overall healing, rather than that she might've sensed the chafing from the repeated stimulation of Oria's velvet gloves the night before. An excellent lesson in how something apparently soft can be unbearably rough, given repeated exposure.

"Grasp the bed post," Oria told him, cool and arch.

"Excuse me?" Momentarily baffled, he glanced at the post beside him.

"You heard me—and you owe me, barbarian." She raised her brows in challenge. "Better, put your back to it and lace your hands behind."

Arousal spiked, and he did as she bade, having to shrug back his cloak to stretch behind him and link his hands together. The newly healed muscles in his arm, chest, and belly tingled. "What are you up to?"

"Whatever I want," she replied, eyeing him. "Does that hurt?"

"Not in the way you mean."

She pushed the cloak more fully off his shoulders, raising herself on her toes to do it, then rounded her hands over his shoulders and chest. Then she reached up to remove the tie that kept his hair pulled out of his face. "You are a gorgeous man," she murmured. "Have I ever told you that?"

"No." And he found himself strangely warmed by her regard. "I'm a scarred and ugly brute, in fact."

She exhaled warm breath over his nipple. "You're so wrong." Her hands worked to unfasten his pants.

"Oria…"

"Be still. Or do I have to tie you there?" Her mouth curved in a sly and sexual smile, reminding him of the times he'd said as much to her.

He dragged in a breath as she tugged his pants down, and the air burnt in his lungs, ragged. The pants only went so far, stopping at the top of his boots and bunching there. He eyed the open doorway, hoping none of his mother's ladies would come to check on them. What an eyeful they'd get—him partly naked, fully erect, ruthlessly exposed, while Oria knelt down before him and formed her long, shining hair into a noose that…

"Holy Arill," he choked out.

~ 7 ~

THERE WAS A lovely power in seducing him this way. Holding his shaft firmly by the root, Oria fixed him in place as she teased him with the silken length of her hair. His eyes glazed over, his face going hard with arousal, those veins in his temples bulging. Her warrior, at her mercy.

He'd been correct that she'd started the seduction with the object of distracting him. No sense at all in them fighting over the mask as she'd resolved to learn how to use it. During the time waiting for him, realizing she was alone with the mask, she'd taken the opportunity to study it. Testing herself as she had with the freezing lake water, seeing if she could have it close and available without losing control of herself, and it.

She could use guile to coax Lonen along, much as he did with her. Two could play that game.

But, as it always did between them, the rush of passion took over, and she forgot that she'd intended anything but enjoying him. Lonen looked incredibly enticing this way, framed by fur and leather, his masculine strength leashed at her request. She began to understand why he liked it so well when he had her at his mercy, bound and crying out her need.

"This is my mouth on you," she murmured, giving him those words back, sliding her hair to tease and tighten. She added hot breath, and he moaned, leaping in her grip. She firmed it, then stroked, wishing she could use her mouth on him in truth, needing more ways to touch him.

Oil. He'd wanted oil.

"Stay like that," she ordered, rising to her feet. Tugging at his chest hair, sharply enough to get his attention, she delighted in the frustrated flex of his muscles. Perhaps all the physical power didn't belong to him. "If you move, I won't play anymore."

His gray eyes glinted with fierce determination. "I could convince you."

"No. I'm resolved." She allowed her long skirts to brush the head of his cock, savoring how his mouth tightened, the groan rising from him like a growl.

"Oria…" He dragged out her name on something very like a plea.

"Are you begging me?" she crooned, then laughed when he snarled. "I'll be right back."

He muttered something as she walked away, swaying her hips more than usual to add to his torment. On the supper table she found what she'd hoped for—a vial of oil pressed from olives. Setting it on the hearth to warm a bit, she stripped off her clothes, putting on his spare leather gloves instead of her velvet ones. They were too big, of course, and thicker than she'd like for this, lined to keep out the cold, but better than the velvet that had chafed him so viciously.

Retrieving the oil, she returned to him, wearing nothing but the large gloves, cloaked only in her hair. She thought she might look silly, but his gaze fired and his body flexed at the sight of her. Immensely gratifying. "Hold still," she purred, then drizzled the warmed oil over his chest.

He gasped, cursing through clenched teeth, and his magnificently muscled thighs tensed.

"Too hot?" she asked innocently.

"You'll find out how it feels when I get my hands on you," he promised, his voice rough.

"*If,*" she replied, with emphasis. "It depends on how good you are."

"Oh, Oria, love. I thought I'd repeatedly demonstrated that I'm *very* good, and—" He threw back his head, body arching and throat straining, as she allowed a drop of the warm oil to fall on the head of his cock. "Fuck!" he shouted.

"Turnabout is cruel, isn't it," she taunted. Pouring more oil into the palm of her glove, she set the vial aside and ran her hands over his chest, rubbing the oil in. He watched her through slitted eyes, the gray sparking silver with promises of retribution. She paused to toy with his nipples, as he did so often to hers, pinching them so he hissed. He strained toward her, not touching her bare skin, but clearly wanting to. Dragging her hands down his body, she knelt again, taking up the vial to pour more oil over his cock, enjoying the sight of the golden liquid coating his turgid member, and rolling off in beads. "We're getting oil on your mother's carpets," she noted, opening her eyes wide as she looked up at him, feigning concern.

"Ask me if I care," he growled.

She laughed—and it felt like ice melting. Even naked she was warm again. Chuffta would be all right. Lonen looked better than he had since before the golem battle. Cupping his heavy balls in one hand, watching his face for the right pressure, she worked his shaft with the other. He liked it hard and fast, she'd learned—a curious opposition to the meticulous patience he showed in tormenting her.

He jerked in her hand, hips thrusting as a groan rose out of him and he ground out a shout of pleasure, his seed spurting to land on her naked breasts. He watched in avid delight, so she kept milking him, rubbing his seed into her breasts, her own arousal so keen she nearly orgasmed then and there.

Lonen sagged a moment, breathing as hard as if he'd run a race. Then he lifted his head and gave her a menacingly silvery glare. "My turn," he said silkily. "Give me my gloves."

Sensual alarm thrilled through her and she started to rise as she pulled them off.

"No." He unlaced his hands, flexing them, then took the gloves and pulled them on. "Lie back, right there. Knees up. Thighs parted."

Trembling, she obeyed, very aware of displaying her slick arousal to him. He gave her a knowing smile. "Don't move," he cautioned her, and went to a cabinet near the bed. His grunt of satisfaction made her shiver again. What now?

He came around the bed, crawling on hands and knees, for all the world like a stalking predator. Naked now, hair hanging around his face in black snarls, he grinned as if he might devour her, holding something in one hand that she couldn't quite see.

"Pull your knees back, love, so I don't touch you."

"What is that?"

He stopped between her spread thighs and held it up, showing her. Carved of some smooth material, it looked like a wooden cock, polished and gleaming smooth. And awfully large. "Is that…"

"Yes," he hissed, his smile wicked. "It absolutely is." He sat back on his heels, lowering the thing and dragging it through her wet folds. She shook, moaning, and he nudged her entrance with the rounded tip. "This is my cock," he murmured, "and I'm going to fuck you with it."

Her moan took on a desperate edge as he pushed it into her, filling and stretching.

"Hold wide apart," he coaxed, pushing it deeper, and now leaning over her, braced on one arm beside her head. "It might be easier for you on hands and knees, but I want to see your face—is that all right?"

The soft question from her predatory lover came as a surprise. She smiled at him. "I want to see your face, too."

"My beautiful sorceress." He pushed the phallus into her, working in and finding her depth. She arched her back at the pleasure, losing all breath. "There we go," he murmured, then began sliding it in and out of her, alternating several short strokes with one or two longer ones. On the deepest penetration, he'd stroke her pearl of pleasure with his thumb.

"Lonen," she panted, in a full frenzy, digging clawed fingers into the furry rug.

"Yes," he replied, staring into her eyes, black mane and molten silver. "Mine."

"Yes," she replied, and convulsed, letting the climax sunder her, imagining that it was him inside her.

And that nothing could ever come between them.

SHE LUXURIATED IN the hot bath as Lonen added another bucket of the heated water. "It's big enough for both of us," she pointed out.

"But not so big that I could avoid touching you," he answered, dipping a cloth in the water and using that to sponge clean himself.

Sometimes she thought he remembered the restrictions better than she did. He'd so thoroughly invaded her intimate self that it was easy to forget he wasn't another part of herself. "Maybe it wouldn't be that bad..." she trailed off at the incensed look in his eye.

He pointed at her inner thigh, where she'd lifted a leg out of the water to soap herself. "And that?" he asked, in a dangerous tone.

She looked, surprised to find a handprint on the inside of her upper thigh, red and rough, as if she'd been scorched. "I forgot about that."

"I only hope it's not a permanent scar," he said, looking grim. "I'm so sorry."

"Don't be." She'd been wild with grief and panic, and his searing touch on her skin had jerked her out of it. "It doesn't hurt and you only did what you had to do to save us all."

"Hmm." He didn't say more, that wordless sound very like his mother's—and one that likely meant he didn't agree but wasn't planning to argue.

"What is this place?" she asked, to change the subject, sure, but also because she couldn't stand the curiosity any longer.

"Part healing center, part religious retreat, part refuge," Lonen said, sitting on a chair beside her, completely at ease with his nudity. His manhood hung lax and heavy between his partially parted thighs. If she could, she'd reach over and stroke him to arousal, just to see the transformation. As it was, his organ twitched, swelling slightly. "Are you listening?" he asked.

Her gaze flew to his face, her own heating with chagrin. "Yes. Sorry."

He spread his thighs wider, bracing his hands on them. "No apology needed. Look your fill—but I'll save the explanation for when you're paying attention."

"I'm paying attention," she replied primly, yanking her gaze away for good measure.

He chuckled, sounding darkly pleased. "Many a man would give a great deal for his wife to look at him the way you look at me. I like to look at you, too."

She didn't have to glance at him to verify that his gaze lingered on her breasts where they thrust above the water. They should both be sated, but desire coiled lazily in her stomach, demanding as ever. "You were telling me why your mother lives here," she reminded him.

"Well, that's a different tale, but I suppose they're interconnected." He sat back in the chair, stretching out his legs to the fire, adjusting himself as he did—most fascinating. "A number of years ago, when the golem depredations had become so great that we began to fear that Dru and the Destrye would be destroyed, my mother and father had a truly epic argument."

"She lived with you then?"

"Yes, and served in the traditional role of High Priestess to Arill, along with being Queen of Dru."

This was something he'd never mentioned all those times that they'd discussed Oria's role in Dru. "I'm not a healer, Lonen. You know that," she felt compelled to mention.

He waved that off. "It's traditional, but not mandatory. Not every queen has been also a priestess of Arill's. It's not a concern."

Apparently part of being married to someone involved letting some battles go unfought. Lonen sunnily declared it wasn't a concern and she wouldn't solve the problem by arguing with him about it. Besides, she could deal with that once they scaled the several chasms between now and her being ratified as queen.

"Was the epic argument an unusual occurrence?" she asked instead. She began vigorously soaping her hair. The luxury of hot water to bathe in was something she'd once taken for granted—and never would again.

Lonen laughed, an affectionate shading in it. "Well, like all husbands and wives, they fought at times. And like all Destrye, they argued loudly and passionately."

Oria had never once heard her own parents argue beyond a mild disagreement. Theirs had been a temple-blessed marriage, a union of perfect harmony. But Oria had opened her eyes to all the assumptions she'd made in her youth, and in that moment she wondered if they'd been truly harmonious or simply creating the appearance of it. Could she herself pretend not to disagree with Lonen? She'd learned to fake the serene state of *hwil*, so she could certainly recreate her mother's demeanor of being sweetly loving and agreeable—along with the surface appearance of a lovingly harmonious relationship with Lonen where they never disagreed. But to what end, to playact for what audience?

"So, you don't mind that I fight with you?" she asked, squinting at him through the suds.

He paused, momentarily confused by the changed of topic, then grinned. "Oria, love—if you stopped arguing with me, I'd be worried you'd taken sick."

"Ha ha." She made a face at him and sunk under the water, rinsing her hair. When she surfaced, he'd scooted his chair closer, leaning his forearms along the tub's rim.

"Seriously," he said, gaze calm, face grave. "I value that you'll be a queen with the force of will to argue with me—as long as you respect that I won't cave to you, either."

She gazed back at him a moment, certain he referred to the mask that they both knew still lay on the bed, its magical hum an alluring background song that teased her senses, like the scent of rich gravy making her hungry for a meal she hadn't known she wanted. He leaned back again, breaking the tableau.

"So, yes—they fought at times, usually loudly, but this was different. By then our scouts had discovered that the golems that plagued us came from Bára, and my father wanted to take all the warriors of the Destrye and set out to make a last stand: destroy the makers of the monsters killing us inch by inch, or die doing it."

Oria soaped vigorously, wishing she could as easily scrub the guilt from her conscience. All those idyllic years of living in her tower in Bára, and she'd had no idea that her people had plagued their ancient barbarian enemy, rather than the other way around. "Your mother disagreed?"

He shrugged in his chair. "She thought we couldn't win. But that's not why they fought. Because the warriors and armies would be leaving Dru, the rest of the people couldn't fight off the golems on their own, so my father planned for them to leave. The women, children, the sick, infirm, elderly, scholarly—anyone *not* a fighter— would travel in a caravan to a land on the other side of these mountains. He wanted my mother to lead them."

She rinsed once more, then stood in the tub, taking the towel Lonen handed her and wrapping up in it. "Do you want to empty the tub?"

"No need." He scooped a bucketful of water out and emptied it down a drain hole, then added more hot water to the tub.

"There's plenty of hot water still," she pointed out.

"I know." He grimaced. "But it feels wasteful, even in this place of abundant water. Old habits."

"It's dirty."

"Your dirt is my dirt." He winked at her cheerfully and sank in with a happy sigh. He fit, but barely. They definitely couldn't have both been in it and not touched. He had a knack for assessing dimensions like that, which she utterly lacked.

"Queen Vycayla didn't want to lead the caravan?" she prompted.

"No. She wanted to come with us to Bára."

"And fight?" Oria couldn't contain her surprise.

"And fight," he confirmed. "Many of the Destrye women have learned to fight in recent years. With us so hard-pressed, it became a necessity, though the men still have a hard time with that. My mother pointed out it was ridiculous to plan to commit our entire fighting force, but confine the effort to the male portion of it. Failing that—as bringing women into battle was a tree far too tall to climb for our more traditional sorts—she wanted to stay in Arill City and defend it in the absence of the warriors."

"That makes sense. Why forsake all the defenses already in place?"

"My father... he had more than a bit of traditional barbarian in him." Lonen gave her a rueful smile as he soaped his hairy self in demonstration. "I come by it honestly. He couldn't abide the idea of the Destrye women in battle—and he was convinced that they'd fall to the golems in his absence if they remained in Arill City. He, and many of his advisors, felt that worrying about the women would be too distracting for the male warriors. My father finally issued an edict forbidding the queen—or anyone at all—from remaining in the city environs once he departed."

"Ah." She understood now—and could see herself making a similar choice. "So Queen Vycayla left in protest."

"Yes and many of the women went with her."

"They don't all look like fighters."

"Not all of them are. Some are healers, priestesses of Arill. Others have various skills and crafts. Some are lovers of other women or have their own reasons for eschewing the company of men. My mother meant to show the idiocy of my father's edict by removing herself from him and the palace, and ended up creating a new way of life."

"Ah. So that's why there was that… tool, you used on me."

He grinned at her, a wicked slant to it. "I found a similar one here before when we visited. I was younger then, and didn't figure out what it was right away. I was hoping I'd find one for us here. I have a number of ideas for ways to use it." His voice dropped into those sensual tones that always undid her.

She decided not to contemplate that too much, as she'd promised to pay attention. "Why did she come here, so deep in the mountains?"

"This used to be the summer palace, and it's one of the few places in Dru with plenty of water, though the winters are harsh. They planted crops for food, hunted, and offered healing services to anyone who traveled here, in exchange for other goods. That's what the white candles in the windows mean—an offer of safety and succor to travelers."

"And they succeeded."

"They did, and proved the point that they could survive without the men to protect them. Even before we left, it was clear my father regretted driving her to such an extreme with his ultimatum. We made the trip and visited a few times before we left on campaign, and they reconciled to an extent. But she refused to return to Arill City unless he allowed the women the choice of staying there or joining us on campaign, and he refused to consider it. Finally, when supplies were readied and we set out for Bára, and the caravan with all the others departed in the other direction, we left Arill City completely empty, as my father had decreed."

She mulled that over, and he took the pause as an opportunity to dunk his head and rinse his hair.

"But they could've come back when the army returned," she said when he surfaced, "like the people in the caravan did."

"Some of them did, sure." He stood, water sheeting off of his magnificent body, and she hastily handed him a towel instead of gawking. She'd meant it when she called him gorgeous. The scars only emphasized everything about him that appealed to her, and she relished the secret glee that she'd found her own barbarian, straight out of the pages of the old books. She'd never quite understood why his large and powerful body affected her so deeply, but some feelings went beyond rational explanation. And to have found a man of Lonen's loving nature with it…she'd been impossibly lucky. She couldn't imagine living without him.

"Do you think she couldn't bear to return, with King Archimago gone?" she asked, feeling her way around the question.

Lonen scrubbed the towel over his face and beard, then gave her a somber look. "I think they both bore a great deal of guilt over the separation, and that they'd both been too stubborn to reconcile. Under the best of circumstances, either would've been bowed by the grief of losing the other. Being estranged like that…"

Oria swallowed, surprised to find her throat tight with tears, her eyes prickling with unexpected grief.

"Here now," Lonen said, easily stepping over the high rim of the tub and coming to her. He wrapped the towel around her and embraced her over it, placing a gentle kiss on her wet hair. "What's wrong? Don't cry."

"Oh, I'm not." Impatiently she rubbed her nose and wiped the tears away. Then she looked up at him. "I don't want that to happen to us."

He gazed back at her, eyes misty gray with like feeling. Though only a moment elapsed, it felt eternal and fraught.

Then he cracked a grin. "Easily accomplished. If you ever try to move away from me, I'll simply find you, toss you over my shoulder, and carry you back."

She wrinkled her nose at him. "You think you could, you brute."

"I think you'd love it," he returned with a wicked sparkle. To prove his point, he lifted her and laid her over his shoulder—though the brutishness was mitigated by his care to make sure the towels stayed between them and their skin didn't touch—and he smacked her upraised, cloth-covered bottom, striding into the other room.

"For now, I'm hungry for food. Even if there is no oil for my bread."

"We could ring for more," she pointed out, breathless from being upside down—and a bit from that sexual thrill. "We might need it for other things, too."

"I like the way you think, my love."

~ **8** ~

H E WOKE LATE—WELL into the morning, judging by the slant of the wintry sunlight streaming into the sitting room. The tapestries remained over the windows in the bedroom, shrouding it in shadow, but the doorway to the room beyond showed considerable daylight.

And no Oria.

Abruptly and fully awake, and with a curse, he leapt from the bed and to the locked cabinet where he'd stowed the mask. Still locked, but he retrieved the key from where he'd put it—hidden while Oria was tending to nature's call, and while he loudly thought of other things—and unlocked it. The mask gleamed with sullen light within. He even touched it, just in case it wasn't real, though Oria couldn't create illusions—not that he knew of, anyway—and found it unnaturally warm. Foul thing.

Breathing a sigh of relief, he locked the cabinet again, and considered swallowing the key. That would provide a few days of reprieve, theoretically, but as for that, Oria could simply have the cabinet chopped apart. Besides, the mask did belong to her, and she did need it. He couldn't destroy the thing, or her knowledge of its existence. They could only work with it.

Finding clothes laid out for him, he swiftly dressed, then pocketed the key. Telling Oria the sad tale of his parents' separation had been interesting—and had affected him deeply, too. He hadn't had much cause to think back to that epic argument, or the reasons for it, over the ensuing years. At the time he'd been headstrong, full of warrior pride and the arrogance of a young man in the prime of his strength. He'd been angry at his mother, laying all the guilt at her feet. She hadn't supported his father. She'd abandoned them all. Stubborn, unreasonable, callously independent, arrogant, cold-hearted. With a wince of deep chagrin he recalled all the faults he'd accused her of, both in his wounded son's heart, and aloud, griping with his brothers.

Never once had he thought about what his father had driven her to by issuing his ultimatum, so determined to have his way. *I don't want that to happen to us*, Oria had said, with that stricken look on her face. He'd made her laugh, distracting her, but for an endless moment the knowledge had throbbed between them that they very well could face an irreconcilable battle exactly like that.

And with far less history of connection between them to see them through it. If his own parents, after four children together and decades of marriage couldn't resolve their differences…

He would learn from this cautionary tale. That's all there was to it.

All vestiges of the dinner they'd shared had been cleared away, replaced by the cold remains of breakfast. He must've been sleeping like the dead if all that activity hadn't wakened him. He grabbed a muffin and wolfed it down, savoring the tang of dried fruit. It only added to the irony of it all, that his mother and her women ate so much better than the royal household in Arill City did.

Determined to find Oria, he stepped out the doors. A young woman leaning against the wall smiled and curtseyed. "Good morning, Your Highness. May I escort you?"

"I'm looking for Her Highness the Queen," he replied, studying her. She seemed familiar.

"Certainly. Queen Vycayla is in her morning room. Allow me to—"

"I meant Her Highness Queen Oria."

The woman's smile turned wry as she gestured for him to accompany her. "Not 'Her Highness' and not 'queen,' yet, I think—or you wouldn't be here to take our lady away with you, Your Highness."

"I see gossip flies with its usual speed," he observed.

"Oh yes. The juicier, the faster it flies," she agreed cheerfully. "And the betting pool grows on what you'll decide, now that you are King of the Destrye."

Decide—about what? He gave the woman a longer look. "I know you... Alyx."

She grinned, and he saw past the white robe and older face to the young woman she'd been, in fighting leathers and training alongside them. The Destrye women had a difficult time going toe-to-toe with the bulkier men, particularly when upper body strength allowed them to wield heavier weapons. Some like Alyx, however, developed the speed, agility, and sheer tenacity to have beaten a number of men, to the male warriors' everlasting chagrin—and not a little resentment. When Queen Vycayla left, Alyx had gone with her.

"Good to see you, too, Lonen," she replied. "Though I never expected to call you my king."

"Believe me, no one was more surprised than I." He exchanged grimaces with her for all that had happened since their mutual youth. Then he realized what she'd meant, that the women fighters wondered if he'd change his father's decree on their status. "Do you?" he asked. "Call me your king."

She shrugged, staring down the hall. "That depends on whether you earn my fealty."

A sticky problem. By law his mother's hermitage and lands belonged to Dru and fell under his rule, but his father had been understandably unwilling to press the point. They'd drawn water from the lake, but hadn't required taxes or tithing. So much so that it hadn't occurred to him to access the stores here to alleviate the food shortage in Arill City. Changing the law regarding the women fighters would cause trouble in various quarters, particularly the traditional and stodgy ones, but that would be a small price to pay for additional food and healthy warriors for the defense of Dru.

Besides, Oria would be pleased. Anything he could do to balance her sacrifices and the inevitable friction for her of living in a foreign culture would be worth it. If she never wanted to leave him, he could neatly avoid the ramifications of dragging her back. That was just good strategy.

He stopped, and faced Alyx. "As far as I'm concerned, Dru needs every warrior we can get. I would be privileged for you and your sisters to fight alongside me."

Something fierce and bright shone in her face, and she went down on one knee, bowing her head. "My king, I offer you my fealty."

He laid a hand on her head, a strange set of emotions passing through him. How angry his father would be. How his older brother Ion would've mocked him for womanly softness and sympathy. So odd that he could miss them with such grief—and also take such perverse delight in defying their ghosts.

"I accept. Of course," he added lightly, drawing her to her feet, "I might lose the throne to Nolan and you'd likely be out of luck there." Definitely out of luck, as Nolan would be outraged that he'd countermanded their father, on top of being the sort of man who couldn't stomach competition from women.

"Then we'll have to assure you are the one to win," Alyx replied, with considerable determination. "Your wife is through there, seeing to her Familiar." She cast him a sidelong look. "I don't wish to question my king, but you're certain this is wise—a foreign sorceress as Queen of the Destrye?"

One day people would stop asking him that. "Yes." He loaded all of his conviction into the affirmation. "More than wise. Oria will be the saving of our people."

Alyx nodded, very seriously. "Then I will serve her and guard her with my life."

She strode off, no doubt to share the news with one and all—which made him realize he'd better tell his mother before she heard it from someone else. He itched to see Oria, to reassure himself of her well-being and bask in her loveliness, but he owed this duty to his mother and the throne.

Which would be her morning room? East side of the house, assuredly, but behind which door? He'd hate to trespass by opening the wrong one. Fortunately—perhaps guided by Arill—Vycayla emerged just then from a room across the hall. Expression set in austere lines of thought, she looked older in the harsh light of morning. The silver threaded thick through her hair, or maybe it showed more because she had it braided back from her face, now that she'd finished dazzling her visitors by playing avatar of the goddess by wearing it long and loose.

She caught sight of him, and her face smoothed into serene lines, making him second-guess that he'd seen signs of age at all. "You're looking much better," she said by way of greeting. "Your Oria says you slept long and hard."

"I did. Thank you for the healing."

She waved a hand. "Nothing I wouldn't do for the least of humanity—or the animal kingdoms. We treat all who come here, regardless of station or relation."

He set his teeth, ignoring the dig. "I've decided to countermand my father's edict. Women warriors will be welcome in whatever capacity they wish to serve."

Vycayla gave him an impenetrable look, the bright winter light casting sharp shadows under her silver-threaded brows and broad cheekbones. "A bit late," she finally said.

"I can't change the past, Mother. All I can do is change the present."

She nodded, pressing her lips together and looking into some internal vision, a dark reverie he hesitated to interrupt, though it stretched out uncomfortably long. Finally she raised her gaze to his. "Did he… say anything? A message for me, maybe."

His heart stuttered, clenching hard. Had no one told her? He supposed he should've been the one to do it. When he'd returned from Bára, thinking the war over, he'd thrown himself into the pressing problems of assuming kingship—and making sure the Destrye could survive the coming winter. His mother always knew what went on in Dru, with people loyal to her keeping her informed. All his life, Vycayla had known everything before anyone else, and he'd grown accustomed to that reality, relied on that assumption. But, had he been thinking, he would've taken the few days to journey to see his mother and tell her of her husband's and sons' deaths himself.

He'd learned that compassion since marrying Oria, understanding how the widowed spouse would feel in a way that his self of only half a year before hadn't been capable of. Now he had to find a way to give her a truth she could live with.

"It happened too fast for last words or messages," he told his mother. On impulse he picked up her hands, holding them in his. Strong and long-fingered, the bones more pronounced than he remembered. With some surprise in her eyes, his mother gazed back, clearly braced for the pain. "The Trom touched him and he died instantly. I doubt Father—or Ion—even realized their deaths were at hand."

She nodded, swallowing hard, her gray eyes shining with unshed tears. "Not a bad way to die, all in all."

"No." He cleared his throat. Tempting to make something up, to tell her that she'd been in his Father's thoughts, in Ion's, but they'd been focused on the war. If they'd thought of her, they hadn't said. "I'm sorry," he said instead, "that I haven't been a better son, that I blamed you for leaving. I'd like to do better."

Carefully, braced to be rebuffed, he put his arms around his mother, as he hadn't done in easily a decade, surprised to find her shorter and frailer than he remembered. Nothing like Oria's delicate and birdlike bone structure, but far from the hearty mother of his childhood. She leaned into him, returning the embrace, then drew back and framed his face with her hands.

"You have always been a good son," she said. "And you'll be a good king. I've regretted not being a part of your life. I'd like that to change."

"Then you'll stay in Arill City?"

"No," she replied firmly, dashing those hopes. "The Destrye cannot have two queens." She looked past him and he turned to see Oria in the doorway. Wearing a borrowed white robe, Oria looked like an angel of Arill, her copper hair full of light as if touched by the goddess.

"How is Chuffta?" he asked her, and she shook her head, mouth set in unhappy lines.

"He still hasn't woken up." Her gaze went to Vycayla. "Are you sure there's nothing else I can do?"

"Nothing that I know of, child," Vycayla answered with professional compassion. "I've done all I can for him. The ways of the derkesthai are mysterious. I think we must simply wait."

"Is there anyone who would know more?" Oria persisted, her eyes hard and intent. Not one to back down easily from any challenge. His mother might see Oria as a child—and his wife was young in many ways—but she possessed a will of steel.

Vycayla glanced at him and he gave a small shrug. Oria deserved the truth, whatever it might be. "There's a colony of derkesthai," his mother conceded, "two days journey from here, in the Taal mountains. That's why I've seen them, from time to time. You could take your Familiar to them if he hasn't awakened by the time you return."

"Return?" Oria looked at him blankly and Lonen winced internally. Terrible timing.

"From the duel and securing the throne," Vycayla explained slowly, sliding him a look as if she'd begun to doubt Oria's intelligence. Or sanity.

"Oh." Color flooded Oria's face and she clasped her hands together. "I see. There's not enough time to visit the colony before the seven days are up. Of course."

"Precisely," Vycayla agreed. "But I can keep your Familiar here.

He'll be safe and warm, in good hands, until you can return and make the journey. If he hasn't woken on his own by then."

Sensitive to the nuances in his mother's assurances, Lonen gave her a hard look. "And the odds that he'll die before we return?"

Oria pressed her fingers to her mouth as if she could take back the sound of distress she'd made.

His mother gave him a resigned glare. "I have no way to evaluate that. We don't have any way to feed him, but he's also partly a magical creature."

"If we left today, that gives us half a day of travel, all of tomorrow, then half a day to the derkesthai colony. Less if we ride fast." He calculated in his head, picturing the map. "Then we could take the diagonal back to Arill City and be back before sunset on the seventh day."

"That's in good weather, and without problems," Vycayla argued. "You'd be cutting it too close."

"Buttercup is faster than most horses," he replied, still in deep thought.

His mother made a choking sound. "Excuse me?"

"My horse." He frowned at her. "You know he's fast—with great endurance."

"I know *that*," she replied, a smile tugging at her stern mouth. "But not that you'd named him *Buttercup*."

"He named himself," Oria inserted with a frown on Buttercup's behalf. "I simply asked what it was. Lonen didn't know before that. I'm surprised a healer of your ability who can look into the wounds of others wouldn't respect the names we choose for ourselves."

Vycayla raised her brows. "Extraordinary." Then returned to Lonen with a firm stare. "It's too risky. You have no idea what they're up to in your absence."

"If you traveled there with your retinue ahead of us, you could affirm my continued good health, suss out the situation, and forestall Rhiten Robson from declaring me dead."

"With Nolan agitating otherwise?" she scoffed.

"You can back him down if necessary. He's as afraid of you as I am."

Vycayla snorted at that. "This is a very bad plan. Needlessly asking for trouble. Are you sure this isn't about sentiment," she said, sliding a glance at Oria, "rather than solid judgment?"

As he wasn't all at sure that his fundamental determination to hold the throne against Nolan's challenge didn't stem more from sentiment than solid judgment in the first place, he couldn't provide a good answer to that. He seemed to have only sentiment left, as nothing made sense the way it used to. Besides which, a large part of him believed that Arill had guided his footsteps to taking Oria as his wife and queen—if the goddess wanted him on the throne of Dru, She'd grace their travels, too. Perhaps Arill Herself had arranged events so they'd visit the derkesthai colony—who could say?

Ultimately, however, Oria watched him with such hope and terror in her eyes that he couldn't possibly make any other choice. So be it.

"Oria needs her Familiar to work her magic," he embroidered on the truth, willing Oria to go along. "I can't win the duel without her, and she can't assist without him. We must do this."

Oria nodded, carefully, though she lowered her gaze to hide her troubled expression.

"Ah, well, that settles it," Vycayla agreed, dusting her hands together, then ringing a bell. "I'll have supplies assembled for you. At least with visiting the colony, if they can't help this one—or if they decide to keep him there—you can choose another Familiar."

Turning to the lady who came to her summons, Vycayla missed Oria's outraged reaction. Lonen gave her what he hoped was a quelling stare, going to her to set a hand on her rigid back. "Let's go pack up our things. The sooner we depart, the better."

Oria flashed him a wry and grateful look. "I couldn't agree more."

"THANK YOU," ORIA said quietly once they were alone in their rooms. "I know you're risking a great deal by doing this."

He gave her a smile as he retrieved the saddlebags. "I promised to do everything in my power to make you happy. Chuffta's well-being is critical to that."

"Even so, I appreciate it." Then she held out her hand, palm up, a determined and expectant look on her face. He scrutinized her empty hand, then raised a questioning brow. "The key to the cabinet where you put Tania's mask, please," she said. A definite command, though at least she added the pleasantry.

"Oria," he began, thinking fast. Not fast enough, as she'd planned this.

"I'm abiding by the rules you set. I didn't argue when you locked it away and hid the key as if I'm a child who can't be trusted."

"Should I point out that you broke that trust only yesterday?"

"But not since. I didn't touch it last night without you and I didn't take the key and open the cabinet while you slept, though I saw in your mind where you hid it."

"You see my thoughts that clearly?" And here he'd worked so hard to cover that.

She smiled slightly. "Things you feel strongly about I see the most clearly. And the mask is amplifying my abilities. You kept worrying about that key and me finding it, even in your dreams."

He didn't know quite what to say to that. He'd known she could read his thoughts and feelings when he married the sorceress. That didn't prevent the revelations from unsettling him, though he had nothing to hide from her. Not anymore, anyway.

"I know you're afraid, Lonen." She closed the distance between them, laying her hands on his chest over his shirt. Tipping her head back, she gave him a long, solemn look, her gorgeous eyes large in her pale face, her lush lips, so torturously kissable and unattainable, slightly parted as she searched for words. "I'm afraid, too. The mask is powerful and I do lose myself in it, more than I've confided in you."

Neither of them was wearing gloves, or he would've put his hands over hers. Instead he ended up waving them in the air. "Then why under Arill's gaze do you—"

"For the same reason you took me to Odymesen's Chapel in the first place," she interrupted in a sharp tone. "I need that mask. More important, I need to learn to work with it—and you need to learn to help me. If we're going to be taking this side trip, that means a lot of hard riding. I might as well use the time productively. Especially since you'll be right there, to supervise." Her mouth quirked with wry impatience as she said it.

"You're giving in, just like that?" Arill forgive him for doubting Oria's sincerity, but... "You're suddenly happy to let me control your access to the mask."

"No, I'm not happy about it," she snapped, eyes flashing with fiery arrogance that perversely reassured him. That was his Oria. "But I also didn't like passing out while I bled from ears, eyes, and nose. So, yes, I'm giving in. You and I are a team. You've said it often enough. I'm going to trust you to take care of me—and see to it that I learn to use the mask without losing myself to it."

"Is this about Chuffta?" he asked her, hesitant to compel her with that kind of debt.

"No. And also yes. You're a good husband to me, Lonen." She smiled ruefully. "I'm trying to be a better wife. Not an irretrievably stubborn one. If that means working with your concerns regarding the mask, then fine."

His heart turned over and he wanted to kiss her with the desperation of a drowning man gasping for air. "You are the best of all possible wives, Oria," he told her, giving himself the weak substitute of running a hand over her shining hair, silky from the washing. "I love you with everything in me, and more than anything else in this world."

"I love you, too," she replied, though a faint line formed between her brows. "We'll get you back to Arill City in time to knock that odious Nolan on his ass, so you can get to the business of being the king you should be."

He didn't tell her he wasn't sure he cared that much about being king. Instead he dug the key out of his pocket and handed it to her. When her eyes sparkled in anticipation, he sent a prayer to Arill that he hadn't made the wrong decision.

~ 9 ~

ORIA ADJUSTED THE fur-wrapped bundle of the sleeping Chuffta. One of Vycayla's many assistants had contrived the sling from the ones women used for carrying recently delivered infants home again. It looped over her shoulders and kept him safely cuddled against her under her fur cloak, while leaving her hands free.

And, thanks to the successful negotiation with Lonen, she now had the mask to use at her discretion—though for now she kept it safely wrapped in its own bag. Time enough to answer its dark siren call. That was a good sign, wasn't it? That she could bide her time before tasting the powerful rush of that magic again. Her arguments had been sound and logical or she wouldn't have been able to convince Lonen. He was far more rational than she was, especially about the mask.

She *had* to learn to use it. So much better this way, that Lonen had agreed.

He stood off to the side, speaking with Vycayla, so Oria checked on Chuffta—for the umpteenth time—parting the furs to peek at him. He did look so much better. Vycayla had splinted his wings and stitched up the bites, bandaging him in places. She'd worked her healing magic on him, too, so that he wasn't even bruised. He might be only sleeping, if not for the utter lack of his presence in her mind.

She couldn't think about that too closely, as scrutinizing that aching empty hole sent flutters of panic through her. The evening before, when she'd found herself alone—and acutely lonely—she'd distracted herself with the mask. Then, when Lonen took it from her, she'd distracted herself with him. Fortunately sex with Lonen worked nearly as well, almost as hypnotically seductive as the mask's magic.

"Farewell, Oria," Vycayla called. "Swift journeys and may Arill bless your endeavors."

Oria lifted a gloved hand in acknowledgement. It was a graceful and generous thing to say, but Oria couldn't yet shed the fury over Vycayla callously suggesting she replace Chuffta with another derkesthai. She'd nearly suggested Vycayla replace her dead son with another, but had bit back those cruel words.

Vycayla didn't understand. None of the Destrye could, really, and Oria had to remind herself of that reality. Even in Bára, no one else had been paired with a derkesthai Familiar in generations, not since Oria's great-grandmother. Oria only received Chuffta because her mother had journeyed to a colony when Oria turned seven. Queen Rhianna had recognized Oria's unusual sensitivity to magic and had known her precocious daughter would need a Familiar to help her through the difficult trials life would hold for her—as Rhianna's own grandmother had.

Oria frowned to herself, thinking back as Lonen embraced Vycayla. Queen Rhianna had said something more before Oria and Lonen fled Bára, something about how Oria would need Chuffta's help in other ways—much as Lonen had said when he lied to his mother about the duel.

Maybe it hadn't been such an untruth. Of everyone around her, Lonen understood her relationship with—and dependence on— Chuffta better than anyone. That was part of why she'd made the concession on him controlling the mask, because her husband did love her. He was risking reclaiming his throne to help her with Chuffta, after all.

She'd simply have to give her utmost to do the same for him. They would make it back in time, he'd win the duel, and then she'd give everything she had to securing Dru and the Destrye for him. Even if it killed her.

Using the mask very well might, but it would be worth it. That part she wouldn't tell him, however.

Lonen mounted behind her. "Buttercup looks sound. How's he feeling?"

She patted the warhorse's shoulder and he pranced in place. "Like a foal again, he says."

Lonen laughed. "I thought he doesn't use words."

"He doesn't. I'm approximating the translation." She glanced over her shoulder at him, always happy to hear his laughter. So she caught his change of expression as he focused past her.

Turning to see what struck him so, she took in the six women in battle gear like Lonen had worn back in the attack on Bára, riding horses laden with packs and weapons. The one leading, with black curling hair in braids on each side of her head, and snapping dark eyes, bowed in the saddle. "Your Highnesses."

"What is this, Alyx?" Lonen asked.

"We're your escort and honor guard," she replied very seriously. "Lest you be outnumbered by the wildlife again," she added, a cheeky sparkle in her eyes.

"You humble me," he said in a dry tone.

Alyx sobered. "With all due respect, my king, my queen," she nodded to Oria, seeming to mean it, "we're all volunteers, committed to seeing you healthy and ruling Dru, no matter what you may face."

"I suppose you do have a personal stake," he observed.

They inclined their heads. "That's how it should be, yes?" Alyx replied. "We give our all to support the crown that supports us and who we are."

Wondering what prompted all that—and the women's emotions, riding so high and full of fervor, she sensed it from that distance—and raised a brow at Lonen.

"I'll explain later," he muttered. "Then let's be off. The wolves await!"

HAVING THE WOMEN warriors along turned out to be both a blessing and a hindrance. Lonen relaxed some of his tense vigilance, no longer solely in charge of their safety. Oria couldn't openly handle the mask, knowing without discussing it that Lonen preferred to keep the existence of the mask, and their possession of it, a secret. They couldn't banter with each other, but also they couldn't argue.

And Oria could discreetly experiment with grien without Lonen interrogating her.

Communing with the mask reminded her in some ways of touching the vast pool of sgath the priestesses had generated back in Bára. Oria had grown up in constant contact with it, so that sgath had been familiar, even soothing. Each of Bára's sister cities had their own reserves of sgath, pulled from the wild magic and made coherent by the meditative efforts of that city's priestesses. Oria had been forced to flee before ascending to the ranks where the arcane process was taught, but it involved the application of *hwil*, to remove the taint of emotion, of the violence of nature, to purify the magic for consumption by the priests.

Naturally, Oria knew even less about how the men wielded their grien magic. They took in the sgath—unable to produce it on their own—and transformed it into active magic according to their own skills and natural talents. Each priest employed his grien magic in a preferred modality, whether manifesting earthquakes or fireballs.

Or creating golems to attack their neighbors.

As a woman, Oria shouldn't have been able to manifest grien. When the temple discovered she could, even though she'd legitimately beaten her brother Yar in her own duel for the throne, they'd declared her a monster, anathema, and exiled her.

However, as Chuffta had pointed out, why would the temple outlaw something that wasn't possible? Clearly a woman *could* wield grien magic, like a man could, because Oria did. Whoever had created that law must've known of the possibility, but considered the ability a dangerous one. Even more than summoning the devastatingly powerful and destructive Trom, as Yar had done. Difficult to believe, as that summoning corrupted Yar visibly from his first attempt.

She shivered at the memory of Yar's eyes turning matte black like the Trom's. He'd tried to hide them behind his priest's mask, but she'd seen them. Just as she'd seen herself in nightmares, with the same inhuman gaze.

That wouldn't happen to her, though, as she'd never summon the vile Trom—or touch that magic in any way. Oria was different, and she'd trust to that difference to protect her. Or did that difference doom her? Her mother had asked the derkesthai for a volunteer to be her daughter's Familiar because of her unusual nature. The Trom had known something about her, calling her Ponen, an old word that meant potential, her mother had explained. But potential for what?

Corruption, certainly. The mask held that, too. When she'd first touched it, back at the tomb, the magic stored in the artifact had felt inert, motionless as a frozen river. But like ice melting in proximity to warmth, the mask's magic had thawed over the last day in her possession. More and more it seemed to reach out to her, begging to be used.

Wanting to be worn.

She would only wear it as a last resort, however. Not only because Lonen would loathe seeing it on her—and very possibly do something extreme, like try to destroy it. She also wasn't sure what it would do to her to actually wear it. No, she'd save it for the point of no return, because every instinct in her screamed that once she took that step, there would be no coming back from it.

You've taken not one, but several steps farther down your path, the Trom had said to her in a dream so real she'd nearly suffocated before Lonen managed to wake her. That warning no doubt reinforced the fatalistic sense that she wouldn't come back from this course of action.

One thing was certain: she had only herself in this. No one could teach her. She'd have to learn through trial—and hope the errors didn't destroy her.

At least, not before she destroyed Yar.

Thinking back through all she knew about magic—male and female—and what she'd learned about using her own, she slipped one finger inside the bag, not touching the polished metal directly, but over the layers Lonen had wrapped it in. Missing nothing, Lonen threaded his arm inside her cloak, winding it securely around her waist—not for support so much as to remind her that he'd been paying attention would be watching her closely.

Fine. Spinning her resentment into gratitude would be an exercise, like transmuting sgath into grien.

Before, when she'd opened herself to the mask's magic, it had overwhelmed her, like the bore tides of Bára, coming in an unstoppable rush, so fast that a horse couldn't outrun the drowning waves. That would be the first step, to manage the flow and control it. Even if that seemed as unlikely as standing before a tidal wave and holding up her hands, asking it politely to stay back.

Intention mattered. Her mother had always said that, as had her teachers. *What people believe becomes real. Don't put attention on a result you do not want.*

So instead of seeing the mask's magic as an irresistible wave, she pictured it as a slow trickle, a soothing sip of water from a cup. Carefully, she drank from the mental glass.

"Ouch!" Oria batted at Lonen's hand, pinching a fold of skin at her hip painfully.

"Had to bring you back," he explained in a rough voice, changing his grip to a soothing caress over the likely bruised skin.

"By pinching me?"

"You didn't answer when I spoke to you and I didn't want to alert our companions that anything was amiss," he explained quietly in her ear.

Up ahead, Alyx led the way, scanning the forest while two other women behind her chatted amiably. Another pair rode behind Buttercup, with the sixth woman at the rear.

Oria sighed. "I see your point. How long was I unresponsive?"

"That I could discern, about fifteen minutes."

And it had felt like only seconds to her. All right then, a drop of water, rather than a sip. "I'll see if I can sample a smaller amount of the magic."

"Oria…"

"Lonen. Look, no blood." She showed him her face, smiling.

He sighed heavily, his chest rising and falling against her back. "Point taken. Go ahead. But I don't like this."

"You'll like it when Dru and the Destrye are safe."

"Not without you," he muttered, but said nothing more, so she let it go.

Once again, she opened her magical senses to the mask, but this time imagining tasting the smallest drop, like the jewelbirds delicately sampling the blossoms on her rooftop back in Bára, before the garden dried up and blew away. At the same time, she did her best to keep awareness of the physical world around her. The low conversation of the women warriors, the crunch of horse hooves on the snow, the scent of mountain air and the soap Lonen had used, his arm warm and strong around her waist and Chuffta a soft weight in the sling around her neck. She kept her eyes closed, the better to focus on the image of sipping that sweet magical nectar—neither sgath nor wild magic, but something else entirely, nourishing and invigorating.

It filled her with a vitality she hadn't felt since leaving Bára—and very carefully she closed off contact again. "How was that?" she asked.

"I didn't notice anything," Lonen replied carefully. "I didn't try to talk to you, but you didn't go inert either, like you did before."

"Good." Excellent, really. "Now I'm going to try something."

"What will you do?" he sounded wary.

She didn't know. "I want to see if I can do something with it."

"Grien magic?"

"Yes—and no. The mask magic isn't exactly sgath, so I'm thinking the active aspect won't be exactly grien. Does that make sense?"

She felt him nod slowly. "Sure."

Something in his tone made her laugh. "You mean, as much as anything to do with Báran magic makes sense?"

He shifted around her, his breath warm against her temple. "You make sense, my sexy sorceress. That's all that matters." Then he murmured several naughty suggestions for how she might use her magic.

Blushing, she cast a glance at the women riding in front of them, though she and Lonen had been speaking too quietly for them to overhear. It said something, that she worried more about them hearing Lonen's flirtations than their discussion of magic.

And yet... he provided a sort of balance to her efforts. The earthiness of Lonen's strong body wrapped around her, along with the vivid images of what they could do together, helped to ground her in the face of the out-of-body disconnectedness the mask's magic created. It helped anchor her in that flood of enticing power. Maybe he'd been right to push her to share this experimentation with him—though he couldn't possibly have predicted this.

"I was thinking something more applicable to, say, dueling or battling the Trom," she informed him tartly, wriggling to back him off.

Lonen laughed amiably and gave her room. "I like my idea better, but go ahead. Just try not to startle the horses."

Wouldn't that be wonderful? She could panic their little caravan and send them in all directions, possibly off the precipice to their deaths. Biting her lip, she hummed in uncertainty.

"Don't worry so much," Lonen said in her ear. "I was just lightening the mood. These are all well-trained horses that won't panic easily. And it's good for you to learn to project magic away from your own people, right? Think of it as an exercise in that kind of control, too."

She nodded, somewhat reassured, though not completely. It would be ideal to practice where she couldn't hurt anyone, but then all of her attempts to use her magic—all her life—had been fraught with difficulty. She would never have the ideal situation she'd once dreamed of, some perfect day when she'd have easy mastery of *hwil*, receive her own mask certifying her as a real priestess, and then be admitted to some vast trove of information that would enable her to know everything and resolve all her doubts forever.

It had been a childish idea of what being a priestess would be like. Somewhere along the way—starting with the realization that no one understood what *hwil* should feel like any better than she did—she'd begun to understand that the powerful sorcerers and sorceresses of Bára were making things up as they went along. No one lived free of doubts and no one possessed all the answers.

Magic came from the world around them, a force as powerful as drought or blizzards or bore tides... or packs of wolves. Maybe it wasn't reasonable to think about controlling the world, forcing it into obedience. Yar saw things that way, and she would do every-thing not to follow his example. She might instead work with nature, coaxing it along and directing the course of things.

The sorcerers had loved to use grien in loud and destructive ways—but they were men and that fit with how they did most everything. She hadn't grown up with three brothers not under-standing that much.

Oria had used her own grien in various ways back in Bára, when she'd been replete with magic—blasting doors open and creating a physical "touch" that affected Lonen. Thus his salacious suggestions. But she'd also brought blooming, fruiting life to dying plants. And grown vines out of stone at the trials. She could communicate with Buttercup and sense thoughts and emotions from people. And Lonen had said she'd made the forest inhale, then blown the wolves over.

"Oria?" Lonen stroked her arm.

"Yes."

"Just checking."

She laughed. "Thinking, not disappearing." She focused on the trees lining the path, how they felt to her. Back in Arill City, she'd held a leaf and sensed the life force in it, its connectedness to the tree it had fallen from, and to the trees that had been its neighbors, the forest overall. Holding that feeling in her mind, she poured a bit of magic into it, imagining a tree up ahead shrugging off its blanket of snow.

Unfortunately, she did startle the horses. At least, Alyx's steed jumped, then danced sideways, ears pointed at the tree that suddenly dropped snow, whoomfing down and sending sparkles of ice through the air.

All of the fighters had their weapons in hand and pointed at the tree and the area around it, warily searching for the cause of the disturbance. All except Lonen, who laughed silently behind her, shaking as he muffled the sound.

When their escort decided no imminent danger presented itself, they moved on. "Well done," Lonen murmured. "It will be very useful to dump snow on the heads of our enemies."

"Don't sweep sand at me," she hissed back. "I wanted something small."

"I know, love. I'm just teasing."

"I know." And she smiled, well pleased with herself. It had worked just as she'd envisioned. A small feat, yes, but also neatly controlled—nearly unprecedented for her. Shaking the tree had only required a bit of magic, too, so she needn't sip more. That would be her protocol for herself: maintain her magical stores without overloading, and apply active magic with precision.

She began to believe they might triumph after all.

~ 10 ~

LONEN MADE A game of observing as Oria practiced her magic in subtle ways, teaching himself to recognize what occurred naturally and what was due to her sorcerous nudging. He did it in part because it gave him something to do. Having Alyx and her warriors along relieved him of the need to scrutinize every sound or flicker of shadow—but he also needed to remain alert. The residual sleepiness from the extensive healing beckoned him to doze, which he couldn't allow. Focusing his attention on Oria, trying to feel her subtle magical shifts, and predicting what she might try next kept him occupied without distracting him entirely.

Also, he wanted to hone his ability to know where *her* attention was. If they were to work together in a productive partnership that would allow her to use the mask without becoming the monster he feared—and would possibly have to destroy, if it didn't kill her first—then understanding how she wielded her magic would be key. As they traveled through the short afternoon and into the early nightfall, he paid attention to when she'd fallen into the mask-induced trances, how long they lasted, and signs that she'd emerged.

He got good at spotting the twigs that curled like fingers, or the flocks of birds that rose from the canopy and then flew in sculpted formations before dispersing. He refrained from teasing her—much—though the sound of her amusement and tart rejoinders reassured him that she remained the woman he knew, and hadn't been taken over by whatever ruthless force occupied the mask.

They made it to a cabin Alyx knew a few hours after dark. Another reason he appreciated that she and her troop had chosen to accompany them. He vaguely knew of the ridge of mountains that his mother had indicated housed the derkesthai colony, but he'd never been there. He certainly wouldn't have known the location of the cabins stocked with supplies for travelers going this direction. He and Oria might've gotten lucky, but they were trusting to fortune enough as it was.

Alyx and her women seemed invested in proving themselves, too, insisting that he and Oria take their ease while the rest of them got the fires going and cooked food. He had to admit, the perks of being king made situations like this far more comfortable.

Oria sat by the fireplace, tending to Chuffta as Vycayla had demonstrated. The derkesthai seemed to sleep as deeply as ever, but his limbs and joints moved easily enough as Oria gently manipulated them, rubbing oil into his scaled hide to keep it supple. Lonen found himself missing the derkesthai's antics. Chuffta would've loved to help tend the fire. He could only imagine how much more Oria must grieve over the lizard's injured state, though she'd said little about it. Neither of them did, somewhat superstitiously avoiding the topic.

Now, however, he crouched beside her where she sat on the hearth, legs curled beneath her and Chuffta on his blanket before her. "Any changes?" he asked, choosing the question carefully.

She shook her head, lovingly petting her Familiar, as if her touch could heal. "He seems weirdly the same, like he's some kind of doll and not a living creature at all anymore."

Lonen frowned to himself, making sure he didn't show his worry. "Well, derkesthai are magical creatures, yes? Maybe they don't react like other animals or people."

She glanced up at him, eyes opaque. "I hadn't thought of it that way. But as we were riding and I was *practicing*..." She lowered her voice so none of the others could overhear. "I worked at listening to other minds—yours, Buttercup's, the other horses, birds in the trees."

"What about the other Destrye?" he asked.

Oria shrugged a little. "I made an effort not to. It seemed like too much an invasion of privacy."

"But you don't mind invading mine?" he pressed, deliberately frowning at her now.

Her mouth fell open, a look of distress on her face. "Lonen, I—oh! You…" She narrowed her eyes and sudden dizziness assailed him, tipping him onto his ass.

Blinking in surprise, he took in her merry smile. "That was you? Well done."

She glanced around, but the others weren't paying attention to them, rather studiously giving them privacy. "Thank you. And no, you have no privacy from me. That way I'll know if you look too long at the pretty Destrye ladies."

"If you've looked in my mind, you know I have eyes only for you, love."

She blushed, making it clear she had a very good idea of the sorts of things he thought about where Oria was concerned, then looked again at Chuffta. "I wish we could get there sooner. Where *are* these Taal Mountains? It seems like we're only going into colder winter, not somewhere…"

"Warmer?" he filled in, crossing his legs and sitting more comfortably. "I wondered about that, too. But the Taal Mountains have a lot of volcanic activity, which would provide a lot of heat for a colony of derkesthai. Isn't that where Queen Rhianna went when she recruited Chuffta for you?"

"She never said," Oria murmured. "She was… vague about a lot of things to do with him."

"Maybe this will be an opportunity for you to get answers then," he offered with a smile.

"Do we even know how to approach them, what to say?" she asked.

He shook his head, keeping the smile in place. "My mother hasn't been there. She's seen them fly and she's studied some about them. But she said you have to be invited into the colony itself. They have considerable ability to defend themselves, as you might imagine."

Oria's brows forked with concern. "Why didn't you tell me that—how are we supposed to get an invitation?"

He shrugged cheerfully. "My mother figured you'd be able to, since you're bound to one of them. Surely they'll recognize and admit you, if only because you bring Chuffta with you."

"So much that's not certain," she murmured, stroking Chuffta's rounded belly, then looking at him, her gaze troubled. "I hope this side trip won't be a gigantic waste of time and effort. We're risking a great deal by doing this, and might gain nothing from it."

"No sense trying to change the direction of the arrow once it's loosed from the bow," he replied firmly. "And we may gain a great deal from it. Remember—Arill is guiding us."

Oria made a face. "I will never understand how you can put so much store in a goddess you don't even know exists."

"It's the barbarian way," he answered cheerfully. "Besides, I put store in you and you are very, very real."

THEY LEFT EARLY the following morning and traveled fast with few breaks, making better time than predicted. Alyx pushed them on to a more distant cabin and, despite the late night, they rose at dawn, arriving at the derkesthai colony after only a couple of hours' ride. It was the morning of the fifth day after Nolan had issued his challenge, and two days' hard riding from there to make it back in time.

Ah well. It would be what it would be.

As his mother had promised, Lonen easily recognized the landscape as their destination. Steam rose from pools of unnaturally colored liquids—oranges swirling with red and pink, and greens as luminescent as Chuffta's flame. If the steam rising thick in the chilly morning air, shrouding the landscape in stinking fog, wasn't evidence enough of the intense heat under the ground, the barren rock terrain with no snow cover proved it. Indeed, as their horses picked their way along the narrow trail—a path they'd been repeatedly warned not to deviate from, lest they fall through a thin crust masquerading as solid ground—heavy snow began to fall. The downy, wet flakes that quickly whitened Buttercup's black mane disappeared as they hit the ground, leaving no sign that they'd fallen. Lonen fancied that he'd hear the hiss of them burning from ice to steam if not for the pervasive popping and bubbling noises the virulently colored pools made.

With the snowfall the fog thickened even more, growing so dense that Lonen could barely see Buttercup's ears, much less the horse ahead of them on the trail.

Oria made a surprised sound, startling a little in his arms.

"What's wrong?" he asked. He hadn't meant to whisper. There was no reason to, but something about the hush of fog and sinister bubbles had him feeling as if they walked into an ambush.

"I hear them," Oria replied, just as quietly. "Lonen—there are so many of them! Lots of minds, a chorus of derkesthai voices."

"Talking to you?"

"No—to each other. I'm not sure they're aware of us yet. It's more like hearing birdsong in the forest."

She sounded rapt and wondering, and for a brief moment he envied her the ability to hear those inaudible voices. He'd only heard Chuffta's mind-voice at the oasis in the desert, when something about the magic there had allowed it. "Can you tell what they're talking about?"

Making a little sound of impatience, she shrugged. "It's like trying to hear one conversation in a vast feast hall where everyone is chattering. I can pick out words here and there, phrases sometimes, but nothing that—aha! They've noticed us."

"Incoming," Alyx called at the same moment. "Stay alert."

"Treat them as friendly unless I say otherwise," Lonen called. "Oria will talk to them."

"I don't like being on this narrow trail," Alyx replied grimly.

"Stay on it," he ordered. "No matter what. The price for deviating is too high."

"They're here," Oria said, and the rhythmic whoomph of wings in the thick air approached them.

Bright green points showed through the fog first, then the slightly darker white bodies in the swirling fog. Three of them hovered before Oria, bobbing in the mist, the one at the leading point of their triangle easily three times as big as Chuffta. It seemed they shouldn't be able to hover like that—certainly not with their wings beating no faster than a relaxed heartbeat—but he let it go. He had no idea how a living creature could breathe burning flame, and yet he'd seen it.

Perhaps one day, when he and Oria had lived long lives together, and produced sorcerous children, he'd be accustomed to the strangeness of magic and the things it wrought.

"We greet you," Oria said aloud, for his benefit and the others, as she could speak to them directly mind-to-mind if she chose. "May I present His Highness King Lonen of Dru, the human name for the lands on which you dwell." She paused, the lull filled with a hiss of escaping steam from something hidden in the fog.

"I am Oria, late of Bára, and now a denizen of Dru, married to Lonen."

One of the horses stamped, blowing out breath through its lips, restless at the halt. Not Buttercup, who remained steadfast and still.

"In time that may be so," Oria replied. "I'm sure His Highness will be happy to entertain negotiations. But we have pressing matters at the moment that—"

She shifted, glancing at him over her shoulder, a meaningful look he couldn't interpret. "I understand," she said, speaking to them again. "I apologize if I offered insult. Of course we will discuss it now. I am clumsy in the ways of derkesthai etiquette."

To his surprise, she laughed then, a delighted giggle. "It's true that Chuffta is not the most discreet of ambassadors." She pushed back her cloak, unbuckling the sling carrying her Familiar against her breast, then unfolded the furs to reveal his quiet form. One of the derkesthai behind the leader zoomed forward, abruptly landing on Lonen's knee, while the other two flew off into the mist. Their visitor, only about twice Chuffta's size, folded its wings with a clap, and dug in. He thanked Arill that he wore thick leather, though he still had to steel himself not to flinch—and that Buttercup knew Chuffta well. Even an unflappable warhorse might be expected to shy under such circumstances.

Given the potential death trap around them, that eventuality became especially daunting.

Oria had fallen silent as the derkesthai examined Chuffta. It bent over the unconscious Familiar, studying him, sniffing, flicking out a forked tongue to taste, and even using the nimble thumbs at the wing tips to prod him. It looked up at Oria finally, and they communed for another long space of silence. Buttercup flicked his ears, betraying the impatience he sensed in Lonen to know the verdict. Lonen clamped down on his frustration. The warhorse was far too sensitive to his subconscious signals. But Lonen really hated waiting. And not knowing.

Oria made a choked sound and he risked leaning around for a glimpse of her face. Silent tears tracked down her pallid skin, her lips on the violet side of their usual pink, from the cold—and perhaps chilling grief. Still she remained locked in silent conversation with the strange derkesthai, and he knew Oria wouldn't appreciate an interruption. Possibly not the derkesthai—who very saliently still had talons gripping Lonen's thigh—either.

An exercise in restraint, then.

Finally, and blessedly, the derkesthai released its pinching grip and took off with another startling clap of wings, immediately swallowed by the thick fog, and increasing snowfall.

"Oria?" he asked.

"We're to follow," she replied, voice thick with tears.

"Follow what?" Alyx called from ahead. "I can't see an Arill-blessed thing."

Oria sniffed, swallowed hard. "The path."

"I don't like it…" Alyx trailed off, a warning in her voice.

"I can see what they see," Oria said, bundling Chuffta up again. "I'll get down and—"

"Absolutely not," Lonen cut her off. "Alyx—follow the same trail. Oria will let us know if we need to deviate."

"Yes, Your Highness," she replied crisply and neutrally, all doubt and caution gone. The horses moved.

"Tell me," he urged Oria. "Are our worst fears realized—is he lost to us?"

"No. Oh, no," she hastily assured him, then hiccoughed on a small sob. "He is alive, and they think they can bring him out of it."

Relief flooded him, a sweet and clean release of tension he hadn't realized gripped him so hard. "Then why all the tears, love?"

She scrubbed a hand over her face. "Because I did it to him, Lonen. I caused this because I'm a monster. It's time we both faced that reality."

~ 11 ~

NO MORE WEEPING, Oria ordered herself. Tears had never solved a cursed thing. Besides, she was more furious with herself than anything else. Feeling so frisky and clever, playing with manipulating the trees and birds along the way, so certain she'd demonstrate to Lonen once and for all that she could handle this ancient gift that was her legacy.

This revelation proved not only that she didn't know what she was doing, but that she was a profound danger to everything good, decent, and right in the world.

"Explain that statement, Oria," Lonen said, with more stern command this time. "I want to know what that creature said to you."

Tukcha would not appreciate being referred to as "that creature," and she was no doubt still listening in. "Be polite," she hissed. "They can hear us just fine."

"Voice or thoughts?" Lonen asked immediately, his mind clicking over into that orderly and suspicious mode that she thought of as his warlord self. Just as he'd cue Buttercup to go from placid companion to ferocious battle horse, he did the same with himself. From concerned lover to calculating king in a flash. He might not even be aware of it in himself.

Something she could stand to learn from, no doubt, though nothing could prevent her from her terrible destiny. "Both," she replied, focusing on the immediate question. "The larger the derkesthai, the more … powerful their thought projection and reading." When the colony guardian, Soldano, had spoken in her mind when the three first flew up to them, the sheer volume in his mind-voice had struck her so hard she felt as if she'd been knocked out of the saddle. What a surprise to find herself still atop Buttercup, secure in Lonen's grip. "Tukcha—the one who landed on you and examined Chuffta—is a healer and she said that what I did, back in the forest when the wolves attacked, that I—" Her voice caught, but she used her fury at herself and her idiotic bumbling to burn the weakness away. "I did something that messed up their brains. The wind didn't knock them over. I put them to sleep."

"And Chuffta got caught in it, too."

"Yes." She could feel his relief and guessed the source of it without bothering to track it back. "And yes, I'm grateful also that I didn't accidentally do it to you, too."

"That's not what I was thinking," he chided her gently. "I'm relieved that they can help him. So it's only a question of waking him up?"

He finished on a hopeful note, ever the optimist. Ahead, the fog changed color, darkening as the large mouth of a cavern loomed before them. The horses' hooves clapped with brighter sounds, hitting solid stone instead of the softer path that had wended through the pools. Alyx directed the others softly, distributing the warrior women into a flanking pattern. Not much time left.

"They haven't said exactly what needs to be done to waken him. I have to go in and consult with them."

"I'll go with you," he replied immediately, as she'd known he would.

"No. All of you have to wait out here."

"Not negotiable, Oria. I'm not letting you go in there alone."

"Then you sentence Chuffta to death," she replied, remarkably calm. She might be in a sort of shock. "And we'll have wasted all this time and effort. You'll have put your chances of claiming the throne in jeopardy, and along with it the futures of both our peoples."

"You're more important to me than—"

"No, Lonen. I'm not. Neither of us is allowed the luxury of putting sentiment ahead of duty."

"Isn't that what you're doing now?" he answered in a quiet but harsh voice. She wished she could see his face, but she didn't dare take her eyes off the cavern. From the dark, mist-shrouded maw, white shapes streamed out, flying soundlessly. The Destrye might see them as more fog, but she knew them for hundreds, maybe thousands of derkesthai, spiraling out into an aerial dance, guard and escort.

"You're putting sentiment ahead of your own safety," Lonen continued, oblivious. "I know what Chuffta means to you, but I won't let you put yourself in danger for…" He trailed off, seeing at last. "What in Arill's name is that?" he whispered in hushed awe.

An enormous white derkesthai emerged from the cavern. Or rather, his snout did. Taller than even Vycayla's manor, with green eyes that would be easily Lonen's height, the giant, triangular face pierced the fog. All the horses but Buttercup panicked, rearing and shrieking as their riders cursed. Even Buttercup twitched, a ripple running whole-body through him and he danced a little in place.

One woman fell, hitting the ground with a cry of pain and her horse pivoted to run.

"Best control your steeds," a voice thundered through Oria's mind.

Wincing, Oria quickly reached for the horse's mind, grabbing it first, then gathering the others carefully, like a bouquet of thorny blossoms. First she stilled them, then she calmed them. Too heavy-handed, as the horses hung their heads in lax resignation, as if she'd beaten them into submission. At least she hadn't had to do that to Buttercup.

"At least they won't cook themselves blundering into a hot pool." The mind-voice of the derkesthai king sounded mildly exasperated with her. **"So you are the ponen. And you've broken your Familiar with unrestrained magic. How distressingly careless of you."**

"Oria, what—"

"Shh," she cut Lonen off. "Yes, Great One," she replied aloud, hoping Lonen would take the cue. "I've misused my magic and harmed my Familiar. I bring him here to be healed. Tukcha indicated it might be possible."

"Tukcha is wise, so I defer to her opinion. You will, of course, accompany him so we may determine if you can be taught. But only you may enter, Ponen. These others will leave come nightfall."

"Thank you, Great One," she answered. "The gift of your permission is beyond price. I understand that only I may enter." She went to dismount, but Lonen remained unmoving. He might have been a granite wall for all the luck she'd have budging him if he didn't agree. She twisted to look at him, his face set in ridged and obstinate lines, exactly as she'd pictured in her mind. She laid a gloved hand on his cheek, and his flinty gaze dropped from the derkesthai king to her face. "I have to do this, Lonen."

"I don't like it."

"I know." And he hadn't even heard the worst part. "I have to go alone, because they'll heal Chuffta only if I agree to their lessons in controlling my power."

"You can come back another time and—"

"No." She looked into his eyes, willing him to understand. She couldn't avoid telling him now. "They won't let me leave. I'm a danger, Lonen."

"You're not," he insisted, but underneath his steadfast love and faith in her, she caught the undercurrent of doubt. He'd seen it in her, how very destructive she could become. Because he loved her, he couldn't face it, not entirely.

"We don't have a choice. I need you to let me do this, for Chuffta, for me, because you agreed to trust me."

His expression didn't soften, though something in his eyes changed, making the color less stony. "You ask a great deal of me."

"I always have." It should've been a joke, but it came out as seriously as she felt.

"We've always asked a great deal of each other," he agreed, then managed something like a smile. "Fortunately we're both capable of tremendous greatness, so it's not a problem."

She smiled back, her heart bursting. "I have to do this."

"I know." With a sigh, he swung down from Buttercup and held up his arms to help her down. Setting her on her feet, he kept a hold of her. "Are you taking the mask in with you?" he asked, the very neutrality of his tone scorching her.

She nodded. "I may need it."

"How long will this take?"

"I don't know," she lied. It had sounded like days, maybe longer, in her mind, though the derkesthai didn't track time the same way humans did.

"Are you coming back to me?" He searched her face as he asked the question, somehow reading the evasion in her.

"Of course," she said, infusing her tone and expression with all the certainty she didn't feel.

His eyes flicked to the derkesthai king, who thankfully remained silent. Perhaps he understood how crushing his mind-voice could be. "That's a dragon, Oria."

"Not the same kind as the Trom have."

Lonen gave her a wry look. "In color only. Tell me the truth."

"I'll do everything in my power to come back to you," she promised. "I've made you promises. I've vowed to be your queen. I won't break my word if I can help it."

"Promises and vows," he echoed. "Is that all we have, in the end?"

"We have love. I love you, Lonen." On impulse she slid her hand behind his neck for leverage, stood on tiptoe and pressed her lips to his.

It burned. And it nearly broke her, feeling the depth of heartbreak in him. And the sheer taste of him flooded her, his emotions mirroring hers with bruising force.

He tore her off of him. "Oria!"

"It's all right," she said through blistering lips. "It will heal." And she'd have that reminder, of what it meant to be human, and loved. Resolutely she walked away, the derkesthai king and the thousands of Chuffta's brethren watching with interest.

"Oria…" Lonen called after her, and she turned to see him standing there, one fist clutching Buttercup's reins, the other hand extended toward her. At whatever he saw in her face, he dropped the hand. "We'll be waiting here for you."

"You have to go at the end of the day. You can't spend the night here. The derkesthai won't let you."

"We'll wait," he replied, implacable.

She stepped into the shadow of the cavern. "If I haven't returned by an hour before nightfall, go back to the cabin where we slept last night."

"What? No."

"You can't sleep out here, and you can't navigate that path in the dark." She glanced at Alyx, who looked both stunned and resolute. "Will you promise me to see that he does as I ask?"

"Yes, Your Highness," Alyx replied grimly, ignoring Lonen's growl of protest. "We'll protect our king, even against his worst impulses, if necessary."

"Thank you." She looked to Lonen again. "And you will leave for Arill City in the morning, whether I'm with you or not."

He made a wordless sound of protest.

"Swear to your goddess that you will," she demanded. "Everything we've gone through will have been for nothing if you don't go claim your throne. Everything I've sacrificed, too. I'll be there to help fight the duel, if I can."

"I can't win without you."

"Of course you can." She summoned a smile. "You always win. That's your nature."

He glared at her, clearly searching for the argument to convince her.

"But you assuredly won't win if you've been declared dead, so you have to get there in time. Delay the duel as long as you can once you're there, but promise me you'll leave the cabin at dawn, no matter what."

"I won't," he ground out. "I'm waiting for you. How can you travel without us?"

"I'll find a way. But swear it now, by Arill, or I won't come at all."

His face went blank. "You would do that to me?"

"Not because I want to. The derkesthai won't let you stay here and I need you to swear you'll journey to Arill City without me, if necessary. I can't concentrate on what I need to do if I'm worried about this."

A muscle bulged in his jaw as he clenched it. "I swear, by Arill's hard heart, that we'll leave for the cabin an hour before sunset, then for Arill City at first light in the morning. Here." He took a pack of food and water that Alyx had been efficiently assembling as they spoke, the warrior woman's mind, as ever, on the practical. "If you're not with us, you'll need provisions. Just in case."

Oria took the bag, closing her eyes in relief, feeling the weight of at least that worry off her shoulders.

"Swear to me," Lonen grated, "that you'll meet me in Arill City."

"I don't believe in your goddess."

"Then on whatever you do hold dear," he snarled, pushed too far.

"I swear on your love then," she said softly, though the stone apron amplified her voice, giving the vow a ringing quality. "On your heart, as that is the most precious thing in all the world to me, that if I have breath in my body, I'll come to you."

She turned and walked into the dark cavern, ignoring the sound of him calling after her. It was the hardest thing she'd ever done in her life.

It was also the first time in her life that she was certain she'd made the right decision.

~ 12 ~

"LOOKS LIKE WE'LL be waiting out the rest of the day here," Alyx said, taking command when Lonen didn't. Buttercup's reins bit into his hand where he clutched them in the fist he'd longed to plant in that dragon's snout. It had looked at him so mockingly, and then mentally *leaned* on him. Lonen had never felt anything like that before, like jaws vising on his will, just enough pressure to make it clear it could break him with a thought.

And so he'd just let Oria walk in there, very likely never to return. Even now, as he contemplated going after her, he felt the impossibility of trying. He could no more force his legs to carry him into the cavern than he could pull Grienon from the sky and have the moon for breakfast.

"Breakfast, Your Highness?" One of Alyx's warriors—Fenive, he thought—stood before him. Not uncannily echoing his thoughts, but offering him a plate of food.

He blinked and saw the other women gathered around a campfire, the scent of warm food wafting over. How long had he been standing there, thinking he planned to go after Oria, while instead he'd lost time? Buttercup, released from the vigil, nuzzled him. "Sorry, buddy," he said to the warhorse. "Thank you," he said to Fenive, taking the plate of food, though he didn't feel hungry. He'd long ago learned to eat when he could, to keep his body fueled.

"I'll make your horse comfortable for the wait, Your Highness," Fenive offered. "I already ate."

"Thank you," he repeated, his head still feeling thick. If the

Great One—ha, to that title—had affected him like that, he could only guess at how the far more sensitive Oria had felt actually hearing its voice in her head. "This is Buttercup," he said, without thinking, introducing the warhorse so he wouldn't treat Fenive as an enemy.

Fenive raised a dubious brow, taking in the ferocious black stallion. "As you say, Your Highness."

"It's his own name," he explained. "Oria asked him."

He felt extraordinarily foolish, trying to explain the ridiculous name as Oria had done with his mother, but Fenive nodded in understanding. "Queen Oria is a powerful sorceress, indeed." She eased the reins from his hand. "Your Highness," she added, inclining her head as a reminder at the plate he'd forgotten he held.

So he ate. The food helped. He paced awhile as the sun parted the clouds, dispersing the fog. At Alyx's urging, he napped while they stood watch, falling asleep hard, then jerking awake from dreams of Oria dying in dragon fire—the harsh scent scorching his nostrils a breeze from the stinking pools, not her burning hair as he'd so vividly witnessed in nightmares.

Unwilling to risk another episode like that, he spent the remaining time working out. Alyx sparred with him, then Fenive and the others. The women warriors did well. They were as fast as he recalled, and amenable to the pointers he gave them on dodging and blocking his more powerful blows.

A few derkesthai watched them, from perches on rocks or sailing in silent circles overheard. They seemed entirely able to fly either with attention-getting claps of sound or with the stealth of apex predators. None of them approached the humans, and they only showed aggression when any of the humans accidentally moved past an invisible line around the cavern mouth. Then the humans were alerted with hissing, flapping wings, and occasional spouts of green flame.

As the afternoon light waned toward evening, the derkesthai's boundary began to expand. More of them ringed the apron of granite, gradually advancing, crowding the group toward the path—or the lethal pools, it became apparent. They would not be allowed to stay, as Oria had known.

Alyx cast an eye at the sun. "About an hour to sunset, Your Highness. Time to go."

Her warriors started saddling the horses again, putting their practice weapons away. Fenive retrieved Buttercup and saddled the warhorse for Lonen while he strained to see some movement, any hint of copper hair, in the depthless shadows of the cavern. None of them seemed surprised that Oria hadn't returned. He'd truly thought she might. In his mind, her voice taunted him for being a hopeless optimist, her eyes sparkling with merriment.

"Your Highness, you promised." Alyx and the others had mounted, ready to go. All save Fenive, who held out Buttercup's reins to him. Before he could protest, Alyx tipped her head at the encroaching ring of derkesthai. "And they seem inclined to enforce it."

Perhaps Oria had ordered them to drive him away. With an irrational spurt of anger, he wished he could give her a serious dressing down for her behavior. The anger died as quickly as it had arisen, quenched by the dread that he'd never see her again.

Saying nothing, he mounted Buttercup. Alyx and two of her women started down the path, Fenive and the other two falling in behind him. It was the same pattern they'd taken on the ride in—one that made perfect sense for guarding an important personage on a narrow path—but he couldn't help feeling a bit like a prisoner being escorted to his doom.

As they rode through the stinking pools, blasts of heat rising from some, the ominous popping and crackling filling the air with forbidding sounds, the rest of his life seemed like the prison he imagined they took him to. Without Oria, the years ahead stretched as bleak as this landscape, as empty as his arms now felt. It seemed so strange to be riding without her in front of him. Where once her vibrant body had nestled, cold air found its way through openings in his cloak. No matter how he tried to close the gaps, the bitter cold crept in.

An omen of his future, no doubt.

He wanted to believe she'd arrive later that night, somehow finding her way to them, but even he couldn't imagine a situation where that would be possible. All day, as each hour dragged by, he'd known the likelihood of her return had diminished that much more. He knew her too well, and he'd understood what she hadn't said aloud.

The derkesthai would teach her to control the power in her, or they would nullify her. Lonen was only a Destrye warrior, a mind-dead barbarian, but he'd sensed it in her, the possibility of monstrosity. Only a few days earlier, he'd considered that he might someday have to kill his beloved, as Odymesen had killed his sorceress, to keep her from destroying the world.

He dragged his thoughts away from that ugly scenario, deliberately summoning his optimism like taking up his iron battle-axe. Did Oria's magic feel this way to her when she strained to use it? Always he'd been able to find a bright side, to anticipate a positive outcome.

Painting the picture in his mind, he imagined Oria arriving at the cabin, maybe only a few hours behind them. The derkesthai escorted her there she'd say with a happy smile, and Chuffta on her shoulder would be bright-eyed and well. And she'd kiss Lonen again, repeating that startling press of her soft lips to his, that all-too-brief flash of contact, while he wrestled back his insane hunger for her and made himself thrust her away.

She's learned control, she would tell him, and now they can touch. All will be well. An idyllic happy ending.

Even without the idyll, she might arrive in the night, tired but fine. There, with him.

As much as he worked at it, though, he couldn't make himself believe it.

DERKESTHAI STREAMED AROUND her as she walked through the dimness, a milky river of an escort whose green eyes provided the only light, parting to allow her to pass, closing in before and behind. Not unlike Alyx's guarding of them. Only the derkesthai weren't protecting her so much as guiding her passage—and preventing her escape. She knew without any of them explaining that once she'd revealed herself to them, they wouldn't let her leave until she passed whatever test they had planned for her.

If she could've run back to Lonen, answered his tortured calling of her name, she might have. If she'd known how the derkesthai king would seize her mind, fillet and gut her thoughts and will like Chuffta devouring his prey, she might not have come here. Not even for Chuffta.

But she had. And with his warm weight cuddled against her body, she walked of her own free will—more or less—deeper into the endless cave. With no going back, she could only contemplate what she faced.

Ponen, they called her, as the Trom had. When that nightmare creature had spoken the word to her, it had sounded so foreign, impenetrable. Even her mother's explanation that the ancient word had once meant "potential" told her nothing. Princess Potential? Meaningless. Now it seemed she very nearly grasped its essence, as if some awakening dimension of herself already knew and she simply had to remember.

For better or worse, she would face the fire and emerge tempered—or perish in it.

Had Tania gone through this? That possessor of the mask and possession of Odymesen. Powerful, but ultimately damaged. Oria had caught the worry in Lonen's thoughts, followed it to the dread that she might become like Tania. However her ancestor had died, it had been tied to the mask and her magic. She hadn't looked deeper than that, as he'd buried whatever he knew, unwilling to contemplate it too closely. It was part and parcel of Lonen's resistance to her using the mask, which didn't matter unless she survived this.

She'd kept the mask in case she needed it after this, and it rode in its pouch dangling from her belt under the cloak. A garment she'd soon have to remove, as the longer she walked, the warmer the cavern became, dropping down toward the volcanic heat source deep inside. So many active minds all around, but remarkably restful for all that. Like Chuffta, the derkesthai seemed able to buffer themselves somehow, so their presence didn't penetrate her own thoughts and emotions.

She could probably live here in relative comfort, at least in that aspect, if they wouldn't let her leave. And if the derkesthai king consented not to kill her outright. Alive, yes, but she'd live out her life as a hollow shell of a person without Lonen. When she first met him, his masculine exuberance was like nothing she'd ever encountered. With his humor, sunny optimism, and sensual nature, he'd filled her up, nourishing an emptiness she hadn't known made her cold and hollow at the core. Marrying him had been like acquiring her own personal sun.

Without him, she'd be consigned to darkness.

Gradually the light changed. Instead of the black of the inside of a mountain, lit only by green eyeshine reflecting off white iridescent bodies, the warm shades of fire illuminated the passage. After a bit, she had to squint, the light nearly blinding, especially when she stepped into the vast dome.

She paused on the threshold, stilled by awe.

The cavern arched above her as high as the tallest towers of Bára and looked to be as far across as the vast Lake Scandamalion. The floor sloped down, filled at the center by a lake, but this one of liquid fire. It glowed with a light too intense to look at for long. All around, the walls and ceiling of the dome glittered with reflected light, refracting and amplifying it. Peering at the wall beside her, she found it studded with crystal shards.

She'd seen a rock like this once. It had been a gift to the royal family of Bára—a round, dull and rough stone on the outside, but when broken open, it was hollow, the interior entirely lined with sharp, jagged crystals. This room was as if she stood inside that stone, only the crystals shone nearly diamond clear, rather than the purple of its smaller cousin.

Everywhere—flying, perched on outcroppings, nesting in hollows—derkesthai thronged. She hadn't imagined so many of the rare creatures, even though the background chorus of mind-voices in her head had indicated their presence.

On a large, flat apron of rock by the lake, the king derkesthai reclined. For the first time, she got a good, long look at his immense size. Bigger than even the Trom dragons, but formed exactly the same as Chuffta, whose body she knew as well as her own, with none of the discolorations or distortions of the destructive dragons. Chuffta had insisted that he wasn't related to the Trom dragons, though she'd doubted his certainty even then. Her Familiar had also been young when they bonded on her seventh birthday. Her mother had always said they were of an age. Could Chuffta have left his colony so young that he didn't remember derkesthai of this size?

Though, as for that, none of the other derkesthai that she could see came close to the size of the king. Guardian Soldano, about four times Chuffta's size, came the closest—which was still as a boulder to a mountain.

"I am the only one like me," the king's mind-voice still thundered in her mind, though with each communication he'd reeled back the volume, as if learning her tolerance.

"How did you grow to such size, Great One?" she asked the question mentally. No need to voice it aloud as he wouldn't hear her across that vast space, and she was alone, without Lonen to listen in on her side of the conversation. She missed him already, with a vital ache, as if she'd left a part of herself behind.

"Can't you guess?" The dragon sounded drily amused—and

somewhat impatient. **"Think,** *human child—what other creatures like me have you seen?"*

"The Trom dragons," she replied promptly, feeling much like a student sorceress in Bára again, answering the peremptory questions of the high priestesses, that sense of being forever inadequate—and doubting her answers in the face of their disdain, when a moment before she'd been certain of them. *"But they're not white,"* she added, *"and not exactly the same as the derkesthai."*

"In much the same way the Trom are like you, but not exactly the same?"

Her legs felt suddenly weak, her head dizzy. The days of riding, short sleep—not to mention tearing her heart out and leaving it behind—and now this terrible interview... She longed to sit. But there was nowhere a human bottom could set itself without injury. Indeed, she saw no path to the relatively smooth cavern floor, only a jagged and uneven crystalline surface sloping down. Even if she could get to that floor, she might regret it, as it looked as hot as the ground they'd traveled past, where the snowflakes hissed into nothing on contact.

Interesting that they'd had a path suitable for horses and people to journey to this place at all, given how insular the colony acted otherwise. Clearly they didn't shun visitors entirely. They didn't exactly welcome them either.

"Well?" the king prompted.

Again, she'd regressed to her student days, when her mind wandered everywhere, landing on everything but what it should. *"The Trom seem far more different from me than the dragons do from you."*

"That's entirely a matter of perspective. Think again."

She didn't like to think about the Trom, with their elongated limbs and black eyes that swallowed their faces, devoid of mouths— or much in the way of human features at all. Like the masks the sorcerers and sorceresses of Bára wore. Like the one hanging from her belt.

The Trom had looked more like person-shaped spiders than

human beings, as if their skin had been stretched over bone with everything else digested away. That image suddenly made her recall what Baeltya, the Destrye healer, had said when she diagnosed Oria as starving to death, how wraithlike and wan Oria had been. She'd gained weight since then and was much healthier, not nearly so skeletal, but the memory stirred unease in her. The Trom killed with a touch, and Oria's sorcerous abilities made her sensitive to touch—but not to the Trom. One had touched her, caressed her cheek like a lover, and she hadn't fallen down dead like everyone else the Trom touched, their bones jellied instantly.

Surely she wasn't like the Trom.

Chuffta weighed around her neck, making it ache. If only she could sit. *"Should Tukcha be healing Chuffta while we talk?"* she asked hopefully.

"No, because you are the one who is going to heal your Familiar. If you can. If you are able to absorb the lesson."

Oh no. Chuffta's life shouldn't ride on her being able to learn these things. All those years of failing to master the least child's magic trick rushed back at her. She couldn't do this.

Which meant she and Chuffta would both die here. She'd break her promise to return to Lonen. The Destrye would perish under Yar's aggression, and the people of Bára would suffer under the tyranny of their mad king. She had to try. Think it through, which meant facing ideas she dreaded.

"Are the Trom… former sorcerers, perhaps like my people, but changed over time by the magic they wield?"

"Yes."

All right then. She'd dreaded that answer, but knowing wasn't so terrible. Perhaps she could learn from their mistakes. *"What happened to them—why are they no longer human?"*

"Magic used incorrectly devours its wielder."

"What makes it incorrect?"

"You tell me."

She wanted to retort that if she knew, she wouldn't be facing this combination of examination and inquisition. *"I apologize, Great One. I am untutored. I left my home city shortly after receiving my mask and lack lessons in how to wield magic correctly."*

"Hmm. Promising. I might be able to work with you then."

That came as a welcome surprise—and gave her just enough hope not to despair. *"Why is that?"*

The great derkesthai sighed heavily, both a mental gust of exasperation and a physical one that blew dust across the stone he reclined on. **"Logic, child. Learn to employ it. If the Trom are former sorcerers, like those of your people, changed over time by the magic they wield, where did those sorcerers learn to wield the aforesaid magic?"**

"In the temples," she replied with dawning understanding, *"like the one at Bára."*

"Where you at least did not learn the wrong way to wield magic."

Excitement flared in her, burning away that dreadful enervation. *"What can you tell me about the correct way to wield magic then?"*

"You must have balance."

Hmm. *"The only balance I know is that of sgath and grien."*

"A good place to start. Like night and day, give and take, water and fire, Sgatha and Grienon. Think of these not as separate, but as a spectrum. If sgath and grien are the extremes, what is in the middle?"

"A balance of both." She whispered it aloud, her voice a surprise after the long silence.

"Indeed."

"So… if a human sorcerer is one extreme, is a Trom the other?"

"That could well be. And thus…?"

"Derkesthai to Trom dragon."

"Yes." His mind-voice, so much more tolerable now, hissed in satisfaction.

"And you… are the balance between?"

"I occupy a point of balance between extremes, yes."

"Are you telling me that a human sorcerer grew you to that size?" She remembered Chuffta's fascination with Tania's mask. How it made him want to be big.

"As a byproduct of other gifts."

"So you retain your derkesthai nature. You're not mindless like the Trom dragons."

"Like creates like."

She understood. *"That's why you want me to learn balance, so I won't become Trom."*

"Yes."

"Is it even possible?"

"We shall find out."

Wonderful. *"How long will this take?"*

He opened his man-sized green eyes even wider. *"Hopefully not longer than you can survive here."*

"Thank you—I appreciate that." She managed to convey that without excessive sarcasm.

"You do have a few things working in your favor. Nothing to un-learn, and your ancestress was able to learn this balance. Perhaps you will be like her."

"My ancestress… the sorceress who gave you your size was related to me?" Oria began to feel that she knew the answer. Ponen.

"The last Ponen before you. The last to have a derkesthai Famil-iar."

"My great-grandmother."

"Indeed. Now, let us talk about the nature of hwil *and how to guide the manifestation of your thoughts."*

She mentally groaned. Back to this. She might as well be back in her tower at Bára. Only this time, Lonen waited for her. And Chuffta.

"Now, this might sting."

When he seized her thoughts and opened her mind, she screamed.

~ 13 ~

ORIA NEVER RETURNED.

Lonen lay awake all night, every scrape of a tree limb and crunching movement in the snow tricking his optimistic heart with the agonizing hope that it might be her.

It never was.

He told himself he was wakeful because he'd slept at midday, during that long nap to kill time while waiting outside of that cursed cavern. A lie, of course. But he lay there, wide awake, going back over the course of events, picking out all the decision points where he could have—*should* have—chosen a different path. He rehashed every conversation with Oria, coming up with better, more compelling arguments. With sick regret, he relived watching her walk into that yawning mouth without him.

He'd made so many mistakes, but nothing matched letting Oria go in there alone. He should've insisted on going with her. Hell, he should've tied her up and tossed her over Buttercup's back and not stopped until they reached Arill City. With a vicious, self-recriminating anger, he bitterly identified with his ancestors who'd kept their captive sorceresses close at hand. At least their women hadn't disappeared forever.

He lay there until the light shifted from black of night to pre-dawn dark, then forced himself to rise as the others did. If Alyx and her soldiers hadn't been with him, he might've gone back to the cavern. Fuck his promises, his vows, his duty.

And fuck the throne.

Though Alyx said nothing, he felt the weight of her gaze, the burden of her expectation. She and her women supported his claim to the throne because of what he could do for them. Oria expected him to follow through because of what he needed to do for both their peoples.

So he'd go without argument. Even though none of it meant anything without Oria.

It should. Once upon a time, long ago, before he ever laid eyes on the copper-haired sorceress, he'd cared about nothing more than Dru and the Destrye. He'd planned to sacrifice himself any number of times for the cause of saving them. Though he'd never wanted the crown or his father's sword, he'd taken them up because it had fallen to him to do so. He'd easily accepted that his duty outweighed his desires.

His life had never been about what he wanted. He could do this just as he'd ridden into battle and as he'd taken the sword of kingship from his father's freshly dead hand. So he packed up and mounted Buttercup and rode hard for Arill City and the palace, ignoring how every fiber of him insisted they went in the wrong direction. They had until sunset the next day to make it back. Nolan would, no doubt, be watching the sun decline, waiting to pounce and seal Lonen's fate at the first possible moment.

He only wished he could face reclaiming the throne with wholehearted commitment. When had Oria become more important than anything else? With each league between him and his wife, he felt the distance strain the marriage bond. He'd become accustomed to it, that connection to her, where Oria burned like a bright spark in his soul. Now it dimmed, and he told himself the distance did it, not that her life force faded.

They rode too fast for conversation. Every hour saved now would allow everyone who supported him to breathe that much more easily. But that left him to the circle of his own thoughts, conversations from the night returning to play over and over.

"He thinks I enchanted you, enough that you'll abandon your duty to

your people for me."

"Not because of magic. Out of love."

"It's the same in the end."

"It's not. Love is something good and pure, not some perversion of magic. If you'd enchanted me, it would be a kind of control, and you don't do that."

He didn't know what he thought anymore. Oria affected him on deep levels—ones he was more aware of than ever, as they throbbed with the pain of leaving her behind—but she'd never tried to control him. She'd given advice, sure. She'd insisted on following her own destiny, fighting with all the obstinacy in her nature, but she'd never controlled him.

Had she?

There'd been that moment when he'd felt the urge to go into the woods and leave Oria there with Buttercup, Chuffta, and the mask ensconced in the saddlebags. One moment he'd been ready to mount up again, the next urgently needing privacy. It had felt much like when the derkesthai king leaned on his will. In the aftermath of how that ill-advised encounter with the mask had harmed Oria, he hadn't thought about it.

Now it only mattered if he ever saw her again.

ORIA FELL TO her knees, sobbing and unable to withstand the pressure of the derkesthai king's mind.

"You're fighting me," he observed remorselessly, but thankfully also pulled back.

"I can't help it," she said aloud through her teeth, too exhausted to project with mind-voice alone, and the Great One seemed to be able to hear her regardless. Reflexively she cradled Chuffta in her arms, though the sling would prevent him from falling.

"You can help it," he replied. *"This is your mind. Who else controls it if not you?"*

Him, at the moment, though she didn't say that. "Some things are instinct. My heart is mine but I don't control whether it beats."

"Ah, but you could, if you trained to do it. Some sorcerers have."

"I bet it took all their lives to learn that," she replied bitterly. The sharp stones bit into her knees through the layers of skirts, and she dripped with sweat, though she'd long ago doffed the fur cloak and other outer layers. The derkesthai wouldn't care if she stripped naked, but the king hadn't let her pause long enough to do so. She'd love to take off the fur-lined stockings at least, but didn't dare remove her boots, lest she burn her feet or cut them to ribbons.

"It may have," the king mused. *"But what else is a life for?"*

"I don't have time for that," she gritted out.

"Everyone has the same amount of time, more or less. Granted, humans have shorter lives than derkesthai, but if you measure yourself against the sorcerers I mean, you are young yet."

"All right," she conceded. Arguing would waste even more time. She shifted to the least pointy spot she could find, hearing her skirts rip with weary resignation. At least the holes would vent some of the heat. She'd never thought, after leaving Bára's deserts, that she'd be too hot again. "Time presses on me because I need to heal Chuffta. I'm in this place with only the food and water I brought in, and I can't live long once that runs out. I've made promises to help Lonen. I can't spend years here."

"Human concerns."

"Well, yes. Because I'm human."

"Yes and no. You are no ordinary human. You aren't even an ordinary sorceress. You are Ponen. To realize your potential, you must rise above human concerns."

"I won't be doing much rising if I die from lack of water."

"There are many kinds of death. You cannot remain how you've been. To become a new version of yourself, the old you will have die."

Oh, that didn't sound ominous or anything. Since they seemed to be taking something of a break, she got out her flask and drank, salving her savage thirst. She also grabbed a handful of the nut, seed, and dried fruit mixture. "Metaphorical death is not the same as physical death," she pointed out.

"I see in your mind a woman telling you that she'd seen people in better condition than you who'd starved to death."

He drew that scene forward in her mind, a strange sensation that she tried to accept without resistance. "Yes, the healer Baeltya treated me—and arranged for me to have better food, the kind my body was used to."

"But why didn't you die?"

"Because I got the right food in time."

"Incorrect. Look with my eyes."

An even more odd sensation, skewing her internal vision to see her own memories as the derkesthai king saw them, like looking at a reflection of herself in a mirror, reflected by another mirror behind that. Through his eyes she perceived different colors, reminding her of seeing through Chuffta's eyes, only magnified greatly.

"Your Familiar will also refine his senses over time. Concentrate. What do you see?"

Strings of energy flowing in and around her, and layers of glowing light, of shades no human eye could perceive. "Is that how magic looks to you?"

"Yes. And how it could look to you, if you will only open your eyes."

She sighed. Always back to this. "If I knew how, I would." She took a judicious sip of water. Already more than half empty. She had no way of knowing how much time had passed, if it might be still daylight. If Lonen had left.

Who was she kidding? It had been ages. They'd all left.

"Let me open them for you," the king suggested, not for the first time.

Lowering her physical lids, she nodded, letting him push around in her thoughts without resisting. Much. It felt like allowing someone to dig around in her gut while she nodded and smiled, only not painful—just impossible to do without flinching. This time the exhaustion worked in her favor. Each time he invaded her mind, she had less strength.

Vaguely it occurred to her that this might be incredibly foolish. She had no reason to trust this dragon, to believe any of his claims. What if he worked with the Trom and this was part of a scheme to destroy her? With an involuntary mental kick, she thrust the derkesthai king out of her mind.

"Ouch!" he scolded. *"If you don't trust me, why are we even bothering with this?"*

"I apologize, Great One," she said, weariness substituting for humility. "It's a reflex."

"You are strong," he replied grudgingly. *"Perhaps too strong."*

"Too strong for what?"

"If you cannot let go of your fears and paranoia, then you will become like the Trom. I cannot save you. Or your Familiar."

Despite the stab of fear they incited, those words gave her an insight, something she likely should've realized earlier, but hadn't, as if a light had illuminated a room. "The Trom seek power to be strong. So they can't be harmed."

"Yes, the human animal drive to kill or be killed. You must rise above that, want something more."

"Wanting to live tops most everything else," she pointed out, adjusting Chuffta, who slept as ever.

"You could have lived and not come here. Why are you here? Why haven't you left?"

"I couldn't just let Chuffta die."

"Exactly. This is the only reason I've agreed to help you. If you had come here for any other reason, I would have simply had you put down."

"You're not helping because Chuffta is one of you, but because I'm doing this out of love, not for power."

"There. Concentrate on the love. Give up protecting yourself, your human concerns."

She didn't have to trust, or even not flinch. She need only think about Chuffta, and how she loved him. How she loved Lonen, a different love, equally as powerful and selfless. And beyond that, a larger circle of love, for family, for the people who'd been kind to her, for the Destrye and Bárans, the deserts and forests crying for water, and even for the moons that waxed and waned, pushing and pulling.

It didn't matter if it hurt, or if it killed her—because all them were worth her sacrifice.

"Ah," the derkesthai king said in satisfaction, and *pulled.*

Oria shattered, her mind splintered, and her body fell like the victims of the Trom had, crumpling into piles of boneless goo. Her flask rolled away, clattering as it tumbled down the rocks.

LONEN FELT A slicing, deep inside, like a knife cutting something a blade should never touch. He gasped aloud, and Buttercup, exquisitely sensitive to his rider's signals, wheeled in place and ran at top speed in the opposite direction. The bite inside him eased and Lonen found himself smiling, ever so relieved to be going back for Oria.

This was right. At last he was going in the correct direction.

If they hadn't been riding so long and hard, if Buttercup hadn't been so recently injured and healed, if the forest path weren't so narrow and twisting, Alyx on her inferior steed would never have been able to catch up with them. He could've ignored her cries, her calls for him to halt, to wait, but when she crowded them on a tight curve, he couldn't allow Buttercup to crush them into a tree with his bulk.

Biting back his frustration, he pulled Buttercup up and Alyx—the warrior woman taking impressive initiative—pushed her horse past them and turned the mare to squarely block the path. The others thundered up behind them, fencing him in. No concerns there. That wasn't the direction he intended to go.

"Your Highness," she panted, out of breath from yelling during the breakneck chase. "How may I assist?"

"By getting out of my way," he replied, only snarling a little at having to state the obvious. Buttercup took a step forward, but Alyx's mare held firm, obeying though her nostrils quivered in agitation.

"Your Highness, we cannot afford to backtrack at all or we won't make it to Arill City in time."

"That's fine. Let Nolan have the throne. He was meant to be king anyway. I won't fight him for it."

Several of the women murmured to each other behind him, and Alyx flicked a glance at them and then to him. The raw betrayal in her eyes might've gutted him, if feeling Oria's pain hadn't done that already. "If you'd treated Prince Nolan as he's treated you, Your Highness, he'd have been officially declared dead when he disappeared on the battlefield. Would you have challenged him for the throne, were your positions reversed?"

"Of course not." He nudged Buttercup another step, closing enough to see the strain in Alyx's throat as she defied him. She didn't give way, however, full of the resolve in her cause that he lacked. Abruptly weariness flooded him. He was so tired of fighting—the Bárans, the golems, his own brother—and of the doubts about Oria, the sun of his life. Oria loved him for himself. If he went to her and said he'd given up being king and wanted only to be a man, with her, she'd still love him.

But she'd be disappointed. She'd look at him with that same expression as Alyx, the sour taste of his failure to measure up in her eyes. Inside him, the knife turned, Oria's pain throbbing like a living wound. "Oria..." he said, only realizing he said her name aloud when he heard the broken sound.

Alyx's face crumpled with compassion, though she didn't yield.

"Her Highness is a strong woman. As strong—or stronger—as any I've met. She wouldn't thank you for turning your back on your mutual cause, on both your peoples, by coming back for her."

She'd overheard a great deal, which should be no surprise. He gave one last look at the path beyond Alyx, knowing he could take it if he chose, then closed his heart to it. "You're right," he told her. "I apologize."

"Take a fast break while we're stopped," Alyx called to the others. "We'll continue to Arill City shortly." She lowered her voice again, shaking her head. "Don't apologize, Your Highness. You have a great heart, which will make you a great king. When there's love like you and Her Highness have, it's difficult to put duty over it. That you will speaks more highly of you than anything."

"With the occasional pointed reminder," he replied wryly, fishing water out of the bags, trying not to think about whether Oria had enough, whether she'd even survive.

"I'm happy to serve as your conscience, Your Highness." Alyx handed him some jerky. "I'm aware my investment is self-serving. I want you as my king, and I'm willing to be ruthless to make sure of it. Though I'm sorry to see you suffer her absence."

"You don't think I'm enchanted?" he asked, before he meant to. Emotional exhaustion getting to him, to ask her such a thing. Though… who else could he ask? Everyone had an opinion about Oria. Alyx seemed to be one of the few who didn't loathe the sorceress on principle.

Alyx chewed her jerky thoughtfully, giving the question such due consideration—and with no surprise that he'd asked—that he knew she'd heard discussions of the possibility. She swallowed, shaking her head decisively. "I don't know much about enchantment, but it seems to me that if the sorceress had magicked you, Your Highness, you'd be a lot happier. Only love, hopeless and impossible, makes anyone this miserable."

"That's… unusual logic."

She shrugged. "Seems to me, Your Highness, that if you wanted an easy way of it, you wouldn't have married a Báran sorceress. You wouldn't be determined to marry her again under Arill's hand either. I've seen how she looks at you—she'd give you the last drop of blood in her body if you asked, whether you made her Queen of Dru or not. I don't know, but if *I* had the kind of power she does, I'd be making you dance a merry tune, not sending you away."

It made sense. So much that he wondered how he'd let himself get confused. "Once I claim the throne, if Oria hasn't returned, I'm coming back for her."

Alyx nodded as if she expected as much. "We'll come with you."

Neither of them mentioned the possibility that there would be nothing left of her to retrieve.

IN THE BEGINNING, there was only the formless void, containing everything and nothing, only potential, nothing yet realized.

The old temple words rolled through Oria's mind, comforting as those early childhood sayings can be. Like nursery songs and the feeling of being loved. Odd to feel that sense of safety as she wandered the void. Formless in a place of nothingness. Alone and yet not lonely.

"Because I'm here with you. I promised I'd always be with you."

She looked, but had no eyes. No ears, either. Still, the voice resonated in her being, requiring no physical senses. Emotion existed in this void, because hope, impossibly keen-edged, stabbed at her. *"Chuffta?"*

"Of course. Who else?"

"You're alive!"

He tutted at her. *"You knew that."*

"Yes and no. Your body…" Memory returned in vivid clarity. *"Are you alive?"*

"The part of me that is eternal is here with you, yes, silly."

Oh no. That didn't sound good. She'd died. She failed that final lesson and her body had died, along with Chuffta's. They were together in the afterlife, which wasn't at all the solace it should've been.

"Not yet, but we will be soon if you don't act. I'm a young derkesthai. I'd like my body back, please."

As did she. *"I don't know what to do."*

He shrugged. *"You're the sorceress. You are Ponen. Take the potential and make form from the void."*

"Oh, is that all?"

"Yes." He mentally flicked his tail.

"But how?"

"Magic," he replied, with crisp certainty, as if the answer had been obvious all along. *"You have all the tools within you, the ability and the knowledge. Use it. And when you give me a body again, make it a big one."*

No, it wasn't enough to use it. She remembered now. She must use it with balance, and out of love. What had the Destrye said about their goddess? Arill made the world from the void out of love and loneliness. She manifested reality to share the delight of being.

Oria tried to be like that, like a pure and perfect goddess, full of love for all creation. She reached for her sgath…

"Not like that," the derkesthai king inserted into her mind. ***"Not the way you did before. You've shed your former body, now let go of the old you."***

She tried, letting it all fall away. A kind of saying goodbye.

"Now: touch the magic. Take it into yourself. Without reservation or defense."

Touch it? Let it flood her? She'd lived her whole life not touching or being touched, living atop her isolated tower, protected from exactly this. Alive but not living. So afraid of dying that she'd walled out all of life.

Of course that had to change, so that she could. She opened her portals, ruthlessly dropping all caution and reserve.

"*Be careful, Oria,*" Chuffta warned. "*Don't—*"

Too late. The wave crashed over her, severing her from every-thing.

~ 14 ~

L ONEN FELT IT the moment Oria died.

The bright, warm spark of her inside him simply flickered out. Gone as if it had never been. Leaving him cold and empty. As much as her pain and torment had tugged at him, as much as he'd hated the gradual attenuation of their marriage bond as he rode farther and farther away from her—this sudden loss was so much worse.

He must have made a sound. A startled cry like a man wounded in ambush, because the two nearest riders ahead of him spun their horses, weapons drawn. The two behind rode up to flank him with their weapons facing out.

"Your Highness!" said Fenive. "Are you hurt?"

Alyx was there in moment, but he was already shaking his head. "I'm fine. Keep riding." No reason to hesitate now.

"Your Highness?" Alyx questioned.

"She's gone," he replied shortly.

They all fell silent, somber with shock, perhaps shared grief.

"You're certain."

"We were magically married. I've been attached to her since that moment. No longer."

As one, the women made the sign of Arill, bowing their heads in prayer. With the forest canopy arching overhead, the early winter evening descending—and the near moon, Sgatha, hanging full, round, and rosy in the sky between the stark branches—the woods felt like a temple. The murmurs of them speaking the prayer for the dead only reinforced the strangely sanctified moment.

Lonen couldn't bring himself to speak the words, or truly even listen. He'd been alone back on that plain before the walls of Bára, and he was alone again. Except for cold duty.

And retribution.

If Nolan hadn't driven them away, Oria and Chuffta would've stayed safe in the palace. Lonen might have only his duty to his people—and Oria's—but that was something. He'd cling to that. And he would make Nolan pay.

The last whispers of the prayer faded away, taken up by the susurrus of a wind high in the bare branches.

"Let's ride," he growled.

This time, he took point. Let the others keep up if they could.

DARKNESS SWIRLED AROUND them, formless and without sign of light. Sgatha had fallen out of sight behind the mountains, and even Grienon on his wild and impetuous path had disappeared over the horizon. In the very early dawn, no habitations had lit lanterns yet.

After riding at a breakneck pace all night, they'd been forced to slow. The horses still sensed the trail, through scent or some sensitivity of their hooves, but the riders had to be wary of unseen dangers.

Besides, not all the horses in their group possessed Buttercup's stalwart endurance. Lonen would've left them behind, if Alyx's warriors hadn't been so determined to keep up—pushing themselves and their mounts to do it. A great deal to prove, he supposed, and because he knew they'd kill themselves trying rather than risk being inadequate, he restrained his snapping impatience.

Finally he agreed to stop for a short break. They'd reached the outlying farmlands around Arill City, the ones scored by the Trom dragons. They knew it because the muffled and crowding shadows of trees had opened up to the echoing space of a flat landscape. And a glimmer of light showed finally, the snow-covered fields picking up the glow from beyond the horizon. In another hour or so the sun would rise, and they'd have all the day to reach Arill's Temple and declare Lonen alive and ready to face Nolan's challenge.

Something truly dire would have to happen now to prevent that. As the worst thing possible had already occurred, Lonen couldn't imagine what could stop him now. He'd fight Nolan, probably kill his brother to exact revenge for Oria's death, and afterward there would be time to mourn.

Besides, Nolan might insist on having the duel right then and there—and Lonen would welcome the opportunity to vent his rage and grief on the prideful sod who'd caused all this sorrow. It would be best if he arrived rested and ready to fight.

So he agreed to Alyx's proposal that they rest in an abandoned farmhouse, one that had escaped the fires and destruction. They gave the horses food and water, ate the last of their own food, and tried to sleep a little.

Some of the women did sleep, with that enviable ability to grab rest at any time. Lonen had once possessed it, but he'd long since passed into an attenuated state of hypervigilance. He'd sleep when he was king. Arill knew he'd never take another queen. His bed would remain empty and Lonen would devote all of himself to his duty.

The image of himself, a mad king in his own right, prowling the palace at Dru in his loneliness, made him too restless to even try for sleep. Instead he joined Alyx on the porch of the farmhouse where she perched on the rail, cupping a mug of hot broth, staring out over the fields. The morning light revealed the burnt landscape with stark brutality.

"I hadn't seen it," she said. "We heard about the Trom attack, of course, and I thought I understood how bad it was. But I hadn't seen it for myself yet."

He leaned against the rail, the frozen landscape much the same as his heart, the scorched earth showing in ridges of scars against the ice-encrusted snowdrifts. Lonen wasn't a farmer, though since he'd become king he'd learned more than he'd ever cared to know about what the land required to bear crops. Looking at the baked earth, so slick it wouldn't even hold snow cover, he wondered how the Destrye could possibly recover these fields. They might have to abandon Dru after all.

The prospect didn't bother him as much as it once had. At least then he'd be far from anything that reminded him of Oria.

"I keep thinking," Alyx continued into his silence, "that if we'd been there, if so many of us hadn't retreated to the hermitage with the queen, we might've been able to help or maybe—"

"Don't," he cut her off. "No one could've done anything. The Trom dragons are unstoppable. We can no more fight them than we can thwart lightning or make it rain."

"I can see that now," she replied after a pause, "what destruction they wreak."

He didn't say anything. There was nothing to say.

"How will we fight them, then?" she finally asked. "I have no doubt that you'll defeat Nolan and claim the throne, but what do we do then? I mean, may I ask what your plan is, Your Highness?" The hastily added addendum to her plaintive question made him smile, though bitterly, because he had no answer.

"My plan was Oria," he confessed. "She could've fought the Trom with her sorcery. We'd thought to drive away their dragons and supplant her brother Yar, so that these monsters couldn't be brought against us again. Without her…"

"Ah." With that breathed sound, more of a sigh than an actual word, Alyx acknowledged the powerful inevitability of their doom.

"I think we'll have to leave," he said. "Take the Destrye and go as far as we can."

"We will of course go wherever you lead, Your Highness."

"Will my mother, do you think?"

Alyx hesitated too long, perhaps searching for a soothingly non-committal answer. Lonen chuckled mirthlessly. "Never mind. I know she won't."

"There will be others, Your Highness, who won't leave. You know that. The ones who've lived here their entire lives, the ones who know they'd die on the journey and would rather lay their bones in Dru, the stubborn, the ones so hopelessly optimistic they'll cling to the hope of victory long after everything points to defeat."

Hopelessly optimistic. How many times had Oria accused him of just that? Countless times. She'd said that nothing could defeat his sunny outlook. Grief surged bitter as the tides of Bára as he—more than anything in the world—longed to tell Oria that she was wrong, something *could* kill his native optimism. All it had taken was her death.

"I won't force anyone to leave," he decided. "Anyone who wants to stay and fight it out can." Maybe he'd stay with them. That would at least end his misery in a noble and fitting way. The king perishing with his kingdom.

"But you will lead the people," Alyx insisted.

"Yes," he conceded. He could hardly defeat Nolan and then refuse to lead as a king should. And there was no question of whether he'd fight Nolan. His brother would pay. "Speaking of which, rouse your warriors. Let's be done with this."

"Yes, Your—" Her words choked off as an arrow pierced her shoulder and pinned her to the porch post.

Lonen ducked before he fully processed what had happened, his iron axe in hand. Even in sleep he kept it near—and it was not lost on him at the moment how fully useless it was against an enemy armed with bows and arrows. Alyx gasped, tugging at the arrow, and another thudded into her, making her cry out. The warrior women shouted from within, and the farmhouse door flew open.

"Stay down!" He yelled. "Fenive, get to an upper window with your bow." He levered up next to Alyx, hating himself for using her as cover as he peered past her hip—but also ignoring her pleas to leave her and save himself.

Bows and arrows meant people, not golems or sorcerers. Another arrow flew past him, narrowly missing his head and hitting the wall behind him. A volley of arrows shot outward from the upper story, toward a low hedge by the road. Using the cover, he scrambled back, breaking off the arrow as he rolled inside.

Destrye arrows, the sort used by the palace guard. Fury boiled up in him, like fire that might erupt from his throat. No longer caring about his safety—a ridiculous concept—he charged out the door, shouting, "Nolan, you fucking coward! Show yourself."

No arrows thudded into him. Silence, except for Alyx's ragged, pained breathing, fell heavy in the crisp winter air. "Hold your fire," a man called, and stepped out into the open, followed by five more.

Twenty more emerged from the copse of trees across the road. And forty more from around the side of the house. All heavily armed, and wearing the uniform of the palace guard.

Lonen and his six warriors couldn't possibly prevail. "This is treachery," he ground out. "You betray your king."

The leader sketched a bow, a reasonably respectful one, given the circumstances. "With apologies, Prince Lonen, we serve His Highness King Nolan. Given your wartime desertion of the Destrye forces, His Highness has taken up the sword and wreath of Dru. He sent us to escort you back home, should you appear."

Lonen bit out a harsh, disbelieving laugh at the insulting words. "An escort? Is that what you call it when you shoot at loyal soldiers in the king's party?"

"We saw only a woman and figured her for one of the prince's camp followers," the man replied. "Lay down your weapons, turn over the sorceress to us, and we'll escort you home peaceably, Prince Lonen."

So that was the way of it. No sense in lying about Oria's fate, however, and better to remove that chip from the bargaining table. "The sorceress Oria is dead," he informed them, tossing his useless battle-axe aside. "I'm going to tend to Captain Alyx. We won't fight you."

Turning his back on them in deliberate dismissal, he checked Alyx's wounds. Mostly attention-getting and not piercing any vital organs, the wounds nevertheless bled enough to kill her if they delayed treatment. "Thanks for the promotion," she said, her lips stretching across clenched teeth in a pretense of a grin. "But don't worry about me."

"We're getting you to a healer, Captain," he replied. "I'm breaking off the arrows. On my mark." She screamed at the first, passed out on the second. He'd have expected the same of any man, so hopefully she wouldn't see it as a weakness. Not an easy burden to labor under, having something to prove. Camp follower, his ass. Fenive arrived just in time to help him slide Alyx's unconscious body off the shortened stakes pinning her to the post, so she took over staunching the bleeding.

Lonen turned to face Nolan's men, who'd assembled in the farmhouse's erstwhile yard. Scanning the faces, he identified several men he knew well—though at least none from his own battalion, which provided obscure comfort—and a number who looked familiar. "So Nolan is too much of a coward to face me in a legitimate duel," he noted.

The leader—who Lonen didn't know at all, which meant he'd likely been one of Nolan's men, probably had traveled with him through the tunnels from the underground lake at Bára—reddened in impotent anger. No doubt they were under orders not to kill Lonen outright. A coup would look bad, whereas compelling Lonen's submission would work entirely in Nolan's favor. A number of the other men, however, shuffled uneasily and wouldn't meet his eyes. This wasn't how the Destrye fought, not though guile and treachery.

"If you wish to challenge His Highness King Nolan to a duel for the throne, you may seek Arill's blessing for it," the leader replied stiffly.

"I'll take it up with the goddess," Lonen answered. "However, since *Prince* Nolan challenged me, and I have been ruling as rightful king since the deaths of my father and Prince Ion, I believe the question of a duel has been resolved."

The leader shook his head. "I'm sorry, Prince Lonen, but you abdicated when you abandoned the throne and crown."

"Don't be ridiculous, Mott," Fenive snapped. "You can't declare His Highness dead until sundown tonight. The seven days aren't up yet."

Mott smiled thinly. "Indeed that's true, but Prince Lonen would have to present himself at Arill's Temple before then."

"So? We're a couple of hours' ride away at best, and it's only just after sunrise," Fenive argued.

The plot dawned on Lonen, and he cursed himself for being so thick and slow. The profound betrayal gutted him—another ambush, one so foul he'd never imagined it possible. "You don't mean to escort us to Arill City, Mott, is it?"

"You don't remember me, do you, Prince Lonen? No, the likes of me wasn't good enough for you and your battalion. But His Highness recognizes worth—and rewards loyalty. It was my honor to volunteer to escort you to Arill's Temple, and I will. Eventually. Well after the sunset deadline. I suggest you make yourselves comfortable. Tomorrow morning should be soon enough to leave."

Fenive made an incoherent sound of anger, but Lonen gestured her to silence. "Captain Alyx will die before tomorrow morning without healing."

Mott gave Alyx's prone body a cursory and contemptuous glance. "Alyx—and you, Fenive—have always offended Arill's eye with your aspirations to men's work. If the goddess chooses to strike you down for your blasphemy, then so be it."

"I believe it was your archer who struck her down, not Arill," Lonen replied mildly.

Mott flushed, hand clenching his sword as if he'd love to use it on them. "Don't you defile the name of the goddess!" he shouted.

"I am still your prince," Lonen answered, striding down the

steps and meeting the point of Mott's sword. "Though you may have been misled over who rules Dru and the Destrye, you *will* give me the respect of rank."

Mott's lip curled. "You won't have to be ritually declared dead if you are truly dead."

Several of Mott's men made sounds of agreement—but more seemed dismayed, shifting uneasily. "Will you kill me then?" Lonen asked softly, leaning his chest into the point of the sword. He'd almost welcome the slicing pain, cleaving his broken heart in actuality as well as metaphorically, followed by the sweet release of death.

"His Highness is right," Mott breathed. "You *are* insane, driven mad by that foul, foreign sorceress who—"

Lonen's hand shot out, seizing Mott by the throat, taking him so by surprise that the sword skidded off Lonen's leather breastplate, carving only a shallow cut. Lonen had suffered far worse and for sorrier reasons. "You don't speak of her," he said, spacing out the words, as Mott was clearly a numbskull. "Am I insane because death doesn't frighten me, that I'd be just as pleased to squash you like the bug you are and lose the throne to my power-mad brother—or because Oria enchanted me to want the throne above all? Both can't be true."

Mott gasped like a fish out of water, unable to breathe, much less answer, and Lonen took a savage satisfaction in it, vising his grip. But the image of the fish reminded him of that day at Lake Scandamalion, when Chuffta landed the stardew fish and Oria scolded him for it. How full of love he'd been—and terror that he'd lose her to the seductive power of the mask. Now he'd lost her entirely and he longed to go back to that moment, to turn time to prevent the cascade of events.

"Prince Lonen, sir, release the captain. Please." Several swords pointed at him, ringing him round with lethal edges. One sharp blade lay against the arm holding Mott immobile, the face above the sword a familiar one. "Please, Your Highness," the man urged, expression contorted with fear and dread. "Don't make us do this."

With a surprising amount of effort, Lonen forced his fingers to open, and Mott fell to a crumpled pile at his feet. Two men moved forward to drag him away. Lonen met the gaze of the man who'd spoken. "Nestor. I wouldn't have expected this of you."

Nestor met his gaze, firming his chin, though guilt crawled over his face. "It hasn't been an easy week, Your Highness. We are simple men. Our loyalty and fealty should be simple also, not a question of choice. We're doing our best to keep the peace."

Lonen supposed he could understand that. Their rightful king had disappeared, slipped out like a thief in the night, with no explanation. Because no explanation was possible. "How are things in Arill City?" he asked.

"Uncomfortable, Your Highness, though guards such as we are not privy to much of what transpires."

Hmm. That meant a lot of political wrangling behind closed doors. And conducted quietly enough that not even servants' gossip carried it to the men at arms. "Did Queen Vycayla and her retinue arrive?"

Nestor glanced from side to side, though who he feared over-hearing such a straightforward answer—one that should be common knowledge—wasn't clear. "Yes, Your Highness. Two days ago."

He said nothing more, and Lonen didn't press. Whatever tran-spired within the royal family was beyond these men. "If you prevent me and my party from reaching Arill's Temple before sundown, you'll be thwarting Arill's divine right to determine who will be King of the Destrye—and jeopardizing Captain Alyx's life."

Nestor, sweat rolling down his temple, swallowed hard. But his sword didn't waver. "Begging your pardon, Your Highness, but you'll have to sort that out with the goddess and King Nolan. We don't dare disobey."

"You'll betray me but not my brother, is that it?" Lonen asked mildly, though he boiled with defeated rage. To come this close and fail... He should've gone back for Oria. Would she still have died if he'd kept going when he tried to turn back? The possibility throbbed with such tender agony that he had to set it aside.

"Your Highness, I—ah, I..." Nestor stammered as he groped for an answer, so Lonen waved him silent.

"Would you at least detail some men to carry Captain Alyx to the temple, so she won't die?" he asked instead.

Nestor swallowed again, still bravely meeting Lonen's gaze though panic lit his eyes. "Our orders are to let none of you past this point. Not until after sunset."

Lonen stared him down another long, endless moment, then called to Fenive. "Take Captain Alyx inside and do your best to tend to her. We might as well stay warm while we wait out this treacherous imprisonment."

He turned his back on the sweating Nestor and climbed the steps to help carry Alyx indoors, glancing back at the sound of boots on the wooden steps. Nestor starting to follow. "Not you or your men, Nestor. You can hold your vigil outdoors."

Nestor bowed, out of habit, stopping himself halfway at an uncertain angle. "And Captain Mott? Sir?"

Lonen didn't bother to look at the man gasping in the snow. "Let him rot for all I care."

~ **15** ~

N EVER HAD A day passed so slowly. As if to mock him, the sun broke through the clouds that had hung over their journey, shining with malicious glee as it glided across the arc of the sky. With each hour that passed, as it became more and more undeniable that he'd lost everything—sacrificed what he loved most to gain nothing at all—Lonen sank further into gloom.

Alyx still lived, but barely. They could do nothing more for her, having stopped the bleeding and closed her wounds. Her ragged panting filled the cabin's silence. Lonen stared into the fire, adding the decision to allow Alyx and her warriors to accompany them to the long list of bad choices, another in the cascade that it seemed he should be able to stop, if only he could go back in time.

A ridiculous exercise, crawling over every detail and choosing the exact spot he'd jump back to in order to change the course of their lives. Selfishly, he wouldn't want to change meeting and marrying Oria, so finding the point where they still found each other, but didn't reach this point of utter failure, was tricky.

Not that he *could* turn back time, but the riddle gave him something to do. By turns despondent and burning with the furious need to act, plotting how he'd change all of this, he prodded his pain over and over. That and plotting his revenge against Nolan at least kept him occupied.

At one point, Fenive sat beside him. "If we found a way to sneak out, perhaps through the back, we could—"

"They outnumber us by too much," he cut her off, unable to

listen to the hope in her voice. No wonder his optimism had annoyed Oria so. "They have the numbers to encircle the house entirely. Any escape attempt would get you all killed and leave me stuck in the same spot."

"You can't just give up!" She sounded aghast, belatedly adding, "Your Highness."

"I'm not giving up. I'm acknowledging defeat. Nolan outmaneuvered me. The game is done—we're stalemated and just waiting for the final piece to fall."

"But Your Highness, we could—"

"No, Fenive. Just no. I'm not getting one more person killed in my bid to hold a throne I never wanted in the first place. Nolan will be a good enough king." Until Lonen killed him, opening the way for their youngest brother Arnon. He'd be a good king—he'd have to be, as the Destrye would be fresh out of Archimago's sons.

"Not good for us," she replied bitterly.

"Then you're no worse off than you were a week ago," he replied. He wished he could say as much for himself.

"That's not true," Fenive shot back. "A week ago I didn't know to hope for more. Now I do and I grieve the loss of that."

"Hope is a terrible tease," he agreed, and she gave him an odd look. "It's better for us to resign ourselves to the grind of fate and hope to hell that Arill has some plan in all this wreckage and disaster."

"Maybe the goddess will provide a miracle yet," Fenive offered.

"That's what it would take: a miracle. I wouldn't advise holding your breath."

Fenive didn't say more—he'd apparently been crushing enough to silence even her youthful enthusiasm. Once he'd believed that Arill had guided him to Oria, that the goddess had led him to marry and love the difficult and powerful sorceress, that She had intended for him to be king and lead the Destrye—and perhaps the Bárans, too—to a peaceful prosperity. He and Oria could have united their people and lived out long lives breeding children born of both races to coax the world back into balance.

But it had all been foolish dreams and wishful thinking. Sparks from the campfire, burning bright as they whirled in their mad dance, then vanishing to ash.

In the morning, once Nestor—or Mott, should he be sadly recovered—Lonen wouldn't return to Arill City. He and Buttercup would go back to the derkesthai colony and recover Oria's body. He'd at least give her a proper burial, and hold vigil over her ashes for the full twelve days, as befitted a true queen.

After that... he would make his plans, and strike Nolan down. He hadn't decided when or how. A future beyond the following morning seemed both infinite and nonexistent. But he felt better deciding that much—that he and Buttercup, riding into the mountain winter. Maybe they wouldn't come back. *Some commit suicide that way—going off into the winter. They say that once you get cold enough, you start to feel warm and sleepy. You fall asleep and never wake up again.* He remembered telling Oria that by the lake, her magical copper eyes bright with interest in her pale face, bloodless from the chill.

Eyes he'd never again look into.

Shouts outside roused him from the depthless funk. Something had the men stirred up. He couldn't bring himself to care.

"Your Highness!" Fenive said from the window, her voice urgent. "You have to see this."

"No, I really don't," he answered. Even standing up seemed beyond him.

"But, the men..." she trailed off, as screaming from outside overtook her words. The roar of flame followed, the unmistakable sound of tornadic fire. "It's a dragon. A real *dragon.*"

The Trom had returned already? A small, petty, and vicious part of him celebrated. There—let Nolan explain *that* away. Let his brother fight the implacable enemy he hadn't believed in. That would be a fair portion from Arill's hand.

But cold duty, his final and unfeeling companion, prodded him to his feet. The Destrye were his people still and always. Even these misguided soldiers holding them hostage only followed the orders of the man who'd declared himself their king. They didn't deserve to die at the hands of the Trom.

Not that Lonen could do anything to save them. He'd tried, and failed.

Surprisingly stiff from sitting still so long, after pushing his body so hard the last few days—and from letting the heaviness of despair settle into his bones, no doubt—he made his way like an old man to the window, bracing himself for the sight of the Trom dragons darkening the sky and setting fire to everything beneath.

Instead, he blinked, the bright sun on the vast whiteness of snow dazzling his vision. Squinting, he tried to refocus, because surely that couldn't be….

"It's Oria!" Fenive clutched his arm, jumping in her excitement. "On a white dragon!"

He couldn't reply, because his breath had guttered out when his heart stopped beating.

It was Oria.

It had to be her, with that distinctive and brilliant shine of copper hair, snapping in the wind like a banner as her iridescent white dragon steed dove, driving the men screaming before it. Bright green flame ripped out, melting the snow in broad streaks.

Men hurtled themselves in all directions, scattering like sparrows before a stooping hawk, leaving their weapons behind in their terror. Lonen ripped open the front door, ran down the front steps, and waved his arms in the air. "Oria!" Her name shredded his lungs, the cold air following hard to choke him. Overcome, he fell to his knees, the snow burning chill through his pants as it soaked in. The white dragon wheeled, spinning midair, then backwinged.

"Oria." He struggled to his feet as the dragon landed, watching him with dancing green eyes that seemed so familiar, though so very large. It bent down, allowing Oria—still clad in her red gown and shadowcat fur cloak, though the gown looked burnt in places, and torn—to slide off his back. She stumbled a little at the impact, but recovered and ran toward him, hair brighter than the sun.

"Lonen!" she hurled herself at him, hitting him like an arrow of intoxicating woman. He wrapped his arms around her, laying his cheek against her silken hair, breathing in her scent—an odd combination of sulfurous fumes, derkesthai musk, and her sweet self—and absorbing her heat. It wasn't possible. Very likely he'd fallen into a delirium born of grief and heartbreak, but at least Arill had given him this gift, this last moment of holding his wife.

"Oria," he muttered, ragged, and like a prayer. She leaned back and framed his face with her bare hands, her touch like the hand of the goddess, sparking through his bloodstream. Her copper eyes, wide and flecked with gold, streamed with tears. She gave him a smile somehow both radiant and tremulous.

"Oh, Lonen. I thought I might never see you again." Burying her fingers in his hair, she dragged his head down as she raised herself up on tiptoe, sealing her lips to his.

He groaned at the unbearably enticing sweetness of her mouth, the incredibly soft give of her lips and the fierce demand as she kissed him, drinking him in and giving back at once. She nearly vibrated in his arms, a tiny sun exploding with magic and sexuality.

From this he understood that none of it was real.

It couldn't be, as Oria couldn't kiss him like this. Never had he felt the sensual slide of her tongue, the piercingly intense sensation of her dewy soft skin under his hands. He must be dying or losing his mind, but if it brought him such delusions, he didn't care. Running his hands through her hair, cupping the back of her head, he kissed her with all the ferocity in him. And the boundaries of the world fell away.

He wandered in a void, formless in a place of nothingness. Magic shimmered all around them.

He was in Oria's mind, feeling what she'd felt.

"Be careful, Oria," Chuffta warned, that distinctive mind-voice Lonen had only heard at the oasis. *"Don't—"*

She did it anyway. She'd been careful her whole life, not to touch or be touched, to follow the rules, to learn the right way. Control and containment and the serenity of *hwil*. Oria opened herself, giving up all control and becoming porous, permeable, and all that nothing poured in—it burst into a myriad of colors, sounds, smells, tastes, and sensations. The wave crashed over her, severing her from everything.

Plunging into it, she gave herself wholeheartedly, without fear or reservation. The frightened girl she'd been—Lonen had never realized the depths of her insecurity, of her self-loathing, how she'd hated her own fragility, how afraid she'd been of exactly this—all of it fell away like ash, burnt in the fire of that unrelenting crucible of wild magic.

After an eternity of tumbling she emerged, changed by her own will, purified to her core being, forged in flames that became her own.

She stood in a vast glittering cavern of crystal, simmering with volcanic fires, the immense derkesthai dragon king splayed across an enormous stone apron next to a lake of lava. The Great One sat up, green eyes round and bright as Grienon.

"Who are you?" The mind-voice, so clearly not Chuffta's, rolled like thunder and lightning at once.

"I am the Sorceress Oria," she declared, feeling the sing of magic, seeing the streaming currents of it in all the world. "I am Ponen."

"And what shall you do with the power you've seized, Ponen?"

"I will be the balance and set things to right."

"Where will you begin?"

An easy answer. She pulled the sling from her neck, unwrapping the sleeping Chuffta. Back in the world, he seemed to be sleeping, still as death, his consciousness in that other realm they'd wandered. But now her eyes had opened and she saw what she hadn't seen before, how magic of her own making had formed a shell around his mind. Winding it back into herself, she freed him from the cocoon of it.

"Finally!" he said, unfurling like a blossoming flower, spreading his white wings exuberantly, then wincing. *"Ouch. What happened to my wings?"*

"The wolves bit you," Oria reminded him, grateful joy filling her. *"And I accidentally put you to sleep with my magic. I'm so very sorry, Chuffta."*

He cocked his triangular head, eyes sparkling bright green. *"Have you learned better now?"*

"I think so," she replied, feeling the sheer power surging through her, capable of anything.

"Then heal me!"

She laughed. *"As you wish, brat. Anything else while I'm at it?"*

His head swiveled backward on his neck to look at the derkesthai king, then back to her. *"Can I be* big?*"*

"Is that what you want?"

"Yes. Oh yes. That and fire. Can I have both?" He fanned his wings in his excitement, talons gripping her arm through the padded sleeve.

"You can have both," she replied gravely.

"There is no going back," the derkesthai king said. ***"You cannot grow small again."***

"Oria can't go back, so neither will I. We are partners in this," Chuffta replied solemnly.

"You must always answer to your sorceress," the Great One put in.

"I shall heed and serve her all my days." Chuffta said the words like a vow.

"I wish you many together."

And Oria spun the magic, twisting it through the living body of the winged lizard, giving the fuel to heal, and to grow, grow, grow. Chuffta flew up into the air, his body billowing with iridescent white magic. Oria pulled the magic through her from all places, giving him the nourishment each part of him needed. Until he landed again, as large as any Trom dragon.

"Now," Oria asked, *"will you fly me to Lonen?"*

"I will fly you to the edge of the world and beyond. To the moons and stars."

Oria laughed. *"Lonen first. He needs us."*

"Then we must go!"

"If I am excused, that is?" Oria asked the Great One.

"Yes. You have much to learn still, but you will learn by doing. When in doubt, return to the balance."

"Thank you, for everything."

"Just be worthy, great-granddaughter of my old friend."

She climbed onto Chuffta's back, a clumsy affair that had her giggling at his mental commentary. *"We shall learn this together,"* Chuffta said.

"As with everything, my old friend," she answered with love and gratitude. Lonen felt it in her and lost all jealousy that had pricked him over Oria's close relationship with her Familiar. She had love enough for both of them, and he was a part of both.

When Chuffta took wing, she laughed with a pure joy that ran over Lonen like snowmelt in springtime, and he rained kisses on her upturned face, savoring the velvety texture of her skin, the clean salt taste of his wife.

"Oh, Lonen," she sighed. "It feels so good to touch you."

"Yes, let's spend eternity just like this."

She giggled, a bubbling brook of carefree happiness. "That sounds good. But we have to get you to the Temple before sundown. It's the seventh day, isn't it?" She glanced at her now giant Familiar. "Chuffta says it is. Why are you sitting in this farmhouse—and who were those soldiers?"

He blinked at her in confusion, then looked around them. At the palace guard, watching in terrorized confusion, and Fenive hanging back with the other warrior women, biting back broad smiles, staring at Chuffta with fascinated curiosity. "This is real?"

"Of course!" She laughed. "What did you think?"

He looked from the enormous Chuffta to Oria, vivid and alive, her cheeks pink from the chill, copper eyes sparkling with humor. "I thought this was a delusion," he told her. "None of this can be real."

"It's real," she assured him, "though I imagine it's a bit of a shock and—"

"A shock?" he broke in, incredulous. He seized her by the arms. Solid and real, yes, but... "Oria, I felt you *die*." Just now he'd been inside her memories when she died.

"Oh, no." She frowned, pursing her lips in sympathy. "I'm so sorry. I didn't think of that—but even if I had, it couldn't be helped."

"It... couldn't be helped." He'd nearly sought his own death rather than go on without her.

"I mean," she continued earnestly, sorrow in her eyes, "I can see now that the marriage bond would affect you like that, you would feel it snap and think the worst, but I had to break all those connections to rebuild myself and my magic in a different way, do you understand?"

He did. He'd seen it in her memories. And the marriage bond— it was there again, stronger than ever. Laughing, he drew Oria into his arms, holding her and rocking as the sheer, shuddering relief flowed through him. "We can touch now."

"Yes. I control the flow of magic into me, so we can touch." She laid her palms against his cheeks, caressing his skin, eyes half-closed as she savored it. "You feel so good. All I want is to touch you."

"I want to take you to bed." He turned, intent on taking her into the farmhouse to do exactly that.

"Not now." She pulled back, laughing. "I want that, too, but we have to get you to Arill's Temple. What was going on here?"

He struggled to think past the overwhelming desire, the need to finally have her in every way. "It doesn't matter now," he told her. "Nolan sent these men to detain me, to keep me from reaching the temple in time."

Oria made a wry face. "I'm not a bit surprised. How did they manage to capture you, though?"

Because he had been surprised, because he'd simply walked into the trap, never suspecting the kind of political treachery that Oria had grown up understanding. Because he'd been naïve and blindly optimistic.

"Because I was a fool—one who doesn't deserve to be king."

~ 16 ~

ORIA SORTED THROUGH the avalanche of thoughts and emotions coming from Lonen. He meant what he said, difficult as she found that to understand.

"He truly thought you had died," Chuffta observed, sounding chastened. *"Though we got here as fast as we could."*

"Faster than would've been possible otherwise, thanks to you."

He mentally preened. *"I like being big."*

"Good thing, as you're stuck with it. More important and pressing, can you carry Lonen and me both to Arill's Temple?"

"Of course, if he wants to go."

"Chuffta will fly us to Arill's Temple," she told Lonen. Then cocked her head at his stubborn refusal, as clear as if he'd voiced it aloud. "You can't let Nolan win with his conniving."

Lonen set his jaw. "I'm done with giving up what I want for the sake of duty. Let him have the throne. Let the Destrye and Bárans fight each other to the death without us. Let's you and Chuffta and I go find a place to live in peace."

She raised an eyebrow. "Like your mother did?"

Anger flashed in him—so much better than that morose despondency—sparking silver in his granite gaze. "She had her reasons. I understand that about her now." He said it pointedly enough that it would've been clear to Oria he felt she wasn't respecting his own reasons, even if she hadn't sensed the thought, and the insult behind it.

For better or worse, however, she had no patience for his turmoil.

"I just flung myself into the jaws of death to be here for you," she replied evenly. "I faced my deepest fears. I don't know if I can explain how agonizing and difficult that was."

Some of the stony obstinacy faded from his face. "I saw… in your memories, when you kissed me."

"Then what, Lonen?" she asked softly, feathering her fingers over his cheek, his skin a miracle, both velvety and bristling with stubble above the line of his beard. He hadn't shaved for a few days, unkempt from what had to have been a wild ride. Turning his head, he pressed a kiss to her palm, the sensation like a lightning bolt. She let it roll through her, savoring all the exuberance of the force of his personality.

"I think I'm maybe not built for this," he answered her, too quietly for any of their listeners to overhear. "I'm a warrior, not a statesman, not a politician. I never saw this coming, this treachery of Nolan's. I can't understand it now. What else will I be blind to?"

"You'll grow into your power like I'll learn mine. You don't have to understand why a man like Nolan has sunk to the depths he has. You only need to keep your own integrity and beliefs."

He searched her face. "I may not know what those are anymore."

"Look around you, Lonen," she replied very seriously, though she wanted to laugh at the absurdity of him questioning himself like this. "All of these people know you're the rightful king. Even those sent against you know it in their hearts and minds. I feel it in them."

He glanced at the man nearest them, one wearing a uniform she recognized as the kind the palace guard wore. Whatever Lonen saw in the man solidified his resolve. "All right then." He nodded to himself, then speared her with a hot stare. "But you *will* be my queen."

"I will," she vowed. "I am in every way that matters already."

"Watching you walk away from me was the hardest thing I ever did."

"It was the hardest thing I ever did." She let the smile break through. "Which makes everything we do from now on easier than that, yes?"

"Look at who's become the sunny optimist," he mock grumbled.

"Yes." She pulled his head down for a long, steaming kiss. "I believe now."

"A miracle," he observed, deep voice murmuring against her lips.

"I sense the hand of Arill in this," she replied, only teasing a little. "Let's go claim the throne."

THE THREE OF them—they strapped the half-conscious Alyx onto Chuffta's back—arrived at Arill's Temple as the sun lowered toward the horizon. With little time to spare, and since they had a dragon to bring them, they decided to go as directly as possible. Which meant entering from the roof. Chuffta assured Oria that the great tree the temple had been built on and around could withstand his weight. As he'd explored far more than she had, she took his word for it.

Oria had barely glimpsed Arill City in the past. She'd arrived unconscious, been confined to a sickbed, caught glimpses from windows heavily covered against the winter chill—and then what little she'd been able to see in the pre-dawn dark when Lonen had spirited them out only seven days before.

Arriving on dragonback gave all the perspective she could want. If they'd had more time—and if they hadn't had the severely injured Alyx with them—she would've asked Chuffta to circle and let them take a long leisurely look at the Temple, palace, and city.

"Next time," Chuffta said. *"Anytime. We can fly every day and all day. We have all the days now!"*

"Once we wrestle with a few teensy problems like duels and the war with Bára."

"Oh, those," Chuffta replied airily, *"so minor I'd already forgotten."*

She laughed mentally, keeping it between them since the sight of the city and temple had Lonen's emotional aura intensifying with a black and bubbling rage. He had his iron battle-axe unsheathed and in his free hand, his other arm wrapped around her waist. As an occasional sweet counterpoint to his violent fantasies of wielding that axe on his brother in revenge, he'd nuzzle her cheek, kissing her bare skin, or nibbling on her ear.

A very odd combination to experience—and she was only glad that he'd soon be able to give vent to all that anger and free himself of it. As for the passion…

Oh, they'd channel that soon enough, too.

Chuffta flew in over the ragtag outer buildings of the impromptu city. Before the war with Bára, before the Bárans had plagued the countryside of Dru with the unstoppable golems, the Destrye had lived in widely scattered small communities. Only the Temple of Arill and the palace, which had begun as a fortress, had been in this place. As the Destrye abandoned their homes and farms, they had fled to the protection of their king and their goddess, building ramshackle shelters in a growing circle around the temple and fortress. With the moat encircling the area, the people ran out of room and so began building up.

Wide and full of wooden spikes, the dry moat had served as a barrier against the golems crossing. On the inside edge, the wooden buildings began, a jumbled pile of scavenged wood built in and around the trees. Ladders gave access to the higher levels, and twisting, shadowed, steep-sided narrow alleys tunneled between. People poured out of these alleys—and doorways and windows and every other opening possible—pointing, screaming, and scrambling in terror.

"They're afraid of me." Chuffta sounded hurt.

"They don't know you're not a Trom dragon," she said aloud

for Lonen's benefit. "We have no way of telling them we're friendly. Hopefully they won't shoot him with arrows," she added, worried.

"We had no success using them against the Trom dragons," Lonen replied in a grim tone. "Of all of us, Chuffta has the best chances. We have to hope they won't shoot *us*."

Good point. "Stay as high as possible, Chuffta."

"I will, though the higher branches tend to be smaller and weaker. And you'll have to climb down farther."

The massive and ancient tree that cradled Arill's Temple rose before them, towering over the rest of the forest. The temple itself, a fantastically airy affair of delicate wooden spirals, spun around the trunk. With hammered metal roofs of copper, it blazed in the afternoon light, a haven of peace and beauty. At the base of the tree sat the palace, square and secure. With walls made of massive tree trunks laid on their sides, it made for an impregnable fortress that climbed several stories. The Bridge of Seofe, which Oria had crossed, looking wistfully out of its windows, arced between the two structures.

In summer, the great tree—with leaves bigger than her head—would shade all the area. As it was, the tree's branches snaked bare and black against the wintry sky. The ones lower down were much thicker than the ones nearer the temple itself. Those higher branches indeed seemed much too spindly for Chuffta to land.

"Any preferences?" she asked Lonen.

He scowled at the rapidly approaching set of possible, and un-likely, landing sites. "As close as you can to that terrace, Chuffta man." He pointed and Oria visualized it for her Familiar. "And pray to Arill the branch will hold."

Chuffta slowed, backwinging a bit. *"This was easier when I was smaller,"* he commented.

"You're the one who wanted to be big," she reminded him, deciding not to look down at how far they could fall if this went wrong.

"Yes, and our lives were easier when we still lived in the tower, people brought us food, and we played all day."

"Oh, is that how you remember it?" she replied drily. *"Watch out for—"* She winced as Chuffta's wing tip clipped a branch, broke it off and sent it crashing down on the shining copper roofs, along with more branches it tore off as it fell. The people who'd started to pour out onto the terrace Lonen had picked all ran back inside.

"Sorry," Chuffta said, sounding chagrined.

"Accidents happen," she said aloud.

"With the side benefit of scaring our welcoming reception," Lonen added with vicious satisfaction.

Wings open for balance, Chuffta lightly perched on a thick branch not attached to any parts of the temple. It creaked ominously. *"I think you should hurry."*

Lonen hadn't needed any urging. He'd sheathed his axe, untied Alyx and was already moving with the unconscious woman over his shoulder as he nimbly climbed down Chuffta's helpfully extended leg. "Stay there," he called to Oria. "I'll come back for you."

She hadn't grown up in the forests of Dru, and couldn't climb a dragon's leg like a tree, but Oria had her own resources. Summoning magic from the living forest, she pulled it into herself and created a cloud of energy between her and the nearby terrace. She floated slowly so she could concentrate on not fumbling the maneuver—particularly when she needed to focus on not being tumbled midair by the gust of Chuffta's departure—which gave Lonen time to hand Alyx over to the healers.

He'd been certain they would observe that much of a truce, accepting the wounded warrior, but palace guards now filled the terrace. With Chuffta's departure, they gained confidence, pointing weapons at Lonen and surrounding him. He'd drawn his battle-axe, holding it two-handed, legs braced widely.

They all gaped when Oria landed light as a jewelbird beside him.

"Nice trick," he muttered from the side of his mouth.

"Thank you." She beamed at him, delighted it had worked so well.

"Though I told you to stay put." A commotion at the back of the ring of guards had the mass of them shifting.

"I was afraid the branch would break and I'd fall." She traded him an angelic smile for his blackly disbelieving growl, but didn't object when he stepped forward slightly, positioning himself between her and whoever approached down the widening aisle in the mass of guards. It gave her the opportunity to drawn on the magic of the forest, replenishing what she'd used and pooling a reserve for the battle to come.

As she'd felt with the fallen leaf her first time in Arill City, the living green magic of the trees filtered in like summer sun through a verdant canopy, sweet and gently warming.

A trio of people approached, Nolan at the leading point of their triangle. The head goose in their fast-traveling vee, Oria thought irreverently.

"Geese bite hard," Chuffta reminded her, sending her images of him playing chase with the irascible flocks of geese that stopped near Bára on their way to other places.

"True." And Nolan looked ready to bite. He wore the Crown of Dru, the wreath of hammered gold leaves that Lonen had left in the palace for safekeeping, and carried their father's sword. Lonen had never cared for the sword, preferring his trusty battle-axe. Or perhaps because he'd had to take it from King Archimago's crushed and still warm hand. Nolan's piercing blue gaze sliced over them like the glittering edge of the unsheathed sword, his mouth grim over his neat and glossy black beard, his fury as honed and lethal.

At his left hand, acting as Nolan's second, their younger brother Arnon kept pace. Oria had always liked Arnon, whose well-trained intelligence had designed the aqueducts and whose incisive wit had amused her during long dinners. At the moment he looked as if he already mourned his brother's death, and he emanated sodden grief. Though for which brother wasn't certain.

Taller than either of them, Rhiten Robson, in the deep green robes of Arill's acolytes strolled, wild mane of purest white shining like fresh snow. His brows bristled with long white hairs that curled with untamed glee, as did his drooping beard and mustache. As when she'd met him before, his pale blue eyes held lively interest—and of the three, he was the only one not roiling with emotion.

"Seize the deserter!" Nolon thundered before he even reached them. "Imprison the false king who brings dragons and sorcerers down on Dru to destroy us."

The palace guard shifted, some of them moving to obey, others stepping out smartly, pivoting to arrange themselves in a defensive formation. One young man saluted and then bowed. "Your Highness King Lonen. Welcome home."

~ **17** ~

"A LBY." LONEN NODDED, as if he'd expected Alby and his loyal men to appear and do exactly this. Inside him, though, something shifted and settled. He *should* have expected this. Oria had been right to remind him that he wasn't alone in this, no matter how he'd felt. The majority of the Destrye viewed Lonen as their rightful king and Nolan as the usurper.

No amount of unfair play from Nolan changed that. It was why he'd been reduced to conniving. It all came clear in that moment, how much Nolan feared he'd lose.

Nolan clenched his jaw, a mad glitter in his eyes, a desperate tension riding him. Arnon flicked a glance at Nolan, met Lonen's gaze, and shook his head minutely.

"Seize him, I say!" Nolan roared, though his voice lacked resonance, perilously close to a young boy's tantrum.

"A point of order, Prince Nolan," Priest Robson said mildly, holding up a finger and looking—of all things—vaguely amused. "His Highness King Lonen has presented himself to me, Rhiten of Arill, at the consecrated temple of the goddess before seven full days elapsed. He is markedly *not* dead, nor is he a traitor."

"Did you not see the fucking dragon he rode on?" Nolan practically hissed at the priest, then pointed his sword at Oria. "Or the black magic of the witch accompanying him? He has allied with the enemies of Dru."

Lonen looked around at the gathering, making a show of it. "Nobody looks to be dead, bleeding or burnt to ash. I say Chuffta, the white dragon, and Sorceress Oria are allies to us all. I have returned in strength, to lead the Destrye to victory and prosperity."

The gathered guard cheered, even those previously holding weapons against him. More cheering echoed from inside the temple, and in waves from below as Lonen's words were relayed through the gathering crowd.

"You are not king!" Nolan shouted over them. "I am heir after Ion, by right of birth order and our father's wishes. You have no claim to the throne of Dru. Resign your claim and I'll let you live."

"If I have no claim, how can I resign it?" Lonen asked.

Nolan growled under his breath, an inhuman and incoherent sound, brandishing Archimago's sword. "Fine. Then die, by our father's blade, as Arill judges."

"As Rhiten of Arill, I agree to arbitrate this challenge for the throne of Dru," Robson declared. "Let no one interfere until the goddess sets Her hand on the King of the Destrye."

The assembly all made the sign of Arill, a murmur of excitement running through them as they all withdrew, forming a circle around the terrace.

"As High Priestess of Arill, I also arbitrate." Head healer Talya emerged from the interior, striding forward serenely enough in her green robes, but with her gaze fixed on Lonen—and especially on Oria—with vicious hatred. The smug curve to her mouth told Lonen all he needed to know about how she'd rule in the contest. A very bad development.

"I believe I outrank you, Talya," Queen Vycayla said, gliding serenely from another doorway. His mother had unbound her hair and it streamed over her white robes, trailing over the polished golden wood of the terrace. Talya gaped at her, clearly astonished to see Vycayla.

"Mother!" Arnon gasped. "You're here."

"Hello, Arnon," she replied. "Yes, I've been here for several days, in fact."

"You have no rank, Mother," Nolan sneered. "Go back to your

rooms, where I ordered you to remain."

"Nolan," Arnon protested, putting a staying hand on their brother's arm. "Our father, the late King Archimago, never stripped Queen Vycayla of rank. You're wrong to treat her so. Why didn't you tell me our mother had returned?"

Nolan yanked his arm away. "You didn't need to know. Go back to your rooms, Mother, or I'll have you taken there under guard."

"You cannot command me, my wounded son," Vycayla replied, sounding sorrowful.

"I can and do!" he shouted, then scanned the gathering. "Who has betrayed me by releasing her?"

"I did." The healer Baeltya stepped forward and bowed deeply to Lonen. "Welcome home, Your Highness. It's good to see your quest has been rewarded with vigorous allies and a return to robust health."

"Better run, little healer," Nolan ground out, fury contorting his face. "Once I've won the challenge, I'll make you suffer as you can't imagine."

"I've already suffered unimaginably," Baeltya returned evenly. "And I look forward to King Lonen righting those wrongs. Your Highness." Bowing, she retreated.

"The challenge has been offered and accepted," the priest intoned.

"The challenge has been offered and accepted," Vycayla echoed. They arranged themselves on either side of the circle formed by the onlookers.

"Name your seconds," Priest Robson said, nodding to Lonen to declare his first, as current king. "Choose wisely, as you may name only one."

"I name my wife, Sorceress Oria," he announced, then felt shock drain cold through his body when both Robson and Vycayla shook their heads.

"Not your wife, boy. Not until Arill seals the union with Her gentling hand." The priest sounded regretful, but firm on the subject.

Arill curse him, Lonen had forgotten that simple order of things. He supposed he'd envisioned a more honorable sequence of events—one where he and Oria had arrived in plenty of time to reassure everyone he lived, to arrange the wedding, and then meet Nolan's challenge in due course. Lonen had yet to get his mental feet under him after all the turnabouts of fortune.

"I request a delay of the challenge then," he replied. "Queen Vycayla, my esteemed mother, has agreed to sponsor our marriage in Arill's Temple."

"Does the challenger agree to a postponement?" Robson inquired politely.

Nolan's hand flexed on the sword, a broad and relaxed smile filling his face, an echo of who he'd been before he'd returned from Bára a haunted man. "No."

The crowd murmured and Robson nodded as if the decision wouldn't doom Lonen. He could perhaps defeat Nolan, but not both of his brothers combined. Arnon might prefer books and diagrams, but he'd been trained as a warrior as they all had, and tempered in countless battles.

"I can still help," Oria whispered for his ears alone, standing just behind him. "They won't know."

"Arill will know," he replied, with a shake of his head. "You must not interfere in the judgment of the goddess."

She made an impatient sound, no doubt considering his refusal stubbornly superstitious. He didn't care. He wanted there to be no doubt of his right to hold the throne.

"King Lonen will have no second." Priest Robson declared. "Prince Nolan, name your second."

"I name my brother, Prince Arnon!" Nolan declared with an excited grin, and some of the gathering cheered.

"Very well." Robson nodded. "Then—"

"A moment," Arnon said, staring hard at Lonen, then to their mother. He swallowed visibly. "I will not serve."

Nolan spun on him, sword to Arnon's throat. "You traitor."

Arnon didn't flinch, simply stared evenly at Nolan. "Kill me, then. I'd rather die loyal to the rightful king than enable this craziness."

"You dare say this to *me*," Nolan gritted out. "Your own brother."

"This is wrong, Nolan," Arnon said quietly. "You and I both know it. Rescind the challenge and pledge fealty to Lonen as king. He will forgive you, work to redress your complaints." Arnon's gaze went to Lonen, a solemn plea in them. "We need every warrior."

Though it grated in his craw like a broken bone from a bitter meal, Lonen nodded. "Before Arill and the Destrye, I pledge it so."

"I. Will. Not. Yield." Nolan shook with the intensity of his fury, a line of blood appearing across Arnon's throat. Vycayla took a step forward, stopping when Nolan snarled at her, like a wolfhound gone rabid.

"A man who commits fratricide, before so many witnesses, with no just cause, may not bring a challenge against the king," Robson explained, as if teaching a class in Destrye law.

Nolan vibrated in frustration, then pushed Arnon away, so that their brother staggered back, caught by the guards behind him. Spinning to face Lonen, he snaked the sword in a lethal arc, then stilled, ready.

"So, it's just us, baby brother," he said with a malicious smile. "Get your sword."

"You have my sword," Lonen noted.

"You'll have to use another."

"I'll use this." Lonen held his iron battle-axe in both hands, the weight of it solid and reassuring. They had been through years of conflict together, he and that axe.

"You'll be too slow, Lonen," Arnon protested before Robson leveled a quelling glare at him.

"Let no one interfere in any way," Robson announced. "Not by sound or movement. Or magic," he added wryly with a pointed look at Oria. Lonen felt her move back, though she remained a warm glow in his heart.

"You will fight until Arill makes Her will known," Vycayla called. "Let the challenge commence."

Nolan launched at him, lethal as lightning and nearly as fast. Lonen barely brought up his axe in time, shifting just enough that the sword bit into the wooden haft between his hands instead of cleaving off his unprotected fingers. For a moment he and Nolan locked in place, nearly nose to nose, his brother's eyes holding nothing sane or rational. In reflex, he shoved, and Nolan danced away, light on his feet, bringing the sword around quick as a striking tree snake.

Lonen dodged, but slowly, hampered by his heavy fur cloak. Stupid not to divest himself of it. But too late for regrets. Nolan was all in, the sword slicing again on the back swing, catching Lonen on his weighted leg—a bright pain of first blood.

He'd yet to swing his axe, pressed into defense by his slimmer, more agile brother. Nolan had always been a quick and clever fighter, and now he fought with all the fury of a man without fear or reservation. Pressing his advantage, he harried Lonen with his lighter sword, flurries of strikes and slices making Lonen feel like a lumbering bear, too thick and too slow.

He'd been fighting golems too long, too accustomed to their methodical and patient ways. Nolan fought with alert intelligence, relentless in his determination to take Lonen apart with ten thousand cuts. He closed in and Lonen swung the double-bladed axe, missing by finger lengths that might as well have been leagues, when Nolan seized the opening to drive the sword into Lonen's gut.

Roaring in pained fury—feeling Oria's terror—Lonen jerked the haft of the axe into Nolan's chin, snapping his head back and reversing the power of his sword. Nolan staggered back, momentarily stunned, and Lonen pursued, bringing the battle-axe around in a diagonal that barely sliced Nolan's chest as he pulled back, but that Lonen continued in a smooth arc, down and up and crosswise again, biting into Nolan's primary sword arm.

That arm dangling uselessly, Nolan still wielded the sword with his other hand, smoothly transferring his grip and bringing it around on Lonen's unguarded flank—again slicing the already wounded thigh. Lonen staggered, that leg collapsing under his weight. And his cloak bit into his neck. Nolan stood on it, a manic grin of triumph making his skin as tight and waxy clear as a Trom's. His sword came up from below, spearing into Lonen's stomach, a spike of fire.

But he paused, face suddenly creased in confusion.

And Lonen brought the battle-axe down on Nolan's skull.

Nolan paused a long moment, eyes wide, the black so dilated it looked oily and lightless, the normal blue barely a bright ring around those lifeless pits. Then his eyes rolled back in his head, and he collapsed.

Lonen went down on one knee, aware of the blood pooling around him, but only able to see his brother's blood on the hammered metal leaves of the crown of Dru.

"Your Highness." Priest Robson put a hand on his shoulder, a firm grip. On the other side, his mother laid her hand on the back of his neck, the healing light of Arill streaming in to give him strength. "You are within your rights to take your challenger's life, King Lonen. Arill has blessed your victory and will forgive you."

But would he forgive himself? "I have no wish to take my brother's life." He sought out Arnon's gaze, his younger brother's face pale and strained. "We need every warrior," he added, and Arnon nodded, lips moving in a silent prayer.

Besides, there had been that moment, right at the end, when he'd seen something...*other* in Nolan. "Oria?"

"Yes, love." She was at his side as if she'd materialized there. Perhaps she had, in her newfound powers.

"Can you look into Nolan somehow?"

"What do you mean?" She laid a hand on his face, copper eyes worried. "Let the healers stop your bleeding."

"Yes, let them do it. But, Nolan—is it possible that he's been influenced? Can Báran magic do that?"

Her eyes widened in horrified understanding. "I don't know of anyone who could do that, but after all we've seen, I won't say it's not possible. What makes you think so?"

"There was a moment." He flinched as someone—Baeltya perhaps—pressed a pad against his stomach wound. "After I cut him with the axe, I saw something in his eyes, his face, that reminded me of the Trom. My iron axe," he added on a pained wheeze.

"And iron cleaves magic," Oria realized, and she wisped away.

"Your Highness, lie back," Baeltya said. Then Arnon was beside him, helping him lie back on the terrace. He stared up at the interlacing branches, a black lace against the twilight sky. For a moment he imagined they burst with leaves of spring green, then realized it was Chuffta, head angled so one great green eye stared at him from a long neck craning over the edge of the terrace. His narrow jaw parted in a kind of smile, furnace hot breath wafting over Lonen, dispelling the chill of encroaching night.

"Chuffta, don't frighten everyone," Oria tsked, wedging her way through the working healers to feather gentle fingers over Lonen's face. "You're right. Nolan had some kind of spell in him. Maybe a long-distance working of the sort that powers the golems. The iron interrupted it, but I'll have to study it more, see if I can get all of it out of him."

"How did this happen?" Arnon demanded from his vigil on the other side of Lonen's head.

Lonen met Oria's concerned gaze, and she read his thoughts. "Yes, I agree," she said. "It probably happened before Nolan made his way back to Dru. We likely don't have the true story of what happened to him in Bára, during the time he was lost to us."

"But you can fix him," Vycayla said, not a question, very nearly a command.

"I will find a way," Oria answered, steel in her voice. "And all the men who returned with him."

Oh, right. Lonen closed his eyes wearily. "We need to round

them up. Arnon has a list. They need to be kept under—"

"We can handle it, Your Highness," Oria interrupted. "*You* will rest and recover, as I'm expecting you to consummate your wedding in fine form."

He forced his eyes open to see her lovely face hovering over his, Chuffta's great visage like a moon behind her. "Excellent incentive," he rasped.

"Good." She kissed him, lips moving against his with unbearable sweetness.

LONEN'S REIGN

SORCEROUS MOONS – BOOK 6

BY
JEFFE KENNEDY

A Looming Threat

The sorceress Oria has finally come into her own—able to wield the power of her birthright and secure in the marriage she once believed would bring her only misery. But the past she escaped still chases her, and the certainty of war promises to destroy everything she's fought to have.

An Impossible War

Once before Lonen led an army in a desperate attempt to stop the powerfully murderous sorcerers of Bára—and he nearly lost everything. Now he must return to the battlefield that took the lives of so many of his people. Only this time he has more to risk than ever.

The Final Conflict

With guile, determination—and unexpected allies—Oria and Lonen return to the place where it all began... and only hope that it won't also be the end of them.

Dedication

For Rebecca Cremonese,
Who gave so much attention and care to every little detail.

ACKNOWLEDGEMENTS

Many thanks to Jim Sorenson and Sage Walker, for encouraging me to persevere and finish this series. And for Sunday brunches and wide-ranging conversations.

A special thank you to Carien, for fact-checking and asking the right questions. And for being there for all these years. Just amazing, isn't it?

Huge thanks, too, to all of you who commented on the podcasts and blog posts, and in the private group, who cheered me on and have been waiting for this conclusion. I hope it's the grand finale you wished for.

Love to Kelly Robson for daily chats, hearts and kisses. Also to Cathy Smith for the same. And to my mom for being a patron of the arts.

And always to David, who loves me just the way I am.

Thank you for reading!

<u>Credits</u>
Line and Copy Editor: Rebecca Cremonese
Cover Design: Steam Power Studios, www.steampowerstudios.com.au

~ 1 ~

"JUST A FEW more moments of your patience, Your Highness," the healer Baeltya said, her tone abstracted as she concentrated.

Lonen stared up at the patterned, arched ceiling of Arill's Temple, counting the interweaving strips of wood yet again. There were one thousand and fifty-two in the central spiral. He should be grateful for Arill's magic—and Her dedicated priestesses who devoted themselves to healing—which made convalescence so much faster, if profoundly uncomfortable. Mostly, however, he chafed at the enforced inactivity. Much easier not to get injured in the first place.

At least his mother, who'd initially taken care of the gut wound he'd received from his brother Nolan during their duel, had left the follow-up care to Baeltya. The junior healer didn't lecture him the way Vycayla, as both the dowager queen and his mother, seemed to feel entitled to do. Not only entitled, but compelled.

If he didn't need her help to ensure he and Oria could officially marry with Arill's blessing, according to Destrye law, he'd be tempted to tell his mother to go back to her hermitage already.

The wedding ceremony was a stupid formality, really. With the duel over and Lonen's claim to the throne of Dru secured, he could declare Oria his wife and Queen of the Destrye once and for all. They'd fought hard enough for it. It still stuck in his craw that he'd had to fight his brother for it.

"Try not to twitch, Your Highess," Baeltya said, sounding more emphatic and less vague. "This is a delicate piece."

"I wouldn't want you to meld my intestines to my bladder after all," he commented wryly.

"You laugh, but given the previous state of your intestines, that's not impossible," she replied in a tart tone, her healing magic twisting in parts of his gut he wished he didn't know about. "That final blow could've killed you—likely would've killed a man in less robust condition—so maybe spend this time contemplating your gratitude to Arill for Her healing gifts."

"I'm grateful," he grumbled. Though he'd much rather be with Oria and his mother as they sorted through Nolan's psyche. He couldn't decide if it made him feel better or worse that Nolan's rebellion and treachery might have been fueled by a sorcerous taint from his time in Bára. And Arnon... Lonen didn't know what to make of his younger brother's changeable loyalty. First Arnon had backed Nolan's challenge, then—apparently somehow swayed by their mother Vycayla's return from self-imposed exile—he had refused to act as Nolan's second.

So ironic that they accused Lonen of being enchanted and duped by his sorceress wife to the point they questioned his devotion to Dru, and now Oria was the only person he felt he could fully trust.

He sighed heavily.

"Your Highness..."

"That was a sigh, not a twitch."

She laughed. "I don't envy Oria in managing you if you're always this difficult."

"She has other ways of managing me than chiding complaints." Which only reminded him that they could touch now. He could finally and truly bed his beautiful sorceress—and he'd instead been laid up for two days recovering. "Will I be well enough to be released after this?"

"In a hurry to leave us? We'll see. Queen Vycayla will have the final word."

"Wonderful," he muttered.

As if evoked by her name, Vycayla swept into the room, asking

Baeltya for a report and not bothering to greet her son at all. With determined resignation, Lonen resumed counting the ceiling pieces and waited for them to conclude their healer conversation. He'd learned better than to interrupt, as it only delayed them, extended his involuntary stay, and earned his mother's scathing remarks about what he didn't know. That's what being king got you—no power in your own household.

His mother laid a hand on his brow, not a soothing maternal gesture but testing his vitality for herself. Her serious gray eyes looked through him, large in her severe face. She didn't show her age much in wrinkles, but time had pared away any trace of youthful softness. With her long hair tightly braided back, her bones seemed to show through translucent skin. She raised a brow at his appraisal. "You're much improved, my impetuous son."

"Improved enough to have the wedding?" he asked. He would've preferred to sit up and have this conversation at least upright if they wouldn't let him stand, but he'd have to fight them both and he'd lose.

"Yes." They both murmured reprimands, gentle hands restraining him as he nearly leapt for freedom. "*Not* this exact moment," his mother added with a hint of a smile. "But we can set a date and plan the ceremony."

"The ceremony will be tonight," he said, using a tone of authority.

His mother rolled her eyes. "You're not some timber brat marrying a milkmaid. This is an event. The King of Dru is marrying a Princess of Bára, who will become Queen of the Destrye. You will be joining two realms that have been at war for centuries. It must be done with appropriate pomp and celebration."

Lonen set his teeth. "No, I'm not marrying a milkmaid. I'm marrying a woman who is already my wife and has been for the better part of a year."

"You didn't marry her under Arill's hand," his mother corrected.

"I *know* that," he replied as evenly as possible. "Which is why we're getting married *again*."

"Don't use that tone with me, boy," his mother snapped. "You're not too big to be turned over my knee and paddled."

Baeltya choked back a laugh. Since Lonen likely outweighed his mother by twice as much, and most of it brawn, that assertion was ridiculous. Never mind the fact that he outranked her. Still... "Yes, Mother," he said with exaggerated deference.

"Better." She patted his cheek smartly enough to sting. "I shall perform the prayers to Arill to determine the most auspicious date and time for—"

Lonen wrapped a hand around her slender wrist, the bones spider-light. "I'm not waiting until spring or some such," he warned.

She relented, smiling with more warmth. "I agree. This is best handled speedily. I'll seek the most auspicious time in the next several weeks."

"Days."

Her smile faded. "Don't tell me my business, boy. I follow Arill's will, not yours—and no crown changes that."

He winced, and Vycayla echoed it, realizing the image she'd evoked. Nolan had been wearing the crown—a wreath of bronzed oak leaves—during the duel. When Lonen had brought the iron battle-axe down on his skull in a desperate move, with his brother's sword already spearing his gut, the leaves had cut Nolan's scalp.

Blood on the crown of Dru. Lonen couldn't shake the sight of it—or the lingering dread that it might be a terrible omen.

"How is he?" he asked quietly.

"Physically he's healed," Vycayla replied with crisp authority. Then shook her head. "Mentally, well... whatever stain they put on him, the iron of your axe only temporarily dimmed it. He's back to his vitriol and ranting. Oria is working on the problem."

"I still think a tincture of iron solution would work," Baeltya commented.

"If it doesn't poison him beyond retrieval," Vycayla replied dry-ly.

"There, Your Highness." Baeltya dusted her hands together to disperse the healing magic and any remanence lingering from her connection with him. "You may sit up."

At last. He sat up, vigor coursing through him. "Thank you. Both of you. I feel like a new man." He stood, brimming with a feverish excitement, pumped his arms and stomped his legs. "Where is Oria?"

"With Nolan in the dungeon," his mother said, then narrowed her eyes. "Why?"

"I intend to see my wife," he answered blandly. And he intended to take Oria to bed and at last fuck her properly, until they both couldn't see straight. His balls grew heavy in anticipation. This long-delayed consummation would be sweet indeed. Maybe he'd keep her naked and in bed with him until the wedding and they could—

"You are not to be with Oria unchaperoned until the wedding night," his mother informed him, as if reading his thoughts.

Lonen paused in the midst of pulling on his shirt. "Excuse me?"

Vycayla drew herself up to her imposing height, slight of build, eyes of steel. "You can sound as dangerous as you like, but you *will* heed me as high priestess of Arill's Temple. This wedding will be done properly. Oria's previous illness is well known, as is the fact that she's a virgin."

"Not so much," he answered with a feral grin. "In fact, we've—"

Vycayla held up a hand. "Spare me the details. So far as the physical consummation of your marriage in a child-engendering act, she is a virgin. And she will retain that state until you are properly married under Arill's hand."

He nearly sputtered as he fumed. "That has never been a Destrye requirement, that a bride be a virgin."

"Yes and no." Vycayla's eyes glittered. "The most sacred of Arill's binding ceremonies are at their most powerful with a woman whose body remains entirely female, who has never taken male flesh inside her."

"Oh, I've been inside her." Fingers, sure, but those counted as male flesh.

"Skin to skin?" Vycayla inquired archly. "Oria says you used gloves and other implements."

Abruptly, self-consciousness swamped him, to be having this conversation with his *mother*—while Baeltya stood by, dark eyes dancing in salacious amusement, though she kept a straight face. "I can't believe you asked Oria about this." Or that Oria had told her.

Vycayla raised her eyes to the heavens, lips moving in a silent prayer. "She will be my daughter. Women discuss these things. And I needed to know, for the ceremony. Arill has chosen wisely for you and we will honor Her hand in this by binding you in Her most sacred ceremony—one that will banish all the bad omens and taint from your kingship and marriage, and that will auger well for the Destrye in the battle to come. This is about more than you and your sexual urges. Do you understand now?" she asked, spacing out the words as if he were still a boy.

He scowled at her. "I greatly regret digging you out of your hermitage."

She smiled serenely. "As does Nolan. You're welcome. Will you abide by this, Your Highness?"

Oh, *now* she used the honorific. "I don't like it."

"You don't have to like it. You must simply agree."

"Don't make me wait too long, Mother."

She patted him on the cheek, gently, pleased with his capitulation. "You've waited all this time. What's a few more weeks?"

"Days."

"We'll see."

He'd been hearing that line since he was a boy, too—and it never boded well.

Finally fully dressed, battle-axe sheathed on his back, Lonen strode out of Arill's healing center in the temple. Baeltya walked along with him, hands folded neatly into the billowing embroidered cuffs of her deep green robes. Everyone they passed bowed to him, crying out their good wishes and joy at his return, an elaborate demonstration of fervent loyalty.

"You'd think they hadn't been bowing and scraping to my brother the usurper only days ago," he muttered under his breath.

"It was an incredibly difficult week," Baeltya replied quietly. "Nolan employed brutal methods to ensure the appearance of loyalty to his claim. Not that I'd expect you to thank him, but he has done you the favor of making the prospect of your reign look very good by comparison. These people are sincere in their delight—and relief."

A group of approaching Destrye warriors spotted him and all went to one knee, bowing their heads and saluting. "All hail His Highness King Lonen!"

They did sound sincere, holding the knee until he'd completely passed. He and Baeltya continued through the dark halls of the palace. Not a beautiful place, but a secure one, it had started out as a fortress, built upon by generations of Destrye and their kings. And with a warren of tunnels hollowed out below. The stairs took them down, past the food storage cellars, and Lonen didn't let his gaze linger on how meager those stores had become. A few more months before the first crops would be ripe, though perhaps Arill would bless them with an early spring.

Perhaps Oria could wield her sorcery to hasten the harvest.

Down another level and they passed the guards—also happy to greet him and congratulate his good health—and into the area used for prisoners. This deep, the earthen walls loomed dark, the great roots of the forest occasionally surfacing like the coil of a sea serpent before disappearing again. For a people accustomed to being outdoors, to climbing the trees of their home, the dungeons imposed their own punishment. Most Destrye chose death over imprisonment.

Nolan, however, would not be offered that option. Not yet.

He paced in a large cell at the end of the tunnel, fenced in by iron bars. Ranting and raving, indeed. His voice echoed down the narrow space, by turns cajoling and ordering. Oria sat very still on a wooden stool well out of reach, facing Nolan. She had her back to the hall, her exotic copper hair caught the torchlight, falling in a straight sheet like polished metal.

Knowing his sorceress, that she'd likely fallen into a deep meditative state as she used her magic, Lonen called out so as not to startle her. "Oria."

She spun on the stool, hair fanning with the movement, her lovely face full of delighted surprise. Running to him, she flew into his arms, a cloud of silk, spicy qinn, and luscious woman. He kissed her thoroughly, feeling he could never get enough of the feel and taste of her mouth, the way she fit against him.

"They let you out," Oria exclaimed when he let her come up for air. "It's so good to see you up." She'd been to visit him regularly while he was laid up healing, but she sounded as if she hadn't seen him in ages. Though they had been separated before their all-too-brief reunion and had no time at all to savor their ability to truly touch.

He ran his hands over her body, ignoring Nolan's crazed shouting and Baeltya's more discreet presence. "I should've taken you into that farmhouse," he growled in Oria's ear, taking the lobe of her ear into his mouth, biting lightly and then sucking on her deliciously sweet skin. She moaned softly, melting against him.

"But look how well everything turned out because you didn't," she answered, pulling back to give him a smile, her copper eyes wide and sparkling, the same color as her hair. "You're the undisputed King of the Destrye and—"

"I dispute it!" Nolan shouted.

"—we'll be married soon," Oria talked over his mad brother.

"Not soon enough," Lonen said, trailing his fingers over her satin cheek, down the swanlike column of her throat.

"Ah, they told you."

"Yes." He lowered his brows threateningly, though his scowl did nothing to dim her radiant smile. "You might've warned me on one of your visits."

She lifted onto her toes and kissed him. "I didn't want to upset you. It will be only a short wait. All is falling into place. Especially now that you're healed."

"Come in here and I'll cut you open again!" Nolan practically screamed. He had his hands wrapped around the iron bars, fisted as he shook them.

With a sigh, Lonen tucked Oria against his side, at least savoring her closeness under his arm. She nestled against him, both of them watching Nolan as he flung himself against the bars, hurtling threats like a tree monkey flinging feces—filthy but without much effect.

"What have you discovered?" he asked Oria.

She shook her head slightly. "The enchantment is there, but it's… slippery. I can't think of a better way to describe it. I can sense it, get near, then it's gone before I can get a good look at it."

"Maybe you need a break," he suggested.

She glanced up with an arch expression. "We can't—"

"Not that," he interrupted. "Is sex all you think about?"

Gratifyingly, she giggled. He ignored Baeltya's snicker. "Let's get out of this hole," he said. "I've been cooped up for days and I want to be outside, to see the sky."

Oria's face lit up. "Would you like to fly? Chuffta says he'd like to."

Her winged lizard Familiar—now a dragon the size of Arill's Temple—likely put it more emphatically. Flying sounded perfect. He hadn't been able to enjoy it the one time before, carrying the injured Alyx between him and Oria during their swift trip to make it in time for his duel with Nolan.

"I would like that." He ran a hand over Oria's hip, contemplating what he might do to her.

Baeltya cleared her throat.

"Oh, brother." Lonen fixed the healer with a baleful glare. "What could we get up to on dragonback?"

Baeltya raised her elegant brows. "If you need me to explain that, Your Highness…"

"You can come with us," Oria invited, slanting him a quelling look. "If you'd like to, that is."

Baeltya's face transformed with rapture. "Truly?" she breathed. "I'd *love* to fly."

"A threesome it is," Lonen declared, just to laugh at their outrage. "Come along, ladies. I'm ready for fresh air."

And they left his treacherous brother shouting his rage behind them.

~ 2 ~

"**W**HAT IS TAKING *so looonnnnngggg?*" Chuffta dragged out the question on an exaggerated moan of his mind-voice. Though Oria couldn't see him—as they had yet to leave the palace—she felt him impatiently furling and unfurling his wings, dancing in place and lashing his tail. She didn't know if she felt his body movements so vividly now because of his greatly enhanced size making every sensation larger, or because her magic had linked them more tightly when she'd used it to make him big.

"Don't hit anything," she cautioned him silently. Like a wolf-hound pup grown too fast, Chuffta had yet to fully comprehend his new size and how his body occupied space. Something crashed behind Chuffta and she felt him mentally wince.

"Oops. But the Destrye have lots more trees."

She sighed. Hearing it, Lonen raised a brow at her as he waved away the cluster of attendants and helped Oria into the shadowcat fur cloak himself. She shook her head minutely, unwilling to explain with so many ears to hear. The Destrye in general didn't know the extent of her and Chuffta's abilities, and she preferred it that way for the time being. Lonen had originally insisted upon it and she'd grown to appreciate his discretion. Who knew what would come in useful in the months of war to come? Her brother Yar might have created more spies than Nolan from the men in his regiment who had emerged from the lake under Bára.

Until the palace guard had all those men quietly rounded up for her to examine, Oria had been focusing her attention on sorting through Nolan's chaotic and vengeful thoughts. Now that Lonen had emerged from the healers' care, he'd likely be expediting the containment of the possible spies. She would study them, of course, but she didn't know what more she'd find out from many minds that she couldn't dig out of one. Especially when that one had been the primary target of whatever Yar and his cohorts had done. That was something that continued to elude her. She might have her power back—and finally the ability to manage it—but she couldn't match the centuries of accumulated knowledge Yar had at his command in the temples at Bára.

"Are you mad at me?" Chuffta asked the question meekly and she realized she'd been too deep in thought to reply to him. Another change with her improved control: she shielded so well that Chuffta no longer "heard" her surface thoughts unless she directed them mentally.

"We're on our way," she reassured Chuffta. *"We had to stop for warm gear. It's winter and even colder in the air. And we have to walk to where you are."*

"I miss being in the same place as you." Chuffta sounded a little forlorn, and lonely. *"I didn't know I'd miss riding around on your shoulder. Remember how I'd twine my tail around your arm?"*

Yes, because it had been only a couple of weeks before, but she kept the amusement out of her mind-voice. Derkesthai had a different perception of time, and Chuffta was a young member of a long-lived race. That hadn't changed just because he'd grown huge. *"I miss having you close, too."*

She really did. Sleeping alone in Lonen's big bed while he recovered had made her realize she hadn't been entirely without company since she was seven—except for those horrible few days when Head Healer Talya had isolated her in an attempt to "save" Lonen from her enchantment. It would have been a great comfort to feel Chuffta's solid little body curled up against her. A price for everything, she supposed. Chuffta had wanted to be big—and she'd wanted it for him—and neither of them had given thought to how that would separate them.

The problem was, the way the solid fortress that was the Destrye palace sat at the base of the immense tree that housed Arill's Temple, a winged creature of Chuffta's size couldn't easily approach. Even if they cleared a flight path for him, there was nowhere for him to land. The Destrye used every handspan of ground inside the moat around the city to keep out the Báran golems.

The haphazard shelters piled up around the palace and temple grounds like sands blown into dunes against city walls, and even the pathways between them were so narrow in places that she, Lonen, and Baeltya had to sometimes go single file as they walked out to cross the moat and meet Chuffta. The Destrye, glimpsing their king, cheered and bowed—and quickly cleared the way—but it was slow going.

"How can it be taking so long?" Chuffta demanded.

"Where *is* Chuffta?" Lonen asked at the same time, his disgruntled tone so like her Familiar's that she had to laugh.

"Outside the moat," she explained, waving forgiveness to a woman who babbled apologies as she pushed a cart full of wood out of their way. Oria raised a brow at Lonen's incredulous expression and gestured at the crush. "Where else did you think we'd put him?"

"I hadn't thought," he admitted. "I'm so used to having him always right there."

"See?" Chuffta said, pouncing on the words as if they proved his point. *"I should be with you. All the time."*

"I don't know where else he'd fit," she explained to them both in some exasperation.

"Isn't he cold outside?" Lonen furrowed his brow in concern.

"Yes. I'm cold allll the time."

Oria mentally rolled her eyes at him. "He's fine. He generates so much heat at his size that he can't get cold."

"Easy for you to say."

"That's not fair to Chuffta," Lonen pointed out. "You know how he loves to sleep by the fire."

"Right! This is not fair to me, Oria."

Oria harnessed her impatience with both of her boys. "Where inside is big enough to put him?" They'd emerged from the warren of shelters that blocked the sky and stood poised on the edge of the wide moat while guards jumped to extend the bridge for them to cross. Chuffta stood on the other rim, tail lashing, his white scales iridescent in the winter light, gleaming where the surrounding snow glittered. He curved his neck in coy welcome, his triangular head elegant and green eyes bright as small suns.

"Holy Arill," Lonen breathed. "I'd somehow not entirely absorbed how truly huge he is now."

"He may have gotten bigger," Oria admitted. Not that she'd worked any magic to do it, but he seemed larger to her eyes, too. Perhaps he was just filling out, like a quickly growing adolescent boy getting his height first, then packing on muscle.

"He's beautiful," Baeltya said in reverent tones. "I mean, you were always a handsome creature, Chuffta, but now you are a true wonder."

He preened, happy to hear Baeltya's words. The healer was one of the few to understand the depth of the bond—and clarity of communication—between Oria and her Familiar. Where other Destrye regarded him as a pet, or even an animal companion with the childlike intelligence of a warhorse or wolfhound, Baeltya grasped how much Chuffta understood their words.

"He appreciates your praise," Oria murmured. "But temper that, as his head has clearly swelled to gigantic proportions as it is."

"Hey! I am perfectly proportioned, thank you—and thanks to you."

Crowds of Destrye had gathered to observe him, and Oria worried that the press might end with some of them pitching into the moat. Dry and deep, the moat held an array of sharpened wooden and iron stakes. In their mindless advances, the golems would fall in and impale themselves, the only sure defense the Destrye had been able to find against the Báran's puppet monsters. Short of chopping the golems to pieces with iron weapons, which exacted as great a toll on the fighter as the golem.

The guards finished extending the bridge—a clever contraption of wooden planks that could be rolled or unrolled with a system of pulleys—and the three of them crossed. Lonen frowned thoughtfully up at Chuffta, assessing him. "What if we built another level on the palace with a roof platform large and strong enough for Chuffta to land on?"

"Yes! Yes yes yes yes."

"Can you do that?"

Lonen gave her an arch look. "I *am* king. I'm reliably informed I can do whatever I want to." His gaze went to her mouth, lingering there as he considered what he wanted to do but couldn't, lust firing hot in his mind—along with the image of her naked and under him. She had to close out his thoughts. The wedding couldn't happen soon enough.

"I meant," she replied in a deliberately prim tone, intended to cool his ardor, "is it possible to do that?"

"The structure is solid enough to bear the weight," he replied, considering, mentally measuring Chuffta as they approached. "We'd have to clear some limbs, but we could put that wood to good use in the construction. We could build a set of apartments there for our rooms—with lots of windows, a balcony for you, and a rooftop garden for summer if you like."

Her heart clutched, her steps slowing. "You've been thinking about this."

"Of course," he replied absently, then looked down at her, his granite gray eyes clear and full of love. "I promised you long ago that I'd do everything to make you happy here in Dru, to give you as much of what you left behind in Bára as I could. I've been mulling for a long time how to give you a balcony and garden again like—"

She flung herself against him, cutting off his words with a kiss.

"Can't you kiss your mate later?" Chuffta asked plaintively. *"After all, you can do that when you're inside."*

Laughing, she broke the kiss. "Chuffta is impatient."

Lonen gave Chuffta—whose head hovered barely above theirs, his breath hot as a furnace—a baleful stare. "There are words for this kind of behavior, Chuffta man."

Chuffta grumbled in Oria's mind and backed off a bit. Baeltya coughed politely from a discreet distance away—though not so far that they could forget the strictures against them doing more than kissing.

"When *is* the wedding?" Oria breathed.

His hands tightened on her. "I'll have an answer when we return, one way or another." His mouth fastened on hers, hot and luxuriant, full of promises. She melted into it, savoring the sweetness of being *with* him. Their separation had felt like an eternity, and they'd had no time since to just be together. In that moment, she could regret that she hadn't taken him up on the offer to run off into the hills with him, that she'd insisted he reclaim the throne. "I swear to Arill," he muttered against her mouth, "if it's more than three days from now, I'm taking you captive, tossing you over Buttercup's back, and escaping somewhere I can ravage you at my leisure."

"You wouldn't have to," she answered. "I'd go willingly."

"Yes, but my way is more fun," he said, the wickedly sensual gleam in his eyes making them glint with silvery light. "Let's ride Chuffta into the sunset right now."

"It's still morning," she pointed out.

"Details."

"And there's our chaperone."

"We can toss Baeltya into the moat."

"I heard that," Baeltya said in a clear voice, a ripple of laughter in it.

Lonen heaved a heavy sigh and let go of Oria. "All right then, I suppose flying will be fun, too."

IT WAS, AND more glorious than she'd ever imagined before she could ride on Chuffta's back. Even before, when she rode along in his thoughts as he flew, it hadn't felt the same—the stomach-dropping dives, and heart-pounding ascents, the rush of chill air stinging her cheeks and Lonen's arms strong around her as she sat cradled between his muscled thighs. Baeltya sat discreetly behind him, circumspect but for the occasional startled squeak when Chuffta did something unexpected.

Between Lonen's proximity and Chuffta's mind filling hers, Oria let both of their thoughts and emotions stream through her like the wind of their passage, like the midday sun hot on her eyelids when she closed them, and the dazzling panorama of the forests of Dru beneath them when she looked. In the distance, white-capped mountains reared against a sizzling blue sky. Somewhere in those peaks, Chuffta's derkesthai kin lived in a colony deep inside a volcanic cavern.

"I'd like to go back someday," Chuffta said, picking up on her thoughts now, with her shields so fully open. *"When we're done with war."*

"Is that not where you were hatched?" she asked. They'd had little time to discuss the colony and what had happened to them there. Also, she'd been hesitant to ask, feeling an odd sense of intruding on something she shouldn't.

"Oh, no. Though I don't remember that much about before I was your Familiar. That's why it would be fun to go back and see those derkesthai, so I can spend time there awake!"

Guilt assailed her, that she'd misused her magic so badly that she'd nearly killed her Familiar. Then the moment she managed to bring him out of the deep sleep she'd put him in, they'd raced away to find Lonen. *"I'm so sorry, my friend."*

"A mistake only—and one that led to good things. You mastered your sorcery, all because of me."

He sounded so proud that she had to smile despite the agonizing regret. *"I think 'mastered' is a bit of a stretch."*

"You made me big. No sorcerer or sorceress has done that in generations. We will be famous! They'll write history books about us."

"Hopefully those tales won't include a tragic ending where we die a fiery death on the battlefield," she commented wryly.

"They won't. We shall be triumphant!" He tossed his head and let out a bugling roar, complete with green flame—which blew back on his passengers, who all ducked with cries of dismay.

"Oops. Sorry."

"Something else to practice," she noted without rancor. She could hardly hold such mistakes against him when she'd committed far worse ones.

"THAT WAS THE most incredible experience of my entire life," Baeltya gushed as they waited at the edge of the moat for the guards to extend the bridge. She turned and curtsied deeply to Chuffta, who returned the gesture with a dramatic sweep of wings. "Thank you, sir, for the lovely treat."

"Tell her I'm sorry about the flame backfire."

Oria relayed that remark and Baeltya laughed. "I can only imagine how much practice that sort of thing takes."

"Speaking of which," Oria said to Lonen. "I'd like to spend time each day practicing riding Chuffta."

He frowned at her. "Chuffta can practice his flaming and flying without you. We need you working on the corruption in Nolan's mind and his men's."

"Three things," she replied. "First, Nolan's men haven't all been located and confined, and I haven't been given access to the ones that have. Second—" She raised her brows at him when he opened his mouth to interrupt, and he closed it again, with exaggerated patience. "Second, I can only spend so much time in Nolan's mind before I need to clear my own head. Third, I need to practice working magic from Chuffta's back as he flies, coordinating mentally with him so that we can do that in battle, if necessary."

His frown deepened. "You're proposing... riding Chuffta into battle, against Bára?"

"Were you planning to leave me at home?" she asked sweetly.

Lonen's expression went carefully blank, his gaze opaque as he scrambled to collect his thoughts. Feeling no compunction, Oria peeked at the stream of them and found him hastily readjusting his assumptions. He *had* somehow envisioned her remaining in Dru, safe from harm in the mighty forests, but he realized Oria wouldn't be able to work her sorcery from so far away, and they'd need her at Bára, as she knew the city and the people. He would learn from his father's mistakes and not risk alienating his beloved wife by ordering her to stay clear of battle. And he'd promised Alyx and the women warriors that he'd change the laws prohibiting women from fighting alongside the men.

He didn't like it... but the course ahead became clear. "Of course you should practice on Chuffta, love," he said, running a hand over her hair. "I wasn't thinking clearly."

Fascinating, to see his sharp mind in action. She smiled, pleased with the result. The bridge reached them, and the three of them crossed over.

"I'm off to find my mother," Lonen told her as they reached the palace entrance, the guards snapping to attention. "Would you like to come along?"

Oria shook her head. She didn't dislike Vycayla, but the dowager queen could be sharp—and not a little intimidating—and as mother to Nolan as well as Lonen, she'd no doubt have questions about Nolan's mental health. Questions Oria had no intention of trying to answer yet.

"No, I think I'll go work with Nolan some more. I'll see you at dinner?"

"How about a private dinner, in our rooms?" Lonen suggested with a salacious smile—and a vivid image of dribbling wine over her naked breasts.

Oria felt her cheeks heat and Baeltya cleared her throat. "Your Highness, please don't make me get stern with you."

"It would be just dinner," Lonen claimed in innocent indignation, as if he didn't even then elaborate on the fantasy, imagining where else he might pour that wine and drink it from.

"I can read your thoughts, remember," Oria said, giving him a pointed stare.

"*I* can read his thoughts and I'm no mind reader," Baeltya muttered back at her. They shared a smile and Lonen grinned without embarrassment.

Alby, Lonen's lieutenant on the battlefield and general assistant otherwise, who'd been discreetly lurking among the collection of attendants relieving them of their winter gear, stepped forward and bowed. "If I may, Your Highnesses, I can resolve this issue by informing you there will be a formal dinner this evening." He coughed into a fist rather than laugh at the dismay on Lonen's face. "To celebrate your return to health, to the throne, your engagement, etcetera."

"By whose command?" Lonen inquired politely enough, though the growl in his voice belied it.

"Her Highness Queen Vycayla." Alby held his head high, but unfortunately ended the sentence on a bit of a squeak that made it sound rather like a question.

"I begin to understand why Nolan imprisoned our mother in her rooms," Lonen remarked thoughtfully, and Oria punched his arm.

"Lonen!"

He caught her fist easily in his big hand, moving faster than she could snatch it back. "Yes, my love—did you need something?"

She laughed, beyond relieved to see the merriment dancing in his gray eyes, the laugh lines crinkling around them. For a time, she'd worried that the trials, battles, and betrayals had killed his irreverent humor and sunny optimism. She should've known her barbarian would be more resilient than that.

"Go see your mother. And be polite," she said, tugging her hand free.

He sighed heavily. "Yes, dear."

She narrowed her eyes at him. "I don't have to marry you, remember. I can still—" She shrieked in laughing surprise as he caught her to him and kissed her breathless, uncaring of their considerable audience.

When he finally let her breathe, he cocked his crooked eyebrow at her, the scars—both old and new—making the gesture a bit twisted looking, and enticingly dangerous. "You were saying, my lady?"

"Nothing," she managed. She drew a deep breath and smiled at the wicked mischief on his face. "Nothing at all."

"Good." He set her on her feet. Seemed about to say something else… but shook his head like one of his wolfhounds shedding water. "Stay out of trouble, wife."

"Back at you, husband."

~ 3 ~

LONEN ENDED UP escorting his mother into formal dinner. He hadn't seen Oria since they returned from flying. Alby had relayed a message via Baeltya that Oria would be occupying other rooms until the wedding, and that she'd dress there—wherever that was, as they all avoided saying exactly, determined to subvert their king's worst impulses by keeping the location a secret—and that Oria would meet him at dinner.

It hardly seemed fair, to be stuck with his sharp-tongued mother instead of his delectable wife, but the situation would be temporary. Very temporary, which had him in excellent spirits. He'd put his afternoon to good use, keeping himself too busy to obsess about bedding Oria. Much. Several dire matters required the king's attention, along with a great many only slightly less urgent ones.

He'd put Arnon in charge of designing a platform and new roof-top apartments, and his brother had leapt at the opportunity to take on the project, with almost embarrassing gratitude. No small part of it had to do with the enforced inactivity of winter, no doubt. But Arnon also seemed to feel he needed to make things right between them. Lonen had told him, in a private, intense conversation, that he understood Arnon's choices. He'd been torn between loyalties to his two elder brothers, one who should have been the rightful king, had fate played out as it should, and one who'd had kingship thrust upon him. Nolan had been convincing in his righteousness and paranoia. Had their positions been reversed, Lonen might have made the same choices Arnon did.

But Arnon didn't see it that way; instead questioning his own judgment and intelligence, because he hadn't realized Nolan wasn't himself. A difficult place for Arnon, who'd always been the cleverest, most learned, and most insightful of the four brothers.

"You gave Arnon a project, I hear," Vycayla commented as they strolled toward the great dining hall, as if she'd heard his thoughts. His mother was no sorceress, not like Oria, but she did have an uncanny knack for reading people.

"Yes. An engineering project that should absorb his energies until the weather thaws enough that we can get back to work restoring the aqueducts." He sounded slightly defensive.

"I'm not criticizing," she replied mildly. "It was kindly done, to give him an opportunity to do you a service, one that will benefit you and Oria personally."

"I don't need him to make anything up to me, I told him that."

"You might not need it, but he does. A wise ruler recognizes what his people need and gives them the opportunity to seize it, regardless of his own feelings."

Lonen snorted. "Never thought I'd see the day *you* called me wise."

"In point of fact, I didn't," she retorted in a tone tart enough to make him wince. "I was speaking hypothetically."

"Ah." He nodded to himself, assuming a sage expression rather than an aggravated rolling of his eyes at his mother. Eye rolling was probably not appropriate for a king, wise or not.

Vycayla stopped, turning to face him. They stood just shy of the short corridor that opened into the main hall, out of earshot of the palace guards stationed there. "I do think you'll be a wise ruler, my son," she said, her gaze unusually soft with sentiment. "When you were a boy, even a very young man, I never thought you'd be the one to show the true mettle of your father and me. You've surprised me, happily so."

"Thank you, I think," he said, feeling his scar pull with the frown. His mother never did pay unadulterated compliments, so he should settle for that and be happy. Then, from the opposite direction, Oria stepped into the hall, Baeltya a step behind her, and all thoughts fled from his mind.

Vycayla turned at his expression and hummed in satisfaction. "Ah, Oria, you look lovely."

Oria smiled, pleased and also a bit abashed, her high cheekbones delicately flushed. They'd put her hair up in one of the elaborate piles of coils and braids the Destrye ladies of court favored, and it looked like a gorgeous crown of copper framing her piquant face. She wore a gown of light green, a sheer layer intricately beaded with copper swirls over a darker silk beneath—which wasn't that much less transparent. The fall of the gown outlined her slender limbs, her full breasts, narrow waist, and gave hints of the vee centered between the graceful arc of her slim hips. The sleeves parted at her shoulders, leaving her pale arms bare, and caught again at her wrists in copper-beaded cuffs. A slit in the narrow skirt of the gown showed flashes of her long legs as she walked toward him. Mouth-watering.

His mother cleared her throat. "Shall we step inside, Baeltya, and give them a moment?"

"Do you think it's safe, Your Highness?" Baeltya's voice rippled with suppressed laughter.

"He can hardly ravish her in the main hall," Vycayla replied dryly.

Lonen, who'd been fantasizing that very thing, quickly banished the image of Oria with her back against the nearby carved pillar, green skirts hiked around her waist and head thrown back in ecstasy as he plunged into her. Oria blushed a deeper pink, so he knew she'd seen it in his thoughts. He only grinned at her with wicked delight.

"You look beyond beautiful, love," he managed once Baeltya and Vycayla discreetly withdrew, and his voice came out rough. "The green suits you,"

"Thank you. It no longer seemed necessary to wear red, like a Báran priestess." She sounded almost shy as she looked down at herself, plucking at the gown self-consciously. "But I feel quite… naked."

Oh, if she only knew. "Are you cold?" he asked with hasty concern. His desert-bred bride had become more accustomed to the bitterness of Dru's winter, but she took chill easily.

Her mouth twisted in a wry smile, and she leaned closer, saying in a low, conspiratorial voice, "I'm using magic to keep myself warm. Is that wrong?"

Indeed, with her so close, he felt he'd entered a warm cloud of summer, with Oria its sun. The spicy perfume of the qinn that the Destrye ladies used wound together with Oria's natural scent, becoming somehow both uniquely her and redolent of home. "I'd like to strip you naked for real and lick every inch of you," he replied in a low growl of need. "Is that wrong?"

Her coppery eyes glittered with answering desire. "In the main hall of the palace, probably yes."

"It would make for good illustrations in the history books." He picked up her hand and kissed the silken back of it, then turned it over to press a passionate kiss to her palm, licking it in demonstration—and allowing the image of taking her, fast and hard against the nearby pillar, to bloom in his mind again.

She snatched her hand away, her breath lifting her breasts enticingly, her nipples hard against the clinging silk. "But perhaps not as we'd choose to be remembered," she noted breathlessly.

"Do any of us get to choose how we're remembered?" he countered, but he took up her hand and threaded it chastely through the crook of his elbow, turning to lead her into the hall for the feast. "I don't know, going down in Destrye history as a king and queen noted for their passionate love for each other would be a legacy I could happily embrace."

She slid him a sideways glance, one that he might've called demure for the way her long lashes veiled her gaze, except that her eyes glittered with wicked amusement. "As long as we're not the great cautionary tale used to teach Destrye children the folly of going to war against the walled cities of the desert, I'll be happy."

"There is that," he muttered agreement, pausing ceremoniously in the doorway so the assembly could rise and then bow to show honor.

"A nice change from the last formal dinner," Oria replied in the same quiet voice as she smiled radiantly for the court.

"Isn't it? It's much more pleasant to rule when people aren't looking for the first opportunity to put a blade in your back."

She muffled a laugh and he led her to the high table on the dais at one end of the room. The Haligne tree Oria had grown from a spoon as a demonstration of her magical skills at their last dinner party spread its limbs over the table, elaborate and sweetly blooming.

"Has that thing grown?" he whispered.

"I think so," she replied, equally hushed—and perhaps awed.

"How, without sunlight or soil?"

"I...don't know." She sounded a bit distressed, so he let it go. Arnon waited for them, standing next to his seat beside their two empty chairs at the center. He bowed again. "Your Highnesses."

"I'm not queen yet, Arnon," Oria replied, taking the hand he offered so she could sit.

"To me you are," he said with some fervency, looking to Lonen also. "Both of you, my king and queen, always."

Lonen gripped his shoulder. Then, on impulse, pulled him into a hug, pounding his back. As he did, he said into his brother's ear, "Relax. We're good."

Arnon returned the hug but shook his head slightly as he withdrew. "I have a lot to make up for."

On the other side of Oria, the dowager queen caught Lonen's eye, reminding him of their conversation with a significantly arched brow. "Fine, fine," he said. "Sit already." He raised his voice as he said it, giving permission to the assembly.

Salaya, his brother Ion's widow, standing by her chair at Vycayla's other hand, moved a bit more slowly than the rest, lingering to give him a nod. Her hair shorn short in mourning, Salaya's striking face stood in stark relief in the torchlight, her gaze speaking something. Then she looked away and sat.

They ate, the mood in the hall light, even festive. Oria received special plates of grains and vegetables, with cheese from the goats and buttered puff pastries, all prepared especially for her. Making happy noises, she ate heartily, the sight doing his heart good. Even his mother carried on pleasant conversations with Oria and Salaya, making an effort to be charming to her two daughters-in-law.

Arnon regaled Lonen with an impressive array of details on the planned addition to the palace, having accomplished a truly astonishing amount of work in the few hours since Lonen handed him the project. Listening—and nodding at hopefully appropriate intervals, since the in-depth explanation of stressors and load-bearing designs meant little to him—Lonen scanned the room, noting who was there and who wasn't.

"Sounds excellent," he said, when Arnon wound down. "As for your questions on the rooftop garden, ask Oria. She might be able to make some drawings for you."

"Oh, perfect." Arnon leaned around Lonen to smile at Oria, who nodded that she'd heard, though she listened to some tale of Vycayla's.

"I don't see Natly," Lonen said, as neutrally as possible, after what he hoped was a reasonable pause.

He didn't fool his brother, however, who gave him a sharp glance. "No. I didn't imagine you'd want to. Not after… last time."

When Natly, his former lover and would-be fiancée, had caused a scene—the one that led to Oria's display of sorcery. "I don't *want* to," he replied, maybe a bit too sharply. "But I've also learned to distrust who's out of sight, lest they be plotting something unpleasant."

That was the wrong thing to say, as Arnon's face creased unhappily, shadows of guilt and remorse darkening his eyes. "Natly is down with Nolan," he said before Lonen could take back the careless words or reassure his brother yet again that he harbored no suspicions or ill will. "I am having her watched. When Oria's not studying him, Natly slips down to the dungeon and sits with him."

"Interesting." And surprising. Though… was it? Nolan had been the target of Natly's flirtations for quite some time before he brushed her off and she set her sights on Lonen, the next prince in line.

"I can put a stop to it," Arnon hastily assured him. "It seemed like a harmless occupation to me, and perhaps good for both of them."

"I have no problem with it." As he said it, he realized he felt quite the opposite. "Is he… rational, with her?"

Arnon shook his head. "Whatever happened, however your iron axe affected him, he hasn't put two rational words together since. And, to be frank, he was hardly better than that in your absence. From the moment he discovered you and Oria had fled in the night—" He cleared his throat, hesitating.

"Go ahead," Lonen urged him. "Speak freely."

Under the table, Oria put a hand on his knee, stroking softly. Not high enough to be titillating—or, rather, not distractingly so, since everything about her had his brain going in one direction—but a gesture of approval. In his peripheral vision, she seemed to be intently listening to Vycayla, but Oria possessed many skills, and had long since perfected the art of listening to several conversations at once—and probably to his thoughts, as well. Experimentally, he sent her a mental kiss, and she squeezed his knee in response. That answered that.

"He flew into such a rage," Arnon said quietly. "At first I agreed with him, that your abrupt escape signaled your guilt and, ahem, her influence over you. I'm sorry for that."

Lonen slipped his own hand under the table and took Oria's, lacing their fingers together, just for the pleasure of touching her. "You've apologized countless times already," Lonen said. "Let it go. I have."

Arnon set his jaw. "I'll decide when I can let this go. It took little time to see his madness—though longer for me to admit it. I was a fool."

Lonen moved Oria's hand up his thigh, noting the twitch of her full lips as she suppressed a smile. She didn't resist, squeezing the muscle a bit. "We are all fools at one time or another," Lonen said to Arnon. "What matters is you refused to support him when it mattered most."

"Seeing Mother here—discovering that she'd arrived and he'd had her arrested and imprisoned..." Arnon shook his head and shoved his plate away, as if the sight of it made him ill. "I have a great deal to make up to you both."

"Then do it," Lonen said, allowing a hint of impatience to creep into his voice. He tried to tug Oria's hand higher, but this time she did resist.

Arnon looked at him in shock, for his words and tone, Lonen realized—not his antics shrouded by the cloth on the table. "I need you," Lonen told his brother. "Even if Oria can cleanse the sorcery from Nolan's mind, I don't think I'll be able to trust him in the same way. You're the only brother I have left who I can rely on. Do what you need to in order to get your head on straight—but get it done. We have a lot to accomplish before the weather thaws and I'm going to be relying on you heavily. So..." He waved a hand in the air. "Get your own load-bearing supports shored up, or whatever."

Arnon's lips twitched, the shadows lightening. "I don't think that analogy plays very well."

"This is why I leave such things to you. I trust you to understand them."

Arnon sobered. "You really trust me—still? After everything?"

Lonen leveled his full attention on his brother, giving up the tussle under the table with Oria. "I trust you *more* than ever, after everything," he said with quiet emphasis. "We learn from our mistakes."

Arnon pressed his lips together, emotion shining bright in his eyes. "Thank you, Your Highness."

"All the times I pressed your face in the mud to get you to show your older brother some respect," Lonen said with a growl, "and *this* is what it takes."

Arnon snorted, sounding a bit more like his old, irreverent self. "You're much scarier now. And you have a super scary wife," he added, dragging his plate back and spearing a piece of meat.

Oria leaned over Lonen, eyes sparkling with mischief. "You have *no* idea, Arnon," and slid her hand up to squeeze Lonen's balls under the table.

A perfectly timed attack, as he'd been drinking a deep swallow of wine—so he choked on it, nearly spewing it across the table. He glared at Oria, who only laughed, a bell-like sound of complete delight.

"But not wife," she corrected, with an innocent smile for Lonen as she squeezed hard enough to make him wince. "Not until Arill says so. Only then will I have him to—"

"On that note," he interrupted, taking her hand off him and keeping it in a firm grip as he tugged her to her feet. "I have an announcement." The room quieted and Oria beamed up at him, mooning at him as if completely enraptured. Who knew that the minx would turn out to have such a mischievous sense of humor when she finally felt well? "The dowager Queen Vycayla, in her capacity as High Priestess of Arill, has determined the most auspicious date for the sorceress Oria, Princess of Bára, and I to wed."

Oria raised her brows at him for withholding that bit of information until now. He smiled at her easily, with lots of teeth, which he intended to use to torment her into shameless begging. The hall briefly buzzed with excitement, then fell quiet as everyone strained to hear.

"In Arill's Temple, as Sgatha rises full and Grienon briefly paces her tomorrow evening, Arill will set her hand as the final seal on our marriage, begun many months ago in Oria's City of Bára."

Everyone cheered, the hall in an uproar of toasts and celebratory shouts.

"Tomorrow night?" Oria practically squeaked, not only because of his arm tight around her. "I didn't expect it so soon!"

He looked down into her upturned face, her copper eyes glinting with gold in the torchlight. "Last chance for second thoughts," he said quietly, cursing himself for a fool even as he said it. As if he'd be able to let her go. No. No, if she wanted out, he would let her go. He would be a better man, a better king than his barbarian ancestors.

"You're truly asking me that, Lonen?" Oria breathed, a straight light in her face.

"Yes," he answered gravely, his heart stuttering to a stop. "I'm asking you to marry me, Oria. And if the answer is no, I'll respect that."

"Hmm…" She looked thoughtful, then burst out laughing. Reaching up, she wound her fingers in his hair, which he'd left loose because she liked it that way. Tugging his head down, she kissed him. "If you tried to get away," she said against his lips, "I'd toss you over Buttercup's back and keep you captive in the hills until you broke down and agreed to marry me. Again."

Deep inside, where the marriage bond connected to his heart and soul, heat and joy burned like the sun over Bára.

~ 4 ~

ORIA HAD THOUGHT that the temporary set of rooms they'd given her were far too spacious and extravagant, especially for one person, for a few short days. Now it seemed Vycayla had been prescient in suggesting Oria move into the suite the queen had lived in before she left Dru, because the considerable space teemed with women, most sewing or crafting something, all of them talking at high volume.

Oria thanked Arill or whoever might be listening that she'd learned to shield effectively. There was a time this kind of crowd—and excited emotional energy—would've had her fainting within minutes. They'd swarmed her rooms at dawn with fabric, patterns, jewelry, and keen urgency just shy of panic. Barely an hour later, Oria had taken refuge in a large, thronelike chair that served to give her an island of space in the sea of giggling and chattering women, sipping the hot tea she finally had a moment to drink inside the dubious barricade of the heavy, ornate arms.

"I could breathe some flame and chase them all away," Chuffta offered, making her smile.

"Thank you, but I'm fine. At least they're all here to bring off the wedding in fine form. I'm grateful for the help."

"Oria." Vycayla approached her chair with a determined lift to her chin, a swath of green silk the color of moss draped over her arms. "We should make your wedding dress from this. It's the best choice. Once you agree, the seamstresses can start cutting."

They'd already taken her measurements—every part of her—in

a dizzyingly fast examination. She'd been relieved to put on her dressing robe and escape their discussion of her body's finest qualities, and what would be best concealed. The Destrye women were honest and frank in a way that Báran women were decidedly not. Only the knowledge that they didn't mean to embarrass her, or insult her in any way, had salved her raw reactions. At least Lonen loved her body as it was.

"So do I," Chuffta pointed out.

"Yes, but you don't count."

"Hey!"

"Oria." Vycayla snapped impatient fingers. "All I need is a yes."

"It's very pretty," Oria offered. Behind Vycayla, Baeltya shook her head emphatically. "But…"

"But?" Vycayla demanded.

Oria looked to Baeltya for clues—and rescue.

"I thought you might prefer this red," Baeltya said smoothly, drawing up a young Destrye girl who nearly drowned in a pile of crimson velvet. "As is traditional for your people," Baeltya added, with a glance at Vycayla.

"Oria will be married in Arill's Temple via her holiest rites," Vycayla argued. "She should wear Arill's colors."

"If I may," Oria began, but both women ignored her.

"Oria is not a priestess of Arill," Baeltya countered. "And this wedding is a joining of Bára and Dru. Dress the king in Arill's colors and Oria in Báran ones."

"Oria may not be a priestess of Arill, *yet,*" Vycayla countered, "but once she marries my son and is acknowledged Queen of the Destrye, then she will be expected to take up the mantle of serving Arill, which means she should begin as she means to go on, wearing Arill's colors." With a triumphant huff, she held out the fabric to Oria. "Yes."

Not a question at all, and Oria opened her mouth, hoping words would come to explain how she felt. A somewhat desperate hope, as she had trouble defining to herself what those feelings were.

"You don't have to capitulate to her, Oria," Baeltya inserted, eyes flashing and dark curls tumbling as she shook her hair back behind her shoulders, thrusting forward the crimson cloth. "This is *your* wedding and you should be able to come to it as the person you are. Who you decide to be after this is your decision."

"I think—" Oria started to say.

"Nonsense." Vycayla leveled a fierce gray glare on the shorter healer, reminding Oria very much of Lonen in battle mode. "No queen—or princess—is wholly her own person. Oria never has been and she won't be going forward. The Queen of Dru is *always* also the head healer and priestess of Arill." Vycayla emphasized her words with the green silk.

"Oria's magic isn't healing. She's a powerful sorceress with skills not seen in Dru for centuries. She will carve her own path." Baeltya shook the crimson velvet.

"Ladies, I—" Once again, Oria got no further. With a sigh, she set her teacup down.

"Exactly," Vycayla crowed in triumph. "Centuries of *tradition*. Therefore, she—"

Oria sent a chilling gust of wind through the room and stood, letting the power glow from her. She might look silly, bundled into her dressing robe and warm socks, with her hair still a tumbled mess from sleep, but the room went silent, all the busy women stilled at their tasks, gaping at her.

"Your Highness," she said, not unkindly, inclining her head and smiling. "Healer Baeltya. I greatly appreciate your efforts to make this wedding truly spectacular, and I know Lonen does, too." A blatant lie there as Lonen felt no such thing. As they parted after the feast the night before, he'd sent her an array of images of what he'd rather be doing than sleeping alone and muttered dire threats about his mother in Oria's ear before Baeltya firmly tugged her away. It made a laugh rise in her heart to think of it, which only added to the warmth of her smile. "The sorcerers of my people make these decisions based on certain arcane messages," she continued, embroidering on the lie shamelessly. "Perhaps if I could see the fabric choices, then the magic will indicate the most serendipitous choice for this most blessed ritual."

Vycayla studied her with a shrewd gaze, not really taken in by Oria's story, but also unwilling to call her a liar in front of so many people. Baeltya suppressed a grin, turning it into a solemn nod. "Of course, Sorceress Oria. If you'll step into the anteroom with me?"

Oria nearly gasped aloud at the sight that greeted her in the next room. The spacious receiving room was positively stuffed with fabrics of all colors and textures. None of the heavy wooden furniture showed, as every surface had been draped with fabric.

"Overwhelming, I know," Vycayla commented dryly from behind her. "Thus I thought to spare you."

Oria gave her a radiant smile, mostly faked. It was that or say something unforgivable. "I dare say as Queen of Dru I'll have to make more difficult decisions than this. I am beyond impressed to see such an array of fabrics," she added to salve Vycayla's irritation. "Are these all created by the Destrye?"

"No." Vycayla softened, and Baeltya tossed Oria an amused smile behind the dowager queen's back as the tall, imposing woman moved into the room, her long fingers testing the various fabrics with tenderness. She'd braided her floor-length hair and left it in a tail down the middle of her back. Even braided, the tip of her hair brushed the hem of her skirts. "The Destrye enjoyed vibrant trade with the lands to the south back in the day."

Back before the Báran golems came, she meant. Before Oria's people drained the lakes of Dru and drove the Destrye nearly to destruction.

"The queen before me and the queen before her collected many of these, and as a young queen I continued in the same vein, seeking out the most beautiful fabrics from every ship and merchant train. They've been stored in chests of wood that banish insects, preserved all this time." She sighed, no longer vibrating with ruthless determination, and waved a hand. "Choose whichever you like, Oria. It's time we had a queen again who looks the part."

Oria hesitated, taking in the severe dowager queen, hair pulled back tightly from her face in that braid, her gown one she must have brought from the hermitage, an undyed woven cloth no doubt spun from crops they'd grown. "There are more seamstresses here than can possibly all work on one gown at the same time, Your Highness," she said softly. "Perhaps the green silk should be made into one for you."

Vycayla looked surprised, glancing at the lengths of shimmering green she'd set aside, her fingers going to it and stroking with that same tenderness. "We'll see," she murmured. Then her gray gaze flashed to Oria's with granite command. "Now choose. We can't spend all morning dithering over this one decision."

Not when they had countless decisions to dither over for the rest of the day, Oria thought to herself, but circumspectly did not say aloud.

"This is why derkesthai don't wear clothes," Chuffta said cheerfully, if a bit snidely. *"So much time wasted on colors. Be the color you are naturally."*

"I think even the Destrye would be shocked if I arrived at my wedding ceremony naked." Oria wandered through the maze of fabrics, her eye unable to settle on one.

"Lonen likes you naked. He—"

"Stop! Don't go there."

Chuffta snickered in her mind, well-pleased with himself. And her eye landed on a length of shimmering copper silk. *"Ooh,"* Chuffta crooned. *"See? That one matches your coloring. Do that one."*

She had to agree, picking up the fragile silk and stroking it, realizing as she did that she touched it with the same affectionate tenderness Vycayla had shown for the green silk. It was so sheer and smooth that it snagged infinitesimally on the skin of her fingers, though Oria would've sworn they were soft and free of blemishes. Metallic threads ran through the copper-dyed silk, giving the overall fabric a magical sparkle.

"That one has been in the stores for as long as anyone can remember," Vycayla said quietly, reaching out to touch it also. "It was old when I was a little girl."

Oria reluctantly let it go. "I'll pick something else."

Vycayla raised her brows in an amused arch. "And save it for what? Perhaps our predecessor was guided by Arill to purchase the fabric for you, for when you came along." She gestured to a patiently waiting seamstress. "This one."

"It really is perfect for you, Oria," Baeltya said with a genuine smile of pleasure. "It could indeed have been chosen by the goddess for you."

"It seems to me that you all invoke Arill to support whatever outcome you'd like to see," Oria muttered before she thought about how it would sound. "I mean—"

But Vycayla laughed, and Baeltya grinned broadly. Vycayla put her hands on Oria's shoulders and steered her back to the living area being used as the workroom. "Now you're learning. I think you'll do just fine as Queen of Dru."

A surprising flush of pleasure suffused her to have the good opinion of Lonen's mother. Not many people in Oria's life had expressed such confidence in her.

"I think you'll do very well, too," Chuffta said, his mind-voice ever so slightly indignant.

"You don't count," she reminded him with a mental laugh.

"Hey!"

"Because you love me and think I'm wonderful no matter what I do."

"Oh. Well that's true."

LONEN ADJUSTED THE fit of his formal clothes. His tailor sprang forward with a chiding click of his teeth to put it back again. "It should hang thus, Your Highness," he said, the deferential tone changing nothing.

Sitting nearby with a mug of ale, Arnon smiled, tight-lipped, suppressing his laughter. Lonen gave him a dark look. "Laugh all you like, brother. You get to wear your usual clothing."

"True," Arnon agreed cheerfully enough, "but then, I have decent clothing to wear. How did you end up entirely with fighting leathers and hunting gear?"

"I've been busy," Lonen muttered.

"Still, I would've thought that Natly, at least… Ah." Arnon hit the realization and closed his mouth over it.

"Yes," Lonen said, holding still as his man produced a cloak of deep forest green and fastened it around Lonen's shoulders with a hammered metal clasp in the shape of a stylized tree. "I didn't want to marry Oria wearing clothes chosen by another woman."

"Good thinking," Arnon murmured. "And the green is a good choice. Honoring Arill. Peace and fertility, rather than war."

Looser fitting that what he normally wore, the silk trousers and shirt fell in crisp lines, in a green so dark it looked black until the light hit it just right. A thick leather belt decorated with hammered metal leaves cinched the shirt at his waist, and the sleeves billowed with so much extra fabric it would hamper him in a fight.

But, as his tailor had retorted when he pointed that out, today was not for fighting. It gave Lonen pause to realize how much anticipating conflict, the daily battles, had become ingrained in his thinking. One day he'd like to be a king who expected every day to be peaceful.

A nice dream, anyway.

"Is everything ready?" he asked Arnon.

"Yes." Arnon set the mug down and stood. "A temporary solution, but the structure should hold for the short time we need it. It will be a good test case for the long-term stress and stability of the final design."

Lonen paused, running those words back through his head. "Is that code for 'it could come down at any time?'"

"Oh no." Arnon shook his head emphatically. "It's code for 'it could come down eventually, but not today.' Which isn't a concern, because we'll dismantle the platform after the ceremony and reuse everything for the permanent structure."

"Hmm." Lonen eyed his man as he approached with the wreath of Dru, his crown, now shining and cleaned of his brother's blood, at least physically.

"You said you trusted me," Arnon said, a hint of doubt creeping into his voice.

"What? No, not that. I absolutely trust that you wouldn't want me crushed by logs on my wedding day. It's that." He waved a hand at the wreath and sighed, his man hesitating in trepidation.

"It's yours by right, and by Arill's clear decision," Arnon said quietly.

"I keep seeing it covered in Nolan's blood," he told Arnon, trusting him with that, too. "I can't get that image of my mind."

Arnon cocked his head thoughtfully. "He wore a crown he stole to a duel. It's not a metaphor, not an omen. Anything you wear to a duel is going to get blood on it. That's just biology."

Lonen blinked at his brother. "That's a remarkably practical approach."

Arnon shrugged cheerfully. "I've always been the practical one." He took the wreath from Lonen's man with a nod and settled it on Lonen's head himself. "Wear it with pride and no remorse, brother," he said. "Arill knows I'm glad it's not mine."

Together they strode out, climbing the stairs to the upper levels of the palace, bypassing the Bridge of Seofe that led to Arill's Temple. Arnon had performed miracles, recruiting an army of otherwise bored and idle Destyre warriors to construct a flat platform atop the pitched roof. They had to climb a ladder for the last level up, but Arnon had at least designed it to rest at a long angle with broad, flat steps, so hopefully Oria wouldn't have trouble navigating it. Other ladies, arriving in their finery for the royal wedding, seeming to be having no trouble.

Atop the platform, hammered metal basins all along the edges held blazing fires which helped dispel the wintery chill as the sun declined to the horizon and the dusky purple evening descended. Arill's tree showed raw cuts where nearby branches had been severed, and the smell of fresh sap filled the crisp air, along with the sweet smoke of the fires. A bower of evergreen bows had been constructed at one end, between sunset and moonrise, and Rhiten Robson waited there in his formal priest's robes the color of new leaves in spring, lavishly embroidered in gold.

Lonen slipped his hand into his pocket, checking that the ring remained safely within, beyond glad that he'd commissioned the metalsmith to begin work on it before he and Oria fled the palace.

"Nervous?" Arnon asked as they bided their time, waiting for the bride and her retinue. The priest kept an eye on the sky, keenly observant of the timing, but Lonen knew his mother wouldn't let Oria be late, even if she had to drag his Báran bride there naked.

"Eager," Lonen replied with a wolfish smile, making his brother laugh. "Recall that Oria and I have been married some months now. This is a formality for me."

"True." Arnon regarded him speculatively. "Were you nervous then? Marrying a foreign sorceress in some arcane ritual of the bloodthirsty Báran people and all?"

"Terrified," Lonen confessed in a wry tone. He met his brother's amused gaze. "I would have given a great deal to have you with me then. I'm grateful to have you with me now."

Amusement fled, gripped by emotion, Arnon clasped his shoulder. "Now and always," he replied in a rough voice. The drums started up and Arnon glanced to the side, eyes widening. He whistled low and soft. "And look how well all of this has turned out for you."

Lonen turned to see Oria rising with measured steps up the long ladder, Baeltya and his mother on either side of her. The last rays of the sun caressed her with loving fingers, stoking the fire in her hair, which fell in a blazing sheet like molten metal, over a gown the same color. Suspended by chains of copper inset with jewels, the fine fabric barely clung to her breasts before falling in a shimmering drape of sparkling light. The same sort of chain draped around her pale throat, holding on a cloak of emerald green lined with more of the copper silk. A gold band crossed her forehead, holding the veil of hair off her lovely, fine-boned face. She smiled at him, her lips painted the glossy shade of good wine, and her eyes shone brighter than any of the jewels she wore.

He held out a hand to her and she took it, looking him up and down. "Who knew my barbarian warrior would clean up so well?" she murmured. "You'd put even a peacock of a Báran nobleman to shame."

"Oh, I'm still a barbarian brute under these pretty clothes," he replied in the same tone. "As I plan to demonstrate with great vigor very soon."

A high flush graced her cheekbones. "I look forward to that demonstration, my king."

"Excellent news, my queen. Are you ready to marry me again?"

"Again and again," she replied with a radiant smile, that only briefly dimmed. "I only wish Chuffta could be here, more than mentally."

"He can and will. Call him."

Oria frowned. "What do you mean?"

Lonen pointed to the cleared area beyond Arnon, who grinned at her in great excitement, practically hopping from foot to foot. "My wedding gift to you both," Arnon said.

Oria's welled with tears, though her joyful smile never dimmed. "Thank you," she whispered, seeming too overcome to speak more loudly.

Moments later, a white shadow passed overhead, the wind of Chuffta's wings making the bonfires flare. Lonen kept half an eye on them, but the drafts quickly waned.

"I'm telling him to be his very most careful," Oria murmured.

Sure enough, Chuffta soon settled on the nearby platform in a roped-off space kept clear for him. The wooden platform groaned ominously—and Arnon frowned, scanning the area, clearly taking mental notes—but it held. Chuffta folded his wings and curved his neck, lowering his triangular head to rest his pointed chin on the platform, for all the world like a cat settling in to rest.

Rhiten Robson cleared his throat and they turned to him. Holding out his arms, he pointed one finger to the setting sun, and the other toward the opposite horizon, where Sgatha's curve emerged, round and the color of a rose from Oria's garden. Like a blue-green jewel, Grienon rose beside her. They'd cleared branches to make the sight visible, Lonen realized, and a breath of awe sighed through the gathering.

A sacred moment, indeed, full of the peace he and Oria would bring to the world.

~ 5 ~

MONTHS AND FOREVER ago, Lonen had promised he'd show Oria how the Destrye did a wedding. He'd grumbled at the lack of celebration at their Báran one—though having the bride collapse unconscious hadn't helped what was admittedly an intense and solemn ritual.

This was the party Lonen had promised back then, when she'd been so uncertain of what the future held. That uncertainty lingered—they had a war still to fight—but for this one night, they could revel in the best sense of the word. Music played, the hides stretched across the hammered metal drums sending a booming beat through the forest, while pipes carved of wood and fashioned of metal wove higher and mellower melodies around the throbbing rhythm. The fires blazed, sending sparks up into the sky, and Lonen guided her through the unfamiliar dance steps, grinning in delight as she held onto him and followed along.

The dances weren't difficult, but they often involved him bodily lifting her to swing her in a circle, making her shriek with surprise and laughter. The Destrye woman did likewise as their partners swung them in wild patterns, making her less self-conscious, the female voices rising high as the men shouted in counterpoint, stomping their feet—a human version of the song made by the pipes and drums.

Arnon's platform shuddered beneath their feet—and once she spotted him lying on his belly, head hanging over the edge as he checked a support—but it held. To be on the safe side, she sent

Chuffta off again, and he went easily, wishing her a happy night with her mate, and anticipating a nice bloody cow from the Destrye herds a short distance away.

She was just as happy not to be in on that hunt.

Lonen lifted her higher and she clutched his shoulders, sending up a whoop with the other women as she nearly flew, the copper and gold ring on her finger glinting against the black-emerald silk of his fine shirt. Lonen's teeth flashed white in his black beard, trimmed close and neat for the occasion, the hammered gold leaves in the wreath nestled in his black curls glinting. Her barbarian king.

The music finished in a triumphant crash, but Lonen didn't set her down. Instead he slipped an arm under her knees, cradling her against his muscular chest. "Have you danced enough?" he asked, a wicked sparkle in his eyes.

She wound her hands behind his neck, under the hair so tidily tied back, ready to see it falling around his face. "Why—do you have a better offer?"

"I'm thinking a more private celebration is in order. If you've enjoyed the party enough. I don't want you to miss the fun."

"I think there will be other celebrations, yes?" she breathed, desire and anticipation flaring as hot and bright in her body as the bonfires. "Other times to dance."

"We'll dance every night, if you like," he said, and she knew he'd follow through on that promise, as he had on every other.

"Then let's go," she said with a smile, caressing the back of his neck. "If it's polite to—"

"I am taking my wife to bed!" Lonen roared, and the gathering of Destrye shouted their approval.

Oria dissolved into embarrassed giggles, covering her hot face as Lonen carried her through the gathering, people calling out astonishingly ribald suggestions. "That answers that," she said, laughing.

"We *are* barbarians," Lonen noted with a toothy smile, agilely descending the half-ladder/half-staircase she'd so painstakingly climbed. "What did you expect when you wedded one?"

She levered herself up, threading her fingers through his thick curls, now coming loose around his face from the vigorous movements of the wild dancing, and kissed him with all the hunger in her. He growled deep in his throat, returning and deepening the kiss. Tugging loose the tie that bound his hair, Oria recognized the feel of it. Bemused, she studied it when Lonen broke the kiss to hasten his stride. The tie was a simple leather one, nothing as fancy as the rest of his garb. It was the one he'd accidentally left behind in Bára when he returned home with his Destrye armies, when she thought she'd never see him again.

She'd kept it, a girlish memento of the exuberantly masculine barbarian warrior who'd so stunned her senses and awakened in her such darkly sexual feelings. When he'd returned—to angrily accuse her of breaking their tentative peace, an argument that ended in her proposing a marriage of state—she'd given the leather tie back to him. And he'd worn the stained old thing to their wedding.

He saw her studying it. "It seemed right to wear it today. When I saw you kept that tie, that's when I knew."

"Knew what?" She arched a cool brow, but her heart swelled tight in her breast.

"That you wanted me," he murmured, a sensual rumble that crawled down her spine to her groin.

"I did not," she replied with indignation.

"You thought about me, fantasized about me."

"I didn't even realize I had it." She added a lofty sniff for good measure, which became a gasp when he took her earlobe in his teeth and nipped, then laved his hot tongue over the sting.

"You had it on the table beside your favorite seat in the garden. I imagine you sat there in your tower and looked out over the deserts toward Dru, imagining what I might be doing."

"I never—"

"You know how I know this?" He moved through the doors the guards opened. Vaguely Oria recognized the rooms as Vycayla's suite, rather than Lonen's old, smaller one. "I know because I was doing the same thing," Lonen continued before she could say anything about the rooms. He set her on her feet and unhooked the chain holding on her cloak, letting it fall to the floor. "I dreamed of you every night, and I'd wake longing for you. I'd look toward Bára, at Sgatha's rosy face and Grienon's fleeting passage, and envy the moons because they could look on you when I couldn't."

"Lonen..." she breathed, uncertain what words could follow that.

He framed her face in his big, rough hands and kissed her with infinite tenderness. "I love you, Oria. I think I loved you the moment I saw you in that window, as if lit from within by magic. You made me believe in the possibility of beauty, of peace and happiness, just by existing."

"I think it was slower for me," she answered with painful honesty, winding the tie between her fingers. "You frightened me so."

Quick concern creased his face. "Do I frighten you still?"

She laughed, letting her magic swell between them, caressing him with it so his eyes flared from granite to silvery gray. "Not in the least. That was more about me, and my own fears and insecurities. I was such a timid mouse."

"No." He brushed his thumbs over her cheekbones. "Never that. I thought you were the bravest person I'd ever beheld, riding out to surrender the city—and make demands of your conqueror."

She made a dismissive sound. "Nonsense, barbarian. You will never conquer me."

"Good." He took her hand and led her into the next room. All the wedding preparation detritus had disappeared, replaced with white candles and bows of evergreen. Bowls of hammered metal caught the candlelight and overflowed with autumn leaves, carefully dried to preserve their vibrant, fiery colors. "A Destrye tradition," he said, gazing around the room with her. "Evergreen for winter, autumn leaves, candles for the summer sun. Unfortunately we have no flowers for spring, but soon enough I'll be able to offer you real ones."

Oria summoned a bit of magic, remembering the pool at the edge of the forest where she and Lonen had rested and he'd told her they were in Dru. Touching one of the boughs of evergreen, she transformed it into a garland of yellow flowers, sweetly scented and with buttery petals.

"Buttercups," Lonen said, a hint of awe in his voice. "Fitting."

"Yes." She returned his smile. "Now we have everything."

"Almost." He pulled her into his arms, lips brushing hers, rapidly becoming a fire that consumed her. "I wanted this first time to be slow, romantic," he muttered against her mouth. "but I don't know if I can be that restrained. Oria…" He groaned her name, his mouth slanting over her throat, kissing, licking, lightly biting here and there, and she went boneless.

"Where's a pillar when you need one?" she returned and he laughed, hoarse and desperate.

"Take off this gorgeous gown or I'll ruin it."

"I don't care." She arched in his grip, happy to have him tear the fragile cloth from her if it got him inside her faster.

"Oh no." He set her away from him and backed up to sit on the high bed, one hand gripping the other, a determined set to his jaw. "You'll wear that dress every year on the anniversary of our wedding, so I can remember this night."

"You might forget otherwise?" she teased, holding up her hair to reach behind her shoulders to unfasten the braided chain straps.

"Never," he averred, gaze intent on her. She swayed a little in place, enjoying his eyes on her.

"What if I get fat? Maybe I won't be able to fit into the dress after I've birthed ten children." She had the chains unhooked but held the copper silk coyly to her breasts.

"Is that how many you plan to have?" He quirked the scarred brow.

"At least. Maybe twice that many."

"Then I'll find more of that cloth and we'll keep adding to it, even if you're as big as Chuffta."

She laughed, delighted with him. Then let the silk fall, pooling at her feet. She wore nothing beneath—any undergarments would have showed through the delicate fabric—so she stood naked but for the simple slippers and the cloak of her hair. The ladies had wanted to put her hair up, but she'd insisted on having it down, knowing how Lonen loved it that way—and only finally agreed to the circlet as a sign of her station. Now she tugged it from her hair, tossed it aside, kicked off the slippers and moved to her husband, fully naked.

His eyes roved over her with a hunger she hoped he'd never lose. In his eyes, she wasn't too thin, and she believed she'd never be too fat. In his eyes she saw the same love she felt, the deep connection throbbing along the bond created long before the Báran priestesses solidified it with magic. A bond they created between them, despite their warring nations and the storied hatreds they'd been taught.

Lonen's eyes rose to her face with wry humor, as if he sensed her thoughts, and she opened her mind more fully to him, seeing herself as he did. "I think one of us is wearing too many clothes," she murmured.

HE LET OUT a shaking laugh and stood. "You blind me, Oria. I lose all sense around you."

"Then let me help," she answered in that smooth murmur, her nimble fingers moving to undo the clasp holding on his cloak, then the belt. She smoothed her hands over his chest as she parted his shirt, leaning in to press her soft lips to his skin—which might as well have been a brand, the way the touched seared through him. He fisted his hands by his sides, trying to control the nearly violent need to seize her and thrust himself inside her sweet body.

"Oria." He marveled at how calm he sounded. "If I promise you can play with me all you like later, would you get on the bed already and spread your pretty thighs for me?"

Her startled gaze flew up to his, the copper hot as melted ore. She pursed her lips thoughtfully and he seriously considered kissing her senseless. "If you promise…" Turning, she climbed onto the bed, pausing on hands and knees to look over her shoulder, the gleaming fall of her hair sliding over her white skin, her gorgeous ass in the air and shapely legs parted to reveal her copper nether curls and the sweet pink flesh between. "But you're still wearing too many clothes," she purred.

He was, as the near-painful press of his engorged cock against the trousers attested. And he'd thought they were loose. Kicking off his boots, he stripped off the pants and crawled onto the bed after her, feeling much like an adolescent boy again, drooling after his first woman. With a mischievous smile, Oria—now leaning back on her elbows, giving him an excellent view of her delectable, pink-tipped breasts—scooted back across the big bed, daring him to come after her.

With an impatient snarl, he snagged one slim ankle, dragging her toward him, and she shrieked with surprise and laughter. Grabbing the other ankle before she could kick at him, he spread her wide and crawled up between her spread thighs, positioning himself at her entrance. Abruptly and completely serious, she gazed up at him, winding her arms behind his neck, lips parted and eyes full of emotion. He lowered himself, sliding his body against hers, savoring the connection of skin against skin, hers softer than the finest cloth. "Hold onto me," he murmured.

"Until the end of time," she replied.

He kissed her, savoring the way she arched into him, her little nipples hard against his chest, and he slipped a hand between them, her hot sex slick and ready, to his immense relief. Making another promise, this one to himself, that he could play with her later, too, he moved his hand under her slim hips, adjusting the angle and pressing his cock slowly into her.

Pulling back, he watched her face, the heavy-lidded look of concentration in her eyes as she felt his flesh enter hers. She was no virgin, not after the many games they'd played—and various implements he'd used on her—but she also had never had a man inside her. It had to be different, especially as he'd been too desperate to have her to bring her to climax a few times before this moment.

She moaned, long and low—and he stilled, worried that had been a mistake and he was hurting her. His arms shook with the effort at restraint, but he made himself wait until her eyes opened more fully, looking at him in wonder. "Don't stop," she breathed. "You feel so good."

With a gusty exhale, he let himself go, sliding into her tight sheath to the hilt until she surrounded him. Her breath hitched and she ground herself against him where their bodies joined, her skin growing slick against his. He dropped his forehead to hers, taking a shuddering breath, willing himself not to come immediately—incredibly difficult with her internal muscles gripping him like a hand.

"Lonen." She said his name like a plea, like a prayer. "Oh, my love. Please."

Unleashed, he moved, sliding out and in again. She bowed against him with a cry, her body a taut arch, thrumming like a bowstring, nails scoring down his back. He pulled back as much as he could bear—and home again, no longer able to be gentle, holding her hips in place as he plundered her sweet body, drinking in her cries of wild pleasure, her magic sparking all along his skin, enveloping him as he fell into her.

Oblivion, black and sprinkled with bright stars, claimed him. With something between a groan and a shout, he spent himself inside of her.

Dragging himself out of the depths, he managed to roll onto his side, loving her sound of protest as he withdrew from her. She followed along, rolling onto one hip and snuggling against him, pressing herself against his skin at every point of contact possible.

"I dreamed of this," she murmured, lips brushing his chest as she said it, a spoken kiss of movement. "Being this close to another person, touching like this—and my dreams never came close to this... *feeling*. I never knew it could be so mesmerizing, delightful, and somehow nurturing."

He knew what she meant. It felt as if she entered his very pores, assuaging a thirst he hadn't realized plagued him until it was slaked. "Any person at all?" he teased.

She laughed softly, a huff of air against his skin that had his groin tightening again, but in a lazy, sated ripple. He could have her as often as he liked, hold her just like this, for always. The knowledge settled something in him, made the trials ahead seem of little consequence, if he could always return to this.

He felt her shift, tipping her head back to look at him, so he opened his eyes. She looked sleepy, equally sated, almost feline in her smug contentment. "For a long time, I thought it would be my ideal mate, you know—the mysterious priest who would be the perfect match, his grien to my sgath—and I imagined this glorious harmony, where we'd feel like one person, where I'd no longer know where I left off and he began."

Lonen ignored the prickle of inadequacy. He'd long ago accepted that he could never be the perfect, harmonious match Oria had expected as part of her sorcerous birthright.

"And now," she continued, threading her fingers through his chest hair, trailing her nails lightly over his skin, "I recognize how meaningless that was. How utterly foolish of me to want that."

"What do you mean?" he asked carefully, the surge of hope proving how little he'd actually ignored that jealous prickle.

She gave him a very serious look. "The keenest joy is finding connection in someone *unlike* me. When I was in the cavern with the derkesthai king, he told me I had to find the balance between extremes, that the purest magic resides in balance of both. In Bára, they always said it was a balance of sgath and grien, but I think they lost the truth of it somewhere along the way. I think it's this." She tugged his chest hair with a mischievous smile. "You and me, opposites, with a seed of each in the other."

He caressed her cheek, brushing the shining hair back from her high forehead. "We make a good team. I never expected to marry a woman like you."

"No." Her smile widened wickedly. "*You* were going to marry Natly!" She dug her nails painfully into his chest, making him yelp and clap a hand over hers.

"Never," he protested, rolling her onto her back and pinning her. "She was like your fantasy perfect husband—a distraction to pass the time until I found the real thing."

"Truly?" She breathed the question, searching his face, and it occurred to him that he might not be the only one vulnerable to that prick of uncertainty.

"Look into my heart and mind and you'll know," he assured her, brushing a kiss against that tempting mouth, savoring the taste of her.

She opened to him, as if she, too, wanted to drink him in. His cock grew against her soft thigh and she chuckled. "Again—already?"

"And again and again and again," he replied as he, unable to resist that lure of being surrounded by her, slid into her body, her sigh of pleasure like a song.

She wrapped her legs around his hips, trailing gentle caresses over him. "And again," she whispered. "And always."

~ 6 ~

WHEN THE LAST deep ripples of pleasure faded, Lonen rolled onto his side again, murmuring an apology for crushing her. Oria hadn't minded though. She'd loved feeling him lose himself in her, his mind going thoughtless but for the sensations of her, his love and delight in her bathing every pore like soaking in a perfumed and steaming bath. She whimpered a little as he slid out of her, leaving her empty again.

"Are you sore?" he asked, levering up on an elbow, a concerned frown twisting his scarred eyebrow, the flickering candlelight softening his features.

"No," she answered honestly, throwing her arms over her head and stretching in luxurious satiety. "I just miss having you inside of me."

He smiled, a hint of surprise coming from him and he stroked a big hand over her body, lingering to cup her breast, tracing the curve of her waist to her hip and down her thigh, his gaze following the movement. Feeling like a cat being petted, she wished she could purr. "I like being inside you," he said, gaze returning to hers, eyes full of silvery heat. "But I promised you other pleasures, too."

"We've done those," she replied. "I like those things, but this is new."

He laughed, levering himself up and going for a basin of water set over a warming candle on a nearby table. Sweet herbs and dried flower petals floated in the water and when he handed her a cloth soaked in it, the steamy fragrance rose up. She cleaned herself, moving leisurely to draw his eye. He stood by the bed, cleaning himself also, his heavy cock now lax. Wicked desire shimmered from him, his thoughts shuttered, and she wondered what he might be planning.

"Believe me, what I have in mind is new also." He held out a hand for her cloth and she gave it to him with a little pout—one difficult to maintain at the sight of his gorgeous behind flexing as he returned the bowl and floating cloths to the warmer. She'd seen him naked plenty of times, but it seemed she'd never get enough.

He joined her on the bed again, tossing back the furs to expose her fully. Pleased with his admiration, she slid her legs together, a sinuous dance for him alone.

"You are so beautiful, Oria," he said throatily, crawling over to straddle her on his hands and knees, "and I plan to taste every bit of your luscious body."

Languidly she slid her arms around his neck, ready to draw him into a deep kiss. And he obliged her, but only with a brush of lips. Instead of sinking onto her, he moved to brush soft kisses along her jaw, to the sweet spot under her ear that made her shiver, then down her throat. She moaned, low and long, a sort of human purr, and he made an answering hum of pleasure.

Her arms fell back heavy as he continued to explore, lingering over the thin-skinned pulse points and slight hollows that sent her senses thrumming. Sometimes he nipped lightly, other times bestowed soft rains of fluttering kisses, followed by hot licks, then drawing her skin into his mouth as if he would devour her in truth.

She dissolved into a flurry of soft cries and pleas. Plucking at his shoulders, she tried to urge him between her spread thighs, but he wouldn't be moved, instead taking her hand in his to deeply kiss her palm, then each fingertip, drawing her fingers one by one into his mouth, an indescribable sensual delight. He kissed his way down her arm, lingering at the hollow of her elbow, then tracing the tender underside of her arm to the near-ticklish skin at the side of her breast. Her nipples tightened in anticipation of his clever mouth on those sensitive points, but he circled around the one without touching, lavishing her breast with sensation, teasing and stirring her to a frenzy.

With a cry of frustration, she seized his head trying to move him to her throbbing nipple—but he only laughed, husky and darkly amused, and took her other hand into his mouth. With infuriating patience, he repeated the performance on the other hand, giving each finger meticulous attention before making his way down her arm, exquisitely slow, maddeningly thorough.

By the time he reached her other breast, still not touching her nipples, Oria had enough. Her magic swirled in the air, raking light claws down his back as she clung to his shoulders. "Lonen," she panted, half in plea, half in warning.

He raised his head to stare her down, his face set in ridged lines of intense arousal, eyes flinty with determination. "No tricks, sorceress, or I'll stop."

"Don't you *dare*," she breathed, lifting her breasts to him, torn between begging and berating him.

He surveyed her with a molten stare, taking advantage of her arched back to slide his hands beneath and hold her there, draped over them. "In time, sweet. But only if you're good. No magic."

With supreme effort, she withdrew the mental claws, drawing the magic back into herself—which only made her feel more like exploding. "Be quick about it," she said through gritted teeth, "or I'm liable to tear the palace apart before I realize it."

He tsked, gently chiding. "You wanted to practice control."

She growled in frustration, choked off when he pressed a deep kiss to the hollow at the center of her collarbones, then licked her, in one long, hot and slick caress down between her breasts all the way to the top of her pubis. He lingered there, dipping his tongue into her belly button, holding her in a firm grip as she writhed and mewed.

A wail escaped her when he flipped her onto her belly. "Every bit of you, Oria," he reminded her in that sensual, graveled voice, gathering her hair and draping it to the side to expose the back of her neck. "You might as well resign yourself."

"You're so cruel," she whimpered, undulating with need as he pressed his mouth to the nape of her neck.

He sank his teeth into the thicker muscle where her shoulder met her throat, and she sobbed at the intensity of it. "Yes," he murmured, licking that spot, gentling her, then nipping at the skin along her spine on his way back up to her nape. "And you're all mine to do with as I will."

She moaned in resignation, letting him play his games, taunting and teasing her as he tasted every bit of her. As he made his way down her back, she lost all sense of time, of the edges of herself. Becoming only her skin and the unending sensations of his hot mouth and raking hands. She didn't protest as he continued past her bottom down her legs, to her toes. The backs of her knees, the hollows of her ankles, the tender arches of her feet, all quickened to his caresses, each dissolving her a little more.

She'd gone blind and deaf, insensate to everything but the dark magic he worked on her body. So when he kissed his way up her inner thighs, she only groaned, unable to bear any more, unable to resist.

When he spread her wide and put his mouth on her sex, she climaxed in a wrenching convulsion that had her tearing at the bed cover. She screamed, spine arching and head thrown back, and Lonen held her plunging hips in his hands, tongue an incredible sensation on her most delicate tissues.

Though he wasn't done with her, licking her through the orgasm, prolonging it, driving her still higher. When she neared peak again, he slid into her, and put his mouth on her nipple, sucking hard as he pinched the other.

Beyond the ability to make sound, she fully and completely shattered, becoming shards of starlight, swallowed in the blackness of night.

ORIA TRIED TO keep to a smooth pace as she made her way down to the dungeons. With every movement, however, each set of stairs she descended, aches and twinges reminded her of Lonen's vigorous lovemaking. He'd wrung her dry, seemingly inexhaustible himself.

The ribald remarks she'd heard the Destrye calling to each other about women walking funny in the morning kept echoing in her head. Apparently, they were based at least somewhat on reality. Though she'd experienced penetration before, nothing had prepared her for her husband's extremely well-endowed efforts. To make matters worse, when she'd commented on it, he'd only looked terribly pleased with himself and not sympathetic at all. Men.

"But you're happy?" Chuffta asked.

"Oh yes," she reassured him. *"Just sore and tired—and not willing to give Lonen any reason to expand his already big head."*

They hadn't slept much at all—just naps here and there—because every time she stirred, it seemed to awaken his insatiable hunger for her. Not that she minded. She'd known from their first wedding night that Lonen was a creative, sensitive, and generous lover—totally at odds with his barbarian mien—but she hadn't quite expected the intensity of being skin to skin with him. Or what access to her skin allowed him to do to her. He'd promised to consume her and she indeed felt entirely as if she'd been chewed up and left boneless.

"Perhaps you should sleep more," Chuffta offered solicitously. *"Or see a healer."*

"I don't need a healer." She mentally laughed, and also cringed, at the thought of telling even Baeltya about it. The thought of Vycayla somehow becoming involved.... No, no, no. *"I'm fine, really. I got used to riding a horse after all, and this is—"* She cut herself off, realizing how Lonen would laugh his ass off at that analogy.

"Why is that so funny?"

"It's a human thing. Listen along as I work with Nolan, all right? Just anything you notice." She nodded at the guard who unlocked the door for her to enter the lowest level of the dungeon. In better times, Lonen had told her as they curled together sleepily, a newly married couple could be expected to stay in their rooms for days—or even go off together somewhere—and he offered for them to take a day or two. But she hadn't needed to read his mind to know that, as much as part of him yearned to closet himself with her, he also itched to get after the business of the realm.

In truth, she should start learning her responsibilities as queen, but Lonen had preempted that impulse by telling her that her priority should be dealing with the sorcerous Báran taint in Nolan and his men. He hadn't said aloud, but they both knew that the first priority for Dru and the Destrye was planning for the inevitable next attack.

Or, rather, forestalling that possibility by taking the war to Bára.

"Do you think we will—go back to Bára and attack them?"

"Strange to think about, hmm?" Strange, indeed, to consider how she'd once stood at the balustrade of her high tower and looked out over the desert, straining for news of the battle she couldn't see. Now she'd be the enemy. But not to destroy Bára. No: to save it.

Nolan's ranting echoed down the tunnel of the corridor, the volume of it seeming to make the torches flicker, though Oria knew that shouldn't be possible. Adjusting her barriers, she steadied herself as she came around the last corner. As usual, he paced his cell, waving hands in the air as he raged.

Also as usual when Oria wasn't there, Natly perched on the stool. She seemed to be trying to talk to Nolan. She didn't hear Oria's approach immediately and started when Oria called out a hello, by way of warning. Glancing over her shoulder and quickly away, Natly brushed at her face. When she met Oria's gaze, her defiant one glistened still with tears.

"I'm surprised you're out of bed already. Your Highness," she added, a beat too late for true courtesy, not quite enough to be insolent.

Oria figured she'd be none too polite to a woman she knew had just crawled wobbly-kneed out of Lonen's bed—more likely she'd be inclined to murder—so she ignored the slight. "I have work to do," she replied with a calming smile and gestured at Nolan. "Any changes?"

Natly bit her lip. The Destrye woman always groomed herself beautifully, fit for the queen she longed to be, so her lips were painted in crisp lines of glossy crimson, her dark eyes artfully highlighted with cosmetics, and her black hair piled in an artful tumble of curls and jewels. Oria was glad the ladies assigned to her had insisted on braiding her hair—adding the gold circlet—dressing her in a new gown and decorating her with subtle cosmetics and discreet jewelry. She wore her wedding cloak. The silk-lined emerald satin was heavy enough to keep her warm in the pervasive chill of the palace without her needing to expend magic to warm herself, but it was a better weight for indoors than the shadowcat fur cloak. Lonen had noted that her wearing Arill's colors would help establish Oria in her new role, too.

Lonen had similarly girded himself for the day ahead, and there had been something companionable and intimate in their shared ritual of donning their costumes as rulers.

And in the knowing that she'd return to him at the end of the day and remove it all again. Had she thought herself sexually exhausted? Apparently not, because the thought of what might occur once night fell had her flushing in anticipation.

Natly noted the blush, narrowing her eyes knowingly. Lonen had likely polished all those bed skills, those many clever tricks of his, with this woman. Once that realization might have made Oria jealous, but not now. To have had Lonen in her bed and lost him...Oria could only feel sorry for Natly, which the Destrye woman would not abide.

"I think he's worse," Natly finally said, her tone far less brash, and Oria recalled herself to the important matters at hand. Natly even stepped aside, not quite offering Oria the courtesy of acknowledging her rank, but making way for them both to observe Nolan. "I stayed until late last night and have been here a few hours. I don't think he's slept at all."

Nolan seized the iron grate barring the cell, shouting incoherently, eyes glassy and wild.

"Did *you* sleep much?" Oria asked without thinking, then wished she could take back the inconsiderate words.

"I couldn't," Natly bit out, her voice and spiky emotions daring Oria to say anything more.

"Nolan is fortunate in your devotion," Oria said instead.

That threw Natly off course, and she paused, reeling back whatever words she'd been poised to hurl at Oria. She gazed at Nolan with a strange expression on her face, her emotions a tangible snarl of worry, anger, fear—and love?

"I loved him once," Natly said, confirming it. "Long ago. Forever ago, it feels like. He didn't love me, but at least he wanted me." Rather than the brash, confidently aggressive woman Natly had presented herself as before, she sounded small in that moment, even forlorn. "Even after he returned, and Lonen... was with *you*, I offered to be his lover—we'd always been good together that way— and he ignored me. As if that part of him had died. I hate what's become of him."

The way Nolan's once-handsome face contorted in his insane ire, spittle flecking his filthy beard, Oria didn't blame Natly a bit. She couldn't imagine seeing Lonen in such a state. And it was all her people's fault. Whoever had turned Nolan's mind—Oria's brother Yar or someone else—the guilt belonged to Bára.

"I'm going to help him," she told Natly, setting the resolve in herself as she said the words. "Maybe you should go rest. Come back later and—"

"You can give me orders," Natly said in a flat, malicious voice, all softness gone. "Because you are Queen of Dru now, and I'll obey.

I won't give you reason to have me exiled for disloyalty. But don't pretend that you care a fig for me." She gathered her skirts and strode off in a brisk, athletic stride, jewelry chiming as she went.

"Good riddance, I say," Chuffta remarked. *"She makes my ears hurt."*

"How can she make your ears hurt when you can't literally hear her."

"I don't know. She just does.*"*

Privately Oria had to agree that the area felt calmer without Natly's prickly presence—which was saying something given Nolan's noisy behavior—though she also felt petty thinking it. Natly had suffered a great deal and lost her planned future. Oria should try to be more generous in her thoughts. She sat on the stool Natly had vacated and cleared her mind. Lately she'd been drawing on the sensations of flying to get there, evoking that calm, in-the-moment peacefulness of simply existing in the world. Back in Bára, Chuffta had helped her meditate by guiding her into trances that at least mimicked *hwil*.

Now she found that she could slip into that state—not *hwil*, which never had made sense to her—but a place of being, in the most profound and basic sense; a point of equilibrium, a still, quiet place she'd found in the inferno of the derkesthai cavern. Lonen's delicious torment had brought her to a similar place, one where she accepted the flow of existing without trying to control it. As if she had immense wings like Chuffta's, she soared on the currents of the wild magic.

Once those unpredictable currents had destabilized her, dragging her under and drowning conscious thought, driving her nearly insane. When she'd begun using the ancient mask of her ancestress, which she and Lonen had dug out of the unnamed sorceress's tomb, the magical artifact had focused and exacerbated the effect—to the point that it had nearly killed her. Lonen had overreacted, wanting to take it from her. But after the trials with the derkesthai, Oria felt confident she could use the mask effectively, with no damage to herself.

But she kept the mask out of Lonen's sight anyway. He hadn't mentioned it since they had found each other again—possibly with so much on his mind, he'd forgotten about it, or thought she'd lost it in the molten lakes of the derkesthai caverns—so she hadn't brought it to his attention. If they took the war back to Bára, then she would need to have the mask in hand. She and Lonen could fight about it then.

For the moment, she'd hold the mask in reserve. She held on to that steady core of balanced self, sailing with the magic, absorbing it into herself and becoming one with it. Not helplessly tossed about, but integrated.

One with the flow of the magic of the world, she moved the flow of it with her. If she let herself, she could spend hours distracted by the rivers and streams of different kinds of magic, each with its own particular quality. They'd be different scents or flavors, if magic was chemical. Or colors, if magic flows were a visible thing. They'd be different notes in a song if magic could be heard, the melodies and harmonies related to the source of that magic.

Gradually, however, she'd begun to learn to accept magic as its own thing. She didn't perceive it with the same parts of herself that smelled, saw, or heard things. It could be that the part of herself that sensed, drew in, and manipulated magic had nothing to do with her physical body at all. Thus, comparing her magical senses to physical ones would only lead her down false paths.

She'd been mulling this, contemplating it in the last days while flying on Chuffta and distracting herself from anticipating the wedding. That had been a good event, no doubt about it, but it felt good to have their personal lives settled, and their political ones, too. Now she could concentrate on her sorcery.

And her first big project: finding the magical corruption in Nolan.

Removing it would be the second ambitious project.

In the still place, she shut out her physical senses, aware only of the world formed entirely of magic. There, Nolan's shouted epithets didn't exist, nor did the hard stool or the chill, dank air of the dungeons. Even she didn't exist, exactly, nor did Chuffta, but they were together, swimming in an endless sea of magic.

"Or flying."

"Yes. I'm going to look in a different place this time. Tell me what you notice."

When she'd tried before, she'd looked into Nolan's mind, the way she read Lonen's thoughts or sensed the wordless images from Buttercup. With no time to spend with Nolan the day before, and lots of time to mull while all the ladies decorated her for the wedding, she'd realized that Yar—or whatever sorcerer had worked this magic to poison Nolan's thoughts—would predict that Oria could read them.

Till now she'd thought that Yar assumed her to be dead. A reasonable assumption, since no sorceress had survived long outside of the walls of her city and its sustaining source of sgath. She herself had thought she'd die. Likely she would have, if not for Lonen's stubborn determination to save her life, and his ridiculous optimism that he could thwart everything the Bárans knew about how sgath and the wild magic worked.

Never mind that he'd turned out to be right.

Oria had realized that whatever opened Nolan's mind to Báran influence could be a two-way connection. The golems could also operate that way. The silicate constructs were given packets of sgath to animate them and instructions to follow, but Oria could receive and well as send through her magic portals. Surely a sorcerer could, too. Which might mean that Yar had been aware that Oria had survived ever since the Golems attacked her and Lonen in the desert. If so, he might've gained even more information once Nolan found them at the borders of Dru.

Worst of all, he might now know everything Nolan knew about Dru and the Destrye.

That realization changed nothing—they could hardly prepare for attack any more than they had—so she hadn't mentioned this possibility to Lonen. Not yet. Not until she tested her theory. If Yar had anticipated that Oria would read Nolan's thoughts, then the taint lay somewhere Yar believed Oria couldn't access.

So, this time, instead of looking in Nolan's chaotic thoughts—an unpleasant experience, regardless—she looked at other parts of his being. Particularly the masculine aspects. Yar wouldn't easily relinquish his ideas of the superiority of male grien and the sorcerers who wielded it. Even though he'd personally witnessed Oria using grien, active magic supposedly beyond the reach of women, that self-absorbed and self-congratulatory ego of his would blind him to the truth. She was gambling that he'd consider anything male beyond her ability to comprehend.

Sifting through Nolan's masculine nature, she found it grounded in the physical body. From there the personality stemmed, partly shaped by the physical, partly by the non-physical. To her surprise, she found that the eternal aspect of Nolan—that which had existed before his birth and which would move on following the death of his body—was neither male nor female.

"This could explain why you can access both sgath and grien," Chuffta noted quietly, observing along with her. *"You've found that the world of magic exists beyond the physical. If you are not your body, then your use of magic is neither male nor female."*

"Balance in all things," she remembered the Great One trying to explain. *"Finding the point of equilibrium could mean between masculine and feminine also."*

He agreed, wordless in their connection in this space.

She moved into the parts of Nolan's identity where his sense of himself as a man resided. And there, she found what she sought.

"EXPLAIN THAT AGAIN," Lonen told Oria, wondering to himself if he'd heard correctly.

Oria huffed out a breath in exasperation, which made her full breasts—nicely displayed in the pretty gown her ladies had dressed her in—rise and fall enticingly. Not something that helped his concentration on the conversation. When Oria had asked to have their midday meal in private, in their chambers, and he'd assumed she had more sex on her mind. But no, she wanted to talk about his *brother*.

"I've already explained it twice," she replied crisply, narrowing her eyes at him. "Focus on what I'm saying, not on my breasts."

He grinned at her, unrepentant. "They're beautiful breasts, and delicious. I'd like to have my mouth on them."

"I shouldn't have suggested a private meal here," she said with rueful resignation. "I wanted a confidential conversation with the king, not a tryst with the man."

"All right, all right," he conceded. With an effort, he wrenched his mind from salacious fantasies and thought through what Oria had explained about Nolan's state of mind. At least thinking about his crazed brother and his backstabbing treachery, regardless of the reasons for it, had the salutary effect of quenching his desire.

"So, if I understand correctly, you found magic that you associate with that of the Báran sorcerers, though not Yar specifically, and it's attached to Nolan in his male sexuality?"

Oria beamed at him like he was a prize student. "You *were* listening! That's exactly what I'm saying."

Hmm. Though it still didn't make any sense. "Are you asking me to cut off my brother's balls?"

She burst out laughing. "No! Not a bit of it. That's the physical. I'm talking about the non-physical."

"Some of us, like your loving husband," he said, pointing his eating knife at himself, "have only the physical world to deal with."

"Is that right?" she replied archly. "What about Arill?"

"She's a goddess."

"Does She exist physically?"

"Well, no, but—"

"What about the healers in Arill's service, like Baeltya and your mother—is their healing magic a physical thing?"

She was making his head hurt. What came of marrying a sorceress, no doubt. "Yes," he decided. "Because I can feel it, therefore it exists physically."

"Can you touch the healing magic? Smell it, see it, hear it?"

"No," he conceded. "But it obviously exists, because it has an effect."

"Exactly," she pounced on the point. "You feel the effects of the healing, but not the magic that induces the healing, because that exists on a non-physical plane of reality."

He nearly asked if it counted as "reality" if it didn't exist physically, but Oria looked so earnest in her explanation, and so excited about her discovery, that he didn't have the heart to tease her about it. He also still didn't know what tree she was climbing. "Oria, my love, can you indulge your barbarian of a husband and reduce this discussion to what actions we can take? Whatever we need to do to fix Nolan, I want to do."

"Well, that's just it," she said thoughtfully. "I'm not sure we should."

He reined in the surge of anger that she'd suggest such a thing— especially since her calm expression and sparkling gaze held no hint of malice or revenge. "Then what?" he asked simply, pushing his empty plate aside and leaning his forearms on the table.

She hesitated, a line forming between her brows. "You won't like this part."

Oh, wonderful. As if he'd liked any of this. "Say it anyway," he said, as calmly as he could.

As she explained her theory, however, that the magically implanted control that guided Nolan's thoughts and actions might actually be a conduit that linked everything Nolan experienced back to a sorcerer in Yar, his rage grew. His fingers itched for his iron battle-axe, leaning against the wall nearby, even though this particular enemy—this non-physical *thing* Oria spoke of—couldn't be hacked apart. It would ease him to have the axe in his hands. He'd agreed to wear the crown of Dru again, but nothing could make him take up his father's sword, the one Nolan had nearly killed him with. He trusted the battle-axe like he trusted his warhorse, Buttercup, like he trusted Oria.

"Lonen." Oria leaned on the table, too, copper gaze intent, a whisper of her essence in his mind drawing him out of his dark thoughts.

He blinked away the red haze. "So he's a spy. All the time that he accused you of being a spy for the enemy, accused *me* of being subverted by you, under your control, *he* was the one. All this time, working to destroy us."

She smiled, crooked and close-lipped, both wry and sorrowful. "It's a clever way to divert suspicion—accuse others of the very thing you're guilty of."

"I could kill him for this," Lonen snarled, all those conversations with Nolan rolling through his head, the plans to repair the aqueducts, their strategy to plant crops in widely varying places and scatter livestock herds so that if one portion met with destruction, they might still have another... all known to the enemy. A few of the Trom dragons deployed to the right places and within the space of an hour they could lose everything, be utterly and finally destroyed.

Oria covered his hand with hers, small and delicate, but fiercely strong. "It's not his fault, Lonen. Don't kill him for that."

"Right. I'll just cut off his balls then," he suggested, intending it as a joke, though it came out far too lethal sounding.

"He didn't consciously betray you," Oria insisted.

"You're sure of that?"

She nodded, absolutely serious. "It's not in his mind at all. Probably to him it feels like he's in a dream. If he's aware at all."

"He acted like himself, for a while."

"Do you want to know what I think they did to him, what happened?"

"Will I understand?" he retorted grimly.

Oria laughed and rolled her eyes. "You may be a hulking brute of a barbarian, husband of mine, but I happen to know what a sharp mind you have inside that thick skull. Of course you'll understand, as long as you're not thinking about sex instead," she added with a teasing note.

Sex, and happy topics in general, had fled far from his mind. He'd grown used to sorcery, being around Oria—but like her, the magic she embodied seemed full of light and the beauty of nature. Things he understood and loved about the world. This conversation… it reminded him of how he used to feel about Báran magic, ground under by the odious stuff. "All right." He sighed, bracing himself. "Explain."

"What would you be thinking about if I came over there, knelt down, and took your cock in my mouth?" she asked.

He paused, disconcerted—and immediately aroused. They hadn't done that yet, her mouth, hot, wet, and tight on his intimate flesh. "I thought you didn't want me to think about sex."

"Where did your mind go just now?" she asked seriously, not flirting at all.

"You know perfectly well, sorceress," he growled at her. "Since you can read my mind, you know how much I want that."

"Could feel it? Imagine me on my knees in front of you?"

His cock had grown so hard he had to adjust it, giving her a wry glance as he did. "Yes."

"Even though it wasn't real," she pressed the point.

"Even so," he agreed.

"So, even though we're having a very serious conversation about something critically important to you on several levels, with a few words I managed to divert your thoughts to something else entirely."

"Something that's never entirely far from my thoughts to begin with," he pointed out. Especially with her in the room. Perhaps one day this hunger for her would relent, but the day after their wedding? Not likely. "Is there a point to this game of yours, Oria?"

"Don't get testy with me. Of course there's a point. I played on your male sexuality to influence the direction of your thoughts, and by saying only a few words."

"A few extraordinarily enticing words," he felt he had to say.

"I acknowledge I had a good idea of which words to use," she replied with a feline smile. "Now: imagine what a clever person with a good idea of which words to use, *and* powerful magic at their command, could do to a man's thoughts."

Understanding dawned, clearing his muddy head. "So, every time Nolan thought about sex…" He trailed off, the enormity of that hitting him.

"Not even thought about it," Oria replied in all seriousness. "Just felt the urge. How many times a day do you feel a sexual urge, even if you don't give it much thought?"

Every fucking minute of every day, with Oria near. "Arill save us," he whispered.

"I realized this in part because of something Natly said, that Nolan used to be a vigorous and enthusiastic lover, but after he returned, she said it was like that aspect of him had died. It occurred to me that maybe it wasn't dead and instead pointed in a different direction."

"So when he felt any urge, his mind went to, what, betraying the

Destrye?"

She shrugged a little. "Of that I can't be too sure. The spell is complex and finely wrought, like a spiderweb of metal wrapped around his sexual being. Probably the suggestions are simple and easily followed. Like commands you'd give Buttercup, so as not to confuse him."

"Don't be insulting my warhorse," Lonen shot back, not angrily, but relieved that he could make a joke during this horrible conversation.

Oria smiled back, looking relieved by his levity, too. "No insult to Buttercup intended. I just mean that if you could give Buttercup instructions to go off and accomplish some task by himself, wouldn't you want those directives to be pretty straightforward? Clear tasks, that could be adapted to circumstances, but nothing so complex that the plan would fall apart if some component changed."

An idea of that formed in his head. "So nothing so vague as 'destroy the Destrye,' but maybe 'become king.'"

She nodded. "At any cost. And there seems to be a kind of intensification built into the spell, so that if he doesn't succeed, it drives him to try harder."

"The more he's thwarted, the harder he tries."

"Exactly." She looked grim as he felt now.

"But, if he can't try, if he's prevented, wouldn't that—" He cut himself off, unwilling to say the words.

"Drive a man mad," Oria said softly. "That's what I'm guessing is happening to him."

Horrifying to imagine. He stared at Oria. Surely she couldn't be so cruel as to want that for Nolan. Even his own craving for revenge, his certainty that Nolan deserved death for his treachery, had evaporated with these revelations. "How can you suggest leaving him that way?" he got out. "Would you leave him to go so mad that he can never be healed?"

"Oh!" Oria's eyes rounded in shock—and a reassuring tinge of horror at the picture he painted. "No, that's not what I meant at all.

You think I would want that for your brother?"

"Then what?" he ground out. "Just tell me."

"I'm sorry," she said. "I—"

"There's your one for the day," he said, reaching across the table to take her hand in an apology of his own.

She returned the smile, acknowledging the days when they'd each apologized to the other so much that they'd set a rule to limit it to one apology for each per day. They'd moved past that at some point in the last weeks, finally easy enough with each other that they weren't forever worrying about their own failings. Perhaps that indicated they'd become more confident in themselves, too. Certainly Oria seemed to have done. She spoke about her abilities as a sorceress in a way she hadn't before.

And Lonen himself had grown, no longer secretly believing himself a fraud and imposter on the throne. He'd claimed the throne through his own abilities and determination, as well as the vagaries of fate. He'd be the best ruler for the Destrye that he could be.

"I think we should let Nolan believe he's succeeding in his goals," Oria said, as if that made perfect sense. When he frowned at her, trying to follow why she'd suggest something so outrageous, she continued. "If he believes he's following directives, the loop of magic driving him should ease off. With every goal accomplished, he should return to a more sane state of mind."

"Are you saying we should… make him king?"

Oria shook her head, then nodded. "I think we should let him *believe* he's king. You have a palace full of subjects utterly loyal to you. If we tell everyone to play along, we can all pretend he's won, that he's actually king—and then we can observe what else he does, and thus learn what the Bárans have planned."

A sneaky plan—perhaps an exceedingly clever one—but fraught with possibilities for failure. "But if he's also relaying information back to Bára…" He said as he thought it through.

"Then we can feed him, and thus them, the information we want them to have."

"If they already know I won the challenge, that I'm king and you're officially my queen, and that Nolan has been imprisoned, won't they be suspicious if that suddenly changes?"

She held up a slender finger, eyes glowing with excitement. "Aha! But *does* Nolan know that? Think back. He knows he gravely wounded you in the duel, and that you both fell. Your iron axe disrupted some of the magical connection, plus you knocked him unconscious, so they can't know what happened after that except that he woke up healed and imprisoned in the dungeons."

"He saw me come find you there, though."

"Yes, but he was ranting, not listening. I'm not convinced he noticed you at all. Even if he did, you weren't wearing the crown or carrying your father's sword."

"He will have noticed you, however. You've been with him a great deal."

"Yes, but what will Yar and his cronies make of that? They won't believe I have magic capable of cracking theirs."

"You defeated Yar in that contest of your magics."

"Yes, but Yar thinks I cheated and that Gallia failed him. She should've been the perfectly harmonious match for his magic—and she was powerful, in her home of Lousá—but Báran sgath was unfamiliar to her. You've met Yar. Which is more likely—that he'll honestly see that his magic is no match for his sister who failed to master even basic *hwil*, much less magics he could do by fifteen, or that he'll decide to blame everyone but himself?"

She had a point there. Her brother had all the brash hubris of youth. Even with maturity, Yar might not gain the strength of character to examine his own weaknesses—and to recognize others possessed abilities he lacked.

"All right," he said slowly. "Let's say we release Nolan from his cell. Why would he suddenly go from being a prisoner to the throne?"

Oria leaned in, expression full of wicked delight. "*We* won't release him. His loyal co-conspirator Natly will free him."

"And I'll be in the dungeon cell in his place?" Lonen folded his arms, trying to look forbidding. In truth, he could see where she was going with this. The plan had possibilities.

"No dungeon cell for you, my king," she replied with a twinkle of amusement.

"Won't Nolan notice if I'm wandering around, not defeated?"

"He might, if you were in Dru."

"I won't be in Dru?"

She shook her head from side to side, terribly pleased with herself. "Neither of us will be. Because while Yar and the rest of the Báran sorcerers are preoccupied with Nolan finally being on the throne of Dru uncontested, executing whatever their next instruction is, we will be leading the army to attack Bára."

He sat back in his chair, the possibilities opening up, laying themselves out neatly. "We muster the warriors and begin shifting the troops to just beyond Bára. Once we're clear of Arill City, Natly frees Nolan in a brave coup. A skeleton staff of warriors puts up a token fight, then declares loyalty."

"Exactly. We wouldn't need a lot of people to make it convincing—just enough to create verisimilitude where Nolan can observe. We leave trusted friends to observe him and notify us of his initiatives. Meanwhile, Yar and his cronies are lulled into complacency, thinking all is handled here until they can complete their conquest at leisure."

"The farther away we are, the longer it will take for anyone staying behind to notify us of Nolan's actions if he does something truly detrimental to Dru," he pointed out, not really arguing but mentally covering the logistics. "And taking an army on campaign in winter is difficult."

"I don't know much about that," she conceded, "but I have three thoughts. One is that pulling all of the warriors out of Arill City would relieve the housing and food problems, making it more likely the rest of the population can make it to spring."

"Not if we provision the army with the remaining food supplies."

"If we enlist your mother in this plan, we could ask for some of their supplies to provision the army. That was my second thought."

She had a cannier brain for this kind of planning than he'd have predicted. "And the third?"

"We travel through the tunnels."

~ 8 ~

O RIA RATHER SAVORED Lonen's astonishment at that suggestion—though the surprise quickly cleared from his face, replaced by shrewd analysis as he worked out the logistics with all the experience of his warrior's mind.

"The tunnels, huh?"

"Yes. Nolan said he and his men traveled from under Bára to the edge of the forests of Dru before emerging to travel the rest of the way overland."

Lonen stroked his chin, considering. "It could work. We know the tunnels are big enough to accommodate a warrior on horseback, though a large company will have to be strung out for leagues."

"Send warriors in small groups, one after the other."

He grunted at that thought. "We could do that, start sending the battalions most ready to leave as soon as possible to secure the entrance to the tunnels and begin sending warriors through. Nolan might not be willing to tell us where that was, however."

"Two things." Oria held up two fingers in demonstration. She'd had time to work on the details of her plan while she waited for Lonen to get free of business and join her for lunch. "The warriors who traveled with him will know, and if that becomes a problem, then I can look in Nolan's mind."

"I can see a problem right now," Lonen said with a frown, tapping his knuckles on the table. "What if those men have the same magical corruption? If they're spies also, then—No?"

He broke off as she shook her head. "I've checked all the ones in custody. None of them have any taint of Báran magic."

"You're sure?"

Oria restrained a sarcastic reply. "Yes, I'm sure. Once I found the magic binding Nolan, I checked those of his men in custody—falsely imprisoned, in light of this information, I might point out—and they don't have it. I wondered why I couldn't find anything different about them, but that's the answer. Only Nolan was tampered with."

"That doesn't mean that's true for those men we haven't located for you to examine," he countered. "Perhaps they're evading capture because they *have* been tampered with and want to be free to spy and conduct their sabotage efforts."

"*Or,*" she returned, "maybe they're evading capture because, oh, I don't know, maybe they don't want to be *imprisoned in the dungeons.*"

Lonen narrowed his eyes in a granite glare. "Destrye warriors are accustomed to hardships of all kinds—and to obeying their king."

Oria gave him a look of disbelief. Why was he being so obstinate? "Oh, you mean like you did? When Nolan wore the crown and ordered you imprisoned by the palace guard, did you meekly obey?"

"Of course not!" he snapped. "That was entirely different."

"Different why?" she asked sweetly, letting his anger wash over her, sampling it.

Emotions, it turned out, were another form of intangible energy. People sensed other people's emotions through physical cues—facial expressions and body movements, the sound of the voice, perhaps even a scent, like wolves smelling fear. Oria had always known that other people's emotions affected her—the stronger the emotion, the greater the effect. But she'd always been sadly at the mercy of them, which was why she'd lived alone atop her tower in Bára, to spare her the draining miasma of the people living in the city.

Now, with her growing mastery of magic, being able to perceive the flows of energy in all its various forms, she'd discovered that emotions were a form of magical energy—a kind that every person seemed able to manifest, whether they harnessed that to conscious purpose or not.

"It *is* different, Oria," Lonen answered her needling through gritted teeth.

"Why are you so angry?" She followed the emotions to the thoughts behind them, sifting for the source. "No one expects you to be perfect, Lonen. It's all right to make mistakes. You imprisoned those men for just cause. Now we know there isn't one. Don't cling to the decision just because you don't want to admit an error."

"Reading my thoughts?" he asked, palms flat on the table.

"Yes," she replied candidly. "You've known from the beginning that I can. Even when I had little control of my magic, your thoughts and feelings have loomed large in mine. If you don't want me to, I can make an effort to close off those channels. All you have to do is say so."

His set expression softened, and he scrubbed his hands over his face, then through his hair, seeming surprised when his fingers snagged on the crown. Pulling it off, he set it beside him on the table. He gave her a wry smile. "It's a bit unsettling, how precise you've gotten at it."

"Part of mastering my magic overall," she agreed. "I'm getting more precise at all of those skills." When he didn't immediately reply, her stomach dropped. Stricken with fear that she'd misstepped, that she'd abused his trust, she asked. "Did I do wrong?"

"No." He looked up from the crown he'd been contemplating as if it held answers, took in her expression, then scooted back his chair. "Come here, love."

Gladly, needing the reassurance, Oria came around the table to settle on his lap, inside the circle of the arms he held open for her. He held her there a moment, then tipped up her chin and kissed her, long and sweet and loving. Heat billowed between them and she melted into it, relaxing against him. A knock on the door had him breaking off the kiss with a sound of regret.

"Your Highness," Alby discreetly called through the door. "I'm to remind you of the time."

"In a moment," he called back, and urged Oria to sit up straight on his knee again, then adjusting the fit of his crotch yet again, and with a rueful smile. "Arnon is waiting for me," he explained. "Unfortunately."

"There's tonight," she offered, hopefully.

"Always." He kissed her forehead. "And no, you didn't do wrong. It's good for me to have a sorceress wife who can glance into my mind and call me on my horseshit. But I want you to examine *all* of Nolan's men. If we can round them up."

"Release the ones in custody," she suggested, "and tell them to carry a message, along with a public proclamation, that these have been examined and absolved of any guilt, and the others can present themselves to be absolved also."

"Clever," he agreed, tugging on a lock of her hair. "If excessively civilized."

"Well, you could go around and bash everyone's heads in with your axe, if you'd prefer."

"I would certainly enjoy that more."

"Poor thwarted barbarian," she cooed.

He pinched her bottom, making her squeal. "I'll just have to take out my barbarous urges on my tame witch tonight."

"Oh, will you?" She tried to look menacing, but the immediate arousal at his words—and the fantasy he painted in his mind—had her breathy and aroused instead.

"Yes, but not now." He stood, easily bringing her with him with his casual strength, and set her on her feet. "It's a good plan, Oria. Let's set it in motion. Come with me to meet Arnon. We can tell him about it and maybe he'll have a solution to speeding up communication between us and those watching Nolan. I don't know how we're going to recruit Natly to the cause. Regardless, we can pick apart the details. Arnon is exceptional at finding flaws."

The face Lonen made as he said that had her laughing. She patted his cheek—gasping when he captured her hand and pressed a hot kiss to her palm, his eyes silvery as he watched her over their joined hands.

"You can thrash out the plan and I'll meet you later," she said, tugging her hand away and folding his kiss into her palm. "But I'll handle Natly."

"Oh you will, will you?" He raised his brows.

"Yes," she replied, with more confidence than she felt, but she suspected she knew exactly how to entice the Destrye woman to cooperate. "I'll see you at dinner."

"Are you going somewhere?"

"Indeed. I also have a solution to the communication problem."

"And that is?"

"I need to make sure I can pull it off. I'll tell you either way tonight. Will you trust me until then?"

He bent over and kissed her, a gentle brush of lips that held a world of longing. "Until the end of time, my love."

"Or at least until dinner," she quipped with a smile, and handed him his crown. "Don't forget this."

"As if I could," he replied in a dry tone, settling it on his head again.

"THIS IS FUN!" Chuffta said, as she emerged onto the rooftop platform. Gone were the wedding decorations, musicians, and beautifully dressed guests. Instead the area swarmed with Destrye working with a great clamor of tools. Some dismantling a section here, others building there. Every one paused to bow deeply as she passed, then immediately resumed work.

Lonen had said that Arnon had taken on the project of building onto the palace with great enthusiasm and determination, but the progress startled her. Chuffta waited on the specially reinforced section where he'd perched for the wedding ceremony—and the Destrye all seemed to be keeping half an eye on him—talons digging into the wood, looking as pleased as he sounded.

"Just don't sit too heavily," she cautioned him. Maybe it was her imagination that the platform sloped down slightly in his direction.

"How am I supposed to do that?"

"I don't know." Visions of the palace collapsing beneath them dashed through her mind. *"Think light."*

"Hurry up and I can be in the air," he replied grumpily. And needlessly, because she was already there.

Drawing on the magic, she created a harness of soft rope over his torso. Having done it several times already made it easier, as if the pattern settled itself into her mind, quickly accessed and recreated. It seemed to come from thin air, but that was an illusion. She'd pulled the fibers from the dead grasses beneath the snow cover on the forest floor. Her magical perception showed her all sorts of aspects of the world that she hadn't perceived before—like that even dead-seeming grasses retained life, and a tangible energy available to be woven into a new thing entirely.

It made sense, now that she knew. Now that her world had resettled into another way of perceiving and being. Bára had been built of stone, but the structures had a beingness of a sort she'd recognized since early childhood. The jewelbirds in her garden, the blossoms they fed from, the soil that nourished the flowers and the water that kept them alive, the stones of her tower—all of them had their own distinct *presence* and nature. All of it connected and needing balance.

It was all so much more complex than the two faces of Báran magical theory, far more manifestations than sgath and grien. And yet, simpler, too. Everything was part of everything.

She climbed up the rope steps of the ladder, settled herself, and fastened the straps.

"I won't drop you." Chuffta sniffed—mentally, and with a puff of

flame—and leapt into the air, wings working furiously to lift them.

"I know, darling." She stroked his neck. *"But this is good practice for us. If we encounter the Trom dragons in battle, or spells from the city sorcerers, then you'll need to be concentrating on dodging and flaming—not staying level so I won't fall off."*

"I shall flame them all!"

"Well, maybe not all.*"*

"Spoilsport."

"No worries—there will be plenty of flaming." Probably far too much, but just as she'd had to pass through the crucible to emerge on the other side, so too would the Destrye and Bárans—and the Trom—to forge themselves into something new. Something once again balanced.

Chuffta winged toward the distant mountains, the ground flying past below. Incredible how swiftly they covered distances it had taken her and Lonen days to travel, even on fleet Buttercup. They flew over Vycayla's hermitage, a few white-robed women working the grounds pausing to shade their eyes against the bright winter sun, gazing up, and waving. Oria waved back, unsure if they could see her, a tiny rider atop Chuffta's immense form, but glad that the news of who she and Chuffta were had spread to them even in Vycayla's absence from the place.

A short time later, they passed over a steep, snow-capped ridge of peaks, and spiraled into the valley below. Even from her high vantage, the steaming hot pools glistened below in violent shades of lime, orange, and even violet. The fiery ones were mostly molten rock, welling up from the volcanic pits below ground. The others were water, but teemed with plants and animals that thrived in the intense heat, lending their strange colors to the broth of their isolated seas.

A triad of derkesthai flew toward them. The one in the lead had once been the largest derkesthai she'd ever seen—until she met their king, and then grown Chuffta to that size as one of her first great magical works.

"Hail Soldano," she projected. *"May we be welcome to the Colony?"*

"It seems you have might on your side," the colony guardian replied, his mind-voice dry.

"Thanks to your and your king." She tried to sound meek and grateful. *"Though we would never bear ill-intentions toward those we call kin."*

"'Kin,' are we now? Then—"

"Leave off teasing them, Soldano." The derkesthai king's mind-voice thundered through hers. Chuffta didn't sound like that—thankfully—despite his equivalent size.

"The Great One is very old and powerful," Chuffta told her quietly, and privately. *"He sounds loud to me, too."*

"Approach already," the derkesthai king commanded. **"I shall meet you outside the cavern mouth."**

Chuffta angled in that direction, the guardian trio wheeling to flank and escort them.

"Greetings Oria and Chuffta," one of the smaller derkesthai, the healer Tukcha said. *"You are both looking well. Especially you, Chuffta."*

Did Oria detect a flirtatious tone from Tukcha? Perhaps so, because Chuffta managed a preening neck curve, even with their rapid descent. Oria held on, glad to be validated in her prediction that she'd need the straps if Chuffta became distracted. She loved her Familiar, but he had a fiery and capricious nature. The wise sorceress recognized that and compensated for it.

"I am very big now," Chuffta informed Tukcha, and Oria rolled her eyes at both his arrogant tone and statement of the obvious.

"So I observe," Tukcha replied mildly, but with enough amused reproof to make herself clear. *"And very handsome and powerful,"* she added, and Oria caught the wink in the healer's tone, probably meant just for the sorceress.

The derkesthai king emerged from the yawning cavern mouth just as Chuffta landed on the stone apron before it. Set a bit above the level of the surrounding pools, the reception area provided a safe place for creatures not immune to flame—like herself—and also created a nicely defensible area for the derkesthai to repel unwelcome visitors.

"I didn't expect to see you again so soon, sorceress. Itching for another lesson?"

The king's thunderous laugh was close to painful, but Oria sat tall on Chuffta's shoulders, for once close to level with the big dragon's eyes. *"I believe I have plenty to work on for the time being, but thank you for the offer, Great One."*

"Hmm. I can't argue with that."

Oria very nearly preened like Chuffta at the implied compliment.

"Then why are you here, wasting my time?" the king demanded. *"I'm very busy."*

"Have an important nap by the lava lake scheduled?" she retorted with impertinence.

The great dragon's jaws opened in a lethal grin, green flames licking around teeth sharp as swords. *"As a matter of fact, yes. What do you want, sorceress?"*

Oria lifted her chin and met the dragon's gaze, and spoke aloud. "I've come to ask you and your people to join our army, to fight with the Destrye to save Bára and destroy the Trom."

~ 9 ~

"I T'S AN AUDACIOUS plan," Arnon commented after stroking his neat beard in silence a few moments. "I have to hand it to your Oria—she doesn't think small."

"She's your Oria, too," Lonen replied without rancor. "Your sister and your queen."

"Oh, yes, of course." Arnon waved that away, still deep in thought. "The communication is a problem."

"That's what I told Oria. She says she has a solution." Tired of sitting, Lonen rose from the study table and paced over to the window, one of the few in the palace proper, and pulled aside the hide covering it to keep the warmth in. The new apartments would have many windows, according to the designs Arnon had showed him. His canny brother hoped to bring back the transparent glass the Bárans forged from the sands surrounding the city—or, better still, with the knowledge to make it themselves. The Destrye knew plenty about forging metal, Arnon reasoned—why not sand?

"If we leave Nolan here, even as a fake king surrounded by people who know better, what's to stop him from summoning the Trom and their dragons to set fire to Arill City in our absence?"

"That would be bad," Lonen agreed. Where *had* Oria gone?

"Then we'd be a scattered people," Arnon continued, "with no base to speak of, our warriors at Bára and the rest of the Destrye isolated refugees."

"Our warriors would be at Bára, regardless."

"Yes, but even if we failed in the attack, the rest of our people would have a somewhat defensible place here. *Some* of our people would survive. At least they'd have a better chance together, with the moat and the stout walls of the palace between them and the golems and Trom. But not if Nolan has the power to undermine that."

"True," Lonen said. "But he won't have real power. We'll have people watching what he does, which will give us clues as to what the Bárans plan."

"Not if the people watching him can't communicate with us."

"I think I mentioned already that Oria has a way around that."

"What is it?"

Lonen shrugged. Still no sign of her. Easy to promise to trust. Not so easy to set aside his anxiety. He felt her presence, however, a bright and vital sun at the other end of the marriage bond—which felt stretched over a distance. Though…maybe less so that it had only a few minutes ago?

"It's a real flaw in the plan," Arnon argued, as if Lonen had denied it. "A horse and rider, even with fresh mounts at intervals and going top speed through the tunnels, would still take days. Overland would take even longer. Birds… maybe we could use birds, but they'd need at least a day each way, and we don't have messenger birds trained to find Bára. Besides, the Trom dragons could burn them from the air. And sending messenger birds could alert the Bárans to our movements and the element of surprise would be lost."

"Also true," Lonen answered, though Arnon hardly needed a response.

"I suppose we could just leave Mother in charge and trust her to use her best judgment. Alyx and her warrior women could serve as her personal guard and—"

"Alyx comes with us," Lonen interrupted. "So do *all* the warriors. Every Destrye who wishes to come and fight will be allowed—no, encouraged—to do so."

Arnon raised his brows. "You mean to stand by that idea, allowing the women to fight alongside the men?"

"I do." Lonen let the hide fall and turned to face his brother, leaning against the wall, arms crossed.

"It will cause problems. You know that our father decreed that—"

"I," Lonen interrupted in a flat voice, "am not father. I will not repeat his mistakes."

Arnon paused, considering. "You think his decision that the women shouldn't come to war with us, a war that seemed certain to end in doom—a debate argued long and hard with a great deal of input from all walks—was a mistake?"

Lonen held his brother's gaze. "Yes. It was a mistake. It resulted in a schism of our people at a time we could least afford to be divided, a fundamental division that reached all the way to the throne of Dru and resulted in our queen exiling herself from court."

"That was her decision, Lonen, and she—"

"Is it a 'decision' when a person chooses to live their life on their own terms rather than bow to having their rights taken away?"

Arnon pursed his lips. "That's a rather dramatic way of putting it."

"Is it? If a person wants to fight the enemy that threatens their home, and someone else says they're not allowed to, that's taking away a fundamental human right. Even the lowliest of animals defend their territories."

"This is different, and you know it." Arnon threw up his hands. "Those women will endanger us by being on the battlefield."

"How so?" Lonen asked quietly.

"Don't play dumb, Lonen. You can talk change and progress all you like, but we are at heart still the barbarian people your Oria calls us. We haven't departed long from the days when women were legally property—ours to protect and cherish. If a woman is in danger on the battlefield, every man nearby will move to protect her. We won't be able to help ourselves. It's pure instinct. Would you punish a man for that?"

"Yes," Lonen replied. No question there. "If a Destrye warrior fails to follow orders, then yes, they will be punished. That's basic discipline every warrior learns along with how to properly hold a weapon."

"But instinct can override their—"

"Have you never had the instinct to run away instead of go forward in the crush of battle, Arnon? Have never had the impulse to do other than your commander ordered?"

"Well… yes, but—"

"There is no argument. We have military order because we have to override our instincts and impulses, for the greater good and strategy. You know that as well as I do, perhaps better."

Arnon raked a hand through his brown curls, stopping at the back of his neck and gripping it. "It's a hell of time to test the theory, Your Highness."

"Oh, *now* I'm 'Your Highness?'"

Arnon grinned back at him, releasing his tense posture and shaking his head. "Absolutely. When I'm arguing with you, giving you my best advice, I'm your brother. When I'm certain you've decided, then I acknowledge that you are my king and have my unconditional support."

"Thank you," Lonen replied, voice unexpectedly rough with emotion. "For both the arguments and the support."

Arnon's smile took on a cocky bent. "Of course, I—what in Arill is *that* noise?"

Lonen had already spun to pull the hide from the window again, leaning out and craning his neck. The beat of thousands of wings thundered through the air, shrill reptilian calls echoing above the lower voiced shrieks of humans. For a panicked moment, he thought the Trom dragons might be attacking, but Oria's proximity—elated and triumphant—thrummed along the marriage bond.

And then he saw them. Arnon, wedged into the window beside him exhaled a giant breath of stunned awe. "Are those…?"

"Derkesthai," Lonen confirmed. "An entire colony. Oria brought them here."

Arnon cleared his throat. "For what purpose?"

Lonen pulled back, looping an arm around his brother's shoulders, letting the hide fall into place again. "Let's go find out."

ATOP THE PALACE, all but a few of Arnon's Destrye workers had fled from the onslaught of derkesthai. The smaller ones—the size Chuffta had been when he easily perched on Oria's shoulder—lit on the branches of Arill's tree. They looked oddly in place there, like exotic white flowers bringing the goddess's tree into bloom early. If Lonen let his gaze unfocus, the hundreds of bright green eyes could be new leaves amidst the living, shimmering wings, unfurling like waxy blossoms.

The derkesthai too large for the branches—fortunately no more than a handful—settled on the platform itself, and Chuffta landed on his accustomed spot, Oria on his back. She seemed to be unbuckling herself, then slid down Chuffta's leg and trotted toward them, an exultant smile on her face.

"I don't know that the struts will withstand this amount of weight," Arnon said, dropping to lie flat and look under the edge.

Lonen had eyes only for Oria. She looked to be wearing fighting leathers like the women warriors did, an adaptation of the standard male warrior's gear, scaled to size and reinforced in slightly different places to accommodate the female form. Only her leathers were a bright metallic copper that seemed to be embossed with scales. She gleamed in the late afternoon light like a derkesthai herself.

"What have you done, Oria?" he called, more forcefully than he meant to, overcome with both her feelings and his own.

She grinned at him, radiant with victory. "I've brought you reinforcements."

He opened his arms and she launched herself at him, wrapping her slender legs around his waist and returning his kiss with passion. Unable to resist, he slid a hand down to cup her small bottom, so enticingly clad in the soft leather. The embossed scales gave it an intriguing texture, and he squeezed, exploring.

She laughed, breaking the kiss. "Like them?"

"Yes," he answered. "Who do I have to thank for these?"

Her eyes danced with amusement. "Alyx provided the leathers, and my army of seamstresses adapted them to fit. Then I experimented a little with the color and design. I want something I can wear on Chuffta's back in battle that will suitably impress the Bárans when we accept their surrender."

"I understand the Bárans care about such niceties," he commented blandly.

"Oh yes," she replied in a mock serious tone. "Can you imagine what terrible terms we'd be forced into if we arrived at their gates dressed like barbarians?"

He scowled at her and bit her neck when she, giggling, dodged his retaliatory kiss. "Just so long as you don't agree to marry anyone else," he growled.

"If you two are finished," Arnon inserted, coming to stand beside them, "Your Highnesses, we really should relieve some of the weight on this platform before it collapses and takes the palace with it."

"Oops, sorry, Arnon." Oria glanced to the side, and the derkesthai, Chuffta included, took wing in a temporary blizzard. "I just wanted you to see them."

Arnon surveyed the departing... it seemed wrong to call them a flock, like birds. Perhaps a squadron? His brother cleared his throat. "It's an exhilarating sight, to be sure, but why are they here, Your Highness?"

Oria wiggled, so Lonen set her down. Even though she was shorter and far more delicate than the two of them, Oria stared Arnon down with all the regal arrogance of her heritage. "My dear barbarian brother of the heart, I can communicate mind-to-mind with these derkesthai."

Understanding dawned. "Over long distances?" he asked.

Oria held up her hands. She wore gloves of the same close-fitting, textured copper leather. "We need to test it, but I figure we can post the smaller derkesthai at intervals that match the range of their communication distance. The relay would be nearly instantaneous—at most a matter of minutes."

"Why only the smaller ones?" Arnon wondered, eyeing the many winged lizards festooning Arill's tree, preening and fluttering thin-membraned wings.

"First, because they can ride on your shoulder. I think all your officers should have one," she said to Lonen.

"We can't hear what they're saying," Arnon replied, bemused, as Lonen nodded at the wisdom of the plan.

Lonen clapped his brother on the shoulder. "You'd be surprised how much they can communicate non-verbally. Certainly they can alert you to problems or point you in a necessary direction."

"And defend you with flame," Oria added.

"I see." Arnon mulled that over, casting a glance at the struts underpinning the platform as they descended the steps. They looked fine to Lonen, but Arnon gestured at his foreman, who at least hadn't fled far, then pointed him at something. "Dare I ask what the big ones will be doing?"

Oria grinned, a lethal smile, full of teeth—and worthy of the most barbarous Destrye warrior woman. "They'll be in my aerial squadron. You and your warriors will handle the Báran city guard on the ground. If the Trom dragons arrive, we'll face them in the sky."

"I'M STILL NOT convinced this is the best idea," Lonen argued, fully aware of his hypocrisy—and relieved Oria hadn't been there that afternoon for the argument with Arnon about women in battle.

What she didn't know, she couldn't call him on, and he made sure to push thoughts of that conversation down deep where she couldn't easily hear it. "There were a lot more Trom dragons at the Battle of Bára than I saw today of even moderately sized derkesthai."

"I'll be on Chuffta to lead the defense, so I'll be using magic. And don't forget the Great One." Oria turned her back and held up her hair so he could unlace the gown she'd worn to dinner. Another pretty one, though not half so alluring as those figure-hugging leathers had been. "He'll arrive when we're ready to depart. Until then he elected to stay warm by his lava lake."

"I'm surprised the others didn't do that, too."

She shrugged a little the loosening gown falling away more. "They were all curious and excited. How could I say no? But, speaking of warmth, did you—"

"Yes, yes," he interrupted. "I set men to clearing a swath of the moat. The derkesthai are all in there with a good supply of wood lighting their bonfires."

"Good idea," she admitted. "I wondered what Chuffta was talking about. It sounds like quite the party. It's not as if any golems could get past that lot."

He pushed the gown off her pale shoulders, indulging himself in savoring the texture of her skin. Softer than silk or velvet, that slight shimmery feeling of her magic coursing through her body, her skin enticed him to savor her more and more and more. He kissed the back of her neck, exposed with her hand still holding her hair out of the way, and she hummed with pleasure.

"I don't like the idea of you facing the Trom and their dragons without me," he admitted, lips moving on her nape in a caress that made her shiver.

"You're going to say that, and after you managed to convince Arnon otherwise?" she countered, stepping away and putting her fists on her hips. Her expression was fierce, but the way her copper hair fell in a cloud around her, crackling with static and catching the firelight, her full breasts bare, small nipples pink and tight—she looked far too lovely and alluring. So much so that it took him a moment to catch up to what she'd said. Arill curse it.

"You read that in my mind?" he demanded. He'd have to get better about not thinking about things she could easily "overhear."

She smiled in triumph. "No. You actually are getting better at hiding thoughts you don't want me to 'overhear.' I read it in Arnon's mind. He kept going over the conversation in his head during dinner. Loudly. You really upset his tidy world."

Deciding he'd do better to distract his wife than argue with her, Lonen snagged Oria around her waist, threw her over his shoulder and carried her to the bed. "I think I'd rather upset your tidy world," he told her as she dissolved into shrieking laughter.

He tossed her on the bed, quickly ridding her of the rest of the gown. She stretched, slender arms over her head, her lovely body pale against her shining hair and the darker furs of their coverlets. Grabbing her ankles, he lifted a delicately arched foot, pressing a kiss to that spot he'd discovered undid her. She moaned, going languid in his grip, then tugged her foot free.

"Think again, Destrye," she said, kneeling up and crawling over the bed to him. Reaching for his belt buckle, she worked to undo it, glancing coyly up at him. "I believe I made a suggestion at lunch I should follow through on."

The memory had his already hard cock throbbing. He brushed a hand over her hair as she freed his cock and pushed his pants down. "Are you sure?" he asked, feathering fingers under her chin, coaxing her to look up so he could see her face.

She'd licked her lips, and they glistened full and wet, her eyes full of sensual desire. "Oh, yes, barbarian," she purred. "Tonight I get to torment you. Isn't that what a good tame witch does to appease her brutish captor?"

He began to reply in kind, but his sally choked off in his throat as her avid mouth closed over him, and his eyes rolled back in his head from the pure intensity of the sensation. Giving himself over, he let her plunder his body, wondering who in fact had captured whom.

~ 10 ~

"**G**OOD AFTERNOON, NATLY," Oria said from her seat at the prettily set table. "Would you like tea or wine?"

The Destrye woman eyed her with suspicion, her gaze then roving over the intimate salon with its dainty table for two. "I've lived here my entire life and I've never been in this room," she commented, hovering by the door, even though the lady who'd escorted her there had closed it discreetly.

"They call it the queen's salon," Oria replied easily. "I understand the Dowager Queen Vycayla rarely used it even before she withdrew to her hermitage, and it was closed off after that."

"Vycayla was never much for afternoon tea and sweets," Natly replied, giving those guilty items a scathing look. "I'm surprised she gave up her rooms entirely. What black magic did you have to work on her to accomplish that?"

Oria decided on wine, pouring them both some. "She called it a wedding gift, certainly a generous one. Possibly being confined here for several days by Nolan soured her on the place. She says she's happier at the temple and my ladies seemed delighted to fix up this little salon again. It works well for me as there are vanishingly few places in this palace where I can have a conversation. Come and sit." She added a tone of regal command, lest Natly continue to play the game of standing by the door.

After a beat—not hesitation, but a demonstration of insolence—Natly strolled to the table and sat. Taking up the metal goblet, she drank the excellent wine in one swallow, setting it down with a smile that was more of a sneer. Oria obligingly filled the goblet again, raising one brow in a dare.

If Natly wanted to get roaring drunk, Oria had plenty of wine and its effects would suit her objectives just fine. Natly, however, seemed to wise up and simply wrapped her hand around the cup, her jeweled nails flashing. "If you want to interrogate me, you'd do better with torture than wine." Natly threw the defiant words on the table between them like a warrior tossing a blade to their opponent, hoping they'll take it up in challenge.

Instead Oria picked up a cookie and nibbled it. Made from crushed nuts and a sugary syrup reduced from the sap of trees, the cookies had a lovely subtle sweetness unlike anything she'd had in Bára. "I don't."

Natly didn't change expression, or alter the hard stare from her dark eyes, but her thoughts stuttered from their determined path. Oria wasn't reading her, exactly—she hoped to keep that invasion as a last resort for dealing with anyone, except perhaps her husband, who deserved what he got—but when Natly was practically shouting her anger and jealousy, a change in the flow came through clearly. "You don't what, Your Highness?"

"Ah, you do know my title," Oria said, sipping her wine and taking another cookie. The flavors complimented each other well. "I didn't think you were too stupid to be making that mistake accidentally. I don't want to interrogate you," she continued smoothly when Natly opened her mouth to say something she'd likely be made to regret.

"Then why did you summon me, *Your Highness*?" she practically snarled.

Oria pushed the plate of cookies toward her, gesturing in demonstration. "Wine and cookies."

With an impatient huff, Natly took a cookie and ate it. Then drank down all of her wine in one swallow again. "There. May I be excused now, Your Highness?"

"No," Oria said in a tone hard enough to freeze Natly as she scooted back her chair. "You will stay until I excuse you. More wine?"

Natly gave her a long and burning look, then held out her goblet. "Might as well, since I'm trapped here."

Oria smiled genially, filling the goblet and topping off her own. Lifting a metal bell from the table, she rang it. "We'll need another carafe of wine, please," she told the lady who popped her head in. Once the door had closed again, Oria relaxed back in her chair. "I have a proposal for you, Natly."

"Our stallion Lonen isn't pleasing you in bed?" Natly opened her lushly lashed eyes wide in pretend shock. "I'm afraid the fault there is yours. He always satisfied me very well. Over and over. But then, I know a great deal about coaxing a man to peak performance— nothing a virgin could be expected to employ. I can't help you, however, as women hold no interest for me. Not enough cock." She smirked over her goblet.

Oria let her run on and wind down, waiting Natly out with amused placidity. One thing about being the magical runt of the litter with three brothers all far more proficient in magic than she, Oria had learned how to handle this kind of vicious needling. The bullies—Yar sprang to mind—fed off their victims' pain. Without a reaction, they ran out of steam. As Natly had, now fidgeting in the face of Oria's silence. Natly took a cookie and ate it, somewhat defiantly.

The silence between them stretched on, broken only by the lady delivering more wine. Oria thanked her and topped off Natly's goblet. She sat back and waited patiently. It was peaceful, after a fashion, especially with Chuffta off playing derkesthai games, practically giddy to have the company of his kind. And she'd given him a pass, since he always complained so bitterly that Natly hurt his ears.

"Fine," Natly snapped, folding her arms. "Since you'll clearly keep me imprisoned here until I listen to whatever ridiculous idea you have, Your Highness, tell me. What is your proposal?"

"I'm glad you asked," Oria replied with a polite smile, as if the interlude had never occurred. "This is hardly a prison. If it is, it's far more pleasant than the cell Nolan finds himself in."

Natly choked on her cookie crumbs, bending her head and thumping her chest. When she raised her eyes to Oria's, hers glittered with hatred—and perhaps a bit of respect. "Do you want me to say you've won—is that what this is about? Gloating is so petty."

Oria restrained the urge to comment that Natly would know. "You told me that you and Nolan used to be lovers. Do you love him still?"

With a sullen stare, Natly shrugged one shoulder, toying with her goblet. "Love," she scoffed. "What is it anyway? An occupation for adolescents."

"So you only offered your affections to Nolan and Lonen because you aspired to be queen?" And to Arnon and their older brother Ion before he took Salaya as his wife, from what Lonen had said.

"Is that what Lonen told you?" She lowered her gaze to her goblet. "It's easy for you to sneer at a woman like me, I imagine, to think that I only wanted to climb the tallest tree I could. But there's not much else for a woman of no family. I don't have *magic*. I have no connections, no property or wealth. All of that is gone."

"Lost to the Báran golems?" Oria made herself ask.

"Yes, long ago, when I was a girl. We used to be the wealthiest family in Dru, with fertile lands for ranching and farming. We even had a small township attached to the lands. Lots of water." She gave Oria a hate-filled stare. "It's desert now. And I have nothing to offer my children, if I ever manage to have any. So don't sit there in your Báran arrogance and judge me for trying to be queen."

Natly's grief and old despair worked like corrosive acid and Oria had to shield against it. "I can save Nolan," she said, instead of offering Natly the sympathy she'd only resent. "That's why you're here. I'm offering you the opportunity to be the agent of his salvation. What you choose to do with his trust from there is up to you. I can say, however, that once the war is done and Nolan returned to sanity and his rank, if you and he decide you'd like to be a Princess of Dru, then His Highness and I would sponsor your marriage in Arill's Temple."

Natly managed not to gape in surprise, covering it with narrow-eyed suspicion. "Why would you do that?"

"We need your help," Oria replied simply. "And you're obviously a woman of spirit and intelligence. Dru needs people like that to rebuild."

Natly considered that. Her brittle attitude relaxed a bit, and shrewd interest showed through. "What would I have to do?"

AFTER NATLY LEFT, Oria rested a moment, rallying her reserves for the next interview. Checking in with Chuffta, she asked, *"What are you doing?"*

"Flying!" he replied promptly. *"And setting things on fire! So fun. Do you want me to come get you so you can play, too?"*

"No, I have to stay here."

"Boring meetings. Burning things is way more exciting."

"You're not burning anything important, I hope?"

"Of course not." Chuffta's mind-voice had a wounded tone. *"We are not stupid Trom dragons. We're practicing precision burning while flying in formation. Lonen told us where we could practice and gave us Mikkon to teach us. Usually Mikkon works with people on horses, so he says it's a pleasure to work with such intelligent and ferocious creatures as us derkesthai."*

Oria didn't know Mikkon, but he clearly had the cleverness to flatter the derkesthai. Clever Lonen to assign him, too. *"Where is Lonen?"*

"Running around, ordering people to do things. The city is all in an uproar, people doing all kinds of things. Shall I send a small one to bring him to you?"

A "small one." Oria suppressed the laugh at Chuffta's name for derkesthai the size he'd been only weeks ago. *"No. I was just curious."*

Lonen had been up since dawn, planning to move the army out to the tunnel entrance. Oria had been up that long, too, verifying that Nolan's men were telling the truth about the tunnel's location, and clearing those stragglers who came in after the offer of clemency.

A polite knock on the door. "Your Highness? Lady Salaya is here for her summons."

"I have to go. Have fun." She sent Chuffta a mental caress of affection.

"I'd say the same, but ugh."

She had to smooth her laugh into a polite smile as Ion's widow entered the room. The tall woman looked somewhat less haggard these days. Lines of grief still bracketed her full lips, but her deep blue eyes held more interest and less angry despair. She kept her hair close-cropped in mourning, so the curls made black whorls against her lighter scalp. Without the elaborate fall of coiled hair like the others her intense eyes and arched dark brows became even more striking.

"Please make yourself comfortable," Oria said, gesturing to the chair Natly had vacated, the plates and goblet replaced, the cookie tray once again pristine. "Would you prefer tea or wine?"

"It's a bit early in the day for wine for me, Your Highness, so tea, if you please," Salaya replied with perfect politeness, but something of an edge.

Relieved not to feel obliged to drink more wine—it was early in the afternoon for her to drink, too, especially when she needed a clear head for all this mental fencing—Oria poured them both tea into finely made ceramic mugs. And because Salaya possessed far more emotional reserve than Natly, Oria opened up her senses to the other woman, seeking the source of her worries. Ah. Salaya believed she'd be run out of the palace, her sons perhaps exiled to prevent competition for the throne from Oria's future children.

"How are Mago and Kavon?" Oria inquired. "I don't believe I've seen your sons since we returned."

Salaya gave her a considering look as she stirred the sweet syrup into her tea. "It seemed wisest to keep them out of sight," she replied baldly. "Though it was too much to hope they'd stay out of mind."

Oria shook her head. "You have no cause to be concerned for their safety. Please have no fears on that account. I can tell you now that Lonen plans to officially name Mago as his heir, should he and Arnon not return from this war."

Salaya sat back in surprise. "What of your sons and daughters, Your Highness?"

"It will be many years before any child of Lonen's and mine is old enough to be considered for the throne. If I bear children, Lonen will address the line of succession then."

"If?" Salaya raised her finely arched black brows.

Oria met Salaya's gaze with frank honesty. It would be good if they could be friends. "I don't know how well a Báran womb will accept Destrye seed. Time will tell."

A smile tugged at Salaya's mouth. "Fair warning: Destrye seed is strong stuff, and the men of Archimago's line particularly… vigilant about planting it. I have no doubt you'll find yourself with child before long."

What a wonderful thought—though they had a war to win and survive first. "If that happy day comes, I want you to know that your sons are safe, and they will always have a place in our court and our household. When we retake Bára, we'll need good rulers for that city, too, perhaps for the sister cities in time."

Salaya dipped a cookie in her tea and ate it with delicate precision, studying Oria. "Then the rumors are true. Your Highnesses are taking the armies back to Bára."

"Yes." Oria imitated her, finding the cookie even better dipped in the hot tea.

"I'm surprised you're telling me. Or that you'd consider putting Destrye princes in positions of power in Bára."

"Your husband gave his life to end this conflict between Dru and Bára," Oria replied with solemn softness. "Your sons lost a father; you lost a husband. I lost a father, too, and brothers. Too many good people, our leaders, have perished and more will be lost still. We must treasure those we have left—and put them to good use to ensure peace and prosperity for both our peoples."

"You really believe you can take Bára, and stop them from attacking us again?"

"Yes." Oria said it with utter confidence. "Taking the city won't be easy, but I am the rightful Queen of Bára. Once the city is once again mine, I won't have to stop 'them' from attacking. We will be one people, Lonen and I will be King and Queen of a united realm."

Salaya smiled. "You don't lack for ambition, I'll say that. I accept on Mago's behalf. What else do you need from me?"

"How good are you at play-acting?" Oria asked.

Her final visitors of the day arrived not long after Salaya left. Much as she loved the cookies, Oria gratefully accepted the platter of savory snacks her ladies brought, along with a heartier wine. She needed something with substance and they wouldn't go down for dinner for a while yet.

Baeltya and Vycayla made themselves comfortable, also helping themselves to the tapenades, nut-butters, and creamy cheeses to spread on the fresh bread. Vycayla raised a brow at the offerings. "You could've included some meats for those of us who aren't vegetarians, daughter."

Oria gazed at the platter in some dismay, as it hadn't occurred to her. "I apologize, Your Highness. My ladies have already grown so accustomed to catering to my tastes that I didn't think of it."

"Hmph," Vycayla snorted. "The Queen of Dru should think of such things when entertaining."

Baeltya rolled her eyes dramatically. "As if you *ever* entertained, Vy. Don't badger poor Oria. She's had to maneuver both Natly and Salaya into going along with this audacious plan. Successfully, too, I believe?"

Oria gave the healer a grateful smile, accepting the wine she poured. "Yes, they both agreed to their roles. Though you two will want to keep a close eye on them, regardless."

"Not me," Baeltya replied. "I'm coming with the army."

Vycayla seemed unsurprised. Oria knew Lonen had officially proclaimed that women warriors were welcome, but she didn't think Baeltya had any fighting experience. "You are?"

Baeltya nodded vigorously. "You'll need healers. I'll be leading a contingent of us. Since we can travel through the tunnels at our own pace, we should be fine."

Oria really wanted to ask if Lonen had agreed to that but thought better of it. They'd discuss it later, when they finally retired for bed. *If* they managed to keep their hands off each long enough to have that private conversation.

"You're staying here, though, Your Highness?" she asked Vycayla.

"Oh, call me Vy already as this impertinent chit does," the queen mother replied testily. "Since you won't call me 'mother.' And yes, I'm definitely staying here to keep an eye on the foxes *and* chickens. You need me to make sure you and my son have a palace to return to."

No, Oria didn't feel right calling Vycayla 'mother'—not while her own mother, Queen Rhianna might yet live. Among the many reasons Oria burned to return to Bára she longed to discover if her mother lived and, if so, what sanity remained to her. With the magic now available to her, Oria might be able to restore her mother to the woman she'd been before her husband's death broke her mind.

"We are more than grateful to be able to leave Arill City to your capable rule," Oria replied fervently, and with complete honesty. The gamble with Nolan became far less risky with the reins of actual power in the former queen's hands.

"It's my privilege and honor to defend my city and people while you're gone," Vycayla said, her gray eyes so like Lonen's bright with emotion. "When do you depart?"

Oria glanced at Baeltya, who'd just come from the war council meeting. She should've realized the healer had attended the meeting out of more than casual interest. "I've been playing tea-party politics all afternoon," she said, "so Baeltya has fresher news than I do."

"The day after tomorrow," Chuffta supplied.

"You could have told me."

"You were busy with your boring meetings." He blew a mental puff of flame at her that had the odd effect of seeming like a child sticking out their tongue. Baeltya was relaying the same information aloud.

"So soon," Vycayla murmured, reaching across the table for the carafe, pouring them all more wine. "I'm amazed Lonen can mobilize the army so quickly."

"The warriors have been on alert since we returned," Oria pointed out, "and they're almost all concentrated in Arill City or in camps between us and the tunnel entrance. We've been sending discreet messengers since we conceived this plan for the camps to begin moving in that direction, and the derkesthai have obliged in ferrying in foodstuffs that you're generously supplying." She nodded her thanks to Vycayla. "Any delay on our part plays to my brother's favor. And we don't want to risk him giving up on Nolan as a tool and sending the Trom to attack here. The sooner Natly 'frees' Nolan and he believes himself solely in power, the more likely Yar will relax into complacency."

"How soon will Natly move?" Baeltya asked.

"As soon as we're clear of the city, I'd think." Oria looked to

Vycayla, who nodded agreement.

"I've got my personal guard at the temple prepared. They'll play along with Nolan as king, while making sure I'm not confined to quarters again," Vycayla said in a sour tone. "Of course, I'll have a tremendous change of heart, beg my son's forgiveness, and cater to his every whim. I hope you're right, Oria, that he'll be manageable if no longer thwarted."

Oria hoped so, too. "As soon as I can, I'll remove the geas on him. If it doesn't disperse with the death of the sorcerer who laid it on him."

"It's odd to hear you speak of these sorcerers being so easily killed," Baeltya said, mulling it over as she swirled her wine. "These terrible monsters had nearly mythic proportions to us before we met you. The stories warriors came back with…" She shuddered and gulped her wine.

"They are men like any other," Oria said. "And, like any man, they can be killed."

"And what of your last living brother, this Yar?" Vycayla asked with a sadly knowing look in her eye. "Will you be able to bring yourself to kill him?"

"If I must, yes."

"Easier to say than do," Vycayla murmured, not without sympathy.

And yet do it, Oria would. Even if her mother begged her not to. One way or another, this last, desperate campaign would put an end to an era of conflict.

One way or another.

~ 11 ~

Lonen watched the last of the warriors and wagon loads of supplies cross the moat, the once-teeming city almost ghostly quiet. They were leaving Arill City nearly as empty as they had on that day so long ago when Lonen accompanied his father and three brothers on a lost cause, while the caravan of non-fighting citizens departed in the other direction. This time, of course, they were leaving the city occupied with the Queen Mother in charge, but a surprisingly large number of citizens had chosen to accompany the army and fight—or assist in whatever way they could.

Those staying behind had consolidated into a tighter ring of dwellings near the palace, partly because those buildings had the best construction, and the logistics made sense—but also to create the illusion of a populated city for Nolan, and whoever might look through his eyes.

Arnon had gone ahead to organize the march through the tunnels from the lead, while Lonen—along with Alyx and three hand-picked warriors for his personal guard—brought up the rear.

Overhead, Oria rode on Chuffta, Baeltya riding behind her, the great form of the derkesthai king beside them, the sky filled with derkesthai of all sizes, flying in perfect formation. Lonen's mother stood beside him, also watching the final departure, her expression stern and expectant.

"Once you retract the moat bridge, don't extend it again for any reason until we return," he told her.

"Don't be ridiculous, boy. If people seek shelter here, of course we'll extend the bridge and let them in."

Lonen bit back a sigh. "Remember who we're dealing with here. These are sorcerers who can animate golems and who've possessed Nolan and subverted his will. It's entirely possible they could create a simulacrum of a Destrye refugee to infiltrate the city."

Vycayla's brows had climbed as he spoke, finishing in incredulous arches. "I've been dealing with the Bárans and their magic since before you were born. I'm not an idiot."

"I know." He allowed the sigh to escape. "Just... be careful. I don't like the feeling that we're leaving you undefended."

Her expression softened. "You are your father's son—but you're balancing what you can control with what you can't better than he did."

Lonen couldn't help glancing at the sky and the copper banner of Oria's hair streaming against the blue. "Nothing like a sorceress wife for lessons in what a man can't control," he commented wryly.

His mother patted his cheek, but for once the gesture felt sympathetic and not condescending. "You'll do fine." Her gaze went to the sky, too. "You two make a formidable team. Send word often, and we will, too." A small derkesthai winged over to land on her shoulder, winding its tail down her arm like a set of iridescent ivory bracelets, and Lonen was vividly reminded of Oria when he first met her. "Illya and I have worked out a system of conversation with yeses and noes, haven't we, pretty lady?"

The derkesthai dipped her chin in a clear affirmation. "I should have done something like that with Chuffta long ago," he said admiringly.

"Yes, well, you can't be expected to think of everything," his mother replied archly, pleased with herself. "Take care of our people, and come home victorious." She embraced him, her eyes suspiciously bright, and walked off across the bridge.

Lonen took his time checking his gear, then mounting Buttercup, who had his head high and tail flicking with excitement, the warhorse recognizing the signs of battle to come. The delay let him reassure himself that the bridge had been properly withdrawn, the city and people safely within. Smoke curled up from fireplaces, hanging low in the chill air, along with the scent of meals being cooked. High above, in the towering tree Arill called Hers, the fabulous spiraling structure of Her temple perched like a beacon of peace.

Taking one last look at his home, he reflected on what it might mean that he left it for Bára a third time. A prickle of foreboding accompanied the realization, and he shook it off, Buttercup lifting his ears in question. "Nothing, man," he said quietly, patting the horse's neck. "Silly human superstitions. Let's be off," he called in a raised voice. Alyx and the others saluted, their faces full of the same eager anticipation thrumming through Buttercup.

Buttercup eagerly kicked into a fast walk, and Lonen lifted a hand to Oria, sweeping his arm forward. She waved back, and the derkesthai squadron peeled off into groups, some going ahead as the vanguard, others fanning out to scout the countryside they'd pass through on the way to Bára.

"ORIA IS READY to meet us at the first oasis," Lonen told Arnon, holding up a candle to read the message Baeltya had penned and the bright-eyed derskesthai perched nearby had brought. As soon as he read the missive, he blew out the candle, the pervasive dark of the enclosed tunnel returning.

That particular element had been left out of Nolan's stories. And—though Nolan's men had mentioned the tunnels were dark—nothing had quite prepared them for the utter lack of light so far below ground. Lonen suspected those men had been so long in the tunnels, making their way back, that they'd become accustomed to lacking sight and had forgotten.

Moving an army of warriors, support personnel, and food supplies through the tunnels without light presented various tactical issues, which Arnon muttered about pretty much non-stop. The tunnel, however, went in two directions only—forward and back—which at least made it impossible to get lost, so that worked in their favor. Other than that, they'd found themselves pressed to handle the foreign experience of being trapped underground for days on end. The Destrye were not a people who dealt with that well. It didn't help that the floor of the tunnels retained moisture, forming stinking pools in places, and soggy mud in much of the rest, slowing their progress.

Added to that, they hadn't brought along enough candles and lanterns for the entire strung-out caravan to have light all the time. They'd concentrated light at the front, in case of unforeseen obstacles, and the rest of them used light only when necessary. They'd discovered, too, that their eyes did adjust somewhat, and if they avoided light as much as possible they were able to make out general shapes of black on black.

Fortunately, the derkesthai seemed able to see just fine, so they winged their way happily up and down the tunnels, carrying written messages and bringing news from the outside world. After a week underground—and without Oria—Lonen found his own grip on reality fraying. Having the connection to her through the marriage bond kept that sun lit inside of him. He had no idea how the rest of them coped.

So, when Arnon argued—yet again—that only Lonen should go aboveground at the break in the tunnel, he shook his head vigorously, even knowing his brother couldn't see him. "Anyone who wants to go above should be able to."

"There are a lot of very good reasons not to," Arnon said, his voice muffled by whatever he was eating. "One, we could be spotted, blowing the element of surprise. Two, the oasis can't support great numbers, so not everyone can go. Three, our eyes are adapted to the depths now and anyone who goes above will simply have to adjust again."

"Four, we are not meant to live like moles belowground and I need our people in top condition."

"A desperate army fights harder," Arnon pointed out.

"Is that true?" Lonen didn't think so. "I'd rather have people remember what they're fighting for. Besides, we need to replenish the water supplies. And Oria has arranged to ferry more candles and lanterns from Arill City."

"We have a relay team to pass things along."

"Isn't it driving you crazy," Lonen demanded, "being underground for days on end like this?"

"Yes," Arnon replied evenly, not sounding anywhere near as crazed as Lonen. His hand bumped Lonen's shoulder, then gripped it. "I just keep reminding myself it's worth it. Every man and woman in this army knows that. Being upside a few hours isn't worth blowing the element of surprise."

Lonen really hated that Arnon was right. "Fine. I'll stay below and so will everyone else. But quietly pass the word among the commanders that anyone who really needs some fresh air, so much so that they'll crack without it, gets to go up."

"No, you go up." Arnon's voice held laughter. "Maybe fuck your wife and take the edge off. *You* need it."

From nearby, Alyx snickered, quickly muffling the sound. "You sound like Ion," he retorted, then regretted it immediately. Their older brother had died at Bára and had been buried there next to their father. As much of them as they could scrape together to bury.

"I think Ion would approve of what we're doing," Arnon said, and they were both silent a moment. "Does Oria have a plan for countering the Trom if the derkesthai can't stop them from landing?"

Lonen had been surprised Arnon hadn't asked it before. The looming question that haunted his own mind. They had iron weapons to fight the golems. The sorcerers they could perhaps counter with Oria's magic—though she'd be one against many.

They had their own dragons to battle the ones the Trom would no doubt bring. But how to battle the Trom themselves, who seemed indestructible and could dissolve an armored warrior with a single touch?

"Yes," he said, with confidence that was a total lie. Oria would only say that she was working on it. He knew her well enough to understand that she meant she had a few ideas that she'd likely have to test in the moment, while they prayed like hell to Arill that one of them would work.

Shouts echoed from ahead, followed by flares of light, and a wave of sound as a message passed back. With the Destrye army strung out a good five leagues along the tunnel—necessary because of the space restriction and to keep the good air flowing—Lonen had appointed a person in each group to be the relay. Their one job was to accurately repeat any message they received. They couldn't afford to have messages from ahead or behind get distorted or changed.

Fenive, who'd gone with them to the derkesthai colony, served as the relay for the king's party, and she came dashing back from the next group ahead, her lantern painfully bright. Lonen closed his eyes until she shuttered it. "Golem attack at the fore," she repeated carefully and clearly, the relay from the group behind them listening carefully. "Unknown numbers."

"I'm going," Lonen said, rising and whistling for Buttercup, who saw better in the darkness than he did.

"We're with you, Your Highness," Alyx said. "Fenive, give us the light."

She took the lantern and the lead, both of them riding as fast as they dared on the uneven surface and through close quarters. Lonen gave Buttercup his head, letting the warhorse choose his footing. Forewarned, the groups of supply wagons and marching warriors crowded to the side, giving them room.

It still seemed to take forever to reach the vanguard, and it occurred to Lonen that the scouts had reported the exit to the oasis was only a few leagues beyond that. Had Oria and her derkesthai squadron landed at the oasis only to be overwhelmed by golems? The thought filled him with rage and terror. An answering pulse along the marriage bond reassured him that Oria was alive and reasonably strong. Though he knew she'd hide any distress from him.

To his great frustration, by the time they reached the vanguard those warriors had dispatched all the golems, leaving Lonen nothing to vent his fury upon. The Destrye were hacking apart the fallen, methodically chopping the pieces into bits too small to cause damage. Spotting a clawed arm, Lonen dismounted and chopped it in half with his battle-axe, a small thing, but satisfying.

"Too bad we can't eat them, Your Highness," Alby said, with a cocky grin. Lonen had put his lieutenant at the fore, trusting his former squire to recognize all manner of trouble.

"Isn't there an old saw about eating broken glass?" Lonen returned, giving the man a smile. The golems weren't made of glass, exactly, but Oria had explained that the monsters were made from the same substance as the Báran glass, but forged differently so as to be flexible, then animated. Their lethal claws, however, had a hard and sharp edge—as evidenced by the bleeding wounds on the warriors in the group. "Casualties?"

Alby sobered. "Two dead. Several severely wounded. They're with the healers."

Lonen nodded, having spotted the group working on their way past. "Were the golems looking for us—could you tell?"

"I couldn't." Alby frowned, troubled. "Do the creatures show surprise? There were an even two dozen of them, marching this way. Our derkesthai scouts saw them before they saw us. We set up an ambush and had them surrounded before they could do much."

The tunnels also made for good bottleneck fighting, thankfully turning with the landscape just enough to create ambushes at blind corners. This was the first time they'd tested it, though. A pulse came along the marriage bond, followed by a bobbing lantern. Oria came striding down the tunnel, light glowing off her copper leathers, Baeltya just behind and beside her. Both women carried swords.

Lonen glanced at Alyx. "Are the swords your doing?"

She gave him a cheeky grin. "Magic is one thing, but there's nothing like a sharp blade to boost a girl's confidence."

Oria had spotted him, slowing her headlong pace, taking in the piles of golem bodies. "You're all right?" she called.

Rather than answer, he strode to her, handed her lantern to someone else, and caught her up in a fierce kiss. He only surprised her momentarily before she kissed him back with passionate fervor. "What was that for?" she asked breathlessly when he let her come up for air.

"I missed you," he said in a low voice. "*And* I thought to keep you from embarrassing me further in front of my warriors."

Her fine, fiery brows arched in disdain. "Me, a small and simple woman, embarrassing a mighty Destrye warrior? Pfft."

"Why are you here, Oria?" he asked, still holding her close. Arill, but it felt good to touch her again.

"I felt your battle rage. And I was close, waiting for you at the oasis."

"Did you see golems there?"

"No." She frowned, extricating herself and scanning the area. "Let me take a look at these. Are any mostly intact still?"

"I'm afraid we chopped them all up, Your Highness," Alby said from a discreet distance.

"Next time leave me a torso or two," she ordered, crisp and offhand, as she knelt by a pile of the biggest pieces. It struck Lonen then how much confidence Oria had gained. With her hair bound in gleaming copper braids woven into a coronet, bound by the gleaming gold circlet of her rank, she looked queenly indeed.

Lonen signaled the others to give her room, then squatted beside her. When they'd been attacked by golems—near this same oasis—she'd been able to absorb the packets of sgath they carried in their torsos where a human had a heart. Not a tangible thing, the sgath magic would nevertheless have been dispersed when they were chopped up with iron.

"Anything?" he asked after a while.

"I really wish I could figure out how to determine who is controlling them." Then she looked at him, the frown still on her face. "I don't like to sound an alarm unnecessarily."

"Just say it."

"I'm pretty certain they were looking for us."

~ 12 ~

"I T'S NOT LIKE reading a letter," Oria said, rephrasing the same information, yet again. "I don't get words and detailed explanations."

"Then how do you know they were looking for us?" Arnon demanded, eyes glinting blue in the flickering light.

They'd collected several lanterns and stacked them in a circle, gathering around them like it was some sort of campfire. With the mounds of still-quivering golem bits stacked along the sloping tunnel walls nearby, it made for a strange scene, even for Oria who'd at least been familiar with the golems as mindless workers in Bára. Outside of their aura of light, the blackness of the tunnel was impenetrable. Murmurs of the vast army behind them echoed uncannily off the walls, and the air sat heavy, both dank and stale.

She didn't know how Lonen had taken a week of it—though she now understood the vibrations of frustration and despair that had seeped through the marriage bond. Never mind the nightmares she woke from in a cold sweat, unable to understand why she saw Bára from the outside, the walls ever fading into the distance—until she realized they were Lonen's dreams. Ones that had abated for a while in Dru and had now apparently returned in full force.

"It's more of a feeling," she said to Arnon, who still frowned at her. Lonen, more accustomed to magic and her inability to put some aspects into words, squeezed her hand.

"How Oria knows is irrelevant," he said, cutting off further discussion with a chop of his hand. "What's the latest from Arill

City?"

"Nolan seems to believe he's king," Chuffta, listening in through her, reported via Illya. *"He crowned Natly queen and Vycayla is barricaded in the Temple of Arill, stalling him as much as possible. Salaya is pretending to be Nolan's ally and relaying information to Vycayla. But Vycayla is keeping Illya in the temple so Nolan won't see her, since you decided that seeing any derkersthai might put his watchers on alert."*

Oria repeated that for the group, then asked Chuffta aloud, "Anything on what his priorities seem to be?"

He paused a moment, and Oria heard an echo of another derkesthai relaying the question to Illya. A kind of muffled sound down another long tunnel. *"He keeps asking for Lonen and Arnon. He's been repeatedly told that they were killed in the coup that resulted in Nolan's liberation, but he demands to see the bodies."*

Lonen looked grim when she related that bit. "It wasn't enough to leave him the crown and sword. Whoever is prodding him doesn't believe we're dead. They suspect. Maybe not this, exactly, but something. So, they're sending golems to Dru, too, to assess the situation through other eyes."

"I'm afraid you're right," she said, exchanging looks with Lonen. They both knew Yar. She'd known her brother longer, of course, but Lonen had a knack for taking a person's measure quickly and thoroughly. "I think we underestimated the ability of whoever is looking through Nolan's mind. We should've gone to more trouble to make his ascension to the throne more believable."

"We took a gamble. Besides, I wasn't willing to offer my corpse to the cause," Lonen replied with a crooked smile. "It was a delaying tactic anyway—and one intended to preserve Nolan's sanity. Had we been determined to keep all knowledge from his watchers, we would've killed him outright."

A silence fell as they processed that. Arnon shook his head sharply and stilled, mouth pressed in a grim line. "I have to say it. We can pass the message back that Nolan should be executed."

"No." Lonen's tone was resolute.

"He's a liability," Arnon persisted.

"He's also my brother who is essentially still a prisoner of war. I will not have him killed."

"He wouldn't have been so gentle with you, even before we went to Bára, and you know it."

Lonen held Arnon's gaze, gripping Oria's hand a bit tighter, then smoothing it where it rested on his knee. "I do know that—which is why I'm not going to do it."

Arnon inclined his head. "I had to argue the point."

Lonen's granite expression broke into a grin. "Yes, you did." He turned to Oria. "Will they know we killed their golems?"

She winced, thinking it through. "They'll know something did, and we might be better off assuming they know that it was here."

Lonen nodded, unperturbed by that. He'd already expected it. "So Yar knows something is up, but not exactly what. But he can at this point summon the Trom and send them to this location. It's what I would do."

"Yar is not the strategist you are," Oria pointed out.

He gave her a warm smile. "But he has advisers. I'm going to assume the worst."

"If he does send the Trom and their dragons," Arnon said, "then we're better off in the tunnels instead of on open ground."

"Unless he floods the tunnels." Oria kicked herself for not thinking of it before. "He could. It wouldn't be difficult. You'd be trapped, along with all the Destrye, and—"

Lonen squeezed her hand hard enough to break through her panic. "We have your derkesthai scouts and messengers, remember? They'll forewarn us if that happens."

Oria relaxed fractionally, though she doubted any warning would come in time to evacuate all these people. And Lonen would no doubt insist on being the last one out. *Could you and the Great One dig down to the tunnels in an emergency?* she asked Chuffta privately.

Depending on the place, yes—but there's a lot of rock on top of the tunnel in a lot of places, which would take a long time."

"It's not exactly a task worthy of one of my exalted status, sorceress," The derkesthai king boomed in her mind. **"Fire would be faster and wouldn't get dirt in my talons."**

"Would fire burn the people inside the tunnel, though?" she asked politely, taking his cranky mind-mutter as confirmation. At least they had something of a backup plan.

"We continue as we've begun," Lonen decided. "But we increase the pace. The best way to avoid a conflict with the Trom and their dragons is not to be here when they arrive. We haven't lost all the element of surprise as they're unlikely to predict we've an entire army in their tunnels."

"We're like fish in a barrel in these tunnels," Alyx muttered.

Lonen nodded at her. "Yes, but if we take everyone aboveground, then we stand a good chance of being defeated at the oasis, far from our destination. We press forward."

"And Nolan?" Arnon asked.

Lonen glanced at Oria. "Let's end the farce. Send a message back for them to take Nolan back into custody. Not the dungeons. If they can find a way to let him believe he's still king to preserve his sanity, do it. He can be confined to quarters—windowless—and Natly may keep him company as she chooses. Vycayla can be regent for Mago, and begin teaching him what he needs to know, should he need to take the throne."

"It won't come to that, Lonen," Oria said softly, but no one acknowledged her words.

"Oria," Lonen continued, as if she hadn't spoken, "mind your scouts. If they spot the dragons before we all reach Bára, I want you and your squadron to disappear. Do not engage."

She gaped at his resolute expression, beyond shocked. "What? Why? We could fight them. That's our job."

He was shaking his head as she sputtered, keeping a firm grip on the hand she tried to yank away. "You will follow my orders, Oria, and I've made them clear: any hint of the Trom dragons and you and all of your derkesthai hightail it out of there."

"None of us will like that either," Chuffta said glumly.

"And tell Chuffta the order includes him and his," Lonen added with narrowed eyes, sensing her rebellious thoughts, if not Chuffta's actual words.

"We could harry them," she said quietly, wishing the others weren't listening so intently, so she could give Lonen a real piece of her mind. "We could be all that distracts them from going after you in the tunnels."

"No way am I spending you and the derkesthai on a delaying tactic. We'll need you at Bára to keep the Trom from landing. The Destrye can handle the city guard. We can take the walls and hold them after—but not if the Trom land."

"We won't be much use to the Destrye if you don't make it to Bára at all," she retorted.

"If the army doesn't make it there, you won't be able to take Bára without us," he replied with cool logic. "Likewise, we won't be able to take and keep the city without the derkesthai holding off the Trom. And we might as well not bother if we don't have *you* to put on the throne and neutralize Yar and his sorcerers. Either we bring all three points of attack to Bára simultaneously, or we abandon this effort."

"To do what?" she replied bitterly, unable to envision what future that might be.

"To live another day. To make a new plan. Promise me you'll obey my orders, Oria."

Her lips ached from biting down on them. "Will you walk with me a ways?"

"If you promise, here and now, before witnesses."

Oria glanced around the small circle, all of them wearing identical expressions of weary determination. Setting off on the war had been exciting, full of anticipation and hope. Now they'd settled into the part that required fortitude—and perhaps far more courage than launching the venture. "I promise to obey your orders in this," she said quietly, and Lonen relaxed his grip on her hand, stroking the back in a caress.

He pushed to his feet, giving his top commanders orders to relay down the line. A detail would be sent to the oasis to pass water down to each group as it passed that tunnel fork, but there would be no pausing. They'd accelerate to maximum pace. Then, sliding an arm around Oria and snugging her close to him, he walked her down the tunnel between segments of the vast Destrye army, alone but for Buttercup following loyally behind and the white shapes of derkesthai zipping along overhead like pale bats in the darkness.

He bent and brushed a kiss against her temple. "I'm sorry," he murmured for her ears alone.

She sighed and leaned against him. "No—you know the strategy and what you say makes sense. I just don't like being out there, knowing you're trapped down here, and I can do nothing to help you."

"Can you hold the water back with your magic, should it come to that?"

"Maybe." She resolved to practice with the oasis water, to hone those skills. "And depending on where you are, Chuffta and the Great One might be able to dig an emergency egress."

"Good thinking."

"It won't be fast enough, Lonen."

His arm tightened. "We'll have pray to Arill that they don't find us—or think of flooding the tunnel before we all get to Bára."

"I have a better idea." Turning under his arm, she faced him, wrapping her arms around his waist, needing that contact with his strong body.

He studied her face with a wary expression. "What idea?"

"Chuffta and I are going ahead, to Bára."

"Hooray! We shall save the day and everyone will write songs about us."

"Absolutely not," Lonen said at the same time, his granite command a low counterpoint to Chuffta's ecstatic warbling.

"It makes sense," she continued, as if neither of her men had spoken. "Chuffta will fly me past the bore tide flats, drop me off, and I'll enter the city by stealth."

"Wait, what? I want to go with you."

"I said no, Oria."

"I'm going to wear Tania's mask, disguise myself to look like any other priestess, and infiltrate the city," she said, ignoring both of them.

Lonen's face set into obstinate ridges, tension vibrating through his body. "I thought you got rid of that vile thing."

"No, I simply let you think so," she replied, holding onto him when he would've pulled away from her. "We need every trick and tool at our disposal. They took my mask, Lonen, and I need one to go unnoticed. I can't take Chuffta, because he'll draw attention."

"I guess that's true," Chuffta agreed slowly.

"You'll wait nearby and help me."

"That's true! I shall fly to your rescue and they'll write songs about that."

"I forbid it," Lonen said. "And you just promised, in front of witnesses, to obey my orders."

"I promised to obey you in that situation," she qualified, watching the anger flood his face, followed by resignation. "You could never stop me from doing this, Lonen. This is the city of my birth, my people, mine to deal with. I need to find my mother." Maybe kill her brother, though she wouldn't say it aloud. The superstitions of the Destrye had begun to affect her. "If I stop the sorcerer sending the golems, I can open up your path."

"We know how to destroy golems," he replied with a vicious intensity, touching a hand to his iron axe. "The Destrye figured that out long ago."

"Yes, I know, but why spend warriors on that, so far from Bára?" When he didn't have an immediate retort, she pressed on. "If I can stop Yar from summoning the Trom at all, then we won't have to fight them in the air. If I can get to him before he figures out where you are, we won't have to worry about digging you out of the tunnels before you drown."

"It would be a great joke of Arill's, to drown the Destrye as our final fate," he said, though no laughter lit his eyes.

"I don't think it would be Arill's joke," she replied very seriously. "And I have no intention of letting it be Bára's."

"Stop him from summoning the Trom…" Lonen echoed, stark realization on his face. "You mean to go right now."

"Yes. It's nighttime in the world above. I can be there and inside the walls before first light."

He set his jaw, his thoughts flying furiously through his mind as he sought an argument to stop her. "I want to forbid you from doing this."

"In point of fact, you already did forbid me, and it didn't take," she said drily.

"I don't like this." His arms tightened on her. "The last time we were separated…" He trailed off, unwilling to speak *those* words aloud.

"We came out of it triumphant," she filled in, reminding him. "Bring the Destrye to Bára, my king. The plan hasn't changed. I'll meet you there."

"You'd better," he muttered on a growl, just before he caught her mouth with his. The scrape of days-old beard contrasted with the hot, soft texture of his mouth. Arousal flooded her, nearly painful after missing his touch for a week. Her breasts tightened, swollen with need, and all her skin cried out for his, feeling stretched to bursting with neglect.

Lonen cursed against her mouth, his hands everywhere over the leathers. "I can't touch you in these things. They're a tease— showing everything and revealing nothing."

She breathed a voiceless laugh. "Just as well. We can hardly do anything with our people advancing at top speed." Indeed, the growing sound of the army on the move filled the tunnel, the section behind them rapidly approaching. "And now there's no time to dally at the oasis. It isn't the same without you."

He kissed her again, a final feel to it that she hated, even as she relished it. "I don't want this to be goodbye," he said with quiet ferocity.

"It's not." She pulled away, taking his hands in hers. "You found me in Bára twice before. Isn't the third time the magic number?"

He smiled back, though it didn't reach his eyes, which held quiet despair. His muffled thoughts echoed it, and she didn't look too closely, lest she begin to weep.

"I love you, Lonen," she said. "I'll see you at Bára."

He dragged her back into his arms, kissing her breathless. "I love you," he murmured into her ear. "I'll find you."

She knew he spoke truly. He would find her. He always had.

CHUFFTA ROSE INTO the night sky, white wings ghostly. The desert air was cool, but not as cold as in Dru. They weren't far from Bára and her hot days that lingered in the baking sands. Sgatha hung round and rosy full in the sky, Grienon sinking fast to the horizon somewhere behind them. Stars glittered thick, their light bouncing off the still oasis water below. And somewhere below that, the love of her life.

"Lonen could've come with us. I've carried you both before, plus Baeltya," Chuffta pointed out.

"I know, but we couldn't have snuck him into Bára any more easily than we could sneak you in." The thought of her muscled Destrye warrior trying to pass as one of the effete Báran men had her smiling. *"And he can't abandon his people. He'll stay with them and lead them until he's the last man standing."*

"That does sound like Lonen."

And that was part and parcel of why she loved him. As much as she hated leaving him behind, they were both doing what they must, according to their natures and the responsibilities they'd been born to. She wouldn't change any of it. She could only hope that they'd triumph in the end.

A SHORT WHILE later, the towers of Bára rose against the horizon. Grienon had made his circuit around the far side of the world and rose again behind the graceful city, a blue-green jewel among the forest of towers. Though the desert sands extended all around like a lightless sea, the windows of the city gleamed with lights here and there, reminding Oria of the lovely rooms those arches and balconies connected to. Somewhere in there was her mother.

She hoped.

And somewhere in there also was Yar, and his wife Gallia, if she'd adapted to the city. Also Priestess Juli, who had waited faithfully on her, along with so many other people who'd populated her childhood. A strange sense of nostalgic familiarity warred in her heart with all the bad memories. The city seemed different now, smaller somehow. She'd seen so much more of the world since she'd fled Bára's walls. While tall and beautifully built, the towers of Bára couldn't match the forests and mountains of Dru.

She'd left this place an ignorant child at the mercy of the forces of the world, and now she returned as a queen and mighty sorceress.

"And I'm big,*"* Chuffta chimed in with smug delight. *"Let the high priestess complain about a few songbirds now."*

Oria laughed, and the odd melancholy faded to the background. She had a job to do, two realms to serve, the populations of both counting on her whether they knew it or not. Very likely she still had a certain vulnerability to the emotional miasma of Bára, the place of her birth, and that affected her on a deep level. Mentally reviewing the balance of her magic, she adjusted her senses to allow in only what she wished for the moment, then opened her magical perception to envision Bára that way.

She gasped aloud. Gone was the lightless desert. Instead, Bára seemed to be a glittering island of magical vectors—all spinning and whirling with fabulous resonances—perched atop a sea of deep rose still magic. Bára's pool of sgath, more ancient and immense that she'd ever imagined. And the walls, the towers, most every building—all shone with blinding blue-green light. The stones of Bára were held together by grien magic, somehow held in an endlessly cycling form, drawing on the pool of sgath.

What would happen if the priestesses of Bára stopped adding to the sgath below the city? Surely those towers would fall one day, then the lower structures, the stone itself crumbling back into the sand from which it was formed. So much made sense suddenly. Of course the temple carefully taught every sorceress she could not live beyond the city walls. In truth, the city itself would not survive if her sorceresses abandoned it. Oh, it wouldn't fall immediately. Maybe not for years, but eventually the sgath would be depleted, the grien spells would fail, and it would all return to the desert.

Tucking that information away, she picked out a quiet spot, well-shadowed both magically and according to her physical vision. *"Drop me over there."* She showed Chuffta mentally. *"Then find a chasm and stay hidden until I call. You know what to do, what to look for."*

"You'll let me listen with you though, yes?" Her Familiar sounded anxious, as he so rarely did, and she sent him a soothing thought.

"Yes. And you'll be only moments away by wing. You'll know if I need you. Watch for the Trom dragons and tell me if you see them. Let me know if—when you see Lonen and the army, too."

"I know, I know. I remember. They're still on the move, fighting more golems." Chuffta set her down on the soft dunes on the moonless side of the city. Now the walls reared above her, seeming not so small at all. *"I liked being able to ride on your shoulder and miss it at times like this."*

"I miss it, too," she replied, deciding not to remind him this time that it had been his idea to be big. Unstrapping her bag and herself from his harness, she climbed down his leg, then got out the red robes she'd brought from the palace and shrugged them on over her leathers. She'd restored the priestess robes to pristine condition with her magic, and added ribbons to Tania's mask. The mask glowed with magic like the heart of a sun, and she had to make sure not to look at it directly. Fortunately, she'd discovered, once she tied on the mask, the contact with her skin dropped it out of her magical perception. It became one with her own magic, an unexpected benefit. For the moment, she left it dangling from her belt.

Reaching up to Chuffta's lowered head, she hugged his jaw, clinging to him for courage. *"Now go. Once you're away, I'll enter the city."*

"I'll be with you."

He leapt into the sky, dusting her with some sand, but not as much as he might have even a week before. He'd gotten quite skilled with flying at his new size in a short time.

His white form receded into the night, like another moon, if moons were that color. Then he vanished, and she could no longer make him out. She turned and trudged over the dunes toward the walls. It wasn't easy going, with the soft sand sliding away and dragging her down. If only she could've had Chuffta set her down closer—but that would have jeopardized them both.

She made it to the wall soon enough, though her leg muscles ached from the unusual exercise. She made her way along it to one of the smaller side gates. Putting a hand against the barrier, she extended her magical senses through it, perceiving what lay on the other side. No one was about, as she'd hoped. These side gates opened into back lots and alleys, for loading supplies, and were barricaded most of the time. The main gates would be constantly guarded, but not these sealed ones. Part and parcel of Báran arrogance, she supposed. No one without magic could open these gates, and no one with magic would be outside the city wanting in.

She untied Tania's mask from her sash, where it had dangled by the ribbons, and donned it, taking the time to weave the ribbons through her braids, tying them decoratively as if her lady's maid had done it. The metal felt warm and strangely close against her face. Eyeless, the mask made a shield against the world she found stifling after living free with Destrye.

It murmured dark things to her, but she understood it now, the way it sought to gather magic and focus it into her, and she mastered it, harnessing the artifact to do her will.

It took only a whisper of grien to undo the magically sealed locks, a bit more to clear away the sand blown against the door. She wedged it open just enough for her to slip through, then closed it again, mentally resealing the lock.

And Oria stood inside Bára, the exile returned.

~ **13** ~

I NSIDE THE WALLS, the familiar feel of home enveloped her. She'd always known—had always been told—that Bára and her sister cities had been built to create a perfect place for sgath and grien to exist in balance. Outside the walls, wild magic would erode the very life of a sorceress.

As with everything she'd been taught, those lessons contained a seed of truth, but had strayed so far from the fullness of truth as to make them into outright lies. Yes, the walls of Bára had been woven with spells that filtered out the magic of the greater world, creating an oasis of apparent peace within. With her expanded senses and understanding of magic, however, Oria understood that the sense of coherence came from homogeneity. All magic but one kind—which the Bárans and their ilk called "sgath"—had been screened out.

That process, along with the efforts of Bára's sorceress population, created the vast pool of magic beneath the city. But, like the Destrye in the tunnels for a week, accustomed to darkness and weak candlelight, then blinded by the sun, living with only one kind of magic had made the Bárans painfully sensitive to any other kind. The men in Bára, trained to draw on magic only from Bára or their sorceress companions, benefited from this system.

The women, however... They'd been made into prisoners, captive livestock bred and trained to feed magic to the sorcerers. No wonder the men used grien so easily. They'd essentially had their magic chewed up by the walls and the women, then fed to them like milk produced by a cow.

The realization filled Oria with cold rage.

"Rage is good, as long as it stays cold," Chuffta advised. *"You're not so good at breathing fire."*

The superior tone in his mind-voice made her smile—and did help restore perspective. She was here to do a job, and she would focus on that. Time enough later, when she was recognized as Queen of Bára, to make changes, both here and in her sister cities.

So many changes she would make.

For the moment, she tucked her hands inside the wide sleeves of her crimson priestess robes and strolled out onto the smooth stones of the paved city paths. The eyeless mask prevented her from seeing the city as she had for most of her life, but her magical perception revealed far more. She understood now how wearing the mask could become a crutch for a priestess. Without the competition of physical vision, even a poorly skilled practitioner could more easily focus on only magical sight. It was hardly the badge of honor that Bárans regarded it as, however. Did a sorcerer or sorceress with real power need to advertise it via something as basic as seeing without physical vision?

The mask did give Oria the anonymity she needed, and she passed citizens and guards with serene equanimity, acknowledging their bows and greetings with a gracious incline of her head—and continuing on her important business.

Whatever a Báran priestess might be doing, it was always important.

In the same way, she strolled over Ing's Chasm and into the palace without challenge. Yar had built a new bridge of stone over the chasm. She recognized his magic instantly, able to observe how he'd woven the stone together with his grien. If she wanted to spend the time, she could likely trace every bit of stone and sand back to where he'd pulled it from. Each bit retained a thread to where it had been before, and where and what it had been before that. Levels upon levels, strands infinitely woven together to create physical reality. Fascinating—and potentially overwhelming.

And nothing she had time for.

Especially because, as she crossed the bridge and entered the palace, the matte black taint of the Trom impacted her senses. Not present, exactly, not at that precise moment, but they'd left their essence behind, as obvious as muddy footprints on the white and gold polished marble floors. She hadn't been practiced enough when she'd encountered the Trom before to differentiate the strength of their recent presence from the more distant kind, so she couldn't pinpoint how old this trace might be.

What would she perceive now when she encountered the Trom again? She'd have to brace herself for that, because even in her formerly dulled state, they had seemed to her like black suns of magic, drawing light inward instead of radiating it. It could be they did that with all magical wavelengths, devouring everything around them.

Somehow, knowing that they'd once been as human as she—and that she carried the potential to become what they were—gave her such a chill of terror that her thoughts began to fragment. What if she became that? The peril loomed beneath her like Ing's Chasm, lightless and bottomless.

"You would never become them, if only because I won't let you," Chuffta assured her with stalwart arrogance.

"I'm holding you to that." Once again, her Familiar's steadying presence helped her regain her sense of self and perspective. She wished she could have him on her shoulder.

"It seems to me that if you were a truly great sorceress, and you made me big, you could also make me small again."

"But what if I accidentally left out important bits?" She asked in her most innocent mind-voice.

He was silent a moment. *"You're right. It's not worth the danger."*

Suppressing a giggle, feeling much lighter, she made her way to her mother's receiving rooms. When Oria was last in Bára, Queen Rhianna hadn't returned to the bedchamber she'd shared with Oria's father. After his untimely death, and how that loss tore Rhianna's mind in half, the queen hadn't been able to face their shared space. Time might have healed that wound, but Oria's instincts said otherwise. Her mother would be sleeping sitting up, staring out the window, perhaps, watching for people who'd never returned to her.

That was, if her mother still lived. Oria could help Rhianna now—show her that she hadn't lost half of herself at all—if only her mother hadn't given up. Though that would have to wait for later. For the moment, Oria had no doubt that Yar would use their mother as a hostage against Oria's good behavior. Better to secure Rhianna first, before Oria challenged Yar and took out his council.

The lack of guards posted outside the Báran Queen Mother's receiving rooms made it easier for Oria to slip inside without being noticed but boded ill for her hopes. Indeed, as Oria passed from one room to the next, she found them all unlit and still with the quiet air of disuse. She'd have to keep looking.

Oria paused a moment by her mother's chair, gazing out the unglassed window that looked out over the city walls and beyond to the desert. A cool breeze wafted in from the distant sea, smelling of brine and moisture—and forewarning of dawn approaching. Oria had stood in that window and seen Lonen for the first time, astonished into freezing like prey at the sight of the muscled barbarian striking down the priestesses guarding the walls of Bára.

So much had happened since then, and yet here Oria stood in the same place, almost as if she'd never left.

"Who are you?" A voice asked behind her, making her whirl with a gasp of startlement as her heart skipped a beat. She should've sensed another person in the room.

A priest in golden mask and crimson robes stepped into the rosy moonlight streaming in the window. A sorcerer, who'd shielded himself from her senses. Even after all this time, she knew that voice.

"Answer my question, priestess," Yar commanded with lofty impatience. "Who are you and why are you here?" His grien snaked out, blue-green fingers to probe her, which she deflected easily.

Would he notice that she did?

Why was he here in their mother's rooms and where was Yar's wife, Gallia? Oria couldn't sense the priestess anywhere nearby, but she also hadn't known her long, and the last time they'd seen each other, Gallia's sgath had been weakened by moving to a new city. Even laboring under that terrible sapping of her native magic—a sensation Oria knew all too well—Gallia had helped them to escape. Oria owed her a life, and she knew exactly how to help her if the priestess from Lousá would be willing to learn.

"Are you even a priestess?" Yar's voice climbed with offense. "It's a crime punishable by death to wear a mask not ritually given to you."

"Hello Yar," Oria said, her voice remarkably steady.

He stilled, grien tentacles of power renewing their attempt to penetrate her mind and body. To no avail, as she sent them spinning into nothing.

"Oria." Yar spoke her name like he'd found a venomous snake in the room. "How are you here? And masquerading as a priestess. I'll remind you, Oria, that's still a crime punishable by execution. But, then, you already have a death sentence on your head for being an abomination, don't you? You only escaped it because we knew you'd die outside the walls. You were supposed to die!"

How very tiresome of him. She'd forgotten over the elapsed months, in her hatred of all Yar had done to the people of Dru and Bára, and intended to do to the Destrye, what a whiny brat he was at heart.

"Where's Mother?" she asked.

"Mother is dead," Yar replied with careless insouciance. "Your fault, of course, She died of a broken heart. Knowing she'd birthed a monster, and one too cowardly to face the temple's righteous judgment, was too much for her to bear."

"Oh no," Chuffta moaned. *"Not Rhianna. We loved her."*

"We don't know it's true. Even if it is, we'll mourn later."

"She waited for you, right here." Yar's voice oozed a manufactured sorrow not even remotely reflected in his emotions. "Day after day while we searched the desert for you, only wanting to bring you home."

"Bring me home to be executed, you mean."

"It's not the fault of anyone here that you're anathema, not even our mother's. It *is* your fault that you lied to hide what you knew went against all that's good and right, and that you attempted to use that twisted, cursed, and demonic ability to steal the throne from Bára's rightful king. You may be an abomination, but your poor, abandoned mother wanted only to lay your body in the family crypt so she could mourn you properly."

"Nothing about me is an abomination," Oria replied evenly, grateful for Chuffta's mental reassurance of that, and the love flowing down the marriage bond from Lonen. It was one thing to know in her mind that she wasn't a monster, and another entirely to *feel* the truth. It took effort to resist the image Yar attempted to paint, especially when her own guilt gave it fuel. She'd abandoned her mother, the woman who'd not only given her life, but had been her greatest—and sometimes only—champion.

"But you denied her even that small peace," Yar talked over her. "She died believing you lost forever." He'd wound himself up, his wiry body tense under the priest's robes. His grien—now thick, blue-green ropes of magic, still unable to find purchase in her— flailed about her body like the tentacles of a sea creature a trader had once brought to Bára.

"Did I—or did you?" Oria retorted. "I think you, at least, knew I was alive and in Dru."

"Found my little spy, did you? I wondered." His grien stabbed at her with sudden, increased force. Enough to sting. If he figured out how she'd changed, he might be able to hurt her in truth.

Oria set all other concerns aside, studying Yar's magic. Strong, yes, but all of one flavor. And she couldn't determine whose sgath he'd filled himself with. It was all Báran sgath, processed and purified until nothing of the individual remained. Where was Gallia?

"How is it that you're alive, sweet sister?" Yar asked when she didn't reply to his accusations. She gave no sign she sensed his invasion, even as he redoubled his efforts to scan her. He was using his magic all wrong—like using a club to slice bread—but a club would smash the bread to mush. "You have no magic left at all." Yar crowed his discovery, incredulous and gloating.

"But I do. In fact, I'm more powerful than ever," Oria replied, very seriously, tempted to lecture him on drawing hasty and false conclusions. "And I can teach our people, so that we need never call on the Trom again. So that we can banish them again entirely."

Yar burst out laughing, a manic edge to it. "Silly sister. As you had little training with the temple and none with grien, you won't know that I can sense these things." His grien buffeted her once more, clumsy, but painful enough to make her scramble to convert it to another wavelength of magic.

"When I scan you, there's nothing at all," he rambled on, hitting her again, even harder. "Is that what the wild magic did instead of killing you? It stripped you of even that crippled excuse for magical potential that you never used. Now you're like your barbarian husband. Queen of the Destrye and just as mind-dead as the lot of them. You're not even a sorceress now. So that's how you lived."

Yar laughed again, grien brightening with renewed confidence. "How our parents used to go on about how you were so *special*, that your latency meant your power would bloom into something spectacular. Giving you a Familiar even. Did it occur to them to give *me* a derkesthai? No! Just for super special weakling Oria. And now it turns out they were wrong, and you have *nothing*. You *are* nothing. How utterly fitting."

"The wild magic is not what we believed, it's true," Oria replied, growing weary of his posturing. "Neither are the Trom. Their foul presence lingers here. How recently have you had contact with them?"

"What do you care? I don't even know why you're here. Could it be that mind-dead brute of a hunk of barbarian meat tired of you and dumped you back at our doorstep? If you've come crawling for forgiveness there's no tolerance for anathema in my reign." He redirected his grien, giving up on her entirely, snaking those blue-green tentacles to the stone walls around them, totally unaware that Oria could perceive exactly what he was doing. And showing her what she'd needed to see—he only reached for stone and earth. That had been his talent, but she'd wondered in the intervening months. She, herself, had an affinity for growing things, but her own magic wasn't limited to that realm. The sorcerer who'd animated the golems had died in the Battle of Bára, so someone had taken his place. She'd thought Yar, perhaps, but clearly not.

She'd have to look elsewhere—but she had to get past Yar first.

"The Trom are anathema, not me," she said, letting him hear the conviction in her voice. "According to temple teaching and our own eyes. You summoned them to attack the Destrye—broaching our treaty—and they devastated the city and Bárans along with our enemy."

"You're still stuck on that? I saved Bára! Sometimes one must cut off a limb to heal the body. Thanks to me, Bára will continue to flourish. I am the hero of this story and *you*, my mind-dead sister, are the villain." His grien fingers dug into the stones, tensing on them as a warrior might flex his muscles, giving forewarning of his intent.

Keeping a wary mental finger on the pulse of his power, Oria tried one more time. "Yar, listen to me. I've come here to help you and Bára. We are not enemies."

He paused, finally assimilating some clues. Yar had always been bright, but too self-involved to be truly observant. "How did you get into the city anyway? This is what we've been seeing. You traitor, you brought the Destrye here. Guards—to me! We're under attack!"

And he yanked on the stones around them, chunks flying at Oria. She deflected them, sending them zooming toward Yar instead, and they slammed him to the floor. He crumpled into a heap, his grien collapsing. Had she killed him?

Stricken she moved closer to check. "Yar?"

A lightning bolt of grien shot out, striking her hard enough to stun, and she staggered back, head swirling like a sandstorm.

"Take *that*, you bitch," Yar snarled.

"Another wave of golems incoming, Your Highness," Alyx reported. Even with the warmth of the light of the stubby candle she carried, the warrior woman looked wan and exhausted. They'd been battling golems nonstop, with barely a pause between assaults. In the eternal night of the tunnels, Lonen had lost all track of time. He had no idea how long it had been since Oria left for Bára.

Only the pulse of her at the distant end of the marriage bond reassured him that she yet lived. The continued waves of golems, however, bore witness to the reality that Oria had not succeeded in defeating Yar—or whoever continued to create and animate the mindless creatures. Oria was alive, yes, but in what condition?

Certainly not in any that would let her help them. At this rate, the Destrye would emerge beneath the city only to be finally and permanently decimated. At least they hadn't been drowned. Yet.

Grimly, Lonen relayed the order for a fresh battalion to move up, to relieve the group that had just spent hours chopping up the previous wave of golems. The warriors jogged past, iron weapons at the ready. Before long, another wave would pass him going the other direction, carrying the wounded back to the far end of the caravan.

"How long can we keep this up?" he asked no one in particular.

Arnon emerged from the gloom ahead, having led the previous defense and yielded to Alby for this one. All the commanders had been taking it in turns. All of them were exhausted.

"If we make the logical assumption that the golems will continue to assault us according to the established pattern," Arnon said, "then I estimate they'll chew through us in another eight assaults."

"Oh, well, is that all? We're fine then," Lonen replied, resting his battle-axe on the floor of the tunnel and leaning against the wall.

"The good news is," Arnon continued as if Lonen hadn't spoken, "I calculate that we've passed under the bore tide flats—at least the tunnels let us avoid that hazard—and if we can keep pressing forward at the same rate, we should reach the underground lake Nolan and his men fell into in fewer than three assaults."

Lonen wondered at the kind of hell they found themselves in, where they'd relinquished daylight and counted time in golem assaults. "What kind of army will we have when we get there?"

"Able-bodied warriors? About a third of what we started out with," Alyx replied somberly.

Wonderful.

"We never planned to take Bára by might," Arnon reminded them. "We did that once before—and only because Lonen figured out how to knock their sorcerers out of action, particularly the one setting the golems on us—and we pretty near decimated our army doing that."

"I don't think bashing our heads against waves of golems counts as guile, either," Alyx commented, dabbing her fingers at a freshly bleeding slice across her cheek. "What did we plan to take Bára with again? I know we gave up on surprise."

"Stealth," Arnon supplied, gesturing at the enclosing tunnel.

"Oh right. I keep forgetting we're not actually mole people," Alyx replied wryly.

"We just need to keep ourselves in optimal form until word arrives from Oria," Lonen told them, not for the first time. "Once defeats Yar, she'll stop whoever is driving the golems at us. The city guard was always sympathetic to her rule. She'll be able to persuade at least some to open the gates."

"And if she doesn't?" Arnon demanded. "It won't do us much good to have crept here all this way if we emerge outside the city walls with the gates barred."

"She will. And, if not, we took the walls with the gates barred before. We'll just do it again," Lonen asserted.

Arnon and Alyx exchanged a speaking look. They'd developed a friendship through this campaign. It wasn't clear if their relationship was of the brothers-in-arms variety or something more intimate. Not that it mattered, but on the rare occasions Lonen found the energy, he amused himself by contemplating the latter. Unfortunately, his first impulse then was to share his speculations with Oria, which killed any lightness of heart.

"Lonen," Arnon said gently, "if Oria hasn't succeeded by now, then we have to face that—"

"She's alive," Lonen said, cutting him off.

"We believe you," Alyx supplied in the same tone. "But clearly she hasn't been able to—"

A tremor shook the earth, dirt, sand and small rocks rattling down from the tunnel roof. A bore tide, thundering above? No... something else. As if, for a moment, reality dislocated itself. The derkesthai perched on Arnon and Alyx's shoulders spread their wings, giving eerie screeching cries that had the two humans covering their ears and cringing.

"What in Arill is wrong?" Alyx shouted.

Arnon met Lonen's gaze. They both knew that feeling, had experienced it before. If Oria had been with them, she likely could have described the color of the magic wave that had just passed through.

"Nothing to do with the goddess." Arnon told her through gritted teeth, pressing his lips together as if he might puke. He remembered that day, too, when their father and brother died. "That happened before when..." He trailed off, unwilling to say the words.

"When the Trom arrived," Lonen finished for him. With renewed energy, he shouldered his axe. "Alyx, pass down the alert. Everyone who can lift a weapon to the fore. Enough of them chewing through us. We're punching through."

She saluted, mounted her horse, and galloped down the tunnel, her derkesthai messenger winging ahead to clear the way. Lonen reached for Buttercup, who stamped with delight, sensing his master's change of temperament—and the opportunity to engage in the fight at last. Thus far, they'd been forced by the tunnel dimensions to face the golems on foot. That would change now. Shouts echoed down the tunnel, the clash of battle engaged ahead, the chants of battalions on the move from behind.

"Lonen!" Arnon said, not for the first time. "Are you mad? Even if we can 'punch through' those waves of golems, what we will we do? You can't face the Trom."

"No, but Oria can." And she'd be facing them all alone if he didn't get there in time.

Arnon kept his grip on Buttercup's cheek strap, a dangerous and bold obstinacy in the face of the warhorse's mighty impatience to be off. "Then let Oria do it," Arnon said, very reasonably, except that he shouted the words.

"We promised her," Lonen replied, leaning over to speak clearly into his brother's face. "I promised her. The Destrye army and the derkesthai squadrons must be ready when Oria signals us, to convene on the city at the same time.

"And if Oria has been taken out of the equation?" Arnon asked soberly. "Without her we can't communicate well enough with the derkesthai to coordinate strategy. Without her magic, we can't defeat the sorcerers. We learned that to our sorrow last time."

Lonen shook his head, refusing that possibility. It didn't bear thinking of—and planning around it would change nothing. "I can't control what the derkesthai will do, and I can't help Oria right now, but I *can* have the Destrye warriors where we'd said we'd be. We won't fail in this."

With that, he gave Buttercup his head. Arnon, cursing, stepped out of the way just in time. Lonen galloped at top speed down the tunnel, bent low over Buttercup's neck so his head would clear the tunnel roof atop the warhorse's towering height. His blood coursed with battle fury and he gave over control to it, letting it flow down the bond to Oria, signaling and fueling her, too.

Enough with measured progress. To hell with this waiting game. Time to engage the enemy, bust out of these cursed tunnels, and finish this war.

And pray to Arill that Oria would meet him on the other side.

~ 14 ~

"**Y**OUR HIGHNESS, WON'T you drink some juice?"

Oria stirred, blinking her eyes, her lids heavy as she opened them to see Juli—her distinctive hair curling around her gold, eyeless mask as she hovered with the proferred glass of juice—and Oria groaned mentally.

Stupid. So stupid of her to have let down her guard, not to have killed Yar when she had the chance. She could've struck him down, and she'd foolishly hesitated.

"Not foolish or stupid. You are not a predator, and he's your younger brother," Chuffta said. *"Killing isn't easy when you haven't practiced."*

"True. Thank you."

Oria sat up and took the glass, happy enough for the drink restore her wits and cleanse her dry mouth. It was her favorite kind of juice. Or, rather, it used to be. Now she understood it had been pressed from a fruit carefully nourished with the water stolen from Dru. The sweetness was a lie, covering the bitter origins.

"It's good to see you again, Juli," Oria said with great sincerity, surprising herself with the rush of emotion.

"Oh, Oria," Juli murmured, sliding her hands into her sleeves, the perfect image of calm composure that the Bárans called *hwil.* "We've missed you so. No—don't move. His Highness King Yar unleashed his grien on you and you're gravely injured."

No, she wasn't—but how odd that Juli couldn't perceive it. Looking at the priestess she'd known for so long with her altered perceptions, Oria understood how Juli alone had been able to touch

517

and tend Oria all those years. Juli had her magic so tightly balled up, along with her emotions, that she almost seemed to be not there, on the magical level. The priestess had become the perfect vessel they'd made her into—a funnel for sgath and nothing more—and for the first time Oria wondered what had been done to her to warp and distort her healthy self.

Feigning the injury Juli expected, Oria lay back, expanding her senses. It had only been a couple of hours, she thought, if that. Nice that Yar had summoned Juli to tend Oria, who he no doubt assumed—in his vast arrogance and the habits of a shared childhood—to be no threat. He'd even tucked her in her old tower rooms instead of a cell, falling into the old patterns of thinking she'd be days up there, recovering.

Not realizing that he'd put her in the perfect position to take over the city.

"What's going on?" she asked Chuffta, while Juli prepared one of her herbal solutions. So funny that the Bárans considered themselves the height of civilized sophistication and sorcery, but the barbarian Destrye were the ones with truly effective healing magic. One of the first things she wanted to do for Bára would be to bring a few of Arill's healers here.

"The Destrye are still fighting through the golems in the tunnels. We're waiting for them to come out," he replied promptly, though she got an impression that he was preoccupied.

"Can't you help?"

"The small ones are helping, but—"

"Would you like us to simply blow flame down the tunnel and melt them all at once?" The derkesthai king boomed the question in her mind. **"That would be easiest, but you didn't like the idea before."**

"No, please don't." She mentally tucked her tongue in her cheek. *"I trust you both to do as you judge best."*

"Hmpf." The Great One's mental snort had a breath of flame to it. Chuffta simply sent his love and turned his attention away again. Before he did, she caught the impression of a deep chasm, a lightless lake—and hordes of golems climbing over mounds of their twitching and broken brethren. Oria sent him her love back. She sent some to Lonen, too. As always, however, he was less defined—just a burning fire of battle rage.

Alive, though. Oria shivered at the frisson of fear, despite the growing heat as the sun rose. It would be a hot day. And by the time the sun set, their futures would be decided one way or the other. Time to start recruiting allies before she went after Yar again—and finally took care of him.

"You have a fever," Juli said, approaching with the cool, soaked cloth. "Let me—" She gasped as Oria seized her wrist, shuddering in horror at the skin-to-skin contact. Yanking at Oria's grip like a trapped animal, Juli dropped the cloth, frenzied in her struggle.

Until Oria sent a calming wave through her old friend. The physical contact allowed her to loosen some of the bonds throttling Juli's free will. As with Nolan, several magical ties worked in a loop through Juli's emotions. Not libido with her, but her longing to be loved. A clever knot that tied that need for love into a need to keep her magic contained. If she wanted to love, she had to give sgath. If she wanted to be touched, she had to give sgath. If she wanted to be loved, she must keep all her sgath and give it only as the temple deemed appropriate. Most insidious of all: Juli herself had created this spell and fed its power with her own magic.

Tempted to sever the vile circle, Oria hesitated, concerned that it might make Juli crazed like Nolan had become. Instead, she offered a suggestion, inserting an alternate idea into the loop. Juli could touch and be touched as she willed. Juli could love and be loved as she decided. Juli's sgath belonged to her, to circulate as she wished.

In her grip, Juli stilled her frantic struggles. Then she relaxed, physically and magically, like a tight flower bud suddenly unfurling into a lush blossom. "You're touching me," she breathed. "I feel…"

"You feel," Oria confirmed, then let Juli go as she got out of the bed. "There's no time for long explanations—just trust your magic.

And don't believe anything they told you."

"Oria, I—what are you doing?"

Oria finished stripping off her robes. "I'm done with disguises. Where are my mother and Gallia?"

"In seclusion in the temple. A great deal has happened while you were… away."

"I'm sure," Oria replied grimly, picking up Tania's mask from the decorative tile beside her bed, the one made for that purpose. Yar hadn't taken it from her, probably hadn't even recognized its power. "They're *both* in the temple?"

"Yes. Here, I'll get new ribbons for your mask and—"

"No need." Oria tied the bits of cut ribbons to a belt loop of her fighting leathers, then strode out onto the terrace, calling over her shoulder. "We don't need to wear them, Juli. They're for focusing magic, that's all."

She gave herself a moment and no more to look around her rooftop garden, dead now, the jewelbirds fled, all the plants and trees crisped except one struggling jasmine. Even her silk shades and pillows had been left to fade and tatter in the relentless burning sun and hot desert winds, frayed bits flapping in the morning breeze. Like her old self, all of that had been lost.

Like her new self, what she built from these ruins would be better.

Resolved, she moved to the stone balustrade, fancying that her hands settled into smooth curves worn there by all the years she'd stood in exactly that spot. As she had then, she stared into the heat shimmer rising in the distance beyond the high walls of the city. No sign of violence, no telltale glitter or the shouts of warriors calling orders. Only the peaceful city, growing busier as the morning waxed on. Opening her senses to the city and its surrounds, she finally and completely used her vantage from the tallest tower in Bára. As she'd hoped, being at this height and back in this place where she'd focused so much attention on her magic magnified her perception.

Then she really and truly *saw*.

"Oria…" Juli had followed her out, sounding bewildered.

"Shh. Watch. Remove your mask, stretch out your senses, and you'll understand."

Oria didn't know if the other priestess did as she suggested or not. She cast her attention on the surging sea that was the mass consciousness of Bára. A beast of thousands of faces, hearts beating, bodies working, magic weaving. The temple taught that magic came from life itself, and Oria perceived that clearly now, how all the people, plants, and animals of Bára created the multitudes of sparks the priestesses then distilled into sgath. Without all those living beings, the city would fail—not only because no one would tend the physical aspects of people's lives, but because the magic that kept a city alive in the midst of this desert would disappear.

All those years Oria had lived on her tower, this had been what sustained and overwhelmed her. If only she'd known…

But she knew now, and that was key. Casting her mind on the surface, she dove through the currents, looking for the ones she wanted, following the scarlet, crimson, and rosy threads of priestess magic to their concentrated sources. Deep within the temple, all the priestesses had gathered with Rhianna and Gallia—in their prison cells. A part of Oria raged at the prettified term, "seclusion." Of all the sorceresses, only she and Juli weren't in that group, chanting and meditating, channeling sgath…

Ah. Channeling sgath to fuel the golem army. A small river to feed that. A larger one went to something else.

Even as Oria moved to cut off the sgath to the golems that blockaded the Destrye, another part of her mind followed the larger channel, back to a group of sorcerers. She recognized a few of them, Vico and Yar among them.

And she knew the spell they wrought.

She turned her thoughts into a blade, severing that spell, choking off the magic that fed it. Under her mental grip, it surged, bulged, and tore itself free with a clang that shook the earth, her tower swaying, and that resonated painfully on every magical level.

Juli felt to her knees, clapping her hands over her ears, as if she could block out a physical sound. Oria, her balance refined from sticking to Chuffta's back through his aerial acrobatics, rode out the waves of reaction, scanning the skies.

Boom. Boom. Boom.

One by one, the Trom dragons popped into existence, the rending of reality sending shudders through several realms. The dragons roared, their flame bright even against the sunlit sky. On their backs, the Trom riders were black motes, sucking in all light. Beneath the net of her mind, the consciousness of the city shuddered, as thousands of minds quailed in utter terror.

Too late.

"Chuffta!" she called.

"We're on our way!"

He must mean all the derkesthai. Oria whirled on Juli, who crouched on hands and knees, mask still in place. "Go find Captain Ercole. Tell him I'm here and I've brought the Destrye, that he should open the city gates to them. Then go to the temple and tell my mother and Gallia the same thing. Let them out so they can help."

"Help... what?" Juli panted, disoriented and confused. Oria pulled the priestess to her feet, using her magic to sever the ribbons of Juli's mask so it clattered to the stones. Juli cried out, clapping her hands to her face. Oria pried them away just as Chuffta landed on the terrace in a gust of wind and sand, great talons clutching the stone balustrade. Eyes wide in a pallid face that hadn't seen the sun in years, a pretty, girlish face Oria had never seen, Juli gaped at Chuffta.

"Is... Is that?"

"My Familiar, Chuffta," Oria agreed. "You remember him."

Chuffta lowered his triangular chin, giving Juli his version of a smile. *"This terrace is much smaller than it used to be."*

"No, you're much bigger." Giving Juli a little shake, she nudged her mentally, too. "Listen. I have to go turn the Trom and their dragons

away from the city. Tell Gallia that I said for them to stop channeling sgath to the sorcerers. Tell her that I'm returning the favor she did me."

"But the Destrye will attack," Juli babbled.

"I am Queen of the Destrye. We're here to save Bára," Oria told her. She stabbed a finger at the sky. "Yar summoned the Trom because he doesn't care who he crushes to keep his grip on the city."

Juli gulped, realization dawning on her face, though hard to say if it would be enough. "What if the Trom land? Their least touch is death."

"No, it's *not*." Deliberately, Oria laid a hand on Juli's pale cheek. "Could I do this before? That's right." She nodded at Juli's widening gaze, her brown eyes that Oria had never seen so pretty with their tawny flecks. "I can control the touch now. That's all the Trom do. They're just like us, with a different magic. Control what happens if they try to touch you."

"I don't understand," Juli nearly wailed.

"Trust me. You know me. Release the others. Stop feeding the sorcerers sgath. The Destrye are here to help. Let them. As soon as I can, I'll join you at the temple." Impulsively, she kissed Juli's cheek, and released her.

"Let's go." With a running start, Oria leapt onto Chuffta's leg and climbed up the rope harness she quickly wove onto him from her dead garden.

"Oria!" Juli called, face stark with uncertainty.

"If you love Bára, do as I ask. Go set the priestesses free. Use your magic. Use it for Bára."

Another dragon swooped over them and Oria ducked reflexively, then saw it was also white. The derkesthai king, with a rider on his back... Baeltya. The healer waved, then pointed at the sky. Chuffta leapt into the air to follow, the derkesthai of all sizes massing behind them in their patterns, turning the sky as white as if the snows of Dru had come to Bára.

They surged up in formation, ready to engage in battle.

"Anything from the Destrye?" she asked, reinforcing her straps and gathering the rivers of magic from her home city and the wild magic beyond.

"They are closer, but not yet through. Maybe Juli will get the others to stop Yar and whoever is sending the golems."

Maybe. Torn, Oria cast about again for that river of magic feeding the golems, but the presence of the Trom had disrupted everything. Instead of a living sea, the magic of the city jumbled in chaos, the streams of it warping and bending around the infinite deep holes that were the Trom.

"She'll have to. Let's go knock these monsters out of the sky."

~ **15** ~

Lonen swung his iron axe with grim determination, ignoring the sweat dripping from his soaked hair into his eyes. The three golems charging him dropped with the single blow—and four more took their place. Emotionless, thoughtless, the monster creatures advanced in relentless, silent waves, tearing with long, saber-sharp claws, rending his flesh with crystalline-fanged mouths if they got near enough.

Far too often, the mindless creatures got near enough, and Lonen knew he'd grown as slick with his own blood as sweat, though he felt none of the wounds. The tunnel had widened as it approached the lake and chasm, and Buttercup waded in water up to his hocks at times. That meant the other warriors, like Alyx at his off side, were in up to their thighs. It made the endless advance that much more grueling.

At least they had light. Not direct sunlight, but daylight filtering down from somewhere ahead. They were so close.

Any moment now, Oria would stop the sorcerer animating these things, and they would fall into motionless heaps. He fantasized it so clearly he sometimes thought—in the nonstop fugue of killing—that it had happened already.

But no.

No, the golems kept coming and coming.

If Oria was alive—he knew she was alive. He could feel her, couldn't he? Sometimes he wasn't sure he felt anything but the strain of his muscles, the pumping of his heart, the endless sweep, chop, advance, sweep, chop—but if Oria was alive, she'd stop the golems. Any moment now they'd fall into motionless heaps.

How many of Arnon's assault waves had this been? Probably the metric had fallen apart with Lonen's decision to make a hard push. No doubt Arnon could chart it, how the force of the Destrye army disrupted the regular waves of golem assaults, compressing them into one unending mass, like life in the tunnels, like the passage of time, squeezed into agonizingly slow progress…

A shout from ahead. Then a roar of dragons, echoing from high above. Lonen renewed his vigorous swinging, mowing down the golems like the farmers did the ripened stalks of grain. If only he could feed his people from fallen golem parts.

And then… the golems collapsed. Just as he'd imagined count-less times in the last exhausting hours. They simply froze mid-movement, then crumpled, bobbing up again to float away like soap bubbles and catch in eddies. Oria had done it!

Buttercup lifted his head, trumpeting a challenge, and charged forward, sending golem bodies surging away on the waves. The Destrye roared also, in one voice, a wave of warriors brandishing weapons as they sought the daylight.

As promised, the derkesthai had been busy while they waited, tumbling rock and tamping the dirt into a ramp leading out of the chasm. Lonen and Buttercup galloped to lead the vanguard, his captains on their warhorses raising flags to gather their contingents.

They rode up and out of the tunnels, rising through the crack of the chasm into full day. Above, a fierce battle rumbled and thun-dered through the sky like the summer storms of Lonen's boyhood. Green flame crackled like lightning, and the dragons and derkesthai roared with earth-rattling challenges.

Trusting to Buttercup, Lonen studied the two biggest white dragons. Chuffta and the Great One, especially from this distance, looked much the same. Both bore a rider. He couldn't make out which was which. Though both seemed locked in lethal battles of aerial acrobatics and flame that seemed certain to end in disaster.

"Lonen!" Arnon rode up hard on his flank. "The gates aren't open."

Lonen wrenched his gaze from the sky and focused on the ground. His job was to get the Destrye in the gates to secure Bára. "Then we'll open them."

Setting up the signal, he turned his army to once again—and for the final time—take the city of Bára.

AT CHUFFTA'S MENTAL alert, Oria seized a moment to look down. The Destrye poured up out of the chasm outside the walls of Bára like ants swarming a fallen beast. The city, however, wasn't prone. The towers stood tall and graceful, remote behind her walls, proudly peaceful—and with gates firmly shut, no sign of activity within, turning a deliberate blind eye to the battle raging outside.

The Báran way of dealing with everything, apparently. But that would change.

As Chuffta dipped in a deep sideways tilt to come about, Oria spotted Lonen, easily distinguishable by Buttercup's black bulk. The warhorse climbed a small outcropping with ease, and Lonen looked to be shouting orders, using his massive double-headed, battle-axe to point the way. Her heart eased. She'd known he lived, via the marriage bond and the reports of the derkesthai, but seeing him hale and vital reassured her on another level. She could swear he looked up just then, the arrow of his distant gaze slamming into her, and the bond between them thrummed. Smiling, she pumped a fist, though she knew he likely couldn't see her well.

"*Duck!*" Chuffta's mental shout came at the same moment he folded wings and dove, a roar of green flame singeing overhead and heating the already crackling air. The dragon dove after them, the Trom on its back briefly parallel to her as Chuffta pulled up again to avoid hitting ground.

It sat astride its mount with no apparent apparatus to keep it there, clinging like spiders can to any surface with ease. And it stared right at her. Calm and without expression on its smooth face, it gazed at her as if they'd met in an elegant salon instead of plunging through the air on flaming dragons. The matte black eyes dominated its spherical skull, draining away the visible light as well as all the magic around them. Oria considered hitting it with her magic, but instinct stopped her.

"Careful." The Great One blazed fire at another Trom and its dragon, herding them away from the city. ***"You might not be able to detach again."***

The last thing she wanted was to create a connection to that monster, one that might doom her to be leashed to it forever if she couldn't break away again.

For the first time, however, she saw for herself what the derkesthai king had told her: how the Trom looked like her own people, slim and long limbed, with fine bones. The way its skin clung to its skeleton made the Trom seem so alien and insectile, but in that face, those pits of eyes... Oria glimpsed the sorcerer it had once been.

Or sorceress.

Chuffta peeled off, ending the moment as he evaded a crash, and Oria—caught momentarily unware, reached for the straps to steady herself, hand brushing Tania's mask as she did. The thing nearly burned her, so hot and bright.

Images flooded her—of Bára, recognizable, but different. A Bára with no walls, perched on a great river, with trees! Feathery branches flowering, the lovely trees arched over the placid water, creating cool shade. In those memories, Oria knew how that shade felt, the deliciously refreshing feel of the water. And overlaying all of it, magic—wild and tamed—weaving and flowing together in balance and harmonious life.

Then a patchwork rush of images: A new moon appearing in the sky, bright blue-green that whirled madly past every few hours. The sun burning hot in a cloudless sky. The river becoming smaller, the trees wilting, then crisping. Desperate efforts to manipulate magic, to affect the weather itself. The walls rising around Bára as the riverbed became desert.

The mask. Oria had named it for her aunt Tania, a woman she'd never known, as the ancient sorceress who'd been buried with the mask hadn't had a name inscribed on her tomb.

So powerful. So ambitious and determined, Oria's mother had told her long ago, before she fled Bára. *Don't be like her, Oria. Find an ideal husband and channel your magic through him. Don't try to do it alone. Don't be like Tania. Promise me.*

But Oria didn't have the ideal husband they'd intended for her. She channeled her own magic—and she wasn't alone.

She reached out with her magic and connected to that Trom.

"Oria!"

"I know what I'm doing." She hoped. The Trom didn't fight her grip, but slithered back up it, filling Oria's magic portals with oily slick darkness. *"Land us inside the walls."*

"Them too?" Chuffta's mind-voice sounded bewildered. *"Ugh! I can taste it through you."* He made mental gagging noises.

"Them too." Concentrating, Oria held firm, resisting the visceral urge to drop the connection, and trying to filter it at the same time, to spare Chuffta. *"Take us to the temple courtyard."*

"But the whole strategy was to keep the Trom out of Bára," Chuffta complained, even as he angled them into a steep glide, heading for the expanse of plaza between the palace and temple.

"I'm changing the strategy," she replied tersely, most of her concentration going to coercing the Trom, who'd begun to tug in the opposite direction. Not to break free—no, its claws sunk ever deeper into Oria's psyche—but to pull her away from Bára and its walls. Which only confirmed to Oria that she had the right idea. *"Tell the Great One to keep all the others away still,"* she added, finding it easier to speak along the time-worn channels between her and her

Familiar.

She felt the pang of concern from Lonen as he observed their descent, and sent him a pulse of reassurance, hoping he'd understand. Then she had no mental space for anything but hanging on to the Trom as they crossed the walls, the magic disruption of them like a bore tide crashing through her consciousness, and then again crossing Ing's chasm. She dragged the Trom with her, forcing its dragon to land.

Golden masked priests and priestesses spilled out of the temple, but Oria focused on containing the dragon, holding its mind along with her connection to the Trom. As soon as Chuffta landed, Oria scrambled down the harness straps, pulling the Trom now opposite her on the stone apron to do likewise. It followed suit, moving with spidery ease, as if Oria weren't compelling it. In truth, Oria couldn't tell if she really was making it obey or if she'd fallen into its web.

"Keep that dragon contained," she told Chuffta.

"On it."

As Oria and the Trom walked toward each other, facing off, she saw Chuffta backing the Trom's dragon to the edge of the precipice. The darker dragon tossed its head but retreated before the much larger Chuffta and his well-placed flame. The priests and priestesses shouted, incomprehensible, male and female voices combined—and Oria spared them no attention.

Every fiber of her awareness focused on the Trom.

"Ponen no longer, I perceive," it rasped in its hoarse voice, as devoid of melody as its frame was of human flesh. "You are one of us now."

"No," Oria replied evenly. "I'm what you could've been, ancestress, had you not lost your way."

Its lipless mouth smiled without mirth. "There are ways and ways, child, and you will find that everything dries up and dies but one thing: power."

"You're wrong." Oria untied the mask from her belt and held it out to the Trom. "I believe this was once yours."

The Trom extended its bare twig fingers. Not unnaturally long, but a once-human hand stripped to skin, ligament, and bone. Without the fleshy palm, the finger bones extended from the knobby wrists, creating an illusion of length. The Trom took the mask and held it, staring down at the shining artifact, arrested. "Not mine," it said. "But one I once knew."

A hint of wistfulness came from the Trom, the first taste of emotion Oria'd had from one of them. "A long time ago," Oria suggested.

The Trom raised its unearthly gaze back to hers. "Longer than you can imagine."

"Longer than anyone should live."

"Who's to decide such things? Some things fade too fast, are gone in a blink. Others last far too long, wearing us down to nothing. We did what we had to do not to die."

"The world changed when Grienon arrived," Oria ventured. "You used magic to keep yourselves alive, then couldn't die."

The Trom inclined its head. "You would do the same."

Oria shook her head. "There are other ways."

"Now there might be, but only because of us."

"That could be," Oria allowed. "But you are not harnessed to us. You do not have to answer the call of Bára any longer. Our battles are not yours."

The Trom turned its head, raising the hand not holding the mask and beckoning to someone with an uncanny undulation of those spidery fingers. As if released from a stranglehold—perhaps he had been—Yar barreled forward, shouting imprecations.

As one, Oria and the Trom regarded his frothing posturing with bemusement. "This one summoned us," the Trom informed Oria, a whisper of dry humor in it. "And you say we do not have to answer? The magic compels us. We do not like it."

"If I promise to break your chains," Oria spoke over Yar's impotent yelling, "will you call off your brethren above?"

"You believe you can?"

"Kill her!" Yar shouted, seizing Oria by the arm in a painful grip and shaking her. "I am the Summoner and I command you to kill her."

"I can," Oria replied to the Trom, ignoring Yar. His grien batted at her, but she held him off.

"Prove it," the Trom said, holding out its hand. "Touch me. If I don't kill you, I'll believe."

Watching the Trom's magic, seeing how the currents of it pulsed to suck all life from whatever it touched, Oria changed her own to both match and deflect. She laid her hand in the Trom's, clasping it in what felt like the beginning of a very strange friendship.

The Trom smiled. "Perhaps you can. But you must kill the Summoner."

Everything in Oria congealed, going cold and dense. "He is my baby brother."

Cocking its head with what might be sympathy, the Trom squeezed her hand and released it. "I know. And I've shown you how. Break our chains now. Kill the Summoner, and we'll go. I'll trust you to make sure we can't be Summoned again."

Yar still had her arm, attacking her with his grien. It felt much weaker now, and Oria became aware that one group stood well back, their sgath still and contained. The priestesses, refusing to feed the priests.

Three women stepped to the fore, hands clasped and faces bare. Juli on one side, the golden-haired Gallia on the other, and Oria's mother, tall and straight in the middle. The queen mother observed her two surviving children with a careworn expression, but a sharp, alert gaze. She met Oria's eyes and dipped her chin.

With a deep sense of regret and righteousness, a conflict Oria knew she'd spend the rest of her life resolving, she turned in Yar's grip and embraced him. Letting the black current reverse, she pulled his life force into herself, feeling him dissolve into nothing, and collapse in a pile at her feet.

~ 16 ~

Lonen had forgotten how high those walls around Bára reared up, the towers dizzyingly tall beyond that. Difficult to believe he'd once scaled that impervious reach. Though he had done it—and had climbed trees far taller. The wall only seemed unscalable now because Oria was behind it, facing one of the lethal Trom.

Buttercup valiantly galloped through the sucking sands at a diagonal from the rock outcropping they'd stopped at after climbing out of the chasm. They made for the trade road, the Destsrye army whooping and shouting in fine aggressive barbarian style behind them. Oria would be amused by it, and Lonen clung to that image of her—alive and laughing, not in a gelatinous pile. He let the feel of her burning sun at the other end of the marriage bond draw him closer, though the gates to the city remained firmly shut.

If he had to climb those walls again, he would.

With a clatter, Buttercup's hooves found the hard-packed road, and he put on a burst of speed, heading for those unmoving gates. Overhead, the dragons battled with guttural roars and blasts of flame.

Then suddenly, the skies went silent.

Responding to Lonen, Buttercup reared up, wheeling in a circle to lash out at whatever had changed. But only white derkesthai remained above. The Trom and their dragons had disappeared.

With a shout, Lonen turned Buttercup and the army back toward the gates, resuming their headlong approach. Hardly daring to hope they might have won, Lonen thought as hard as he could at

Oria, praying to Arill that she could hear him.

And the gates opened. The city guard of Bára poured out, lining either side of the gates, raising swords… and then laying them down. Without pause, Lonen and Buttercup galloped full speed through the tunnel in the wall, a space Lonen remembered all too well from long hours taking and holding it against the city guard.

As they emerged from the shadows, the enormous white figure that was Chuffta landed in the wide courtyard. On his back Oria perched, copper hair streaming wildly from her aerial battles, a broad grin on her face.

They both leapt from their mounts and ran, catching each other up in a hard embrace. Her light, lithe body vibrated against him, thrumming with magic and victory. He kissed her, hot and long, savoring the flavor of his sorceress queen.

When they parted, both out of breath, he gave her a cocky grin. "The last time you surrendered Bára to me, you rode a white horse instead of a white dragon. It seems you've come up in the world."

"Well, it's important to dazzle the barbarian hordes at your gates," she replied with a saucy smile.

"Where do we stand?" he asked, sobering.

"Yar is dead." She grew somber, too, haunted shadows in her copper eyes. "I killed him. Lonen—I used the Trom power to do it. I dissolved him while I held him in my arms."

He gazed back at her, letting her see and feel the love and regard he held for her. "You used the tools at hand, Oria, to do what you had to as queen of two realms. You restored the balance, yes?"

Her eyes filled with tears. "I hope so," she whispered.

"You did." He gave her all his confidence in that truth. "And now we move forward. The Trom?"

"Gone," she answered. "That's a story."

"All right then." He let her go and found Arnon and Alyx standing nearby. From behind Oria, a group of three women riding horses and dressed in priestess robes, but not wearing masks, approached. "I suppose we have a great deal to sort out."

"Yes." Oria sighed, sagging briefly against him, then straightened. "The city council and temple are in complete disarray, but let me introduce you to women you've met, but may not recognize. You'll remember my mother, Rhianna."

The tallest woman, with the look of Oria, dismounted and came toward him. Remembering the epithets the queen mother had hurled at him before, Lonen gave her a cautious bow. "Queen Rhianna," he said, straightening, then putting an arm around Oria to draw her to his side. "It's a pleasure to see you alive and well."

She gave him a severe look, noting his possessive gesture. "How gratifying. I offer you two things: my apology for what I said about your suitability as a husband for my daughter, and my thanks, for saving her life. Your Highness," she added with a wry twist of a smile that reminded him oddly of his own mother.

He looked down at Oria, who had her face tilted up to his, an echo of the same amusement in her smile. "Oria saved herself," he said, as much to her as to Rhianna. "And Bára, it seems."

"Because I have the ideal husband," she teased. "And this is Juli, without her mask."

The pretty young woman with tousled red curls gave him a smile and a bow. "Your Highness. Good to see you returned to our walls."

Lonen grinned back at his one-time co-conspirator in handling his then new and skittish foreign bride.

"And this is Gallia," Oria said, drawing forward the elegant blonde. "You encountered her briefly at the duel that had me excommunicated from Bára. We have her to thank for so much, including saving my mother's sanity."

"That's putting it strongly," Gallia demurred, staying a careful step back from Lonen and casting her gaze downward. Remembering how Oria had said his presence affected her before she learned to manage it, Lonen made an effort to pull his thoughts and curiosity back. Oria stroked a hand over his forearm in appreciation.

"It's not." Rhianna gave her daughter-in-law a fond look. "Gallia took Oria's advice and sought out my friendship. She sat with me daily, helping me come out of a very dark place."

"You helped me through my dark place," Gallia returned. "Leaving Lousá weakened me in ways that I never expected—or could've dealt with on my own. That and being married to Yar—" She cut herself off, looking anxiously between Oria and her mother.

"Yar nearly killed Gallia," the queen mother said baldly. "He drained her dry, trying to force her to adapt to Bára's sgath. "He was… not kind to her. Something I shall bear the guilt for to my dying day."

"His actions were not yours," Gallia countered. "You're not responsible."

"I am." Rhianna nodded to herself. "I raised that boy to be who he became. I mourn my son's death, but I don't regret the necessity of it. I'm only glad I had the wit to raise a daughter like Oria, too." She opened her arms and Oria ran to her, the tears falling freely now. They rocked each other for a long moment, then Oria stepped back, holding out a hand to Lonen, drawing him into their group.

"Juli rallied the priestesses to cut off the flow of sgath to the priests," Oria explained to him, wiping away her happy tears. "Gallia had been gradually draining Yar already. They were able to cut off the flow to the golem army."

"And Nolan?" he asked. "Yar or one of his priests had a magic hold on my brother. Is it gone or is it too soon to know?"

Oria glanced at Gallia, who considered. "We cut off everything. There should be no grien leaving Bára now."

Oria's eyes took on that abstracted look she got when speaking to Chuffta mind-to-mind. "Chuffta asked Illya, the derkesthai with Lonen's mother," Oria explained, for everyone's benefit. "The spell binding Nolan seems to have snapped when that sorcerer was cut off from Bára's sgath. He's disoriented—he remembers very little of what occurred since he fell into the chasm on the battlefield here— but seems to be more himself."

Her face echoed the relief Lonen felt, as that scar of guilt and worry unknotted itself. Behind him, Arnon and Alyx spoke to each other quietly, sounding equally pleased.

"How do you have so many derkesthai?" Rhianna asked her daughter, then cocked her head to eye Chuffta askance. "Is that really Chuffta?"

Chuffta lowered his great head to rest his pointed chin on the ground, blinking his bright green eyes at Rhianna fondly.

Oria laughed. "Yes. I used my magic to make him big."

"Apparently," Rhianna replied faintly, still raptly staring.

"Thank you for him, Mother." Oria became very serious. "I don't know how you knew I'd need him, but I did."

Rhianna looked back at her daughter. "My sister Tania told me to get him when you were born, before she left Bára. She recognized in you what our great-grandmother had. Tania had special insight that way, an admirable skill."

"But you told me not to be like her," Oria exclaimed.

Her mother sighed, looking to Lonen. "I wanted my life for you, and for Tania, and that was selfish. I think you're both better off having followed your own paths. At least I hope so in her case, wherever she may be."

Gallia cleared her throat. "Speaking of having cut off all of the priests' grien, we'll need to remedy that soon, or vital spells like those powering the walls and the orchards will collapse."

"We'll have to determine which priests can be trusted," Rhianna put in gravely.

"You can learn to do it yourselves," Oria corrected decisively. "I'll teach you. The trustworthy sorcerers can learn to filter the wild magic—and so can you—and the sorceresses can learn to wield active magic."

"But women can't use grien," Juli blurted, then looked chagrined at Oria's laugh.

"There is no such thing as sgath or grien," Oria corrected gently, not without compassion. "Those are constructs, created long ago to bind us to our roles. We don't need them any more than we need the masks. In time, even the walls can come down. The time we needed that barrier to protect us has passed."

"Including protection from the Destrye," Lonen added. He glanced behind him to see Alyx and Arnon, exhausted and covered in blood and other nameless substances, but grinning with hope. Beyond them, the Destrye warriors mingled with Bára's city guard, some in conversation, renewing acquaintances from the time the Destrye had occupied the city in peace. He squeezed Oria's hand. "We are one people now."

"Which means I'd like Arnon—" Oria looked to Lonen's brother, who stepped forward with a bow. "Arnon, can you set up a system to start ferrying food and water through the tunnels back to Dru?"

"Of course, Your Highness. I look forward to the challenge."

"We're sending food and water to Dru?" Rhianna asked, eyebrows climbing in her pale face.

"It's about time Bára began making up for all it's stolen from Dru over the years, don't you think, Mother?"

Rhianna opened her mouth, gaze sharp, then closed it again. She nodded in resignation. "Perhaps so. But don't strip us bare, I beg you." She said it to Lonen, but Oria answered.

"There is no more us and them." Oria looked up at him with an affectionate smile. "Teamwork, yes?"

"Absolutely," he agreed. "And we'd best get to it. There's a great deal of work to do."

"True, but..." Oria's smile turned flirtatious. "You're awfully filthy, barbarian. As Queen of Bára, I'm commanding you to bathe and make yourself fit for my presence."

"Is that so?" he murmured, remembering Bára's luxurious baths and the fantasies he'd nurtured about Oria in them the last time she'd issued that command. "Maybe I'll toss you over my shoulder and carry you there."

Her eyes sparkled with laughter, and she rose up on tiptoes to reply in his ear. "I do recall promising *total* surrender, once upon a time."

"And thus the conquered becomes the conqueror," he replied, turning his head to capture her mouth with his.

Heedless of all watching them, Báran and Destrye alike, Oria and Lonen kissed, celebrating a lasting peace and partnership. And all around them, people and derkesthai cheered.

~ Epilogue ~

ORIA AWOKE, ALONE in the bed and with late morning sun streaming in. She stretched, muffling a groan, her body heavy and sluggish. Even though she'd clearly outslept Lonen, she felt like she could sleep for days more.

"Sleep as many days as you like," Chuffta suggested. But his bright green eye appeared in the window, blocking the sunlight. *"How are you feeling?"*

"Eleven months pregnant, thank you."

She rolled to her side and used her hands to push herself up, the way Baeltya had taught her. *"It's much better our way,"* Chuffta commented, watching her. *"Lay the eggs and wait for them to hatch instead of carrying them around inside you."*

"I'll keep that in mind for next time." As a first order of business, she relieved her poor, crushed bladder, then pulled on a robe and opened the glass-paned doors to step out onto the rooftop terrace. The autumn sun filtered through the fiery canopy, the surrounding forest a spectacular display of color. Chuffta lolled on his platform nearby, soaking in the sun, the tip of his tail flicking in lazy delight. The planters surrounding the terrace overflowed with flowers, vines, and even small trees and bushes. As the Destrye had ventured out of Arill City over the course of the summer, reclaiming lost homesteads and discovering new ones, they'd vied with each other to bring back anything that flowered that their queen might not already have in her garden on the roof of the palace.

Combined with the plants from her Báran garden, coaxed to

verdant life from seed and shoot, the array made for an exotic bouquet unlike anything else in the world. Arnon had surprised her with the once-dying jasmine tree from her tower garden in Bára, having it brought through the tunnels along with food supplies, calling it a belated wedding gift. Songbirds from all over—even a few hardy jewelbirds—gathered in the branches or flitted from flower to flower. The flora and fauna of Bára and Dru complimented each other with a surprising amount of balance and symmetry. A sorceress's garden sustained by her magic and careful attention.

Arill knew she didn't have the energy for much else.

"She's awake," Lonen called out, coming through the doors she'd left open.

She opened her arms and he gathered her close, carefully maneuvering around her distended belly, kissing her thoroughly. "I was worried you'd sleep through lunch," he teased.

"I already missed breakfast, apparently," she replied with a smile. "I'm starving."

"Good thing I'm king then, because I have ordered a feast fit for a queen." A queue of servants streamed out the doors, carrying platters of food they arranged on the table set in a pool of warm sun.

"How many people are you planning to feed?" Oria asked, raising her brows and laughing.

"At least three," Lonen answered, laying a big hand on her belly. "You, me, and this one. What's your guess today—barbarian warrior or sorceress?"

"Could be warrior woman or sorcerer," she reminded him.

"Copper hair, though."

"And gray eyes. A handsome combination."

"Maybe he'll be a mighty thewed sorcerer," Lonen suggested with a sparkle in his own gray eyes as he helped her into a chair.

"Or she will be," Oria retorted, giggling at the expression on her husband's face. She took his hand. "No matter who our children are, magically gifted or not, mighty warriors or not, we'll love them and teach them."

"Just so long as they aren't annoyingly over-analytical engineers like Arnon," Lonen mock scowled. "I can't love that."

"I heard that," Arnon said, strolling out from inside, Alyx with him, smiling warmly at Oria.

"This is a private lunch," Lonen pointed out. "And the royal couple's private quarters, need I remind you."

"Good thing the queen has a soft spot for me." Arnon gave Alyx a nudge with his elbow, and Oria a jaunty wink. "We received a message from Nolan. He and Natly have settled in at Lousá and are making headway with diplomatic relations."

"Helped along, no doubt, by the promises of wood and water from Dru," Lonen commented cynically.

"In exchange for for what they can send us," Oria reminded him. "It balances out, and we're all benefitting from working together instead of warring."

"I know, I know." Lonen pretended to scowl. "Hopefully we won't get bored with all this peace and prosperity."

"I'm sure something will come up for you to bravely battle," she soothed.

"In the meanwhile," Arnon said, and presented her with a sheaf of scrolls and a gallant bow.

"Ooh, thank you, Arnon!" Eagerly, Oria unrolled them, scanning the designs with an eye grown considerably more practiced.

"Dare I ask what those are for?" Lonen canted his head to look.

"Addition to our apartments," Oria said, handing him one. "The baby will need a room with access for their derkesthai Familiar."

Lonen grunted, studying it. "Surely not yet."

"Which?" Alyx quipped, giving Oria's belly a jaundiced eye. "The baby or the Familiar, because to my unpracticed eye, our queen looks ready to pop."

"Ugh," Oria replied, rubbing a hand over the uncomfortably stretching skin of her belly. I feel like could. But I meant the Familiar. I want to incorporate our child's room into the framework for the greenhouse, which I need in place before the first frost." And hopefully before she had the baby.

"Greenhouse?" Lonen echoed.

"Yes," Arnon replied with enthusiasm, waving his hands at the rooftop garden. "I'm framing in all of this and Oria will conjure the glass."

"That way the plants will survive the winter," Oria explained. "Come spring, I'll remove the glass again."

"Handy," Lonen commented in a dry tone.

"Yes." Oria gave him her sweetest smile. "I am. And you promised to give me whatever I needed to make me happy here in Dru."

He lifted her hand and kissed the back of it, gray eyes glowing with love. "And have I?"

"Always and forever," she answered.

TITLES BY JEFFE KENNEDY

OTHER FANTASY ROMANCES

A COVENANT OF THORNS
Rogue's Pawn
Rogue's Possession
Rogue's Paradise

THE TWELVE KINGDOMS
Negotiation
The Mark of the Tala
The Tears of the Rose
The Talon of the Hawk
Heart's Blood
For Crown and Kingdom

THE UNCHARTED REALMS
The Pages of the Mind
The Edge of the Blade
The Snows of Windroven
The Shift of the Tide
The Arrows of the Heart
The Dragons of Summer

THE CHRONICLES OF DASNARIA
Prisoner of the Crown
Exile of the Seas
Warrior of the World

SORCEROUS MOONS
Lonen's War
Oria's Gambit
The Tides of Bára
The Forests of Dru
Oria's Enchantment
Lonen's Reign

THE FORGOTTEN EMPIRES
The Orchid Throne

<u>CONTEMPORARY ROMANCES</u>

Shooting Star

MISSED CONNECTIONS
Last Dance
With a Prince
Since Last Christmas

<u>CONTEMPORARY EROTIC ROMANCES</u>

Exact Warm Unholy
The Devil's Doorbell

FACETS OF PASSION
Sapphire
Platinum
Ruby
Five Golden Rings

FALLING UNDER
Going Under
Under His Touch
Under Contract

EROTIC PARANORMAL

MASTER OF THE OPERA E-SERIAL
Master of the Opera, Act 1: Passionate Overture
Master of the Opera, Act 2: Ghost Aria
Master of the Opera, Act 3: Phantom Serenade
Master of the Opera, Act 4: Dark Interlude
Master of the Opera, Act 5: A Haunting Duet
Master of the Opera, Act 6: Crescendo
Master of the Opera

BLOOD CURRENCY
Blood Currency

BDSM FAIRYTALE ROMANCE

Petals and Thorns

OTHER WORKS

Birdwoman
Hopeful Monsters
Teeth, Long and Sharp

Thank you for reading!

About Jeffe Kennedy

Jeffe Kennedy is an award-winning author whose works include novels, non-fiction, poetry, and short fiction. She has been a Ucross Foundation Fellow, received the Wyoming Arts Council Fellowship for Poetry, and was awarded a Frank Nelson Doubleday Memorial Award. She serves on the Board of Directors for the Science Fiction and Fantasy Writers of America (SFWA) as a Director at Large.

Her award-winning fantasy romance trilogy *The Twelve Kingdoms* hit the shelves starting in May 2014. Book 1, *The Mark of the Tala*, received a starred *Library Journal* review and was nominated for the RT Book of the Year while the sequel, *The Tears of the Rose* received a Top Pick Gold and was nominated for the RT Reviewers' Choice Best Fantasy Romance of 2014. The third book, *The Talon of the Hawk*, won the RT Reviewers' Choice Best Fantasy Romance of 2015. Two more books followed in this world, beginning the spin-off series *The Uncharted Realms*. Book one in that series, *The Pages of the Mind*, has also been nominated for the RT Reviewer's Choice Best Fantasy Romance of 2016 and won RWA's 2017 RITA® Award. The second book, *The Edge of the Blade*, released December 27, 2016, and is a PRISM finalist, along with *The Pages of the Mind*. The next in the series, *The Shift of the Tide*, came out in August, 2017. A high fantasy trilogy, The Chronicles of Dasnaria, taking place in *The Twelve Kingdoms* world began releasing from Rebel Base books in 2018.

She also introduced a new fantasy romance series, *Sorcerous Moons*, which includes *Lonen's War*, *Oria's Gambit*, *The Tides of Bàra*, and *The Forests of Dru*. She's begun releasing a new contemporary erotic romance series, *Missed Connections*, which started with *Last Dance* and continues in *With a Prince* and *Since Last Christmas*.

In 2019, St. Martins Press will release the first book, *The Orchid Throne*, in a new fantasy romance series, *The Forgotten Empires*.

Her other works include a number of fiction series: the fantasy romance novels of *A Covenant of Thorns*; the contemporary BDSM novellas of the *Facets of Passion*; an erotic contemporary serial novel, *Master of the Opera*; and the erotic romance trilogy, *Falling Under*, which includes *Going Under, Under His Touch* and *Under Contract*.

She lives in Santa Fe, New Mexico, with two Maine coon cats, plentiful free-range lizards and a very handsome Doctor of Oriental Medicine.

Jeffe can be found online at her website: JeffeKennedy.com, every Sunday at the popular SFF Seven blog, on Facebook, on Goodreads and pretty much constantly on Twitter @jeffekennedy. She is represented by Sarah Younger of Nancy Yost Literary Agency.

jeffekennedy.com

facebook.com/Author.Jeffe.Kennedy

twitter.com/jeffekennedy

goodreads.com/author/show/1014374.Jeffe_Kennedy

Sign up for her newsletter here.

jeffekennedy.com/sign-up-for-my-newsletter